Closed Campus, by Charlie Rott, is a horror story and a very captivating one at that. But rather than give away clues about the book, I will say that it's a good read because Rott compels with the story and prologue so much that you get wrapped up before you even know it. No time is wasted in getting down and dirty, so it's set up nicely for the course and it flows with ease until the last word, especially if you like reality based scary stories.

I wish I could talk more about the author but this is a case where I can only say she's a good writer and should be proud of this work, and as a long time writer on the subject that is a compliment when everyone's work is important to them. And I liked this read for more reasons than the subject matter, I also watched some horror the same week. It wasn't easy because I found myself comparing stories and whatnot to stay interested because I review a lot of material. I was able to digest it all because of how well the book flows and it's another great testament to the author herself.

The first thing Closed Campus achieves, is the excellent characters and the choices they make and things they get into among the overall picture. If you like nail biters you'll enjoy this book, and if you like no punches pulled in the language department it's right up your alley and that is where the braveness belongs to both the author and readers. This isn't your mother's horror, but it isn't tasteless either, it's everything the opposite can muster and worth reading repeated times over. In fact, the first thing I wanted to do was read it one more time, but time eludes so I will do that when it allows.

McGinley's School for girl's is on a man-made island three miles from of Lake Michigan, and that is the set location in which the title and storyline are based, but once you're into the story it becomes obvious why that's so important. The path that leads to there is explained and it's never a smooth ride into such an institution, nor is there always an easy way out. And without giving it all away, it's worth noting that it works on all the blood pumping nerves as the suspense wears on and on.

You will find fascinating characters, like Rashida, Andrew, Fulmer,

Lacey and Naomi getting into the troubles that find them there and the subsequent troubles within, as you're taken down the Closed Campus trail of everything a good modern horror story is worth. It's both thrilling and chilling, but more adult minded than campy when it comes to all seriousness about it. This book is on par with all the boarding school stories of the past, and adds new twists to such tales, but that is only one reason I found it to be undeniably good.

- Garth Thomas, Reprospace Reviews™

This is definitely a timely novel. Charlie Rott's Closed Campus is the story of Sarita Teymouri, seventeen-year-old daughter of Syrian immigrants. Sarita is the victim of constant harassment from a coterie of female classmates, harassment extending over years, culminating in Sarita accidently killing her chief tormentor with a knife wound to the neck. Authorities charge her with involuntary manslaughter and imprison her at an island reformatory until they deem her rehabilitated and ready to re-enter society. It's at this point that the novel takes off in earnest.

McGinley's School for Girls is where the bulk of the novel's action takes place. Ava Halsey, a veteran of the conflicts in Iraq and Afghanistan, administrates the "school" and Rott does a masterful job of crafting her as a true antagonist for readers to loath from her initial introduction onward. There other school staff and officers are the expected assortment of "good" and "bad" cops and Rott only develops some of them as fully rounded characters important to the novel's development.

Bennett includes scattered footnotes along the way to explain some of the slang and lingo used in an institution such as McGinley's. Older readers familiar with the crime genre or fiction with a penal setting will find such footnotes unnecessary, but it's a wise move for readers with a novice understanding of such language. Bennett handles the first person narration quite well – Sarita is a convincing character throughout the book and her motivations and reactions never stretch credibility.

Rott renders the secondary characters, particularly the inmates Sarita serves time with, with a keen eye. She doesn't bite off more than she can chew with an enormous supporting cast and, instead, focuses reader's attention on a few figures among the several hundred inmates housed in the school. She depicts physical action with energy and urgency, but her descriptive powers serve her well in this area and others.

She depicts the school and its environs with vivid clarity. Sarita's time in isolation, "the bunker", is a highlight in the novel and one of Rott's finest set pieces. The novel gains momentum as the characters and plot develop further and the author shows herself to have a near masterful command of pacing. The evolution of the inmate's plans unfolds in a believable manner and the responses from characters like Halsey are likewise credible. Rott does an exceptional job of generating suspense as well.

The ending is thrilling and fast paced. Rott will gratify readers with how she wraps up loose ends and Sarita emerges from the narrative forever changed by the experiences depicted in Closed Campus. The novel has something to offer every reader. It is entertaining, well written, rife with first class characterizations, and handled in an intelligent way that never panders for the reader's attention. Charlie Rott has written a fine contemporary novel about the world we live in today and a top-notch action and suspense yarn for those who appreciate that sort of fiction. It's a book well worth your time and one that bears revisiting.

- Jason Hillenburg, Reprospace Reviews™

Closed Campus

**REASON FADES
AS FEAR
GROWS STRONGER**

Charlie Rott

Closed Campus
First edition, published 2020

By Charlie Rott
Copyright © 2020, Charlie Rott

ISBN-13: 978-1-952685-06-4
Cover Photo by Denny Müller on Unsplash

Published by Kitsap Publishing
www.KitsapPublishing.com

Prologue

It's Friday afternoon and I'm sitting at a table in the school cafeteria. For the first half of the lunch hour, it was just me and my sister, Amira. She had to get up and leave for some reason I don't recall. It's my final year of high school and I'm just trying to get through it without any serious problems. Helena's presence is going to complicate things. Right now she keeps looking over at me with her two friends, all three of them snickering. My family came to the U.S. when I was still a toddler. My sister had only just been born. Since I was so young, I don't remember anything about Syria or the journey here. Just the stories my parents tell. Here at school I get along with some people, but most avoid me. Amira has it worse since she wears a hijab. I've seen it get ripped off her head at least twice since we started coming here. The one time I shoved the person responsible, I ended up suspended for a few days.

"We can't have you assaulting other students," the principal told me. I'd never been so frustrated in my life. I was warned after another similar incident that if I got into another fight, that it could lead to expulsion. A french fry hits me in the side of the head and lands on the table in front of me. Keeping my eyes focused on the table, I can hear Helena and her friends laughing about it. A minute goes by and another one lands in my hair. I brush it out and stare daggers at her. Next it's a piece of celery whizzing by my head.

"Nice aim," one of her friends chuckles. Helena's about my size with dark brown eyes, messy, wavy, black hair with plenty of flyaways, a round face, and pale skin. Her nose is a little crooked from a fight she started with me several months back, and never does she fail to have a smug look about her. Placing my fingers on the apple sitting before me, I begin turning it a little at a time; my other hand supporting my head. This happens more often than I care to admit. And each time it does I'm the one who has to remain calm and act civil. Next come the taunts. One of her friends performs a loud fake sneeze and sloppily hides a slur in the middle of it. Clenching the apple in my hand I grit my teeth and stand up from the table.

"Watch out, she's mad," Helena taunts, a malicious grin across her face. I stroll by her and start heading to the front of the building. I need to get away from her. It's the end of the week and I just don't have the energy to deal with this sort of thing. After exiting the cafeteria, I step out the front doors and seat myself behind one of the pillars that line the front entrance. About a dozen other students are out here, all of them doing their own thing. Talking, laughing, and unaware that I exist. As I examine the apple, all I can think about is how much I'd like to chuck it at Helena. Yeah...how am I suppose to explain that to my parents? Sorry, I lost my temper, now how about finding a new school so I can rush to finish my last year and graduate on time?

I take a bite out of the apple and stare off across the street. Right on the other side is an old apartment complex, decrepit and decaying. It's in good company around here. Even the school is falling apart in some places. Storms have been bombarding the city over the past month, and in that time there have been parts of the school that have taken damage. Most of it involving the roof and courtyards. Trees have been tilted, and in some cases brought down altogether. Some of the old rusted fences have fallen apart and water damage is obvious in various parts of the building. On top of the physical damage, the city's been reeling from economic trouble for years.

About ten years ago, the country went through a recession, but there's little I recall of it. The scars still remain in the form of abandoned buildings, vehicles ditched in various places, and what still thrives here left to rot. There's something strange about old buildings. There's an odd feeling I get when I stare at them. I start to wonder who once walked through there and why. What they were doing that day or month, whether they worked there, lived there, and any number of other things. A decaying structure void of life and brimming with memories long forgotten. Yet I still feel like if I maintain my gaze for long enough I might just glimpse a ghost or two. Once I'm finished with the apple, I stand up and toss it into a nearby trashcan. After taking one last look at the abandoned building, I make my way inside and step into the restroom a short distance from the doors. In the middle of washing my hands, Helena and her two friends walk in behind me, chatting away as they go. They fall silent as they lay eyes on me.

"You're still here?" Helena snorts. "Jeez, I thought maybe you took a hint and went home." The water shuts off and I stand still with my head bowed and my hands on the edge of the sink. "Hey, I'm talking to you!" Helena snarls, grabbing my shoulder. I spin to face her and shove her away from me. She stumbles and her friends catch her as I exit the restroom, drying my hands on my jacket as I go. She follows me out of the restroom and out the front doors. She runs up behind me and returns the shove I gave her. I stumble and turn to face her.

"What? You're ignoring me now?" she growls.

"Trying," I answer.

"Well good luck with that, cuz I'm not going away," she taunts.

"Neither am I," I answer. "Deal with it." She shoves me again and I clench my fists. I can't even begin to describe how much I want to hit her. Instead I turn and start walking away, which just makes her even angrier.

"Hey! Where the hell do you think you're going?" she shouts, walking toward me.

"Away from you," I answer, turning once more to flash an obscene gesture. I turn back around and continue walking. Helena doesn't say anything and I start down the nearest street. I doubt I'll get expelled for skipping class and right now I really need to find a place to cool off. Not far down the road is an old house, part of an entire neighborhood that's been empty in all the time I've lived here. Behind one of the houses is a tree with a wooden platform, halfway up and about fifteen feet off the ground.

For two years now, it's been where I go when I need to get away from people. If I'm being honest, I feel like I've been abusing it over the past several months. My love for abandoned structures is what drew me to it in the first place, but to be honest, there's a heavy sadness that lingers in the area. Just off the main road by about five-hundred feet, it seems almost as if it's not apart of this world; as if it belongs to an alternate timeline. More than anything it's a reminder of the way we've seen people either moving away or dying at an alarming rate. They lose their jobs, they get sick and end up swamped with hospital bills, some struggle with addiction, and soon the houses are empty.

I never found out which ones, but there's a rumor that two of the houses played host to suicides. Some of the houses even still have broken down vehicles in the driveway; rusted and sitting on the rims through long deflated tires. Arriving at the house with the tree, I look up at the wooden platform as I approach. There's no indication that anything was ever built on top of the platform, and because of that I have to wonder if maybe the former occupants left before they could finish it. Looking out on the town from the platform, I can see the rooftops of the nearby houses, some of which have large holes. A flock of birds fly by me and I start to hear faint voices approaching from down the street. Once they're close enough to hear, I peer down from the edge of the platform and over the moss-covered wooden fence below me. It's Helena and the others. They must be looking for me.

"I've seen her come this way at least a few times," one of her friends says, looking around the empty street.

"Probably lives here," Helena snorts. "Spread out and look for her. Yell if you find anything." The other two nod and the three of them split up. Helena and one of the others disappear further down the road and the third girl stays near me. For a moment I consider climbing down, but I'm certain she'll see me if I try. For about five tense minutes, I wait on the platform, flat on my stomach with my arms in front of me and my chin resting atop my palms. At the end of those few minutes, she enters the house, making a great deal of racket by tripping on something just inside. Now's my chance.

I pull myself toward the edge of the platform and peer over the side of it. There's no sign of her. I wait and listen for a moment, then drop back down onto my stomach when I notice movement just beyond a shattered sliding glass door attached to a room near the back entrance. Just a little longer. Please don't see the ladder, please don't see the ladder. Sure enough, her footsteps pause and then soon pick up again. Looking back over the edge of the platform, I wait and listen for a second time, and this time I can tell she's further back in the house. I quickly descend the ladder and turn to see her watching me.

"Hey! I found her!" she shouts, racing out the back door toward me.

"She's over here!" I race through the gap in the fence and tear off down the street. I turn the corner and take off down an alley. Less than a minute later I hop over a small wooden fence and fall flat on my back on the other side. Within seconds she catches up and sprints right past me. Once her footsteps fade, I take a deep breath and cover my face with my hands, letting out a muffled groan as I do so. Helena and her two friends, Tara, and Phoebe, have had it out for me ever since I first met them in the 8th grade. Last year Helena's father began campaigning for office as the only challenger in the race for California governor. He's been talking about abolishing sanctuary cities, referring to people like me as criminals and cockroaches, regardless of how or why we came here, and his supporters are eating it up. Helena's hatred of me seemed to intensify not long after that.

One of the few remaining safe-havens in this crumbling country, I have hope that he won't get elected, but this same sort of thing has been taking place in other states over the last several years. State by state, the country is going mad. An Indian man, a Sikh, was gunned down on his front porch about a month ago. He lived about two blocks from me and I'd seen him around from time to time. When the police finally caught the man who did it, he screamed about "invaders" and threatened to kill others. The case has been a hot-button issue in the governor's race. My phone starts ringing in my pocket and I take it out to see that it's Amira calling.

"Hello?"

"Hey, is everything all right?" she asks. "I just came back to the cafeteria and couldn't find you. Not at the table, not out front..."

"I left campus to cool down and now Helena, Tara, and Phoebe are out looking for me," I explain. "Phoebe just about caught me, but I think I lost her. I'm near that abandoned neighborhood, hiding in someone's back yard."

"One of the abandoned yards?" she asks.

"No, I jumped over someone's fence," I answer. "And I'm really hoping no one's home." I sit up and glance at the sliding glass door twenty feet away. A dog has its paws up on the window, barking and snarling at me. The owner is nowhere to be found.

"Well, if I were you, I wouldn't stick around to find out," she replies. "Why's Helena looking for you, anyway?"

"I wish I knew," I answer, rubbing my eyes.

"If she's harassing you, you should report it," she says. "At least that way it's on record."

"That might be hard to do without admitting to skipping class," I counter. I hop the fence and start back toward the school at a brisk pace; occasionally glancing over my shoulder as I go.

"I suppose that's true," she admits.

"I'm on my way back," I say. "I'll be there in a minute. Just wait for me out front." I hang up the phone and continue down the street. Seconds after doing so, Phoebe races up behind me and jumps on my back. Both of us crash onto the sidewalk. I throw her off and scramble to my feet. She chases after me and grabs the collar of my jacket in another attempt to drag me down. I spin and slug her in the cheek. She drops like a stone, landing on the edge of someone's overgrown front yard. I look down at her for a moment and see that she's out cold. Voices down the street catch my attention. It's Helena and Tara calling for Phoebe. I'd better get out of here before they find her. I hurry back toward the school, hoping the entire way that Tara and Helena don't find Phoebe for a while. For some reason I can't quite explain, I feel sort of guilty for just leaving her there. No use trying to help. I'm already in over my head and I'm sure she won't be appreciative when she wakes up. When I at last reach the school, I spot Amira standing outside. She sees me coming and waves.

"I'm gonna go get my bag and leave," I say as I approach. "Come with me or don't, but I'm not sticking around any longer."

"What happened?" she asks as we head through the main entrance.

"If I tell you, are you gonna keep your mouth shut at dinner tonight?" I ask, brushing by a few people in the crowded hallway as I speak. Amira lags behind me for a moment and catches up soon after.

"I'm not keeping my mouth shut about anything," she insists. "Now what happened?"

"I'm not having you squeal on me again," I growl, walking along the wall. "Unless you can promise me that you won't, and mean it, this conversation is over." Reaching my locker, I put in the combination and yank it open. My bag tumbles out and I catch it just before it hits the floor. Amira remains silent as I close the locker and start back toward the main entrance.

"Did you hurt someone?" Amira asks.

"I dunno, probably," I shrug.

"Which of course means you did," she says. "Whatever, I'm not sticking around to take the heat while you run off. I'm going with you."

"Fine by me." I stop when I reach the commons and see that a bunch of people are gathering near the doors. Amira and I try to see what's going on and as soon as I have a clear view, I spot Helena and Tara helping Phoebe through the front entrance. The side of Phoebe's head is covered in blood. She seems lucid and is clenching her teeth in pain. Amira punches me in the arm and glares at me.

"Seriously?" she growls, keeping her voice low. "You do that and then act like it's not a big deal?"

"I didn't see any blood when I left," I whisper. "She must've hit her head on something. I knocked her out and she fell, it wasn't my fault! She jumped me right after I got off the phone with you. Probably not as bad as it looks."

"Either way you're getting expelled for this," she groans. "Now what do we do?" Phoebe is handed off to two teachers who take her into the main office. Helena catches my eye and nudges Tara before pointing at us both.

"Come on, we need to get the hell out of here," I say, grabbing Amira by the arm and leading her through the crowd.

"Do they all have to stare at us like that?" Amira mutters. Dozens of people in the hallway have noticed us trying to leave and are now glaring at us. We brush past several other students and into an empty pocket in the hallway where no one is standing. We both trot down the stairs and out one of the side exits. I look back over my shoulder and watch the doors close. So far so good. Moments later I hear someone shouting at me and we both turn to see Helena and Tara coming toward us. Both of them look furious.

"Teymouri!" Helena shouts.

"Go, run," I urge, giving Amira a light shove. She resists and I scowl at her.

"I'm not leaving," she insists.

"Get out of here! Now!" I order, shoving her harder. It's too late. Helena and Tara are now a short distance away. My heart skips a beat when I see that Helena has a knife clutched in one hand.

"You're in deep shit, Teymouri!" Helena growls, eyeing me with disdain. "The fuck did you do to Phoebe? Huh?"

"Nothing," I lie, backing away with Amira at my side.

"Like hell it was nothing!" Helena shouts. "We found her with a gash in her head!" I didn't mean to tear her head open, I was just trying to protect myself. Too bad Helena's never going to see it that way. She looks like she's about to explode. Her face is already red from running all over, but some of the more concentrated shades around her cheeks are no doubt from rage.

"She jumped me and she got hurt. End of story," I growl.

"Looked more to us like you hit her with a rock!" Tara snarls. "Like you were trying to kill her!"

"I didn't hit her with a rock and I wasn't trying to kill anyone!" I protest. "I hit her, yeah, but that was with my fist...and that's because you guys were stalking me! Maybe if you weren't doing that, this wouldn't have happened!"

"It also wouldn't have happened if you'd stayed in your own damn country!" Helena snarls, walking toward me. I turn and shove Amira again.

"Get the hell out of here!" I shout. "Go!" I look back and Helena is sprinting straight for me. Amira takes off down the street and Tara gives chase. Helena slashes me across the face before I even know what's happening. The blade catches part of my forehead, the bridge of my nose, and slices my cheek in one motion. I kick her in the stomach and she stumbles backward, doubled up in pain. Without giving it a second thought I throw her down and dive on top of her. I pin her arm down on the ground, take the knife, and stumble to my feet with blood dripping down my face as I go. Tara catches Amira and drags her down. She pins her and rips her hijab off her head before tossing it into the street.

I rush toward them and Helena runs at me a second time. She knocks me to the ground and the knife tumbles just out of my reach. I reach out to grab it and she punches me in the cheek twice. I hit her back and throw her off. Some of my blood is smeared across her hand and arm. As soon as we're both on our feet again she lunges at me and I punch her in the stomach. She shrugs it off and jumps on my back, sending us both crashing to the ground. She grabs my hair and slams my face into the ground. Now close enough to reach the knife, I snatch it up and impale her forearm with it. She screams and lets go, giving me time to get back up.

Once back on my feet, she grabs my arm with both hands and the two of us begin fighting for control of the knife. We both stumble and Helena is the first to lose her balance. She falls backward into a bus stop shelter, pulling me down with her. The knife sinks into her neck and she shrieks in pain. I stumble to my feet with the knife in my hand, blood all over both it, my hands, and forearms. Helena tries to get up as blood gushes from her neck. She passes out and falls to the ground in a heap as blood pools around her.

"What the hell did you just do?" Tara shouts, a look of panic now present on her face. Amira is still on the ground, bleeding and grimacing in pain. Without thinking I brandish the knife at Tara.

"Get off of her! Now!" I order. Tara gets to her feet and puts her hands up in surrender. My heart is racing so fast I'm sure it will burst from my chest at any moment. I drag Amira to her feet and hold her up until she regains her footing. Students who heard the fighting are coming out of the building while those who witnessed it are standing around staring in shock.

"Can you run?" I ask Amira, snatching up her discarded hijab. She nods and remains silent. "Hurry up! Let's go!" I take off down the sidewalk with Amira in tow.

* * *

The next half hour I spent vomiting in the restroom. How I managed to wait until I got home is beyond me. Amira phoned both our parents to tell them what had happened. I've never seen her so panicked in her life.

"These girls attacked us, Sarita stabbed one of them!" Amira quavered. "I think one of them is dead!" When our parents arrived at the house, my father was livid. Not at me, but at Helena for having slashed my face. Our mother arrived right behind him. Both times I almost had a heart attack when they came to the door. Sooner or later I knew the police were going to show up on our doorstep. When they did twenty minutes after my mother arrived, both of my parents attempted to keep them away from me. It didn't matter, though. They both stormed in with guns drawn and threw me on the floor. They handcuffed me and the next thing I knew I was sitting in the county jail. Over the next month-and-a-half I stayed there, awaiting a hearing.

The incident made national headlines. The media took it and ran, demonizing me in every way they could. Seventeen-years-old and people are out in the streets calling for my execution. When I was transferred to another facility following a series of violent incidents, angry crowds threw whatever they could get their hands on. Two of the windows on the bus were damaged by flying rocks. I was assigned a public defender, a woman who looked exhausted enough to fall asleep at the drop of a hat. When I was at last sent before a judge, she told me I was being charged with voluntary manslaughter. Voluntary? It was an accident, she pulled me down. I didn't mean for her to die, I just wanted her to stop. The judge asked me if I understood what was happening and the charges being brought against me. I was numb.

It was explained to me that if I were to go to trial and lose, I would likely receive the maximum sentence. My other option was to take a plea bargain, admit guilt, and reduce my sentence as a result. From there I would be allowed to avoid prison and instead be sent to a reform school. Two years at a place called "McGinley's School for Girls." Thinking about that day still makes me feel sick. Everything that could have gone wrong did. It all happened so fast, I hardly had time to blink.

McGinley's School for Girls wasn't a place anyone wanted to wind up. Most of the people who survived their time there came back to tell a series of horror stories. The only reason I knew what the place was and what went on there, is because there was a girl whose violent death on the island five years prior, had caught national attention. Her name was Iris Eston and she was sent to McGinley's for stealing a car. Two inmates who served their sentences at the same time as Eston came forward after they were released, and claimed that they'd seen Eston shot in the back during an escape attempt.

People were quick to accuse them both of lying, and still more said Eston must have deserved it for trying to escape in the first place. One of the two girls, Adria Morris, claimed some of the inmates were beaten bloody for trivial infractions, that the guards used excessive force often, and that the woman who ran the place, one Ava Halsey, turned a blind eye to almost all of it. From what I gather, Ava Halsey is seen as a hero in Michigan where McGinley's is located. She's a decorated war veteran who fought in Iraq and Afghanistan. She's known for having risked her life to rescue a fellow soldier during an ambush.

On camera, when she was being interviewed by reporters, she seemed mild-mannered and strict, but nothing like the monster Adria painted her as. Adria claimed that Halsey took part in the abuse at the school, that she locked people in solitary until they hallucinated, that there were beatings so violent that inmates were picking their shredded clothes from the wounds. The deck was stacked against Adria and the other former inmate, and eventually they both vanished. The investigation into the facility never turned up anything unusual and Adria was called a "liar" and a "traitor" for the accusations she made against Halsey. In a country overrun with out of control nationalism, someone like Halsey is nigh untouchable.

The bus ride to the facility was agonizing and crossed multiple state lines. There were about a dozen of us being shipped to the school. I still remember one girl who was herded onto the bus looking as though she was about to keel over. She tried several times on the trip to request medical attention, but each time she was denied and told to "suck it up." She would die about twelve hours from our destination, leaving the rest of us to sit with the body. Now, here I am, sitting with my head leaning against the window of the bus. We're less than thirty minutes from our destination. Checking my sock, I see the napkin I tucked inside of it is still there. The only hope I have left on this trip. Yesterday we each wrote down contact information and other details on two napkins. The girl whose body now sits slumped in one of the seats is the niece of the person we're supposed to take the information to; assuming we make it out of McGinley's alive.

"Oh my God, are you gonna do something about her?" one of the girls shouts at the guards. Her name's Rochelle and she and another girl, Savannah, have been the closest I have to friends on this trip. The dead girl's head is slumped against the window and thumping against it every time we hit a bump in the road.

"Did I say you could speak?" one of the guards replies. "Keep your mouth shut!" Rochelle shakes her head and looks away. Savannah rolls her eyes and looks down at the floor. Rochelle's the same age as me with warm sepia skin, long coiled hair, and deep brown eyes. She's a about five-ten with a slim build. Savannah is pale with green eyes and stands about an inch shorter than me at five-four with straight sandy hair. She seems a little more shy than Rochelle and wears a pair of black, rectangular-framed glasses that she keeps nervously adjusting.

After the bus comes to a stop, we're taken off and led onto a ferry. In the middle of the lake before us, I can see the island where the school is located. The ferry bobs up and down in the water as we speed toward the island. I keep hoping for some kind of miracle. I have no idea what, but I just want something to happen, something to make them turn back and take me home. It's just a bad dream, right? If I try hard enough I'll wake up in my own bed and none of this will have ever happened. If only that were possible...

Chapter 1

Welcome to Hell

That was the first thing the headmistress said to us. We'd just arrived on the island where McGinley's was located. A man-made island three miles from shore and seated in the frigid waters of Lake Michigan. The ferry ride was over and done with before I even realized it. I was so lost in my own head I didn't bother to pay much attention. Once we arrived on the island we were herded onto the docks, then into the intake center. There they lined everyone up in time for the headmistress to begin what I assumed was the usual introduction.

"This is not a vacation...this is not a free ride!" the headmistress bellowed, pacing up and down the line. She'd introduced herself as Ava Halsey moments before. She's about six feet tall with blood red hair, shoulder length and pulled back into a bun, and a beige complexion, dusted with freckles. She has cold gray eyes and the right side of her face and neck are peppered with scars from shrapnel that struck her in the war. Her uniform is only a little different from the other guards. Olive green with dark brown belts, collars, and boots. Brass name tags are situated on the upper left of each guard's torso and show the first letter of their given names and full last name. The sleeves go down to the elbows and some of the guards wear matching baseball caps while others go without. The same concept applies to the brown jackets some of them have on. Some have them, others don't. Yellow and brown rank insignias are visible on the shoulders of each guard, jackets or not, giving off a military-style feel to their appearance, and the only color on each uniform other than brown or green.

"Here at McGinley's you will learn to be proper citizens, so that you can become productive members of society. Do what you're told, stay in line, pay attention, and you may just succeed. Some of you might think I'll send you back to the mainland, to prison if you screw this up. There is no screwing up in my facility. You will stay here until you are well enough to leave. You will be rewarded with shortenings of your sentences if you behave yourselves. I decide if your sentences become longer or if they become shorter. Cross me or my staff and any progress you do make, will be wiped clean. Is that understood?" Everyone nods.

"I asked you a question!" Halsey barks.

"Yes ma'am!" we chorus...all except for me. I hoped it would go un-noticed, but it would seem I wasn't the first to show defiance here. It was less than three seconds before Halsey was on me. Her clipboard in one arm out before her, flipping through the pages clipped to it.

"You seem familiar," she drawls, glancing over the papers. "You look like that Muslim girl I've heard so much about."

"I'm not a Muslim..." I mutter. She stops and grabs my chin, her eyes piercing my own.

"I didn't ask for your feedback," Halsey growls. She lets go of me and steps back a pace, continuing to sift through her papers. "Sarita Teymouri. Here for the murder of Helena Liggman."

"It wasn't murder..." I reply. "They charged me with-"

"Manslaughter, I can read just fine," Halsey interrupts. "There may be a difference on the outside, but here it's the same as murder. I have no time for semantics. I don't care what the circumstances were, the fact is that you took a life. According to this you're turning eighteen in three months. You're lucky it didn't happen after that. You would have been much less likely to have come here. I hope you thanked your judge on the way out..."

"Crazy bitch..." I mumble under my breath.

"Excuse me? What did you say?" Halsey demands, glaring at me.

"Nothing," I answer.

"Didn't sound like nothing, now what was it?"

"It doesn't matter," I insist.

"If you and everyone else in this line are planning on eating today, you'll tell me what you just said," Halsey growls.

"I said you're fucking crazy!" I snap. She swats me across the face and grabs me by the hair.

"You will learn respect here at McGinley's," she snarls. "I'll let you off with a warning this one time, but if you do this again I will march your happy ass right down to the bunker. Do you understand me?" I glance to my right and see Rochelle looking at me, mouthing "Just say yes."

"Yes..."

"Yes what?" Halsey demands.

"Yes, I do," I reply. She swats me across the face again.

"Let me explain how this works," she growls. "When I ask you a yes or no question, you give me either a yes or a no and always a 'ma'am.' Is that understood?"

"Yes...ma'am..." I grumble. I have to force the last part out through gritted teeth.

"Excellent..." Halsey smirks, stepping back. "Getting back on topic, you will now be shown to your dorms. I don't want to hear a peep out of any of you. No fussing, no complaints, no smartass back-talk! Is that clear?"

"Yes ma'am!" we chorus. She glances at me, then motions for the guards to lead us out of the room. We're led down a long hallway filled with bare light bulbs hanging from long frayed cords above us.

The tan walls are covered in splotches of white paint, as though someone was covering something up. My first thought is that it might have been blood. The bunker, the place Halsey threatened to send me, is an old World War Two era underground structure on the north side of the island. The island, known as Hailstone Haven, was known as Fort Hail during its time as a military installation. It was abandoned in 1959 and stayed that way until McGinley's was founded here in 1973. Remnants of the old infrastructure still remain on the island. The watchtowers, now occupied by gun-toting guards, are an example of how some things haven't changed.

Most of what was left behind has simply been repaired and re-purposed. The spotlights have been altered, upgraded to something much more modern and powerful, the towers repaired, the guns carried by the guards are more powerful, more accurate. Two ferries float alongside the docks, waiting to retrieve new arrivals. Adria told stories of watching some of the more troublesome students taken off to the bunker, only to see the staff dragging the body back up to the surface in a tarp, but the government never found any evidence of wrong-doing on the part of the school. Maybe they never even looked to begin with.

In the dorm we're given the rundown on the rules and regulations. The limited amount of items we're allowed to have at our bunks is the first thing discussed. One pillow, a pillowcase, two sheets, that sort of thing. Three uniforms including the ones we're wearing. Black jackets with white shirts and blue jeans. We're given limited toiletries, a single comb, a toothbrush, two towels, soap, that sort of thing. Five minutes to shower once every other day and so on.

Next we're assigned jobs. I'm assigned to a custodial crew with Savannah and Rochelle. It's not until the following day that we start working. On that day, we're in the back of the building, cleaning out one of the restrooms. The first in a long line of chores that the three of us would be tasked with until the end of our sentences. I ring the mop out and glance out into the hallway. For a moment I thought I heard footsteps. My heart had skipped a beat, thinking it was Halsey or one of the staff coming to check on us again. I know one of the guards is nearby, but she seems disenchanted with her job. She was the one to lead us down here. A woman of average height with a deep umber complexion, short black hair, and dark gray eyes. She's a few inches taller than me with a larger frame and a tired look about her, giving her the appearance of having struggled to sleep for a number of days. Once we were out of earshot of the other staff, she told us to call her Nicole and to drop the "ma'am stuff."

"What are you looking at?" Rochelle asks, waving to get my attention. I glance back into the restroom and see that Savannah is looking at me too.

"Nothing," I reply, shaking my head.

"Nicole coming back or something?" Savannah asks.

"No, I don't think so," I answer. "Thought I heard footsteps, but I don't see anyone."

"Maybe it's the ghosts," Rochelle teases, nudging me with her elbow. "They're coming to take your soul away. That's what my sister told me, anyway. Not that I believe it."

"Ghosts?" I repeat.

"The girls who died here, right?" Savannah asks, continuing to wash the mirrors. I place the mop back on the floor and start cleaning the edge of the room and what I hope isn't the remains of a blood puddle.

"She's not right in the head anymore," Rochelle says, opening one of the stalls. "My big sis, that is. Place screwed her up good. Spent a lot of time in the bunker."

"Did she happen to give you a rundown on the rules before you came here?" I ask, dipping the mop in the bucket.

"Yeah, how'd you know?"

"I'm a big sister myself," I explain, wringing out the mop. "If my sister was coming here and I'd been here before, you can bet I'd be telling her everything I know. I assume that's why you were telling me to just agree with Halsey yesterday?" She nods.

"Halsey's no one to mess with," Rochelle replies. "It's just better to avoid trouble with her. Go along with it. Things work out better for everyone that way."

"I see."

"That said, I'm already wishing I wasn't here," Rochelle continues. "I keep thinking about that Eston girl who died here. Wondering if it's worth trying to escape."

"I hear that," Savannah cuts in. "Only slept here one night and I already want out."

"Anyone else miss their bed?" Rochelle asks, moving to the next stall. "I know I do."

"It's not just that, it's the bugs crawling all over the place," Savannah explains. "It's disgusting. I think a spider bit me while I was asleep." She lifts one of her pant legs and I see a red mark on her ankle.

"Anyone know if they have poisonous ones around here?" Rochelle asks. "Didn't think about that until just now."

"Any that are here probably came from the mainland," I answer. "I don't think there's anything to worry about around here. Friend of mine lived in this state before we met. She talked about getting spider bites all the time. Still alive and well." I dunk the mop in the bucket and pause for a moment.

"You hear something again?" Savannah asks. I look out into the hallway, but again there's nothing.

"I'm telling you, it's the ghosts," Rochelle chuckles. "They're coming for you. Take the murderers first." She holds up her hands and bends her fingers like claws as she speaks. She reaches out and grabs the sleeve of my uniform and I brush her hand off.

"I didn't murder anyone," I growl. "It was self-defense."

"Yeah and so was my case," she sighs. "Guy ran up and grabbed me when I was coming back from the bus stop. I guess his girlfriend ran off on him and I kinda looked like her or something. I thought he was trying to kidnap me or something, so I stabbed him. Ran off bleeding and the next thing I know I'm in handcuffs. How about you, Savannah? What'd you do?"

"Drug possession," Savannah answers. "With intent to sell. Needed some quick cash. Someone I know got into some trouble a few weeks before and because I'm such a 'good friend,' I guess," she continues, making air quotes with her fingers. "I opted to help her. She owed some people some money and said she was gonna get killed if she didn't pay up."

"And what happened to her?" Rochelle asks. Savannah shrugs.

"Hell if I know," she says. "She ran off when I got arrested. No idea if she got caught or not. Not that I care at this point."

"Someone's coming," I interrupt.

"More ghosts?" Savannah snorts. Moments later, Halsey steps into the room with Nicole behind her.

"I didn't happen to hear any talking in here, did I?" Halsey demands.

"No ma'am," Rochelle, Savannah, and I chorus.

"I should hope not," Halsey mutters. "Work doesn't get done if you spend all day chatting." She turns to face Nicole, who shrugs.

"What? Am I supposed to say something?" Nicole asks, sounding annoyed.

"You're supposed to be watching them," Halsey growls. "Now stand here and do your job. You wanna get fired?"

"No ma'am," Nicole sighs.

"Didn't think so," Halsey mutters. "I'll be back later. If I find that you've been neglecting your job again, I'm shipping you back to the mainland. Do you understand me?"

"Yes ma'am," Nicole grumbles.

"Good, now get to it. All of you!" Halsey orders. She leaves the room and heads back down the hallway. When she's out of earshot, Nicole shakes her head and mutters something under her breath.

"Looks like you hate it here almost as much as us," Rochelle says.

"Am I right?"

"What gave it away?" Nicole chuckles. "Listen, I don't care if you three talk, so go right on ahead. I'll tell you if she's coming back." She steps back out into the hall and leans her back against the wall, just to the left of the doorway. After we're done with the restroom, we clean the second one beside the first. In that time, Halsey never returns.

Chapter 2

Nightmares

The first month goes by with little trouble. The other inmates and I begin to fall into a routine. Up at the same time every morning, sometimes we're even pulled from our beds by guards for little more than their own amusement. I was one of the unfortunate few who found themselves targeted for such behavior. The first time it happened, I smacked my face on the floor and split my lip. The guard got upset and demanded to know why I felt "entitled" to bleed on his clean floor. He then dragged me to my feet before shoving me to the end of the bunk. While I stood there, he walked up and down the row of bunks, explaining that because I had bled on the floor, the rest of the room was going to give him and the other guards twenty push-ups. Anyone who refused was threatened with punishment.

I stood there feeling frustrated and powerless while everyone else suffered for something that wasn't even my fault. He then began pacing back up and down the row, picking random inmates to angrily "thank" me for having gotten them in trouble. By this point there were already a few other inmates who'd been in this position more than me, but at the same time I worried what it would mean for me during the nighttime hours. The night before, I'd been woken up by screams from another inmate being dragged from their bed and beaten. A new girl named Jackie who came in on the same bus as me. The guards came in and just stood there laughing, egging them on while two inmates took turns attacking her. The whole dorm woke up and the guards threatened to shoot anyone who tried to help her out. They use rubber bullets in their pistols, but getting hit with one, especially at close range, is not something I want to experience. Eventually Jackie passed out with what I assume was a concussion and was carted off to the infirmary. Needless to say, I didn't sleep well from that point on.

At the end of that month, nothing else had happened in the dorms, other than a few spats over missing items. When you're allowed so little it becomes tempting to steal from others. The final night of that month I tried to stay awake as long as I could, the way I'd done every night since I was blamed for bleeding on the floor. Eventually I dozed off and found myself having a series of strange dreams. None of them made any sense. They were mere fragments of everything that'd happened in the past few months, all twisted into some demented movie by my over-stressed mind. Toward the end I was walking down a long, dark hallway with a flashlight in my hand. The further I went, the more I began to feel I was being followed. Panic set in as I felt a blade pierce my side. My eyes snapped open and I sat bolt upright.

My first thought was that someone had attacked me in my sleep. When I didn't find a wound anywhere, I lay back down and stared up at the ceiling as sweat dripped down my temples. This continued for two hours. I wanted to leap from the bunk and run. It didn't matter where. The need was just to get far away from something that wasn't even real. After the two hours ended, my eyelids grew heavy and I started to drift off again. The dream faded into memory and I saw nothing else like it for the rest of the night.

* * *

Later that day, I would find myself once again working with Savannah and Rochelle, this time cleaning the chow hall.[1] It's after dinner and most of the staff and inmates have gone to their dorms. One of the girls tried to escape today and that's become the topic of discussion for us. Nicole's been assigned to watch us again and is sitting on the far end of the chow hall, reading a newspaper and smoking a cigarette. She slipped us a bit of food before she retired to her current spot. A voice crackles over Nicole's radio and she jumps to her feet and snuffs her cigarette on the inside of a nearby trash can.

"Copy that, I'm heading there now," she says into the radio. She nods

---

[1] Cafeteria

to us and trots out of the room.

"What was that all about?" I ask. The others shrug and we stand in silence, listening.

"You hear that?" Savannah whispers. Screams and shouts can be heard somewhere down the hall. The three of us begin moving closer to the double doors as the shouts grow louder. An inmate comes racing into the room and collides with Rochelle. She's covered in blood and holding a kitchen knife. The both of them tumble across the floor and the girl slugs Rochelle in the face before scrambling to her feet. Rochelle rolls and catches her ankle, sending the girl crashing onto the floor. Rochelle races to her feet, snatches up the knife, and is shot twice in the chest right as the first few guards come charging into the room. She shouts in pain and falls to the floor.

"On the floor! Now!" the guards scream at the rest of us. One of them brandishes a pistol at me and I drop to my knees and lie on my stomach with my hands on the back of my head. Savannah does the same, but the other girl refuses to comply and instead runs for the doors on the opposite side of the room. She hops over one of the tables and nearly collides with another group of guards who've headed her off. They fire off a half-a-dozen rounds and the inmate screams and grabs at her face as blood seeps between her fingers. She's forced down on the ground by four guards while a fifth cuffs her hands behind her back.

"Fuck Halsey and fuck McGinley's!" the girl screams. "Get off of me! Let me – don't touch me! My eye! I can't see!" One of the guards hits her twice in the back with a baton, interrupting her screams. Nearby, Rochelle, now with her hands cuffed behind her, begins to curse under her breath. Each of us has a guard looming over us with their pistols pointed at us. They start requesting medical staff over the radio. The girl they were chasing is still on the floor screaming and cursing at the top of her lungs.

Moments later, the three of us are dragged to our feet and put against the wall. The medical staff arrive with a gurney and whisk the girl on the floor away. Blood is all over the floor where she fell and just as much of it smeared across her body. It's impossible to tell how much is hers and how much is from someone else. The rest of us are led from the room. Once at the end of the hallway, I notice a set of bloody foot and hand prints on the floor and wall. We round the corner and I see an unconscious inmate lying in a pool of blood on the floor. Three of the medical staff are trying to stem the bleeding.

"Quit staring and keep moving," the guard behind me says.

Chapter 3

Trust Issues

Two days would pass before I heard anything about the girl who was shot in the chow hall. Her name is Noami Beckham and the rumor going around is that the girl she stabbed was planning to snitch[2] on her about something. What it was I'll probably never know. More than anything I'm just shocked by the display of force. I thought for sure I was going to witness a murder. I haven't heard anything about plans to discipline the guards, but I suppose I shouldn't expect it. Maybe I never heard, maybe Halsey said something behind closed doors, but I doubt it.

It's now the third day since the incident and dinner just wrapped up. I'm sitting up on my bunk, legs crossed with a book in my lap. Over near one of the exits I can see two girls I've seen around campus in the days since the chow hall incident. I'm certain I've seen them even before that, but from what I've heard, they know Naomi. I don't know either of their names, but one of the three is clearly in charge of the others. The girl I've pegged to be the leader is about the same height as me with a warm brown complexion and deep brown eyes that appear almost black. Her jet black hair is wavy and long, hanging a few inches past her shoulders. She usually wears it up in a bun, but appears to have let it down for the night.

Her eyebrows are bushy and one has a scar running through it that appears to have been caused by a knife. The lack of hair in that spot

---

[2]To rat someone out in this context. Also refers to someone acting as an informant. Snitching is frowned upon by inmates and doing so can place that person in serious danger.

makes it much more obvious. The second girl has straight, ginger hair with freckles peppered across her face, part of her neck, and her arms. She's about five-two with a petite build, a light complexion, and hooded gray eyes. Her hair is cropped short in a pixie cut. She brushes her bangs away from her face as she speaks to her companion. The third girl isn't present in the doorway, but she's a couple inches taller than the leader girl and has straight, dark brown hair and green eyes. She has a beige complexion and a round face with prominent cheekbones. She keeps her hair in a single braid that hangs over her right shoulder. She seems very tense and uptight, as if she was expecting to be ambushed at any moment.

I turn my attention away from them and focus on my book. Minutes later the red-haired girl approaches me and stands at the base of the bunk, staring up at me. I almost fumble my book when I see her and look back at the doorway. The other girl is gone.

"Umm...hi?" I say, closing the book and setting it beside me. Her stony expression converts to a grin and she steps back a pace, keeping her arms crossed in front of her.

"Sarita, right?" she asks. I nod.

"Yeah, what do you want?" Movement to my left catches my eye and I turn my head to see Savannah and Rochelle coming toward us.

"Well, I was hoping to speak to you in private," the girl sighs, eyeing the others.

"What's going on?" Rochelle demands.

"Just talking," the girl responds.

"I hope so," Rochelle replies. Her expression and tone are friendly, but it's obvious she's faking them both. Savannah appears curious, but doesn't seem to be as concerned as Rochelle.

"You're from C Dorm, right?" Savannah asks.

"That's right," the girl answers. "I'm Mika. Nice to meet you all."

"Is there a reason you wanted to talk to me?" I inquire. Mika turns her attention away from the others and backs up a few paces.

"You going somewhere?" Rochelle asks, crossing her arms and tilting her head.

"Just making sure I can see all of you," Mika answers. "Nothing personal. But yes, Sarita, I wanted to talk to you, and like I already said, I was hoping to do so in private."

"You two mind backing off for a few?" I ask Rochelle and Savannah. They both look up at me and then exchange glances.

"I don't think she's looking for a friend," Rochelle says, looking first at me, then at Mika. "Something seems off."

"It's nothing bad, I promise," Mika replies.

"Promises don't mean much in a place like this," Rochelle answers.

"Who was that girl I saw you talking to a minute ago?" I ask.

"That's Leah," she answers. "I'd prefer not to say anything else until these two leave. It'll just be a second."

"Anything you have to say to her you can say in front of us," Savannah says.

"That's the thing," Mika sighs, shaking her head. "It doesn't work that way. Jitterbugs[3] like you need to understand that there are rules here. Sometimes hearing certain things can get you into trouble. What I have to say is for Sarita only, and so long as she's the only one who hears it, there won't be any problems."

"Get lost," Rochelle growls. I let out a frustrated groan and climb down from my bunk.

"Just do what she asks," I order, looking at Savannah and Rochelle.

"Come on, Sarita, you know this is shady as hell," Savannah replies.

"It only looks that way, trust me," Mika says.

"Trust you? Pff...yeah, right," Rochelle growls. Mika rolls her eyes.

"What I have to say stands to benefit all three of you, but right now I only want to talk to Sarita," Mika responds.

"I'm having a hard time believing that," Savannah declares.

"Look, let's not make this harder than it is," Mika groans. "One minute, all right? Just one minute. I'm not about to get thrown in the bunker over a talk, okay? One minute. That's all. Then I'll leave, and if she says no, I'll leave and never come back." There's a tense pause as Savannah and Rochelle take some time to consider what Mika's just said. After about a minute, Rochelle nods and looks at me, then Mika.

"Okay, fine," Rochelle says. "One minute and we're gonna keep an eye on you the entire time." Mika smiles and doesn't respond, leaving Savannah and Rochelle to return to their bunks in silence. Once they're gone, Mika glances around and makes sure that no one is listening. There aren't any other inmates within about fifteen feet of us. Most are

---

[3]New inmates

sitting at the tables near the windows and few others are sitting or lying on their bunks.

"Okay, it looks like I have a time limit, so let's cut to the chase," Mika says, locking eyes with me. "Here, this is for you. Don't look at it until lights out. After you read it, make sure you flush it, and do NOT get caught with it." She removes a kite[4] from her pocket and hands it to me.

"What is it?"

"Just wait till later and find out," she says, walking away. "And don't tell anyone about it. This is between you and me. I'll find you at breakfast. We'll talk more then." She leaves the room and I watch until she disappears. Once she's gone I take one last look at the kite and place it in my pocket. Something about this doesn't seem right. I turn to head back to my bunk and almost collide with Rochelle and Savannah.

"What did she say?" Savannah asks.

"Nothing, she just handed me a kite and walked off," I answer.

"Did you read it?" Rochelle inquires.

"I was just on my way to do that," I answer, brushing past them and climbing up the side of my bunk.

"We can't help if we don't know what's going on, Sarita," Rochelle calls up to me. I peer over the side of the bunk and look down at them both.

"If there's anything weird going on, I'll be sure to let you know," I say. "Right now I don't think that's the case. She did say she'd come find me in the chow hall tomorrow. We'll find out more then."

"All right, fine," Rochelle sighs. "We'll talk tomorrow." They both return to their bunks and as soon as lights out arrives, I unfold the kite and read the message inside:

We know about the note, the bus incident, and Halsey does too. She's looking for you and the note. We'll help you, but only if you agree to our terms.

I'm a little taken aback by what it says. It seems almost like a mix between helpful advice and a threat. An hour passes before I leave my bunk and make my way to the nearest restroom. Right as I walk in I hear one of the stall doors close and lock. I step into the one beside it.

---

[4]A message, usually written on a small piece of paper.

Since someone's in the room with me, I opt to at least try and make it seem like I'm not here for anything unusual. So I walk in, stand there for a few moments, staring down at the floor, and then crumple the kite up and toss it in the toilet. After I flush it, I walk back out and pause by the other stalls. All of the doors are sitting ajar and the girl I heard earlier is nowhere to be found. Did she leave without me noticing?

It's hard to get that crap Rochelle said the other day out of my head. Ghosts and whatnot. It's not like it's impossible to sneak out of a stall without being seen, but still, I'm certain I heard someone close and lock the door. I even heard her moving around a minute ago. As I exit the restroom, I'm feeling a little paranoid, like someone's watching me. Hard not to feel that way when there's security camera's all over the place, but something about this feels different. Like I can almost feel the pair of eyes staring at me somewhere close by. I've always had a vivid imagination and as I'm walking down the hallway I try to suppress it; though my racing mind is making that difficult.

* * *

That night I sleep somewhat soundly. Can't say the same for some of the others in the dorm. Twice I was sure I heard someone pacing around the room. Since the guards sometimes pop in to check on us, I dismissed it as nothing more than that and fell back asleep. It was more annoying than anything. When I reach the chow hall with Savannah and Rochelle, there's no sign yet of Mika, Leah, or the third girl.

"So they know about the note, huh?" Rochelle says. "Great...I had a feeling that would backfire. Now I feel almost stupid for suggesting we write them in the first place."

"It was a smart thing to do, regardless of whatever's going on with this Mika person," Savannah replies as the line moves along at its usual sluggish pace. "It's not like any of us wanted to let McGinley's and whoever else runs this shitshow get away with killing one of us."

"True, but she's just gonna wind up getting forgotten if we don't safeguard that note somehow," Rochelle responds. "If these other girls want it, that could complicate things. Will complicate things..."

"I don't see Mika yet," I say. "Hopefully she's still planning to show up. I was hoping we could get more out of her."

"There she is, by the door. She just walked in," Savannah says. I

16

glance at the main entrance and sure enough I spot Mika making her way through the crowd.

"Hard to miss her with that hair of hers, huh?" Rochelle observes. Minutes later the three of us are gathered at our usual table. Sure enough, Mika plops down beside me a short time after that, much to Rochelle's dislike.

"Did you read it?" Mika asks, taking a few bites of food.

"I did," I answer. "But I'm not sure what to make of it. Sounded like a veiled threat." She gives me a confused look, shakes her head, and clears her throat.

"No, no, no, you've got it all wrong," she insists. "It's meant to be an offer."

"What kind of offer?" Rochelle inquires, staring at Mika. Mika holds up her index finger and then sets her hand down on the table in front of her.

"This isn't a press conference, I'm not just taking questions from everyone," she replies. "But Sarita," she continues, looking at me. "We meant what we said. We know Halsey's on the hunt for that note and there's no telling how long it'll be before she sniffs it out. It could be tomorrow, it could be two hours from now, it could be next week when she finally finds it. The longer you have it, the greater the risk."

"And what's the risk involved with you?" I demand. "Why are you so interested in the note, anyway?"

"We're not the only one's interested, nor are we the only inmates who know about it," Mika says. "Word spreads fast around here. Most people here are on your guys' side about it. They're cheering you on, they want you to wipe the floor with McGinley's. Hell, I do too. But that note alone is not enough. You wanna take this place down for good, then you're gonna need our help to do it. I'll see you out at the bleachers by the track. These two can come along if they want," she gestures at Rochelle and Savannah, "but they aren't going to be apart of the conversation. Not right now." She stands up and moves to another table where I can see Leah and the third girl sitting. Leah catches my eye for a moment, then looks back at Mika. Rochelle and Savannah stare at them for a minute too, then turn their attention back to me.

"That was quick," Savannah mumbles. "She didn't really tell us much."

"Easier to talk in less crowded areas, I'm sure," Rochelle says. "She's starting to annoy me a little."

"A little?" Savannah snorts. "Last night you said you wanted to smack her."

"Places like McGinley's are full of people running all sorts of scams, side hustles, that sort of thing, and some of them are fine, but others... let's just say you don't want to get caught up in them. Mika might seem friendly, but she could be a straight up psychopath for all any of us know."

"She knows that Naomi girl, so I guess that's not too far-fetched," I admit.

"Which is why we're taking her up on her invitation and going with you," Rochelle says.

* * *

The track is situated on the yard[5], out back behind the main building, known simply as "Building B," where Halsey's office, the chow hall, and several other places are located. The streets are named the same way. A Street, B Street, etc. A Street runs between Building B and Building A, which houses the dorms, and connects to C Street. Half-way down C Street is a gate with a team of guards stationed on both sides. It's part of a series of gates and fences that divide the island into various sections. Walking about a third of the way down C Street gets you behind Building B and onto the yard. About a five minute walk. That's where Rochelle, Savannah, and I all head next.

When we arrive, the bleachers are in view, and a dusty dirt track becomes visible near it. I don't usually come out here after meals. I'm always too tired from working and never awake enough in the mornings. Even with what's going on at the moment, I still feel tempted to go back to the dorm like I usually do at this time, and just stretch out on my musty old bunk for a bit. Maybe then I could get a quick nap in before the day's grueling routine kicks in. An entire month of this and I still haven't gotten used to it. Now I have Mika and Leah to deal with on top of it. Near the bleachers, I spot Mika standing with Leah and the brown-haired girl I often see with them. Mika spots us and waves

---

[5]The area within a prison where recreational activities, including working out and sports, take place.

us over.

"Good, good, you didn't run off on me," Mika says with approval. "All right, like I said, your partners[6] here need to stay back for a minute. Got it?" I glance at Rochelle and Savannah, then back at Mika.

"Yeah, fine," I say.

"You sure you guys aren't up to anything shady?" Rochelle asks.

"Depends on your definition of shady," Leah chimes in, her arms crossed in front of her. She shrugs and shifts her weight.

"That doesn't seem all that encouraging," Savannah says.

"We're not here to make trouble," Mika insists. "But you gotta understand something. We have our own interests to protect, and right now you're not the only one taking a risk."

"Your partner turned someone into Swiss cheese a few days ago, I think we're the one's taking the bigger risk here," Rochelle declares.

"That won't happen again," Leah assures us, shaking her head. "Well...we don't expect that to."

"Come on, let's quit wasting time," Mika says, gesturing toward the track. "We don't have all the time in the world." I nod and follow her toward the track. Three girls pass by us, one of them giving me a dirty look as they continue along the track in the opposite direction. One of the three bumps her shoulder into Mika as she passes and we stop as we watch the three of them walk off snickering.

"Friends of yours?" I ask.

"Not exactly," she answers, starting down the track, away from the others. "The tallest one, that's Tala. The one who just bumped into me is Kelly, and the other one is Leilani." Tala is about four inches taller than me with straight, black hair and green eyes. She has a light complexion and prominent cheekbones with a port-wine stain birthmark on her left wrist. Leilani has wavy hair with gray eyes and is about an inch shorter than me. She's a little bony with thick eyebrows, a light brown complexion, and a gap in her front teeth. Kelly is taller than Leilani and shorter than Tala with waist-length blonde hair tied in a single braid down her back, cold brown eyes, and a light dusting of freckles on her face and arms. There's something about the way she looks back at us that makes me want to hit her more than the others. Something about the way she smirks and carries herself almost as if she thinks she's

---

[6]Friend, associate, someone you hang with.

royalty.

"I hate 'em already," I mutter, walking alongside Mika. She chuckles and tilts her head back, looking up at the cold, overcast sky above.

"Yeah, a lot of people do," she says, leveling her head and glancing at me. "Most of us in C Dorm either fight with them, try like hell to ignore them, or just go along with whatever they're doing."

"I guess I lucked out as far as dorms," I reply. "There's not really anyone in B Dorm like that. The usual arguments and crap, sure, but no one deliberately causing trouble all the time. I only just...well, sort of met those three, and already they get on my nerves. Can't imagine being in a dorm with them for any length of time." Mika chuckles again and scratches at the back of her neck.

"Yeah they have a way of getting under peoples' skin," she says. "Part of it is that the guards tend to favor them. Bunch of snitches, that's what they are...and they're rewarded for it. Not just that either. They're used to interrogate other inmates, break them down over time, get them to fight so guards can swoop in and detain them. Sometimes sit and listen for anything unusual and report back."

"That sounds frustrating..."

"Oh trust me, it is," she replies. "If I had it my way, me, Leah, and Ariana would just beat the snot out of them. Or maybe take a leaf out of Naomi's book for that matter. Hell, I'd love to stick Tala in the neck. I swear to God it's like she stalks me every chance she gets...and I'm certain that's why she's out on the track, trying to learn something damaging."

"Who's Ariana?" I ask.

"The other girl over there with Leah," she answers. "The nervous looking girl next to her."

"Right, I see her."

"Leah's kind of like you in a way," she continues. "She's a refugee from Guatemala, but that's all I know."

"How do you know that about me, anyway?" I demand.

"That you're a refugee?" she asks.

"Yeah."

"Guards hear stuff in the media and then we hear them talking about it in the halls," she explains. "Best we have since we aren't allowed to watch or listen to anything."

"I see. Still a little creepy that people seem to know so much about me here," I say.

"It's all just details from your case, nothing too personal," she replies. "It caught national attention from what I heard, but it's not like anyone here knows your favorite color or anything, so don't worry too much about it."

"Yeah, I'll keep that in mind," I sigh. "Is it just you, Leah, Ariana, and Naomi?" She shakes her head.

"No, there's Tia too, but she's somewhere else at the moment. And obviously Naomi's not around either since she got locked up, but that's different."

"Why did Naomi get locked up, anyway?"

"Well she stabbed the shit out of Emily for one," Mika snorts. "Come on, I heard you were in the chow hall when they took her down."

"I was, but I didn't hear anything else about this Emily person. I heard her last name was Parsons and there was some rumor about why it happened and that's it."

"And for right now that's all you need to know about it," Mika answers.

"What exactly are you guys up to, anyway?" I inquire.

"Like I said back in the chow hall, you're not the only one who wants to see this place go down," she answers. "The note has to escape and so do you. Understand?"

"I think so," I say. "Seems like a long shot, doesn't it?"

"Not as long as staying here for a full two years, or more if Halsey feels like it, and then hoping you're still sane enough to file a lawsuit," Mika replies. "The rumors people have heard, the ones I'm sure you're plenty familiar with, they're all true. This place destroys minds as much as it does bodies; if not more so. We're no good to anyone if we're so damaged we can't even fight the already uphill battle that's waiting for us out there."

"Good point," I admit. "Just to be clear, are you asking me to be apart of planning this, or are you just interested in taking my note along with you?"

"I did say you had to escape to take this place down, didn't I?" she chuckles, grabbing and shaking my shoulder. "So are you in or out?"

"You said last night that this stands to benefit Rochelle and Savannah too," I point out. "Are they going to be apart of this?"

"That's up to Naomi," Mika answers. "Since she's not here, I can't say for sure if she'll want those two to help out. She's locked up till the end of the month, so I won't know until then. Right now we know she's interested in recruiting you and that's it."

"What happens if I say no?"

"Who's gonna say no to an escape?" Mika chuckles. "Don't tell me you've gotten comfortable here already. Look, I'll say this much. If you say no, then that's fine, you're fine, just as long as you keep your mouth shut. But Sarita, I'm gonna very be clear about this. If you utter one peep to anyone about what we discussed, well...we know where you sleep."

"I never heard a thing," I answer.

"And I never said a thing. Now are you backing out or joining?" she asks.

"I haven't decided," I answer. "I need to think about it."

"Well lucky for you we've got a few weeks for you to mull it around if you want," she answers.

"I won't need that long," I answer. "It's just a lot to take in, that's all." Moments later, Tala and the others pass by us. Once they're out of earshot, the conversation continues.

"While you're thinking it over, how about we discuss what to do with the note from the bus?" she suggests. "Go down to the restroom between our dorms at 11:47 tonight. I'll take the note from there and we'll make sure it's safe."

"Why such a weird time?" I ask.

"I'm showing up five minutes after that," she explains. "Can't have it seem planned if anyone happens to see. Security cameras all over the place, we have to cover our bases, you know?"

"Yeah, I guess that makes sense," I reply.

"Then I'll see you there," she says.

"I never said that," I counter. "Look...this is a huge risk on my part, I'm sure you get that, but I made a promise that I intend to keep. If I let that note go and something happens to it, then Rachel Caine's death becomes another statistic."

"Hey, I get it," she says, holding her hands up in mock surrender and letting them fall back to her sides again. "We're asking for a lot of trust here."

"And for all I know you could be setting me up."

"If you want inmates that'll set you up, try Tala and her goon squad. We're nothing like that, I promise."

"It's like Rochelle said last night. Promises don't mean much."

"Look, I'm telling you, Halsey's after you and that note, and the bunker is not someplace you wanna get sent," she continues. "Even Tower B is a crapshoot. Hold onto that note too long and that's where you'll end up. And it looks like Tala and the others found their way to Leah..." She stops in place and the two of us stare across the track and toward the spot where Leah, Rochelle, and everyone else are standing by the bleachers. Near them are Tala, Kelly, and Leilani who are focusing their attention on Leah and Ariana. Leah seems to be the primary focus and Ariana looks like she's ready to fight while Rochelle and Savannah are standing by watching the scene unfold.

"Come on, let's go see what's going on," Mika says, starting toward the group. Once we reach them the insults are already flying and Leah is trying to convince Tala to back off. Rochelle and Savannah have stepped further way, both appearing to want to avoid whatever might happen.

"What's going on over here?" Mika demands, approaching Leah and Ariana. I rejoin Rochelle and Savannah and we continue to watch.

"She's claiming I stole something again, that's all," Leah answers, gesturing at Tala, who glares at her.

"Probably because you did," Tala responds.

"Well I must have a doppelganger in here, cuz I never touched your damn locker," Leah answers.

"I've got a lighter missing, Reyes, how do you explain that?" Tala demands.

"You sure you didn't lose it or something? Drop it somewhere while you were out lighting up?" Leah asks, holding her middle and index fingers as if she's clutching a cigarette between them. "Everyone knows you're Fenton's pet! You smell like smoke all day long and she just ignores it."

"That doesn't explain why it's missing!" Tala snarls, clenching her fists.

"She just told you why," Ariana cuts in. "I see your klutzy ass dropping shit all the time!"

"Was I talking to you?" Tala demands, pointing at Ariana.

"Get lost, Tala, no one stole your lighter," Mika orders, pointing behind Tala. "Take Tweedledee and Tweedledum with you."

"The fuck did you call us?" Leilani demands, taking a step forward.

"You heard me, now get going," Mika growls. "No one asked you to come here."

"I didn't need an invitation," Tala snarls. "That bitch stole from me." She points at Leah as she speaks. "That's why we're here. If she knew how to respect other peoples' shit we wouldn't be having this problem."

"You must've passed by her a few times on the track," Mika responds. "You were out there with me a little bit ago. Why'd it take you so long to come over? Huh? I don't think this is about your missing crap, now beat it!"

"And what are you gonna do if I don't?" Tala taunts. "I ain't leaving until I know what happened to my property."

"Come on, let's get out of here," Rochelle mutters. "This doesn't have anything to do with us."

"Fine by me," Savannah murmurs. Less than three seconds pass before we all stop again.

"I bet the ginger passed it off to that Muslim girl," Kelly says. Rochelle gives me a confused look and I shake my head.

"You didn't really take anything from her, did you?" Savannah asks, keeping her voice low.

"No, I didn't," I insist.

"We've got trouble either way," Rochelle says, gesturing at Tala, Leilani, and Kelly as they approach. Tala is the first to approach me and Rochelle and Savannah step up beside me.

"Back off, she doesn't have your lighter," Rochelle growls. Tala gives her a shove which she returns.

"Get the hell out of my way," Tala demands. "If she doesn't have it she can show me herself."

"She doesn't owe you that, now piss off," Savannah growls. Mika races up to us and stands beside me.

"She doesn't have your lighter, Tala! This doesn't involve her!" Mika says. Tala reaches into her coat, produces a shiv[7] and brandishes it at Mika.

"You need to get out of my way, you little pest!" Tala snarls.

[7]A homemade knife or stabbing weapon.

"Hey there's no need for one of those," Mika says, the tip of the blade pressed up against her cheek. "Let's all just calm down, okay? I'm sure we can think of a solution." Right as she finishes her sentence, she grabs and twists Tala's wrist, then slugs her in the jaw. Tala drops the shiv and Savannah snatches it up and throws it out of reach behind us. Kelly punches Mika in the cheek and Leah and Ariana come running up behind Tala and the others. Leah leaps onto Leilani's back and drags her to the ground, punching her in the kidney with as much force as she can muster. Tala throws Mika backward and Ariana kicks Kelly in the back, sending her crashing to the ground.

Tala comes after me and I dodge two punches while taking a third to the stomach. The wind is knocked out of me and Savannah and Rochelle both attack Tala, dragging her down and kicking and stomping her. A gunshot rings out from the nearest watchtower and I feel the round graze my ear. It hits the grass behind us and sends dirt flying into the air. These aren't the usual rubber bullets. They're live rounds. What the hell is going on? They're actually going to try and kill us over a fist fight? Guards come racing onto the yard and one of them, Rashida, the Deputy Headmistress, begins shouting at the man in the tower.

"Hold your fire, McClain!" she bellows. "You fucking idiot!" She grabs her radio and continues shouting into it. "You'd better pray you missed! You hear me? Start praying, Matt!" The three guards with her beat her to us and she brings up the rear. A vein along her temple is throbbing and appears ready to burst. Rashida was at the intake center when we first arrived on the island and since then I haven't seen her much. Her jet black hair is tied in a braid and sticking out the back of her uniform's baseball cap. She has piercing brown eyes, a light brown complexion, and a heart-shaped face. Her right forearm is covered in scars from severe burns, matching similar scars on the same side of her neck. She has bags under her eyes, contrasting the sharp alertness in them, and stands at about five-ten with ramrod posture.

According to what Rochelle told me and Savannah not long after we first arrived here, Rashida's the soldier Halsey's known for having rescued. The guards order us up off the ground and line us up in a row. The entire time I'm fearing the moment a bullet might come sailing through my chest. It never does, but the realization that it could has sent me into panic mode. Rashida waits near us with one other guard while the other two search for the missing shiv.

"I swear to God, I'm gonna take that idiot's head and smack it into a wall," Rashida grumbles.

"I wouldn't let too many people hear you say that," cautions the guard closest to us. "Especially now."

"Everyone knows how I feel about it, it's not like it's a big secret," Rashida replies.

"I'm just suggesting that you make things easier on yourself," the guard replies. "Things have been tough the past few years."

"If that trigger-happy lunatic keeps firing off live rounds like that he'll be the one having a rough time," Rashida threatens. The other two guards find the shiv in the grass and one picks it up. They walk back over to us and Rashida takes the shiv from them. She examines it, then turns to face the rest of us.

"All right, so which one of you had this?" she demands. No one responds. "Really? No one saw anything? No one knows where this came from? Which of you pulled this? I don't see any blood on it. That's a good sign. No blood on any of you, no one got stabbed. Lesser charge for the one responsible. We have cameras watching every angle of this island, ladies. Admitting to owning this lessens your punishment, you know the rules. So if you don't want to say who had this, then fine. We don't need you to."

* * *

Rashida stood there for another minute or so before telling us "have it your way" and ordering us to be cuffed and walked back to the main building. There we were lined up outside her office and forced to stand and wait while she kept an eye on us. A guard went to check the surveillance footage of the yard and when they came back they seized Tala and took her down to Halsey's office alone. After about 30mins or so we were released and ordered back to work.

Mika would show up again at dinner that night, only to remind me about the note and then she was off again. Back to the table with Leah and Ariana. I didn't know what to do, so I resolved to stay up and wait for 11:47pm. That's where I am now. Lying on my side, staring at the clock from atop my bunk. I have five minutes before I need to leave. The note is in my hand and the room itself is about as close to silent as it'll ever get. One of the guards just walked through a few minutes ago, his footsteps echoing through the room and sometimes lost amid the various degrees of snoring.

He's long gone and right now I'm thinking I'll just hand the note off. I've been afraid to lose the note ever since I brought it here and began reading it off and on to memorize it. I'm confident that I can make a complete copy of the note if I have to, but there's still a fragment of self-doubt involved. I've repeated the information letter for letter, number for number, in my head multiple times, but I can't help but wonder if I might somehow forget. I won't have the note to look at if I'm uncertain or I feel like I mixed something up, and making a copy, if Mika's right about what's happening, just seems like asking for trouble. If I were to do that then it would defeat the purpose of both memorizing it and passing it off to Mika.

With a minute to go, I sit up and swing my legs over the side of the bunk and start down the ladder. As I'm making my way through the dorm I'm half-expecting a guard to spot me and shout. It never happens, but I'm on edge and waiting for it regardless. Out in the hallway I start hearing voices and spot two shadows cast from an adjacent hallway. For a moment I consider running back to my bunk, but it soon becomes clear that the shadows are shrinking; their owners walking away from me. I can't make out much of what's being said, but the sound of a static-ridden voice in the background of the conversation tells me that it's two guards. Once they're gone, I start toward the restroom. Upon walking inside, I find the place empty and begin pacing back and forth in front of the stalls. For a moment I consider at least standing inside of one until Mika arrives. At first I decide against it, but soon figure it would look a little less odd if someone else comes in. I'm inside the stall for about a minute before I hear someone walk in. After waiting for about thirty seconds, I hear Mika mumbling about me being late and step out of the stall to greet her.

"Oh, you're not late after all," she observes, turning her head toward me. I stop a few feet from her with the note in my pocket and last minute doubts running through my mind.

"You sure about this?" I ask, taking the note out of my pocket.

"Sure as I'll ever be," she says with a shrug. I give her an irritated look and pull my hand back, clutching the note tighter.

"I'm serious."

"So am I!" she replies. "Look, we don't have all the time in the world. Maybe I don't seem trustworthy, I get that, but handing me the note will spare you a month in the bunker. Or if you want, you can just walk right back out of here and pretend this never happened. We could get along fine without you, but it would be easier to have you on board."

"Excuse me?" I demand. "You can get along fine without me? Real assuring, asshole!"

"Hey! Keep it down!" she warns, placing a finger over her lips. "Guards come by here every now and then. You wanna get us both in trouble?"

"I'm not sure this is a good idea," I say. I pocket the note and cross my arms in front of me. Mika shakes her head and rolls her eyes.

"Look, Sarita, I didn't mean it like that," she assures me. "I'm just upholding what I told you earlier, about backing out. You're free to go if you want, but don't think you can just go out there and keep your nose clean to avoid trouble. Trouble will find you, and when it does, it's not gonna be pretty."

"How do I know that this, what we're doing right now, isn't going to cause trouble?" I demand. "What if you lose it? What if it's an innocent mistake?"

"I'm not inclined to let Halsey find something that valuable," she answers. "Relax, all right? I've got this. It won't get lost. We can't take everyone with us when we leave, we'll need to call witnesses, people who can support our case when we get out. That note's invaluable."

"And that's why I'm not so keen to give it up," I explain, removing it from my pocket again. "And how do you know these people aren't going to die or be useless by the time we need them?"

"Well, you have faith in them, don't you?" she responds. "The risks me and the others are taking aren't much different than you when it comes to this, but if we lose their contact information, it makes it harder for us. For them. So we'll make sure to hang on to it. I can assure you of that much." She reaches for the note and I hesitate for a moment before handing it to her.

"Okay...fine..." I say. "I'm in. If there's a chance I can get out of here sooner than later, I'll take it." She smiles and puts the note in her pocket.

"Glad to hear it," she says. "One last thing before I go. Just know that I won't be around much. I'll come talk to you every now and again to let you know what's happening, but don't freak out and think we've abandoned you, okay? It's all apart of the plan. We have to keep our heads down until Naomi's back out. We're being watched closer than ever since the whole thing with Parsons. We can't act yet and we need to wait for the heat to die down first. Got it?"

"Got it."

"Good," she smiles. "I'll see you around. If you need to talk to me about anything related to this, I'm out at the track most days. If I'm not walking, I'm sitting somewhere nearby. Just make sure you don't abuse the privilege, okay? And if you do, make sure no one follows you. We don't need any eavesdroppers ruining this for us."

"I understand," I say with a nod.

"And while we're on that subject, you should keep an eye on the people around you, Sarita," she continues. "There's always someone like Tala walking around, looking to rat on people. Don't give them the chance to do it. Don't write anything down, don't talk to anyone but me or Leah, if she happens to come see you, about any of this. I'll come find you in a few days or so; let you know how things are going. Just stay in line and don't cause any trouble till then. Or after...you get the idea." She exits the room and after about a minute, I follow suit and make my way back to the dorm.

Chapter 4

No Going Back

Over the following weeks, Mika would keep her promise and give me various updates. There were a few searches in my dorm, all ending with the removal of several unknown items. I was never sure if any of those searches were intended to find the note. It seemed likely that Halsey would want to keep something like that low key. At the end of the month, Naomi was at last released from the bunker, looking tired and haggard. Missing an eye now she wasn't hard to pick out. Bandages are wrapped around her forehead and over her injured eye.

Rochelle, Savannah, and I are in the middle of cleaning a storage room. I'm finally at the point where I'm used to the work. I haven't gotten sore from it in a long time and if anything it keeps my mind busy. Every few nights it seems like I have the same nightmare over and over again. The most annoying part is that I can never remember what it is. I just know that it has something to do with the day Helena died and that I'm somewhere in that abandoned neighborhood. Beyond that there's nothing. Last night was another one of those nights where I had the dream and all day I've been trying to stay as busy as possible in order to take my mind off of it. Nicole's watching us again and in the time she's been doing so, she's been talking with us about various topics. Right now it's McGinley's.

"Whoever thought this place up didn't have rehabilitation in mind," Nicole says. "It was about money and that's it." She's just inside the room, leaning against the wall and smoking as she often does. She has one arm crossed in front of her, hand clutching her belt, and the other arm hanging beside her with her cigarette pinched between two fingers. "I've been working in this place for nine years," she continues, blowing a puff of smoke into the air. "McGinley's doesn't make anyone better, it makes them worse. But noooo...tell Halsey that and she says I'm crazy. Then she threatens to fire me for the umpteenth time. She isn't gonna fire me. She's got no one else looking to work here. Job security in the most screwed up way possible, that's what that is."

"Nine years?" I say. "How old were you when you got here?"

"Twenty-six," Nicole answers. "Waste of a life." She takes another drag on her cigarette and blows another puff of smoke toward the ceiling. "I'm not bothering you three with this, am I?"

"The story or the smoke?" I ask.

"The smoke."

"Doesn't bother me," Savannah replies. "How 'bout you two?"

"Not one bit," Rochelle says with a dismissive wave.

"Same here," I add.

"Hey, Rochelle, do you remember the name of that girl that got shot in the chow hall?" Savannah asks.

"Yeah, I think it was Naomi or something," Rochelle responds.

"That's her," Nicole confirms. "Naomi Beckham. Real troublemaker around here. Kid's been here for almost eighteen months now. She wasn't like that at all when she first came in. Timid and shy, not much different than that other girl that got beat down in your dorm that one night."

"Who, Jackie?" I ask.

"That her name?" Nicole asks. "Hmm...I thought it was Jamie for some reason. One of the new ones who came in with you lot, right?"

"Yep, she was sitting near us most of the way here," Savannah says. She leans against the wall and slides her back down it until she's in a seated position.

"Yeah, she seemed pretty anxious on the bus ride here," I recall. "Can't imagine how she's feeling after what those other girls did to her."

"If she's scared, she won't be for long," Nicole sighs. "Give her enough time and she won't be much different from Naomi. Mark my words." I lean the broom against the wall and cross my arms.

"So what brought you here?" I ask. "Why work in a place like this?"

Nicole takes a moment to think and shakes her head.

"Stupidity," she snorts. "Nah...money. Money's the only reason. Employment rate out there's terrible. Should count myself lucky that I never had kids. Couldn't afford them. Christ, my life is out of control. Never thought I'd be here at thirty-five. I remember back when I was a kid, I wanted to be a cop. Make the world a better place, that whole idealistic ball of nonsense that it was. Pff...yeah...I did become a cop. Then I more or less got fired after I turned on my idiot partner."

"What did they do?" Savannah asks.

"Killed some kid and then lied about it," Nicole mutters. "He was 22, the kid he shot. Iraqi immigrant...my partner made up some bullshit story, said the kid was armed. Kid was reaching for his wallet and got shot six times for it."

"How'd that happen?" I inquire. "I mean, what led up to the guy getting shot?"

"He was moving some stuff into his new apartment, taking it out of the back of a truck he and his brother rented out. Some nutjob saw this poor kid walking up the stairs with a fricken pressure cooker on top of one of the boxes. And I guess to them that looked suspicious. So someone called the cops, said there was a 'suspicious looking man' walking in and out of the building. We got there and my partner started interrogating him, the two of them are standing there arguing, and I'm trying to moderate while the guy is telling us he lives there. Then he goes to reach for his wallet and my partner shoots him. Dead before he hit the ground. After that I refused to take his side. He resented me for it and when the matter eventually found its way to the court, he was acquitted."

"Not surprising," Rochelle murmurs, stretching her arms over her head. She tosses a handful of garbage in the nearby trashcan and leans her back against the wall near Savannah.

"Then everything started to go south for me after that," Nicole continues, poking her head out of the doorway for a moment. "Suddenly I was a traitor for not lying about that guy's death. Found a dead rat in my mailbox one morning. Got death threats tacked on my front door, then two weeks after that a brick comes sailing through my dining room window. I went in the next day and quit my job there on the spot. Left town a few days later. I didn't feel safe anywhere in that city.

Came all the way here to Michigan after that. All the way from Florida. Left my family and friends behind. My entire life got left behind. I knew if I tried to get work here in this state as a cop, everything I did back there would come back to haunt me sooner or later. All my money went into the move, I was a month away from losing my apartment, and then one day I see an ad for this place. Looking for correctional officers. I thought maybe I'd stomach it for a little while, just long enough to get on my feet, pay off some bills, then I'd go start in a different line of work somewhere."

"And why didn't you?" Savannah asks.

"Few folks who left before me, they all ended up homeless because of the reputation you get for being associated with McGinley's...that and a million other things. Savannah, you should probably get up, Rashida's coming to take over." Savannah gets to her feet and Nicole hands me the broom.

"She's more relaxed than Halsey, but she can still be pretty strict," Nicole warns. "You three stay out of trouble." Rashida steps into the room moments later, first looking around the room, then at Nicole.

"Halsey wants to speak with you in her office," Rashida says to Nicole.

"What about?" Nicole asks.

"She didn't say," Rashida shrugs. "I'd hurry up if I were you. You know how she doesn't like to wait." Nicole gives a slight grin that fades almost as fast as it appeared.

"Yeah, I'd rather not ruffle the harpy's feathers too much," Nicole chuckles, striding past Rashida and moving out into the hall. "Wish me luck."

"Good luck," Rashida replies, her face expressionless. She turns to face us and crosses her arms.

"Well, ladies? You just gonna stand there or are you gonna get back to work?"

* * *

That night I find myself struggling to sleep. It takes me until almost eleven-thirty to fall asleep the first time. When I wake up it's after two. My dreams are keeping me awake. I'm staring up at the ceiling, my heart still racing from the dream I just awoke from. In it I was back at school, walking through the darkened hallways, not knowing why I was there. I got the feeling that something or someone was wandering around in the halls with me, but I never saw more than a few strange shadows. One of which was creeping toward me before I woke up.

After a while I drift back off to sleep, about ninety minutes after waking up. Right at 6am, the staff starts marching into the dorm and shouting for us to get up. I feel as though my body is made of lead. It takes all I have to get out of the bunk and stand at attention. The guards make their usual rounds, inspecting everything to make sure we all have our beds and other belongings in order. As I expected they would, they found an inmate to harass and began giving her grief.

"What is this?" one of the guards demands, pointing at the bed behind the girl. She's close enough for me to see that she appears to have made it just fine.

"It's a bed, sir," the girl replies. Her remark gets her slapped across the face. She loses her balance and catches the bunk to keep from falling over.

"Would you look that! We got ourselves a goddamn comedian over here! Any of you girls think she's funny?" the female guard shouts, pacing back and forth down the row of bunks.

"No, ma'am!" the rest of the girls chorus.

"You hear that?" the female guard taunts, turning back to the inmate. "Your act isn't cutting it. Why is that?"

"It wasn't an act, ma'am," the girl replies.

"So you're sassing me?" the male guard surmises. "Is that what you're telling me?"

"No, sir!" the girl answers.

"So it was an act?" the female guard asks.

"No, ma'am, I was just answering truthfully."

"The truth is that you half-assed making that bed!" the female guard barks, pointing at the bunk as she speaks. "And because you think you're so funny, you're gonna remake it while the rest of your dorm-mates pay for your fuck-ups!" The next twenty minutes are spent with the guards forcing everyone else to do push-ups while the girl remakes the bed. By the time we get to the chow hall, my arms feel like rubber. Sitting down at one of the tables, I find myself joined by Leah. I'm a little taken aback by her sudden appearance since she's rarely spoken to me. Almost every update on the plan I've received so far has been from Mika. She eyes me for a second, then glances past me and over her shoulder before looking back at me.

"So, has Mika gotten on your nerves yet?" she asks.

"No, why?" I ask.

"Just thought I'd ask," she says with a shrug. "Between you and me, she can be a little much sometimes. All that aside, how about we get to the point of why I'm here?"

"And that would be...?"

"The gist of it is that we're ready to start moving forward with the plan again," she explains. "Mika already told you everything she could, but now it's Naomi's turn to have a word with you. That's why I'm here."

"What else could there be to talk about?" I inquire. "Mika laid out the basics of it already." She swallows a bite of food and sets her fork down.

"You'll have to ask her when you see her," she says. "I'm just here to take you to her."

"Should I be worried?" I ask, raising an eyebrow. She shakes her head.

"No, I don't think so," she replies. "I know Mika said you agreed to join us, but Naomi's the one who makes the final call on that. I'm guessing she just wants to see how serious you are. Maybe assign you a role in this, that sort of thing. If she does, it won't be anything too risky or complicated. Trust takes time to build, which I'm sure you already know. Mika told me you were hesitating like crazy."

"I'd like to think that most people would, considering where we are," I answer.

"It's not criticism," she says, taking another bite. "It says to me that you think about things, that you look before you leap, that sort of thing. It's a good trait to have...so long as you don't go overboard with it."

"Like overthinking things?" I ask. She nods.

"There will be times you'll need to think on your feet if you're serious about coming along with us," she warns. "So I hope you can do just that."

* * *

Rochelle and Savannah joined us a few minutes later. They both seemed a little uncertain about having Leah around, but there didn't seem to be as much tension as when Mika spoke with us. Once we're through eating, Leah leads me out to the hallway and out of the main building. Rochelle and Savannah are allowed to come with us, but told that they need to follow the same routine as last time and stay by the bleachers. The four of us walk in silence all the way to the track. Once we arrive, I spot Naomi walking along it. She glances in our direction and beckons me over. I take one last look at Leah and the others before proceeding.

Naomi smiles as I make my way over to her. She stops and waits for me to join her before she speaks. Maybe it's just the memory of what she did to Parsons, but I can feel a sense of dread in my stomach as I approach her. The bandages around her head and over her eye are void of blood, but appear that they haven't been changed in at least a few days. Her one remaining eye is a warm shade of amber. She has thin lips, an oval face, and copper skin. Her layered hair is a wavy dark brown, held behind her head in a ponytail that hangs down to her shoulders. She's a few inches taller with a strong build.

"Hello, Sarita," she says. "Nice to meet you."

"Likewise," I reply. "So...what's up? Why'd you need to see me?" The two of us begin walking along the track as I speak.

"Before we get to that, I want you to consider something," she says, clasping her hands behind her back. "Have a look over there and tell me what you see." She points past me as we approach the first turn in the track. Off behind a chain-link fence are a few dozen crude headstones in a small field. The sight of it makes me shudder.

"It's a graveyard," I observe.

"And why do you think there are graves on this island?" she continues.

"Because inmates die here," I answer. "What's your point?"

"The point is that I want you to be aware of what could happen to you," she says. "I'm sure it's crossed your mind more than once, but I want to be sure you understand the gravity of it. I think you know the longer you stay here the more likely it is that you'll end up in one of those graves. The plan we've pieced together could hasten that process." My mind begins to race. Images of the graveyard flash through my mind, accompanied by visions of watching my lifeless body being thrown into a freshly dug grave.

"Not sure I like the sound of that," I say.

"It's a scary thing to think about," she says.

"Who said anything about being scared?" I reply, sounding braver than I feel. Naomi smiles and chuckles as we continue down the track, both of us facing forward.

"That'll change eventually," she says. "Assuming it hasn't already. Either way it's best not to show it. Wouldn't want someone to use that against you." She gives me a smirk that sends a chill down my spine. "From this point on, your time here is about survival and nothing else. Got that?" I nod and clench my teeth in apprehension. "Just so we're clear, you understand that this is a very dangerous undertaking, right?"

"Yeah," I nod. "I understand."

"Good. And you understand that once you're apart of this, there's no going back?"

"No more chances to back out, I take it?" I inquire. She nods.

"So you understand, then?"

"I do," I answer.

"So you're in?" she asks.

"I am," I respond.

"Good to hear," she says with a smile. "I'm not gonna tell you the whole process just yet, but I will give you your first task...if you think you can handle it."

"No problem," I declare. "What is it?"

"Halsey finally found one of the notes you guys took from the bus," Naomi explains. "We don't know if the girl who had it talked or if it was someone else who heard about it, but the point is Halsey's planning to raid your dorm tomorrow morning and she's going to be looking for you." My heart skips a beat and begins to feel as if it's struggling to keep beating.

"Sounds like Mika was right all along," I say. "What am I supposed to do about the raid?"

"Halsey's going to come find you, and since we have the note hidden somewhere else, she's going to be frustrated when she doesn't find it on you," Naomi explains. "I've had a lot of time to deal with her, to see what she does to inmates, and how she acts. My best guess is that she'll take you back to her office and try to get you to tell her where it is. But that's not going to work, because you're going to find the first opening you can and run out of the office and into the chow hall. You'll see Leah in the hall as you go, but she's not going to help you, so don't expect it from her. Do go into the chow hall and try to keep Halsey busy trying to catch you for as long as possible."

"And what's this going to accomplish?" I ask.

"Halsey has a skeleton key we need for something later on," Naomi explains. "I'm going to steal her key ring and run it out to Leah. As long as Leah can get a good look at it, she can make an exact copy of it in the shop, where she works. Halsey will no doubt take it back once she realizes it's gone, but like I said, Leah only needs to see it. Think you can do that?"

"What's going to happen to me if I do this?" I ask. I'm dreading the answer, but I'm pretty sure I already know.

"You'll likely get tossed in the bunker," she says. "And so will I. But for stealing her keys, I'm doubtful that she'll leave us down there for long. Maybe a few days or so. No more than a week." I'm starting to feel sick to my stomach.

"You make it sound like it's not that big of a deal," I say.

"Compared to what she could do, it really isn't," Naomi insists. "Trust me, there's worse things than getting locked up around here. She's decided the bunker was too good for me on a few...few...crap, what was I saying?"

"Something about worse punishments than solitary," I say, looking at her with concern. She seems lost in thought and remains silent for several seconds.

"Yeah...yeah, she's...I don't know what's going on with me," she murmurs. "It's kind of hard to think after you've been in solitary for long enough. That's actually why I asked to see you out here instead of just talking to you in the chow hall. It's still a little weird being around people at the moment."[8]

"And now the bunker really sounds bad," I mumble, looking away for a moment.

"It's no walk in the park, especially once you've been in there for a

---

[8]Inmates who spend long periods of time in solitary confinement often suffer from hallucinations, difficulty thinking and concentrating, panic attacks, decreased impulse control, increased aggression, and paranoia, among other things. After being released from solitary, inmates can struggle to re-adapt to life outside.

week or so," she admits. "Messes with your head and...just give me a minute, I need to get back on topic. Um...shit...the keys. The key ring, you think you're up to it?"

"Yeah, I can get her to chase me, but...I don't know if I want to end up in the bunker for it," I say.

"If we don't get the key, this plan can't work," Naomi says. "It's vital. Parsons was supposed to do it and she chickened out." "Is that why she...you know...?" I ask with caution.

"It was more than that, but Sarita, I already told you that there's no backing out," she replies, giving me a stern look. I take a moment to think about it and take a deep breath. It looks like I don't have a choice. This is going to suck, I know that much...but if we can escape, it'll be worth it.

"Okay...fine, I'll do it," I say. "But I'm not going to like it..."

* * *

My conversation with Naomi ended a few minutes later. I left the yard and went back to my dorm with Rochelle and Savannah until it was time to get back to work. I ended up sitting up on my bunk while Rochelle and Savannah talked with one another nearby. I didn't want to risk letting something slip so soon after speaking with Naomi. The three of us just finished working in one room and now Rashida is leading us to the next room. Naomi added on to what Mika said about possibly cluing Rochelle and Savannah in at some point, but right now she doesn't think it's necessary. They're both on standby as of now. We're taken to a large storage room and ushered inside. Rashida stands by the door, leaning her shoulder against the frame.

"Does she have to stare at us?" Rochelle mouths, taking advantage of Rashida's averted gaze. I shrug and go about my work. In the back of the room is a hallway that sits just far enough away from the window to remain in complete darkness. I start toward it, feeling a little on edge. I hit the switch on the wall a few times, but nothing happens.

"Come here, kid," Rashida beckons. I start toward her and she takes her flashlight off her belt. She hands it to me and points at the hallway. "There should be another switch at the far end of that hallway. Now get to it." I start toward the hallway again, sooner than I want to. I switch the light on as I come to the opening and brace myself before proceeding further. At the end of the hall I can see part of a hand sticking out from behind a corner. Below it is a shoe, similar to the ones we're assigned to wear. Whoever it is, they move away from the corner as soon as the light washes over them. I clench my teeth and continue. When I reach the end of the hallway, I stop at the edge and start looking for the switch. Unable to find it, I begin to wonder if it's further in.

"I don't see the switch anywhere!" I call to Rashida.

"You're not looking hard enough," Rashida responds. "It's there somewhere." With a deep breath I turn the corner. Nothing. No sign of anyone. I hear footsteps behind me and spin around. Nothing again. Just old boxes and old desks; the type you'd find in a typical classroom. Chairs are stacked up alongside them. There looks to be enough for about twenty to thirty students. Something about it seems strange. I never thought that a place like this would have need of such things. Judging by the thick layers of dust, they've been here for quite some time. Something tugs on my sleeve and I gasp and shine the light around the room. The switch has to be around here somewhere. I start searching the walls with my heart thudding in my chest as I go. To my relief I find the switch and flip the lights on. I turn off the flashlight and start back down the hall. Still no sign of whoever I saw.

"Hey, you found it, kid," Rashida says while giving a few sarcastic claps. She holds out her hand and I hand the flashlight back to her. She turns and retakes her position near the doorway. I take another look down the hallway. Was I just imagining it?

* * *

When the day comes to a close, the others and I make our way to the dorm. I haven't told either of them about what I saw at the end of that hallway. Once in the dorm I find it almost full. A handful of the other girls must still be out somewhere. For a moment I glance at the empty bed near one of the corners. It belonged to the girl that Naomi stabbed. One row over is yet another vacant bed. This one is where the girl with the other note is supposed to sleep. I don't see her anywhere in the room. So far it's starting to seem like Naomi is telling the truth. If I don't see the girl tonight, I'll assume she really was caught. I go straight for my bunk and climb up onto it. Less than five minutes pass before Rochelle shows up at the base of the bunk.

"Hey, you awake up there?" she asks. I crawl to the foot of the bed and look down at her.

"Yeah, I'm up," I say, peering down over the edge of the bunk. "What's going on?"

"Nothing much," she answers. "Just wanted to know if you felt like sharing what Naomi had to say. You didn't talk about it all day."

"It's the same as I said earlier. I have to hold my tongue for now," I explain. She shakes her head and takes hold of the bunk with one hand.

"And how long is that going to be? Hmm? A day? A week? A month maybe?"

"Why are you so worried about it?" I groan. She looks away for a moment and shifts her weight.

"It's like I told you from day one, Sarita," she says. "I have your back so long as you have mine. You don't survive in this place alone. Right now I'm just concerned that what you're doing might come back to haunt you."

"I know what I'm doing. It's fine, you don't need to worry about me."

"Yeah, actually I do," she protests. "If something happens to you, then that makes things harder for me and Savannah."

"I get that, but if I go running my mouth it could cause trouble for all three of us," I explain. "Just trust me on this one. I'm not about to backstab you."

"Who said anything about backstabbing?" Rochelle says. "Why, you thinking about it?"

"I think you know me better than that," I grumble, scratching at the side of my neck.

"I've barely known you for more than a couple of months," she counters. "I don't know everything about you."

"Well I can tell you right now that you got me seeing shit after you mentioned ghosts that one day," I growl. "How's that for starters? Care to know anything else about me?"

"Will you chill out? I'm not trying to get you to spill your guts or anything. And uh...what is this about seeing things?" she asks, letting the arm clutching the bed fall to her side.

"Bad dreams, that's all," I lie. I'd rather not explain the whole 'magical disappearing inmate' from the restroom...or what I saw in that hallway. I might've just not heard the girl leave the restroom, but today was a lot harder to explain.

"Yeah, sure," she snorts. "Seeing things usually means you're awake when it happens." Rochelle was the one to bring up the idea of hauntings here on the island. Maybe she knows something about it?

"Well...there's been two so far," I say. "One I don't think was anything special, but...in that room today...when we were with Rashida and she lent me the flashlight, I thought I saw someone back there. Could of sworn it was another inmate. I saw parts of the clothes, clear as day. Thought maybe someone was hiding back there, but...there wasn't anyone there when I turned the light on. Just boxes and other junk." Rochelle's eyes widen a little and she averts her gaze.

"Great, now I'm gonna have a hard time sleeping tonight," she mumbles.

"You're not the only one," I reply, glancing off in the direction of one of the exits.

"You feeling all right?" Rochelle asks. "You seem a little on edge." I blink a few times and look back down at her.

"I'm fine," I assure her. "Just have a lot on my mind."

* * *

Hours later I find myself sprawled out on my bunk, feeling anxious about what I saw in the storage room. Part of wonders if whatever it was might start following me around. Feeling anxious is nothing new to me, but ever since I got here it's been taken to a level I've never experienced before. The stress of being watched all the time, questioning the motives of others, and the constant looming threat of various forms of punishment. Despite my efforts to stay awake, I end up dozing off. I wake up sometime later and glance at the clock. Less than two hours have passed. I'm going to be too exhausted to work if this keeps up. I sit up and climb down the side of the bunk. I don't need to use the restroom, but it's the best excuse I have to go for a walk at the moment.

Out in the hallway I feel a cold breeze wash over me. It felt almost as if someone just sprinted past me. For a moment I stand there in the silence, listening and looking for the source of the breeze, but I never spot anything unusual. Turning away from the doors, I start walking toward the restroom. When I arrive, I push the door open and find myself standing in the commons at the high school. The door shuts behind me while I stand staring in shock at my surroundings. The building is cold and abandoned with few lights on. I spin to grab the handle of the restroom door and find that it's vanished. Footsteps start up nearby and I pause with my breath held. As they grow louder, I spot a figure approaching me. Little more than an outline can be seen.

"Looks like I found you..." says a familiar voice. My blood runs cold. There's a brief pause, followed by the striking of a match. The flame burns bright, revealing the ashen face of Helena Liggman. "Hello, Sarita." Blood has seeped into her hair and soaked into her shirt and jacket. Her lips curl into a sinister smile just before the match goes out. I sit up on my bunk in a panic. Sweat is dripping down my face. I look at the clock to see that it's almost time to get up. 4:51. The dorm's going to get get torn apart in about an hour. I lay back down, stare up at the ceiling and take a few deep breaths. At some point I slip into a dreamless sleep that ends the moment 6am arrives. The doors on both sides of the dorm swing open and guards begin shouting for us to get up.

Chapter 5

Key Issue

"Everyone up! Get on the floor! Right now!" the guards bark. I climb off the bunk and before I have a chance to do anything else, one of the guards shoves me to the floor and points his pistol at me. The same thing happens to a handful of others. Soon the entire dorm is lying face down with their hands on the backs of their heads. Halsey steps into the room and begins walking toward me.

"Get her up," she orders the guard behind me. He holsters his weapon and drags me to my feet by both arms, holding them behind my back once I'm on my feet. Halsey stands back with her hands on her hips as two other guards begin rummaging though my locker, checking under my mattress, and in my pillow case. No stone remains unturned.

"Nothing here," one of the guards reports.

"Keep checking," Halsey orders. "She said this one has the other note." She gestures at me and returns her hand to her hip. The two guards double check everything and again turn up nothing.

"Nothing here, ma'am," the second guard reports. "There's nowhere else to look."

"Stay here and keep searching," Halsey instructs. "It can't have just disappeared." She grabs my upper arm and escorts me toward the door. Once there she turns to address the room. "Search everything and everyone in this room," she barks. "Every locker, every bed, every potential hiding place you can find! Do I make myself clear?"

"Yes, ma'am!" the guards chorus.

"Strip search 'em if you have to, just find that note and bring it to me

"

as soon as you have it!" She turns to leave and I'm escorted from the room and down the hallway. Soon we come to her office. I'm led inside and forced to sit in a metal chair opposite a desk. Above me I can hear the faint humming of the halogen lights. The floor is a faded tan color comprised of smooth cement. Folders, pens, and papers are scattered across part of the surface of the desk. A flat-screen monitor stands near the opposite end with a keyboard and mouse in the middle. File cabinets are placed against the wall to my right with an analog clock hanging above it. Several photos that appear to have been taken overseas during Halsey's multiple tours hang on two of the walls.

In them are various soldiers posing alongside one another with a vast desert behind them; Halsey often part of the group. One photo shows Halsey in a dress uniform without her facial scars. Others show various places she's traveled. One particular photo catches my eye. It's difficult to tell at first, but one of the photos is of Halsey and Rashida, standing together in a hospital sometime after Halsey was injured in an IED blast. Halsey is standing beside Rashida who appears as if she isn't all there; her eyes are dull and her gaze unfocused. Rashida's arm and neck are bandaged and she's holding onto a crutch. Her right foot is missing along with half of her lower leg. Halsey's expression seems to convey a mixture of relief, perhaps due to both she and Rashida having survived, and an eerie gloominess.

The two of them appear a second time in a photo taken prior to the blast. In it they both seem different. Rashida and Halsey's eyes both contain the life they lack in the second photo.

"That was in Afghanistan twenty-five years ago," Halsey says, taking a few steps toward the first photo. "And this is two years later," she continues, pointing at the second photo. "IED caught the vehicle we were in. Killed everyone but us two. Rashida took the worst of it." She paces back toward her desk and sits on the edge of it with her arms crossed in front of her, staring at me the entire time.

"Why am I here?" I demand.

"Good question," she replies. "Why is Sarita Teymouri in my office? Hmm? I think she knows the answer to that...yet she'd rather play dumb for the sake of someone else. Right?"

"Play dumb?" I repeat. "About what?"

"You're not fooling anyone, Teymouri," she says, shaking her head.

"Why don't you make this easier by telling me where the note is?"

"I don't know anything about a note," I lie. She lets out a frustrated sigh and stands up. She walks back behind the desk and opens a drawer. There she removes a dirty fast-food napkin with black lettering scribbled across it. She walks back over to me and holds it up for me to see.

"You've never seen anything like this before?" she asks.

"Not since the last time I ate out," I retort. Her eyes widen for a moment and her tired expression becomes a scowl. She crouches down in front of me with the napkin pinched between two fingers.

"You don't need to have an attitude with me," she says. "I'm trying to help you."

"I don't believe you."

"You know what gain time[9] is?" she asks, cocking her head.

"Yeah, why?"

"Telling me where you put the second note could earn you a decent amount," she answers. "You could leave sooner than two years. You could go back to your family and put this all behind you that much faster."

"Like I said, I don't know anything about a note," I lie.

"Look, I know how this goes," she continues, folding the napkin in half. "You try withholding information for a whole host of reasons, the main one being the code of silence amongst the inmates here. Keep your mouth shut, don't talk to the guards, mind your own business, all that nonsense. It always ends up backfiring somehow, Teymouri, I can promise you that. Most often the way that happens is the liar gets extra time added to their sentence. Is that what you want? Two years isn't enough for you? Surely you're not that stupid, Teymouri. The girls who come in here are master manipulators and I can promise you they aren't on your side. The best thing you can do for yourself right now is to keep your nose clean, head down, and do your time. Otherwise you make this much harder on yourself."

"I don't know anything about a note," I insist. "I've never seen anything like the one you showed me."

"There were thirteen inmates on that bus, Teymouri, and there are exactly four-hundred-eighty-seven on this island at the moment,"

---

[9]Time off your sentence for good behavior.

Halsey growls. "I would say that that narrows it down quite nicely. There's plenty of empty cells in ad-seg[10], the bunker, and plenty of other jobs I could transfer you to that would make you reconsider before long. I could lock all of you up with plenty of room to spare and I could give less of a rat's ass about how long I'm 'allowed' to lock you brats up. Here, I make the rules, not any of those meddling clowns who love treating criminals like you with a light touch."

"Fourteen."

"What?" she asks, looking confused.

"There were fourteen of us on that bus," I declare. "You forgot Rachel. Rachel Caine, the girl your staff murdered. Maybe you didn't count her after she died, but she was there and I saw what happened." She slaps me across the face and glares at me.

"I'll be damned if I ever let a punk kid like you, a miscreant convicted of murder, tell me what I'm guilty of!" she hisses, brandishing her index finger inches from my face. "You're playing a very dangerous game, and I'm trying to give you a way out, but you won't find me losing sleep over it if you refuse to cooperate!"

"I didn't murder Helena," I declare. "She attacked me first. She pulled the knife, she came after me. Not the other way around."

"She's dead isn't she?"

"It was self-defense," I growl. "She slashed me with a knife and I went to disarm her."

"Sure, whatever you say," she taunts.

"Fuck you!" I snap. "You weren't there and you don't know what happened! I'm so sick of people like you thinking you know me!"

"Actions speak louder than words," Halsey counters. "From what I understand you had a history with that girl. I'm not interested in arguing with you so here's an idea, Teymouri. How about you get with the program and give me the note before you make this harder than it needs to be?" She stands up as she speaks, glaring down at me with an intense anger. I stand up and lock eyes with her; looking up at her from my lesser height. For a moment I forget what I'm supposed to be doing. She seems plenty upset. I should start looking for an exit soon.

"Yeah, keep asking me for something I don't have!" I half-shout. "I don't have a note, I never had a note, whoever told you I did is a liar

---

[10]Administrative Segregation, i.e. solitary confinement.

and so are you!" She tosses the napkin on the desk behind her without taking her eyes off of me.

"I know what you're trying to do and it's not going to happen," she growls. "I won't let it."

"What are you talking about?" I demand.

"You think I don't know who Randall Adams is?" she snorts, crossing her arms. "You and whoever else is involved in this is trying to wait out their sentence and run to him so he can spread a filthy pack of lies about my facility, just like he did five years ago after that girl died." Adams is part of one of the two largest news agencies in the country. He's a well known reporter and author and has managed to fight off countless attempts to discredit him. Five years ago, an extremist group began trying to discredit journalists like him and it's believed that they're being funded by several politicians and several of their donors; some of whom are believed to be members of the group. Adams is the best chance we have to be believed.

"Cuz that'd be the end of the world," I mutter. Halsey grabs me by the cheeks, clamping her hands tightly against them. One of her eyes twitches as she glares at me.

"I have worked too long and too hard to let a worthless little crap like you ruin what I've built from the ground up," she hisses. "You can sit here and fight with me all you want, but the fact of the matter is that you will not win. I've been running this facility for well over twenty years and I've had plenty of hopeless little girls like you pass through my doors, and I've seen every trick in the book. I've got news for you, Teymouri! I will find that note, and it doesn't matter if you tell me or not! When I do, you're going to wish you'd behaved yourself back on the mainland." She gives me a rough shake and lets go before stepping back. "If you think you can hold out on me for the remainder of your sentence then you're dead wrong!"

"I beg to differ," I retort. She shakes her head and sits back on the edge of her desk again. Dammit, this isn't working. If I'm to have any chance at running off and keeping ahead of her, she can't be two feet in front of me. She'll catch me before I even get to the chow hall.

"All right, clearly you're itching to do this the hard way," she says, crossing her arms. "Remove your socks and hand them to me."

"What? Why?" I demand.

"Just do it!" Halsey snaps. After a moment's hesitation I pull both socks from my feet and clutch them both in one hand. This is the only chance to make a run for it. Without a second thought I hurl both socks in her face, causing her to recoil and forcing her to briefly take her eyes off of me. I race out the door, and bolt out into the hallway. Just as planned, I see Leah talking to someone by the wall. I race past her, turn the corner, and keep running. Seconds later I crash through the double doors to the chow hall. Inside I crash into another inmate who's on her way out. She and I both tumble to the ground. Halsey darts in behind me right as I get to my feet. She drags me to the floor as other guards begin to close in on us. Naomi had better be quick if she plans to get the keys. I can't tell if she's even here.

Halsey pins me down on my stomach and the second she takes hold of my arms, she lets out a yelp. Naomi has just smashed a meal tray over her head. Halsey's grasp loosens and Naomi begins wrestling for the keys. She manages to remove them from Halsey's belt, but the two guards coming toward us are too fast. They drag her off of Halsey and Naomi fumbles the keys. I snatch them up and struggle to get to my feet. One of the guards grabs my foot and I kick her off before jumping to my feet. Halsey restrains Naomi on the floor while the other two guards block the exit.

"Get the hell off of me! Get off!" Naomi screams.

"She stole my keys!" Halsey shouts, pointing at me. I jump onto one of the tables and leap off on the other side to slow the nearest guard down. By this point about a dozen or so inmates are cheering and shouting at the spectacle. I dart down another row of tables and find that the second guard has headed me off. I backpedal and turn to see the other guard blocking my escape. Two inmates rush from a table behind the nearest guard and tackle him to the ground. The other is tripped by a third inmate at one of the tables beside her, giving me enough time to get away. I race back toward the doors and burst through them. Once out in the hallway, I head back toward Leah's position. As I'm passing her, she sticks out her foot and trips me. I crash to the floor and tumble across it like a rag doll. The keys fall out of my hand and she runs to retrieve them.

Confused as ever, I scramble to my feet and see her wink at me. My entire body aching from the fall, I race down the hall only to be tackled seconds later by one of the guards from the chow hall. I scream in pain as I land, the places I bruised twice already hitting the floor yet again. The guard cuffs my hands behind my back and drags me to my feet. Halsey comes walking out of the chow hall with Naomi and the second guard right behind her. Halsey's got her hand over her right eye and blood is dripping between her fingers. Another wound is present on the side of her head, most likely from the tray. She storms over to me, letting the hand over her eye fall to her side. Blood drips from between her eyelids and down onto her uniform. She grabs me by the front of my shirt and glares at me with her one good eye.

"You're in for a world of hurt, you little shit!" she hisses. "I hope it was worth it!" She lets go of me and covers her eye again, wincing in pain as she does so. "Take these two to my office, cuff them both to their chairs and make sure they stay put. I'm going to make a quick visit to the infirmary. I'll be back whenever they finish with me..." She walks off and the guards escort us to her office.

Chapter 6

Isolated

Over forty minutes later Naomi and I are sitting in Halsey's office, cuffed to the chairs we've been placed in and the two guards watching us standing beside each of us. Neither of us have spoken a single word since we arrived. The silence is starting to get to me. The clock on the wall is ticking away. Occasionally someone in the room clears their throat, or the guards' boots tap on the floor. Just when I'm beginning to wonder how much longer it'll take for Halsey to get back, the sound of multiple voices begin to emanate from the hallway. The voices grow louder and soon the door opens. Two guards step inside, followed by Halsey. Halsey's head is wrapped in bandages that cover one of her eyes. Blood has seeped through them around her eye socket.

"Sorry to keep everyone waiting," Halsey mutters, eyeing Naomi as she moves to the center of the room. "It would be a massive understatement to say that I'm disappointed in you two. Especially you, Beckham!" She backhands Naomi across the face and she yelps in pain. "Before we begin, I would just like to impress upon you the seriousness of what you two have done. Assaulting staff, stealing my goddamn keys! You two just about started a riot in the chow hall! First Beckham takes my keys, drops them, and then Teymouri takes off with them. Why? Care to explain what that was?" Neither of us speak. For over a minute, we all sit in an uncomfortable silence. "What's the matter? Neither of you feel like talking? Hmm? Stand them up and cuff them," Halsey orders. "We're taking them to the bunker." Two guards step forward, undo the cuffs on the chairs, then cuff our arms behind our backs. They escort us out of the room and down the hall with Halsey bringing up the rear. Halsey closes the door and takes the lead.

We make our way down the hall and past several guards and other inmates. Soon we reach an exit and step out into the frigid air. Halsey radios for a transport van to meet us along the street. She and the guards walk us to the intersection where they force us to sit on the curb while we wait for the transport vehicle to arrive. Minutes later, a white van pulls up in front of us and Naomi and I are herded inside. The guards follow us in and sit beside us on the benches that span the length of the interior. Halsey closes the doors and makes her way to the front of the vehicle. The van shifts a little as she climbs into the passenger seat and closes the door. The van moves forward and stops after a few hundred feet. They must be stopping at the gate I saw down the road. After a few seconds, the van picks up speed again and continues. It turns once to the right and then again to the left before coming to a stop. Halsey opens the back doors and the guards escort us out of the vehicle. We're led down a long cement path that leads between the island's two water towers. Two large buildings stand side by side straight ahead.

Something catches my attention near the base of one of the water towers. A figure is moving along the fence that surrounds it. It disappears the moment I blink. I glance at Naomi, but she's looking at the ground. Halsey doesn't seem to have seen it and there's no telling whether or not the guards did. We reach the end of the path and begin walking alongside another building. The path begins to narrow and a small structure in the middle of a large patch of grass comes into view. As we approach, two large, black steel doors can be seen. The doors are chained shut with a large padlock hanging in the center. Halsey unlocks the doors and pushes them open. Inside is a staircase leading down. By the time we reach the bottom, we must be well over twenty feet below ground. At the bottom of the stairs, I can see a series of simple and robust lighting fixtures along the walls. We're led down a long tunnel and past multiple steel doors. We stop at the end of the tunnel and Halsey turns to face us.

"Here's where you'll be staying," Halsey says. "Don't make the mistake of thinking that this is all I have in store for you. Especially you, Beckham." Halsey opens one of the doors and stands by the doorway as Naomi is led inside. She's forced down onto her knees, then her stomach where her cuffs are removed. She's instructed to stay put as the guard that led her inside keeps her pistol trained on her. Once she's back out in the hall, Halsey closes and locks the door. The same process is repeated with me and moments later I find myself lying face down on the cold cement floor as the guard steps out of the room. Halsey closes and locks the door. She and the guards' footsteps echo in the hallway, fading as they move toward the exit. Soon they vanish altogether.

* * *

Hours later I'm lying on my back, staring up at the ceiling. Judging by how tired I feel, I'm guessing it's sometime in the evening. It's hard to sleep with the lights on, though. There are only two, one on each side of the room, and each of them somewhat dim. The middle of the room is the closest I can get to sleeping someplace dark. Even so, the lights are still visible on the edge of my periphery. I try placing my forearm over my eyes. The light gets blocked out, but it's difficult to keep my arm where it is. Another hour later and I drift off to sleep. Nothing good comes of it. I'm back at the school building, sitting outside by the front entrance. It's dark and the moon is full, floating in the clear winter sky.

Footsteps sound from somewhere nearby and Helena steps out from behind one of the pillars that line the front entrance. Her head is still bloodied and her knife clutched in her hand. I begin backing away. For every step I take backward, she matches it with one toward me. My heart begins to pound and I turn and sprint for the door. She catches me right as I take hold of the handle and plunges the knife into my back. My eyes snap open and I sit up screaming in a panic. I scramble to my feet and collide with someone standing behind me.

I scream even louder as I stumble backwards and fall to the ground. The figure standing before me is a decomposing Helena. Her skin is green and rotting, some of it peeling from her face and arms. Her jaw hangs open at an impossible angle and her eyes are sunken and shriveled. She begins walking toward me, her arm outstretched as if to grab me. I stumble to my feet and race to the other side of the room. When I turn to face her, she's gone. I remain standing in the corner of the room where I can see every inch of it. An unknown amount of time passes and soon my eyelids are feeling heavy. More than anything I'd like to sleep...so long as I can avoid dreaming.

After a while longer, I begin to teeter back and forth, almost falling at least twice before sitting down. I pull my knees up to my chest and wrap my arms around them, still keeping an eye on the rest of the room. Eventually I fall back asleep without realizing it. When I wake up again it's because a tray is being pushed through a slat at the base of the door. I stare at it for over a minute before crawling toward it. The meal is sub-par at best, but right now I'm just glad to see it. Once I'm finished with it, I leave it by the slat and sit back in my corner. With no clock or windows, it impossible to tell how much time has passed. It must be after 6am if they're handing us breakfast. At least...that's what I assume. Could be after noon for all I know.

Sometime later I can hear Naomi shouting and cursing up a storm across the hall. It's faint and I can't make out what she's saying. The boredom is starting to get to me sometime after she settles down. I stand up and start pacing back and forth across the room. Counting my steps as I go. One, two, three, four, five, six, seven, turn, repeat. I'm not sure how long this goes on, but it could be at least forty-five minutes or more. When I'm too tired to continue, I move back to my corner and continue to keep watch. More meals pass and I start to really focus on the sound of dripping water on the opposite side of the room. It's been doing it the entire time I've been in here, but only now has it started to bother me. For a moment I glance at the pipe where the water is dripping from. It's up along the wall and just below the ceiling. Water is dripping down onto a patch of mold that runs along part of the wall and around where the water is landing. No matter how hard I try I can't seem to ignore the sound of it. Not until I hear Naomi unleash a second round of angry shrieks. She bangs on the door several times and the sound of it reverberates through the hallway outside. This keeps up for what has to be at least half-an-hour. When she at last stops, the tray is pulled out of the slot and a fresh one replaces it.

* * *

Hours of poor sleep follows, as do various dreams. At one point I awake to find a tray of cold food and its usual companion of a bottle of water. I pass on some of the food, seeing that it has become soggy and melded together. Just looking at it makes me feel like vomiting.

Last night I dreamed I was back home. It was like I'd traveled back in time and stopped Helena's death somehow. One moment I'm walking through the school building, spotting her along the wall talking to two people, the next I'm back at home sitting around the dinner table with my family. I kept asking them what happened, but they didn't understand. After a short time I started to feel like I was losing my mind. The dream seemed so real.

When I woke up it took me a few minutes to make sense of my surroundings. For that short period of time I was panicking. I didn't understand why I was in this old cement room. Then, bit by bit, everything came rushing back to me. Everything that led up to this point. Helena, the courtroom, the prison bus, all of it. My bruises from the other day are much more visible today. The soreness is a little less, but it still aches to move certain ways. Despite this, I stand up at one point and pace back and forth in the room. This time I count ten steps, turn, and repeat the process in the other direction. Eventually I tire myself out. Soon I find myself lying on my back staring up at the ceiling, drumming my fingers on the floor beside me.

That annoying dripping sound is back again. I've been getting angry at what feels like the drop of a hat since yesterday. My thoughts go back to Halsey, the plan to escape, wondering if Leah got what she needed or if she's been caught. A foul stench wafts through the air, sending me into a panic. Images of that corpse-like Helena I saw flash through my mind. I sit up and glance around the room. It takes me a minute, but I remember now. There's no "traditional" toilet in this room. Instead one of the corners has a grate with water beneath it. It's "flushed" on a timer three times a day. As disgusting as it is, I'm just thankful that there's a couple rolls of toilet paper in an aged plastic dispenser near the "toilet." Low quality, but better than nothing.

I lay back on my side and close my eyes. When I hear footsteps pass by me, I sit up and look behind me. Nothing. I wait for a few minutes, but I never see anything. Maybe someone's in the hall. A guard or something. I'm probably just hearing that. Lying back down, I close my eyes again. This time I start to doze, but my sleep is again interrupted by the sound of footsteps. This time in front of me. I even feel the wind on my face as if someone just strolled by. Sitting up again, I glance around the room. Unnerved, I race back to my corner and sit with my legs up against my chest. After a while I doze off a second time, and this time I jump to my feet screaming because I could swear a hand just grabbed my hair.

The corner isn't safe anymore. I know I'm being ridiculous, but part of me is still uncertain. The first explanation that goes through my head is that my hair got caught behind my back when I sat down. It must have gotten pulled when my head rolled to the side as I was falling asleep. Still...I'm certain I saw Helena in here the other day. I sit beside the door and lay down on my side again. My eyes close for a moment, and again I hear footsteps. This time when I open my eyes, I see an inmate pacing back and forth on the far side of the room. She's counting her steps under her breath as she goes. She's about my height with deep brown skin, matching eyes, and her shoulder-length, curly hair pulled back into a ponytail. She has thin eyebrows, a small scar on the side of her chin, and an exhausted look about her.

What I find most disturbing is that she's bleeding from a gunshot wound to her back and leaving a trail of bloody footprints on the floor as she goes. One, two, three, four, five, six, seven, eight, turn. Eston. That's who this is. I recognize her from the photos circulated by the media after she died. Why am I seeing her here? Is she real? Am I awake? A mixture of terror and curiosity washes over me. For over a minute I just sit and watch her pacing back and forth, back and forth. Naomi's usual round of screaming and shouting causes me to turn my head toward the door. She's pounding on the door again. When I look back at Eston, I see that she's vanished along with the blood. For the next twenty minutes or so, Naomi keeps kicking and punching the door. After she stops, I drift off to sleep again.

* * *

"It's about damn time!" Naomi's shouts are faint, but I can hear more than just her voice through the door. Are they letting us out? Pressing my ear to the door, I can hear her arguing with at least two guards. Halsey can be heard among them. After a few moments, the door to Naomi's cell closes. Halsey comes up to my door and pounds on it three times.

"Teymouri! Respond if you're awake!" Halsey shouts.

"I'm awake!" I shout back.

56

"Lie face down away from the door with your hands on the back of your head. If I see you standing up or otherwise disobeying me, I'll leave you in here another week! You have thirty seconds!" A week? There's no way it's been that long. Has it? As much as I'd rather not give her the satisfaction of ordering me around, I do as she says. Last thing I want is to risk even more time in this place. Seconds pass and the door opens. Two guards come into the room and cuff my hands behind my back. They each take one of my arms and drag me to my feet.

"Escort them to Tower B. I trust you won't need me to babysit you?" Halsey says as we step out into the hallway.

"No ma'am," one of the guards replies, shaking his head.

"Good," Halsey responds. "I'll be there to fill these two in on their new assignments as soon as I can. Just put them in their cells and wait in the control room for me."

"All right you two, get moving," the second guard says, pushing me forward. Halsey walks out the door and down the hall, leaving the rest of us to follow after her.

Chapter 7

The Tower

Halsey leads us out of the bunker and closes and locks the doors behind us. We follow the same path we took to come here and Halsey splits off halfway. Instead of going with us to the street, she heads toward one of the two buildings near the water towers and disappears inside. One of the guards radios for a transport vehicle and the cycle repeats all over again. Naomi and I are led to the street where we're forced to sit on the curb. Both guards keep one of their hands on their holsters. Across the street and to my right, I can see someone standing in the graveyard. My view of it is partially obstructed by a building beside it. It's difficult to see who it is. I blink a few times and the figure remains. Just standing, staring at one of the makeshift headstones. The van pulls up seconds later and blocks my view.

We're led into the van and seated along the sides again. Minutes later it stops and a guard comes to open the back of the vehicle. Once outside I can see that we've arrived at one of the corners of the island. A smaller island is linked to it through three bridges. Two footbridges and one made for vehicles. One of the footbridges has collapsed in the center. Half submerged, the broken section can be seen sticking up out of the water. The other footbridge is a short distance away from us. I glance toward the opposite side of the road and see one of the patches of farmland. Dozens of inmates are chained together at the ankles and toiling in the field.

Armed guards stand nearby with rifles at the ready. I glimpse two girls who are struggling to keep pace. One of them stumbles and falls to her knees. Another girl urges her to get up as two guards close in. She's ordered to her feet, but isn't able to get up. The guards continue to threaten her, but she remains on her knees. One of the guards steps back and keeps his rifle ready while the other unlatches the girl's ankle shackles. The guard orders her to stand and she leaps to her feet before breaking into a dead sprint.

Three shots ring out and the girl is struck in the back and leg. She falls to the ground and rolls with the momentum. The guard who shot her catches up to her right as she's trying to get up and pulls her back down. Another guard with a rifle joins the shooter. As we're being led away I can hear inmates shouting and cursing at the guards while they order them to keep in line and stay put. I have to wonder how many times this place has seen a riot and how long it will be before it will happen again. Our group approaches the gates to the footbridge. One of the guards unlocks the gate and the rest of us step through. He closes the gate behind us while we wait and then trots ahead to meet us at the second gate. There the process repeats before we're taken down the cement path leading to the tower entrance.

Inside the lights above us flicker and buzz, illuminating a smooth cement floor covered in cracks and grime. For some reason, this building appears to be in worse shape than the others on the island. It's as though no one's done any maintenance in a while. The few buildings I've been in so far weren't pretty, but they weren't this rundown. The atmosphere feels different. The air is heavy and the faint sound of screaming and shouting can be heard coming from further up in the tower. A series of reinforced windows pepper a wall that circles the base of the tower. What I assume is the control room is just beyond the windows in a separate structure. A handful of guards are sitting inside, their attention turned toward monitors or books. One of them looks up at us for a moment and turns his attention back toward the monitors.

Just inside the entrance and to the left is a pair of double doors, obstructed by a partial ceiling collapse. Two beams have come down in front of it, both sitting at an angle. Yellow barrier tape is strung in front of the doors, the black lettering reading "caution." Buckets and other miscellaneous items are sitting near the doors, further preventing them from opening. We turn to the right as we step inside and begin walking down the hallway. Ahead of us is a door on a track with a large, faded letter S across it. A small room lies beyond the door, sealed with another identical door only a few feet away from the first. The closest door opens as we pass. The guards stop us and one of them peers inside. Beyond the second door is a large room with little light. The only working bulbs are on the far side of the room. Everything else is pitch black.

"Sorry about that," someone in the control room says over an intercom. "Door's been on the fritz for a while."

"Did you report it to maintenance?" one of our guards asks. I can see the man who spoke from the control room shake his head.

"Doesn't matter," he replies. "They've been out here at least five times since summer. Just keeps breaking for some reason. I'll try closing it again. It'll just open again, though." He flips a switch and the door closes. It starts to move back, stops after about three inches, then closes again.

"Making a liar out of you today, isn't it?" one of our guards chuckles.

"Eh, come back after you get the inmates situated," the man in the control room says with a shrug. "I'm sure it'll have opened up again by then." I turn my attention back to the dark room and feel my heart skip a beat. Standing just inside one of the few patches of light is a dark figure. Blood is dripping from one of the arms and collecting in a puddle on the floor beside it. The guards push us forward and I lose sight of the room altogether. Naomi notices me staring at the room as we begin moving again.

"You all right?" she asks. "You looked like you kinda zoned out there for a second."

"Yeah. Yeah, I'm fine," I answer. We reach yet another automated door and wait for the control room to open it.

"Just a sec, that one's having issues today too," one of the guards explains.

"I hate coming in here," one of our guards murmurs. "I never like being so close to Sector S."

"You could always quit," the other guard suggests.

"Every job has something about it you don't like," the first answers. "Tower B is a perfect example." The door opens and we're led through to the other side. A short distance away is a steel staircase. When we reach the third floor we're herded into individual cells. They remove our cuffs and lock us in before heading back downstairs. I glance through the small window on the door and watch them disappear to the floor below us. Naomi kicks her door and the sound of it echoes around the room outside the cells. I can hear her muttering something to herself, but I can't understand it. Someone is moving around in the cell to my right, but I didn't see who it was.

Cameras are watching the room outside, but none exist in the cells. After seating myself on the end of the bed, I lie back and stare up at the ceiling. I regret it within seconds. The lights are still on at this hour and who knows if they ever bother to turn them off? They never did in the bunker, but here things seem different. I can't stand the suspense at this point. Leah's back at the main line[11] and we can only speculate as to whether or not she's been able to make the key. I'll just have to trust that she has it under control. Right now there's nothing else I can do. I roll over on my side and curl up on the bed. I'm out within a few minutes.

* * *

When I wake up again I have no sense of how much time has passed. The girl in the cell to my right is the reason I woke up. She's taken to pummeling the door and shrieking at the top of her lungs. The doors are thin enough to hear better than in the bunker. I'm tempted to yell for her to shut up, but I doubt it'll do any good. Regardless, the idea of letting out some of my frustration seems appealing. Not like I can do much else in here. I sit up on my bed and place my feet on the floor in front of me. It's been days since I've been allowed to shower and I feel disgusting. All the running and walking back and forth I did in the bunker had me working up a sweat.

For a moment I hold my face in my hands and groan through my fingers. More thuds in the other cell vibrate through the floor. The sound of her window getting struck is what's driving me up the wall more than anything else. The thud is always followed by a rattling sound. It's like that dripping water in the bunker. I just keep locking onto certain noises. Just when I'm about to lose my temper, she stops. For a moment I expect to hear another slam, but nothing happens. Why didn't one of the guards come up here and yell at her? Well...we are three stories above the control room. Can't imagine they feel like walking up here.

---

[11]The area in a facility where the majority of inmates are housed.

I lie back on my bed again and try to relax. Before I can even manage to doze, the sound of footsteps coming up the stairs echos through the tower. Moving to the window, I watch Halsey and three guards coming into the room.

Halsey orders them to get us out of our cells, then heads back down, saying she'll meet us there. Naomi and I, along with another girl I don't recognize, are removed from our cells. The slat on the door is opened and we're told to put our hands through. They cuff them together and open the door. Outside the cell I can see the other girl better. Judging by Naomi and the girl's body language, they seem to know one another. If I'm not mistaken, Mika mentioned someone named Tia. I wonder if this is her? She's the same height as me with light brown skin, emerald green eyes, and wavy titian hair. She has a narrow chin, prominent cheekbones, and a slight gap between her two front teeth. After everyone's out of their cells we're led downstairs and escorted to the door with the letter S painted on it. We're lined up against the wall where Halsey is waiting for us.

Chapter 8

Search Party

Halsey removes a manila envelope from under her arm and opens it. She removes two prisoner intake forms from inside. When I left the bunker she mentioned something about a new assignment. This must be part of it.

"Here's what you three will be doing today," Halsey says handing Tia the papers. "Pass these to the others and make sure each of you get a good look at the faces of these two girls."

"What exactly are we doing?" Tia asks, passing the papers to Naomi.

"Right now you're listening, Ellis," Halsey replies. "These two girls have been missing for about sixteen hours now. They got loose and took off into the area behind you. Sector S. I've sent two separate teams of guards down there, but they failed both times to locate these two inmates. My guess is that it's because of the way that they always come running back within thirty minutes, like a pack of scared little children..." She turns and glares at the guards behind her as she finishes speaking. Some of the guards look away, some pretend they haven't heard anything, still more look down at the floor. "Pathetic...every one of you," Halsey growls. "Don't any of you get too comfortable. Two of you will be escorting these inmates into Sector S. Is that clear?"

"Yes ma'am," they chorus.

"Good...now, as for the three of you," Halsey continues, turning back to us. "This is how it works. I don't know if you'll find these two alive, dead, or something in between, but regardless you're to bring them back out of Sector S. Understand?"

"Yes ma'am," we chorus. When the papers reach me, I'm surprised to see their names are Ariana Miller and Mika Sato. The photos are unmistakable. What's going on? Is this some part of the plan I was kept in the dark about? And if it is, did something go wrong? Halsey takes the forms from me and places them back in the envelope.

"Now that you know what they look like, you can get to work," Halsey says, looking at each of us.

"How are we supposed to bring them back if they're dead?" Naomi asks.

"On your backs, of course," Halsey replies. "If not that, then get one of your teammates to help you. Simple as that." I cringe at the very thought. "All right, you and you," Halsey says, pointing to two of the guards. "Richards and Martin. You're going with them. The rest of you are staying here in case they need assistance." Richards is a woman of average height with golden-blonde hair, hazel eyes, and a rosy complexion. Her hair is wavy and tied back in a short ponytail. The backs of her hands have a sandy texture to them, and a slight redness is present on her cheeks. Martin is a tall man with light brown hair, cut short, with dark brown eyes, a very short, scruffy beard, and tough, beige skin.

"What? Why us?" Richards demands, an apprehensive look on her face.

"Because I said so!" Halsey growls. "You wanna keep your job? You take these brats into Sector S and you don't come back until you locate the missing inmates! Now get going." Halsey points at the door and the guards hesitate as both it and the one behind it open for us. Halsey glares at me, then clasps her hands behind her back. A cool breeze washes over us and I clench my teeth. The guards glance into the darkened room for a moment while the rest of us wonder if they plan to move. "Hurry up!" Halsey barks. "Chop chop, let's go! Move it!" The guards herd us through the door, their flashlights the only source of light, save for a few dim bulbs inside the room. The doors shut behind us and I glance over my shoulder to see Halsey speaking with the remaining guards.

"Hey, Laura? You have your spare light on you?" Martin asks from the back of the group.

"No, why?" she answers.

"Why the hell not?" Martin demands.

"It's busted, Jeff, I haven't had it on me in days," Laura grumbles. "It's not like I expected to be here right now."

"You know people talk about their flashlights getting drained down here, right?" Jeff grumbles. "How do you go days without replacing equipment?"

"I don't want to hear it!" Laura responds. "I get it, all right? Let's just get this over with. Sooner we find the inmates, the sooner we can never come back down here." We're led out of the room and into a much larger one with half-decent lighting. It's dim, but most of the room is visible. The place looks trashed; like a storm came through. It reminds me of the room with the dark hallway the other day. Chairs and desks are scattered about, suggesting that this too was once a classroom. Along with the upended chairs and desks, a larger metal desk is flipped over near a wall. Beside it are two smashed computer monitors, both of them old and outdated. On the wall to the left is a TV mounted in the corner. For some reason it's on and showing a display of static. The sound coming from it is faint. Bloodstains cover parts of the floor and at least two windows have their own spatters. It's hard not to wonder what took place here. My first thought is that a riot broke out. Something crashes against a nearby window and some of the lights begin to flicker. It continues for a few seconds before they return to normal.

"The hell was that?" Jeff says, searching for the source of the noise.

"Probably one of the missing inmates," Laura says with a shrug. "Come on, let's go check it out." I glance through the window and feel a knot in my stomach. There's a girl behind the glass, but no one else seems to notice her. She has her bloody hand pressed against the glass, most of her head and face hidden in the shadows. All I can see is a sinister smile as she smears the blood across the window. When she's finished she turns and vanishes into the shadows. Outside the room, I see Laura shining her light around the darkened areas. She orders Tia and Naomi to check the area, but neither of them turn anything up.

"Nothing here. Let's keep moving," Laura orders. I stop for a moment and Jeff gives me a shove.

"Keep moving," he growls. "I don't want to spend all night down here." Yeah, like you're the only one who doesn't want to be here. As we're led further in, we pass by a few rooms along the hall. Pipes, machinery, and tools scattered about, are contained inside. One of the doors slams shut and everyone turns to face it. Laura prods Tia with her flashlight and pushes her forward.

"Go check the room," Laura orders.

"No way! You do it!" Tia snarls.

"Do what you're told!" Jeff barks. Less than a second after he speaks, the door swings open and slams into the wall. The impact shatters the glass in the window, sending bits of debris scattering across the pavement. Both guards look terrified. Jeff pushes me forward and demands that I go look.

"Why do I have to do it?" I demand.

"We're waiting..." he says, pointing at the door while he stares down at me. I let out a frustrated groan and move toward the door with caution. The guards shine their lights behind me as I walk into the room and look around. The room is barren with little more than a few loose bolts lying on the floor.

"There's nothing in here!" I call. I start back out of the room and feel someone shove me from behind. I crash to the ground and roll onto my back. Inside the room I catch a glimpse of a shadow figure. It darts through the wall and vanishes before I can get a good look at it.

"You saw that, right?" Jeff whispers to Laura.

"I saw her stumble," Laura murmurs. "Relax, she's just screwing with us." I get to my feet, keeping an eye on the room as I do so. The guards continue to argue.

"Yeah, the door was her too, right?" Jeff argues. "Don't you sit there and act like everything's fine!"

"I don't wanna hear anymore, Jeff!" Laura growls. "Not another word of it! We're wasting time, now let's get moving."

"I vote we tell Halsey we didn't find anything," Jeff mutters.

"You wanna go back and deal with her, then fine!" Laura snaps. "But don't involve me in it! Halsey's not going to let us back out of here till we find something."

"Hey! You!" Jeff barks at me. "Quit jacking around and get over here!" I curse under my breath and join the others. From there our group continues further into Sector S. We make our way down the U-shaped hallway and to a giant set of gates. Beyond them I can see a small bridge leading over a long row of pipes beneath it. Laura is the first to head across. Once she's halfway over, something snares her ankle and pulls her off the bridge. She yelps and drops her flashlight. She crashes down onto the pipes below with a dull thud that echoes throughout the facility. Everyone else stops and stares in silence. Jeff prods Tia and orders her to assist Laura. She rolls her eyes and sits down on the edge of the bridge with her legs dangling off. She turns and places her palms on the bridge with me and Naomi standing beside her, ready to help her if she needs it. She lowers herself down until she's dangling off the bridge with both hands. Naomi picks up Laura's flashlight and shines it down on Tia.

"Can you get down there all right?" Naomi asks.

"Yeah," Tia grunts. "I think it's only about a foot or so. I can't see where my feet are going to land, though." Naomi uses her light to illuminate the area below her feet.

"You're good," I say. "Just drop down and try not to slip." Tia takes one last look over her shoulder and drops down. She lands on the pipe with a thud.

"I don't see her," Tia reports, pacing up and down the pipes. "I think she might've fallen through or something. Spaces look big enough."

"This is just great..." Jeff mutters. "One of you get down there and help her." Naomi grumbles something incoherent and follows after Tia. She hands me the flashlight and uses Tia's method to get down to the pipes. There she starts looking down through the spaces between them. Naomi looks back up at us and stands up.

"I see her!" Naomi says. "Looks like she's unconscious. There's something on her ankle, but I can't see what it is."

"Get her back up on the pipes," Jeff orders. "And be quick about it." Tia drops through the pipes and beckons for Naomi to stand in a certain spot. I can hear Tia grunting and straining as she pulls Laura up. Naomi kneels down on the pipes and leans down to take hold of Laura's wrists. She pulls her up while Tia pushes on Laura's feet.

Tia then climbs back up and begins trying to remove something wrapped around Laura's ankle.

"I need a light on her ankle," Tia says. I shine my light on Laura's ankle. A thick, black cable is wrapped around it.

"How on earth...?" I murmur.

"Wait, that's what pulled her down?" Naomi asks. "You've got to be kidding me.”

“Halsey this is Officer Martin, I need medical down here immediately,” Jeff says over his radio. “Richards took a spill, she’s unconscious.”

“Come on, let’s start getting her up on the bridge,” Naomi says, looking up at me. Tia and Savannah drag Laura to her feet and start trying to get Laura’s arms where Jeff and I can reach them.

“Halsey, I’m not screwing around,” Jeff says over his radio as he kneels down alongside me. “We need medical down here now. Halsey, are you there?” He waits for a response and curses when he doesn’t receive one.

“One of you hand me her radio!” he orders.

“We’re a little busy here,” Tia grunts. “Can it wait a second?” I grab one of Laura’s wrists and hold her up while Tia takes the radio from Laura’s belt. She tosses it to Jeff and he tries again to contact Halsey.

“Halsey!” he half-shouts. “Halsey, are you hearing me? Richards is down, send someone down here.” Still nothing. Only static comes over the radio. Jeff grips the radio in his hands and puts his own back on his belt.

“Sarita, get her other wrist,” Naomi instructs. I set the flashlight next to me and reach for Laura’s wrist. Jeff grabs the other and we both heave her back up onto the bridge. He stands up and grips the radio in his hand.

“Halsey, this isn’t funny!” Jeff growls over the radio. “Come on! Are you even there?” A female voice answers seconds later.

“Yes? What is it?” the voice asks.

“Who is this? Where’s Halsey?”

“What do you need?” the voice asks, ignoring his question.

“I said multiple times that I need medical at my position,” Jeff explains, intense frustration in his voice. “Officer Richards is unconscious, we’re in Sector S near Tower B.”

“And how did that happen?” the voice inquires.

“What the hell does that matter? Just get someone down here!” Jeff snarls.

“I’m sending someone to your location,” the voice replies. “Wait there.” Static comes back over the radio and Jeff is left pale and shaken up.

“Something wrong?” I ask, feeling more anxious by the minute. Jeff kneels down beside Laura as Naomi finishes pulling Tia up onto the bridge.

"Come on, wake up, Laura," Jeff urges, giving her a shake. "Wake up, dammit!" He shakes her again and this time her eyes begin to open. She mumbles something incoherent and moves her head a little. "Hey, can you hear me?" Jeff asks. "Can you sit up?" She nods and Jeff helps her into a seated position.

"What happened?" she mumbles.

"Something pulled you off the bridge," Jeff explains. "I don't know what it was, but we're leaving."

"What are you talking about?" Laura asks, blinking several times in rapid succession. "We haven't found the other inmates, have we?"

"Doesn't matter, we need to leave," Jeff urges, helping her to her feet. "I don't care what Halsey does, anything is better than being stuck down here." Laura pushes him off and cradles her head in her hand. She looks around, then at Jeff.

"You need to calm down," Laura orders. "What happened while I was out?"

"I was trying to get Halsey on the radio, but I wasn't getting through," he explains. "Someone whose voice I don't recognize got on instead. Kept acting weird and then she said someone would come find us and that's the last I heard."

"Wait, what do you mean by a voice you don't recognize?" Laura asks.

"Laura I've been working here for ten years, we haven't hired any new guards in five. I've spoken to every one of them and I can tell you right now that that wasn't anyone we work with," Jeff answers. "I don't have an explanation and I'm not sure I even want one. Whoever it was, I don't want to be here when they show up." He starts walking back across the bridge and stops when Laura grabs his arm.

"We're staying here!" she declares. "I am not getting fired because of you!"

"That'll be the least of our worries if we don't get the hell out of here!" Jeff snarls, wrenching his arm loose. "Stay if you want, but I'm not sticking around for act two!"

"Fine, go back!" Laura snaps. I back away while they continue arguing and make my way off the bridge and to where Naomi and Tia are chatting. Naomi spots me and beckons me over.

"What's going on?" I ask, keeping my voice low. Tia glares at me and opens her mouth to say something, but Naomi stops her before she can.

"She's solid[12], relax," Naomi says to Tia. Tia nods and steps back with her arms crossed. "This is Sarita, the one Mika recruited. She's risked a lot to get us where we are."

"Oh, right, right," Tia nods. "Nice to meet you, Sarita. I'm Tia." She shakes my hand and then clasps her hands behind her back. "I've been busy with everything on my end. Forgot Leah mentioned you before I got locked up in Tower B. Speaking of which, I assume Leah got the key?" She glances first at me, then Naomi.

"Yeah, she did," I nod. "She was looking at the key ring just before the guards caught me."

"Do either of you know if she made the copy yet?" Tia asks. Naomi and I shake our heads.

"No, we both got tossed in the bunker right after that," Naomi explains. "Thing's didn't exactly go according to plan. I fumbled the keys and Sarita jumped right on it. Ran them out to Leah for me."

"Very nice," Tia says, nodding in approval.

"All that aside, I've been itching to ask you about Ariana and Mika," Naomi continues. "What happened with that? They should have been out of here by now. I mean, come on. Two search teams before us and still no sign of them? Doesn't make sense."

"They might be out for all I know," Tia shrugs. "That is, if they made it to the exit on the other side of the island."

"If they did find their way out, I'm sure someone would've noticed and brought them back to Tower B by now," Naomi counters.

"I suppose that's true," Tia admits. "I hate to say it, but it wouldn't be hard to get lost down here. At least two miles worth of tunnels, maybe more. I don't know about you, but I'm worried that the plan might be starting to fall apart. What do we do from here?"

"We keep moving forward with it, that's what," Naomi answers. "For now let's just work on finding Ariana and Mika. We need to make sure they held up their end and stockpiled some weapons near the other exit."

"Do we really need them, though?" Tia asks. "We're supposed to

---

[12]Someone who always has your back, no matter what.

sneak out on the supply ferry. If we don't catch the next one, we'll have to wait an extra month. That means more time for us to be caught with everything we've gathered. It has to be this next one or not at all."

"You think I don't understand the urgency?" Naomi snorts, shifting her weight. "I realize we're on a time limit here. And yes, we do need the weapons."

"What for?" Tia inquires.

"We're risking getting caught," Naomi replies. "Not just by the guards on the island, but the ones that'll be on the ferry too. We need to cover all our bases. Not everything has gone the way we hoped at this point, it would be careless not to prepare for the worst. Now is not the time to cut cor-"

"C.O.'s[13] are coming," Tia interrupts, watching the guards come toward us.

"All right ladies, we're heading back," Laura says, stopping at the nearest end of the bridge. She motions for us to follow her.

"Fantastic..." Naomi mumbles. I can't decide whether or not this is a good thing. On one hand I see why Naomi's frustrated, but on the other, I'd much rather get out of here before something else happens. I've had my fill of this place and it looks like the guards have too. A loud squealing catches our attention and we all look up to see the gates closing.

"Shit! No, no, no, no, no!" Jeff panics, sprinting across the bridge. By the time he reaches the gates they've already closed, the force of which shakes the facility. Jeff crashes into the gate and begins frantically searching for a way to open them again. Laura trots over the bridge and stops a few feet behind him. Jeff curses and kicks the gates before stepping away and pulling on his hair.

"Find a switch, there has to be a switch or something. Help me find it," he says to Laura. Still dizzy from hitting her head, she makes her way along the wall, searching for anything that could have activated it. Tia, Naomi, and I all start fanning out to search. Tia's the one to find it.

"Hey! I think this is it over here!" Tia calls from the other side of the bridge opposite to the gates. Jeff brushes past the rest of us and joins her by a lever attached to the wall and seated below a faded sign. Most of the letters have long ago been worn away.

"Out of the way, let me take a look," he orders. Tia steps away and

---

[13]Correctional Officer

Jeff shines his light on the faded sign. He takes a moment to examine it and reaches for the lever. Laura by this point is rushing toward him.

"Hey! Wait! Don't touch that!" she shouts. Jeff stops and lets his hand fall to his side as he turns to face her. Laura shoves him away from the lever and stands in front of it.

"What? What is it?" Jeff demands.

"That lever's faulty, you'll fry yourself if you try to use it," Laura explains. "You never heard what happened down here?"

"The girl they found with cables around her neck or something else?" Jeff asks.

"The girl who electrocuted herself with that lever," Laura answers. "It was back in 2010. Some inmate was down here and tried to close the gates. Died on the spot." Jeff looks over Laura's shoulder at the lever and then steps further away from it. He shines his light around the room and then looks back at Laura.

"Well if the lever's no good, what do you propose we do?" Jeff inquires.

"It would be best for us to keep moving toward the other exit," she answers. "Besides, we still have two missing inmates to locate."

"And you're going to walk around with a concussion while we do that?" Jeff asks, sounding incredulous.

"I'm fine, okay?" Laura insists. "I've been through worse."

"If you say so," Jeff says. The two of them glance back at the gates and Jeff shines his light across them one final time. Laura looks back at the lever, then shakes her head in frustration.

"This shouldn't have happened," Laura groans, clutching her radio. "I'm gonna try getting Halsey on the line. Maybe she can get someone to hit the lever on the other side."

"If I get out of here alive, I'm putting in my two weeks," Jeff says, ignoring her. "There's something not right about this island and I knew it the moment I set foot here." He stands in silence with the rest of us as Laura tries multiple times to get a reply from Halsey and the other guards back at Tower B. When her attempts fail, she gives up and tilts her head back, staring up at the ceiling with a look of intense frustration on her face. After a moment she levels her gaze and turns to face the rest of us.

"Come on, let's get going," she says. "Staying here is just wasting what light we have left."

"I'm all for getting out of here, but the last thing I want to do is go further into these tunnels," Jeff says. "The gates closed somehow, that means there's power running to them. I say we look for another way to open them."

"We would just be wasting whatever light we have left, Jeff. We're you the one getting on my case for not having my spare light?" Then change the next part that reads, "Halsey will just send us back in," to "The gates are stuck and there's nothing we can do." Laura counters, taking two steps toward him. "Halsey will just send us back in. Now forget about the gates and let's get moving before this situation gets worse." Jeff takes a moment to consider what she said and nods in agreement.

"Right...fine," Jeff murmurs. "We'll keep an eye out for the other inmates as we go, but I'm not stopping for anything." He walks past us and turns the corner. Laura beckons for us to follow.

Chapter 9

Exit Strategy

It's now been twenty minutes since the gates closed on us. We're about five-hundred or so feet further into the tunnels, checking any potential hiding places as we go. The unusual activity we've been experiencing isn't showing any sign of slowing down. I can tell it's starting to get to everyone in the group. Some more than others. Laura and Jeff are shining their lights around the tunnel as we go, sometimes in response to sounds that turn out to be nothing unusual. Somehow I still feel like we're being followed...and maybe we are. Maybe Mika and Ariana are somewhere nearby, watching us and sticking close. The near silence is soon broken by something flying past Tia's head and striking the wall to her right. The group stops and begins looking around.

"Who's there?" Laura demands as she and Jeff shine their lights around the tunnel. Everyone remains frozen, listening for any other signs of life.

"Laura, do you see anything over there?" Jeff asks. "Whatever got thrown at us?"

"Nothing yet," Laura responds. "Just forget it. Let's keep moving." Footsteps sound somewhere ahead of the group and again we stop and listen.

"This is getting ridiculous," Jeff says, shining his light back and forth. "Enough games! Get out here where we can see you!" His voice echoes down the corridor and fades into oblivion. Again we're met with silence.

"We need to quit stopping like this," Laura says. "We've got a long way to go." I glance over my shoulder, then look back at the front of the group. My eyes widen as I do so. Up ahead is a strange looking girl standing off to the side. She's caught in the flashlight beam for only a moment, but it's long enough to get a good look at her. Her skin is ashen gray and her hair singed. She's facing away and I can't see her face. Her arms are covered in burns of varying severity and bones and muscle are visible in some places. Her clothes are scorched and the smell of seared flesh lingers in the air. When Jeff's flashlight swings back toward where I saw her, she's already gone. As we move further into the tunnels, the air grows colder. Soon I can see my breath in front of me. The hum of nearby machines can be heard in the background as we take a left at the end of the corridor.

"You sure we're going the right way?" Jeff inquires.

"It's been a while since I was down here, but I'm pretty sure we are," Laura answers.

"Pretty sure?" Jeff snorts. "They should have maps down here in these rooms, right? Place is like a maze. Can't imagine they wouldn't have some on the walls or maybe stashed away in a desk somewhere."

"I've seen a couple down here before, but they weren't in the greatest shape," Laura replies. "If it'll make you feel better, have one of the inmates go look for one."

"You got an idea of where to start?" he asks.

"Pick a room, any room," Laura answers.

"Everyone slow down a bit," Jeff orders. He shines his light around the tunnel and begins looking around at the available rooms. At this point in the tunnel it begins to take a sharp left curve to a fork. One smaller tunnel is blocked by two heavy steel doors to the left and to the right the main tunnel continues, curving into what I assume is a U shape. A few lights are buzzing overhead in various spots, providing very little light. Once we reach the second bend in the main tunnel, multiple rooms come into view. Jeff halts our group and turns to face us.

"You two, split up and start checking the rooms," Jeff orders. He points to me and Naomi, then assigns her to check the rooms in the main tunnel, and tells me to check the rooms in the smaller tunnel.

"Go check and see if there are any lights on in there," he says to me. "Come back if they're off. Otherwise I'll assume you're fine." I nod and make my way down the passage and to the double doors. Once there I have to throw most of my weight behind my effort to push the door. When I manage to squeeze past I can see that someone barricaded it. How long ago I can't tell. It's dark except for a few patches of light and all I can see is another tunnel leading left at an angle and moving straight away from me after a short distance. I look back at the others and see that they're still moving, albeit at a slower pace.

"How's it look in there?" Jeff asks.

"Some of it's lit, some of it isn't," I reply, walking back over to him. He takes his smaller, spare flashlight from his belt and hands it to me.

"Now get to it," he says, pointing at the doors I just returned from. Halfway to the doors, I look over my shoulder and see that the group is still moving.

"Hey! What about me?" I demand. "Can't you stop until I'm done?"

"It's called incentive," Jeff responds. "Hurry up and search and you won't be left behind." I can't decide of I'm more annoyed or scared. I don't like the idea of getting left down here. I push the door open and step past the barricade. After flipping the flashlight on, I examine the barricade. It looks like two small crates of various machine parts and rusty tools. Small, but very heavy, nonetheless. Looking around the tunnel I notice a few scrape marks along the path, indicating that the crates were likely pushed or dragged. Continuing down the tunnel I come to another sharp right turn and another pair of double doors leading out into another tunnel. A faded sign points left with the words "Plant Drainage." The same sign also points right with the words "Eastern Tunnel Access."

I follow the tunnel labeled as "Eastern Tunnel Access," and soon come to a room to my left. There I stop for a moment, shining my light through the window on the door. I step inside the room, the door creaking as I do so. Now in search of both a map and an inmate, I start looking through the lockers and file cabinets in the room, all the while thinking about the burned girl in the tunnel. It doesn't take long before I'm checking over my shoulder every minute, always expecting to see something. I bump a wrench off one of the desks and nearly have a heart attack as it clatters on the floor. I steady myself and continue searching. Once I reach the final cabinet, I hear a thud outside the door. My light flashes across the window to see a red hand print on the window. My heart skips a beat and the lights in the room begin to flicker, including my flashlight. The room goes dark for a split second, and when the lights return, the hand print is gone. I glance around the room one last time and bolt outside.

For a moment I take a breather and glance around the tunnel. It's too far for me to run back and see if the others are still close by. By the time I get back here to look they'll just be that much further away. Unless I just lie about having searched the place. Are they going to know or even care if I do? Something is here with me, but a map is going to be vital if something happens to our only guide. She's already got a concussion as it is. I trot further down the tunnel and peer into the next room I come to. I push the door open and start rifling through cabinets. I make my way to one of the lockers and a few boxes topple out in front of me.

I start pushing them aside when my eye catches something rolled up in the locker. I snatch it up and unroll it to see that it's an old map of the area. I tuck the flashlight between my neck and shoulder for a moment and glance over the map. It's faded, but it'll have to do. I roll it up and tuck it under my arm, then start back out of the room with my flashlight in hand. Before I'm even ten feet from the door, one of the cabinets near the doors creaks open. Against my better judgment, I spin and shine the light at the locker. Through the crack in the door, I can see an eye staring back at me. My heart races and I bolt for the door.

"Wait! Come back!" someone shouts as I stumble out into the corridor. I trip over my own feet and crash onto my stomach. The map rolls several inches away as I get to my feet without looking back. Further down the tunnel I come to yet another pair of heavy doors. When I can't get them to budge, I turn and shine my light on my pursuer. She shields her eyes with her forearm and stops in place. Whoever it is, she's holding a flashlight with a very dim beam.

"Can you maybe point that somewhere else?" she asks, still shielding her eyes.

"Are you...are you alive?" I ask, lowering the flashlight. She lowers her arm as I do so and it's then that I recognize her as Ariana.

"Only by sheer luck," she answers. "Look, do you know the way out of here? I got all mixed up when I hid."

"Were you the one who barricaded the door back there?" I ask.

"Yeah, that was me," she nods. "They sent you in to find us, didn't they?"

"They did," I confirm. "The guards are too scared to come down here and do it themselves. Speaking of guards, we should probably hurry. Come on, this way." I race to the end of the tunnel with Ariana in tow. Once we make it back to the main tunnel, I see that our group has disappeared.

"Dammit! Come on, we need to hurry. The others are up ahead somewhere." We start down the tunnel, walking as quick as we can. I'd run, but the flashlight doesn't reach as far as I'd like.

"You all right?" I ask her, noticing that she's been quiet since we left the smaller tunnel.

"Yeah...just...watching for...things," she says, glancing over her shoulder. "I don't know what's going on with me. Two hours down here and I started to wonder if I was losing my mind or something. Swear to God I keep hearing voices, footsteps...something grabbed me before I hid in that locker."

"Did you happen to see what it was?" I ask, thinking of the burned girl I saw.

"I have no idea," she says, shaking her head. "I didn't stop to think, I just ran. You ever hear about the history behind this place? Why they abandoned it?"

"No, what happened?" I ask, shining my light across a nearby door.

"Well, I can't say for sure that anything I've heard is for real," she admits. "Mostly rumors...but the version I've heard is that they used to have inmates working down here in teams. Maintenance and the like. That part might be true since Halsey's got everyone working all sorts of jobs all over the island. Why not here too, you know? She says it's to build character, teach us skills, but it's really just a way for this place to save money. Have the inmates do all the labor for free and you save a ton."

"Sounds pretty messed up when you say it like that," I say.

"Slave labor sounds messed up no matter how you say it," she replies. "It's not like we're doing it willingly or getting paid for that matter. Go on, try throwing down your tools the next time you don't feel like working. See what happens. And the shop, the farmland, the stuff they make and grow, it's free labor for companies working with McGinley's.

They save money by having us do the work while they pocket the cash."

"That doesn't sound like a rumor to me," I reply.

"Yeah, that part is true," she says. "Kinda went a little off topic. Kinda...distracted, I guess. Sorry."

"Did they always do that here?" I ask. "Have the inmates do everything and profit off their labor?"

"Not exactly," she answers. "I've heard they used to have classrooms around here and that they used to educate the inmates, help them graduate on time, give them head starts on college, that sort of thing. Something changed somewhere along the way. Did you come in through Tower B?" I nod.

"Yeah, I got locked up in there and this is my punishment," I explain. "Mine and the others. Tia and Naomi are down here too."

"How did that happen?" she inquires. "I mean, I knew Tia was locked up, but Naomi...that's news to me."

"Long story short, she attacked Halsey," I explain. "It was pretty brutal. I'll let her explain it later, but yeah...I saw the classroom back there. Near Tower B. Or what's left of it, anyway. What else do you know about this place?"

"Well, I heard that this place, Sector S, was abandoned in 2011 and that they tried a few times to continue working down here, but that it never lasted long. Seems Halsey can't get anyone to stay down here long enough to do anything productive."

"And why was it abandoned in the first place?" I ask.

"Oh, right, I was working up to that. I heard there was a girl here named Vesna around that time," Ariana continues. "I was looking for her grave a couple weeks ago, but none of them have any names on them. Just numbers. So who's to say if she was real or not? The story goes that Vesna cracked while she was down here. She was working with a team of inmates and just...snapped, I guess. No one knows what prompted it, but she killed the other three inmates with her. Beat them all to death with a wrench. Then she doused herself in gasoline and set herself on fire." It feels like I was just punched in the gut. That girl I saw, the one with the burns. Was that Vesna? Or was it someone else? Laura mentioned there was a girl who got electrocuted. Maybe they're the same person? Seems possible that the story could have gotten distorted over the years. Two different versions of one event.

"Hell of a way to go," I remark, feeling my palms beginning to sweat.

"You're telling me." Somewhere up ahead I hear a door creak open and the two of us pause. Moments later Naomi exits one of the rooms with something folded under her arm and a flashlight in her other hand.

"Christ, don't scare me like that!" I snarl. She jumps in alarm and heaves a sigh of relief.

"Ariana?" Naomi asks. "Where did you find her?"

"Hiding in a locker back there somewhere," I answer, gesturing behind me. "Come on, let's keep moving. Walk and talk, the rest of the group ditched us."

"Really? I hadn't noticed," Naomi snorts, trotting after us. She strolls up alongside me and eyes the map under my arm. "That a map you found?"

"Yeah, back in the room where I found her," I answer, nodding toward Ariana.

"Did you check yours?" she asks. "Mine was a little difficult to read in spots."

"Same," I answer. "We'll have to compare once we catch up to the others. Just hang onto it for now."

"Something touched me!" Ariana shrieks, clinging to me so hard I struggle to breathe.

"Get off of me!" I choke. Before I can do anything, both our flashlights begin flickering and soon go out.

"What the...?" Naomi panics, slapping the flashlight against her palm. "The hell's going on? It was fine just a second ago." Something wrenches my flashlight out of my hand and tosses it away. Before I can react, I feel someone throw me to the ground. Ariana yelps and tumbles to the pavement near me.

"Let go!" Naomi snarls at someone unseen. She yelps and tumbles backward. Her flashlight hits the floor and rolls away. A tense silence ensues. I can hear footsteps circling around us.

"I can't find it!" Naomi says. "Crap, where is it?" Somewhere nearby, she's scrambling back and forth in search of her missing flashlight. Moments later our flashlights flicker back to life. Naomi begins making her way toward hers. I see her feet in the flashlight beam as she approaches. She reaches down to pick it up and before she can do so, it rolls a few inches away. She stops and stands staring at the light. She hesitates for a moment and goes to retrieve it a second time. She swipes it up and begins shining it around the tunnel. I pick up my flashlight and help Ariana to her feet. She's gone pale and begun to shake.

"I don't want to be here, I don't want to be here, I did not sign up for this!" she panics. Somewhere far off behind us, I hear a loud crash and the sound of twisting metal. "It's coming back!" Ariana shrieks, bolting down the tunnel. "Out of my way! Move!" She races past me and Naomi grabs her in a bear hug.

"Will you chill out!" Naomi bellows. Another crash echoes behind us, this time accompanied by the sound of shattering glass.

"Let go of me! Let go! It's gonna kill us!" Ariana shrieks, struggling to get loose. Another crash and the tunnel shakes.

"We're leaving! Go, go, go!" I shout, stumbling past the both of them. I catch my foot on a piece of debris and stumble several steps before regaining my balance. We race further down the tunnel, occasionally looking back. The tunnel turns right and we pass by two large rooms as the tunnel takes a second right turn at the same angle. Everyone stops as we hear the haunting groan of twisting metal coming from further ahead. To our right is a series of three rooms, all stacked side by side. Naomi points to the one furthest to the right.

"In there!" Naomi shouts. "Hurry!" She has her map partially unfolded in front of her. The three of us race through a nearby door and slam it shut behind us.

"Find something to barricade it!" Naomi orders. She begins searching the room as she folds the map back up.

"Over here!" Ariana calls, waving us toward a heavy crate. It takes all three of us to get it to budge. Outside, the noises are getting closer and more frequent. The room shakes with the force of a small earthquake as lockers tip over and loose objects shuffle across the floor.

"Faster!" Ariana grunts. "It's almost here!" What sounds like a massive pipe crashes onto the ground outside. Another crash and the sound of shattering glass. The room shakes again and more items tumble from shelves. Once the crate is in position, the three of us back away and begin looking for something else to place in front of it.

"Help me move this! Hurry!" Naomi urges, pointing at a desk she begins sliding across the floor. The ceiling lights swing and two of the bulbs burst, sending a shower of sparks down upon us.

Ariana helps her move the desk into position and I start racing around the room, looking for a way out. Another crash causes me to stumble and almost lose my footing. Naomi races over to a damaged section of wall and waves us toward it.

"Over here!" she shouts.

"What are you doing?" I demand.

"There's another room behind here!" Naomi shouts over the noise. "Find something to break the wall with!" The three of us spread out and begin searching the room for anything we might be able to use. Naomi swipes up an old pipe wrench and begins slamming it against the broken portion of the wall. Pieces of concrete begin to crumble away with each stroke, but she's not making much progress. Something slams against the door and the three of us jump in alarm.

"Hurry up!" Ariana panics.

"I'm trying!" Naomi snarls, slamming the wrench into the wall with all her strength. A large chunk of the wall cracks and she strikes it several more times. The door is struck a second time, and this time the desk slides forward several inches.

"Hold the barricade!" Naomi orders. "Keep everything where it is! We need as much time as possible!" I nod and Ariana follows after me. The two of us push the desk back into place just before the door is struck again. We're both pushed back with the desk while Naomi continues hammering away at the wall. Another chunk falls loose and she glances back at us. The door is struck a fourth time, and this time it's hard enough to cause both of us to lose our balance. We both rush to our feet in time to see the desk slide another foot. Naomi turns and hits the wall several more times. The final piece comes loose and falls to the floor. She turns and beckons for us to follow. I squeeze through the opening and step into the other room. Naomi follows, then Ariana after her. The three of us race out of the second room and out into another tunnel. Inside the first room, the door crashes open and the desk is thrown onto its side.

"Go, go, go!" Naomi urges, pushing me forward as she speaks. The three of us race down the tunnel, panting and tripping over debris as we go. We turn a corner and Ariana trips on something. She nearly falls and catches herself at the last second. The two of us catch up to Naomi who urges us to keep moving. Minutes pass and we stop, panting and out of breath in the middle of a four way junction. The three of us look around to see if anything is following us. The noises have faded and nothing that we can see is moving around.

"This way...in here..." Naomi pants, leading us toward a room to the left of the tunnel we exited. The three of us pile inside and close the door behind us. Ariana collapses onto her knees, her palms planted on the floor in front of her. Naomi brushes a few things off a table and then lays her map out across it. I help her weight down the corners with anything I can find, and Ariana drags herself to her feet a minute later.

"All right, let's figure this out quick," Naomi says as the rest of us gather around the table. "First, I want to know what happened. When was the last time you saw Mika?"

"Why are we worried about her all of a sudden?" Ariana argues. "We've got something out there stalking us! Something big from the sound of it! Shouldn't our first priority be finding a way out?"

"Without Mika, a key part of the plan falls apart," Naomi contends. "We need to find her and I want to know where you last saw her."

"I am NOT going back out there to find her!" Ariana declares. "She's probably dead for all we know!"

"And what if she isn't?" Naomi replies, leaning on the table as she speaks. "I'm not saying we go back the way we came. We searched most of the area already on the way here. Just that last portion where that...thing, whatever it was, chased us here. So I'll ask again. When was the last time you saw her? I want to know if we have even a remote chance of finding her further in."

"Look, I have no idea if Mika's still down here or not," Ariana answers, shaking her head. "We got separated after about two hours. She said she was hearing voices and it was freaking me out so I told her to just keep searching the rooms, you know? Next thing I know, I hear her screaming bloody murder, like something dragged her off. Then I start smelling burnt flesh, and don't ask me if I know what it smells like, I lived near a crematorium for five years. So then I ran off and hid because...you know, those freaky stories people tell? The girl who set herself on fire down here? The next thing I know I see this one happen to wander into the same room." She gestures at me with her thumb as she finishes speaking.

"What direction did you hear the screams coming from?" Naomi asks.

"Sounded like they were heading down this direction, but after that, who knows?" Ariana continues. "She could be anywhere. If whatever just came after us found her, then I doubt she's still alive. She's not the first inmate to disappear and turn up dead down here. Remember that girl they found in here last year? Mattie or whatever? Cables wrapped around her arms and legs, strangled with another. The guards found her up on some pipes like twelve feet in the air, left there after she was already dead, and where she couldn't have possibly climbed! I say we cut our losses and get out of here while we still can!" Strangled with a cable? Jeff mentioned something like that earlier. Part of me was happier not knowing all the details. Now I can't get the image of it out of my mind.

"There were rumors that the staff made that up to discourage anymore escapes!" Naomi argues. "They rely on fear to keep people out of here, so why not add to the stories with something new?"

"Did you already forget that we got chased down here by something strong enough to rattle the tunnels?" Ariana counters. "Why would they have to make anything up when they've got the real deal lurking around down here?"

"I meant the last part of the story!" Naomi replies. "The guards were probably lying about where they found her. How does anyone know they were telling the truth? We weren't there to see it!"

"There's no way you can still believe that after what we just saw," Ariana says.

"I never said I did," Naomi grumbles. "Getting back on topic, we'll keep an eye out for Mika on the way out. Now let's find the quickest route out of here and get moving."

"Looking for her will slow us down!" Ariana protests, throwing her arms into the air. "None of us are getting off this island if we're dead! I don't know about you, but I am not spending eternity here, lying in one of those makeshift graves." She points behind her as she speaks and then steps away from the table, still facing Naomi with an anxious look in her eyes.

"Then help me find a way out of here!" Naomi rages, thumping her fists on the table.

"I found one," I say, pointing to the map. "If we go out this direction and cut through here, it will get us to the exit near the docks." The two of them take a moment to examine the map, then look at me.

"What?" I say with a shrug.

"Never mind, let's just get going," Naomi says, removing the map from the table. "We've got work to do."

Chapter 10

New Direction

Outside the room, we shine our flashlights down the tunnels and listen in the silence. For now everything appears to have quieted down. We follow the path I pointed out on the map, keeping a close eye on our surroundings as we go. Some of the doors in the tunnel are covered in patches of rust and grime, and the few flickering lights seem close to going out. Up along the highest part of the right wall are a series of air vents and plumbing. I spot a couple of ladders leading up to some crawlspaces as we go. One of them is broken with its lower half lying on the pavement below. The metal is twisted where it broke, making it seem like something powerful tore it in half.

I've folded my map in a way that's easier to hold with one hand. My flashlight is held in the other. Every now and again I feel that familiar sense of being watched. I turn away from the broken ladder and look behind me. Nothing. I turn back around and shine the light up near the top of the same ladder. The beam washes over a pair of shoes jutting out of the crawlspace. After blinking a few times, the shoes remain and I turn to the others.

"I think I found something," I report. "There's a pair of shoes up there." I use my map to point to where my flashlight is aimed. Ariana turns to look where I'm pointing and Naomi does the same.

"Where at?" Naomi asks. With the light still trained on the nearby ladder, I lead the others toward it. The three of us gaze up at the top of it.

"The ladder's busted, let's forget it and go," Ariana says. She starts to walk away, but Naomi grabs her by the wrist and pulls her back.

"Stay put," she orders Ariana, pointing at the ground in front of her. "Getting separated is how you get killed." Ariana nods. Naomi hands her map and flashlight to Ariana, then turns and approaches the broken ladder. She reaches up to grab it and finds that it's just out of her reach. She jumps for it a couple of times, then turns and tries to get a running start. Again she misses.

"Sarita, come here for a sec," she says, dragging the broken section of ladder aside. "I need you to boost me up. Ariana, keep your light on the ladder." I hand the map off to Ariana and pocket my flashlight while she uses Naomi's flashlight to illuminate the area around the ladder. Naomi finishes moving the broken ladder segment and I stoop down with my fingers laced together in front of me.

"Ready?" Naomi asks, placing her foot on my palms. "One, two, three!" I grit my teeth as I lift her up to around waist-height. She grabs the ladder with one hand, reaching down toward me with the other. "Toss me your flashlight." I take it from my pocket and toss it to her. She pockets it and starts climbing up the ladder. It rattles a little as she goes. After a minute she disappears into the small tunnel at the top and switches her light on.

"Oh dear God..." she gasps.

"What? What is it?" Ariana demands. There's a pause and Naomi backs out of the tunnel and looks down at us.

"Stand clear of the ladder," she orders.

"Is it Mika?" Ariana inquires. "Is she alive?"

"Yes it's her, and no, she isn't," Naomi answers. I feel a knot form in my stomach the moment she says it.

"It's just like last year..." Ariana murmurs, looking down at her feet. Naomi crawls back into the crawlspace and comes back again with something in her hand. She pockets the flashlight and clings to the ladder.

"Sarita, come over here for a sec," Naomi says. "I'm gonna drop something down to you."

"What is it?" I ask.

"A radio," she answers. "Ariana, shine your light up here so she can see." Ariana shines her light on Naomi and I can see her holding a radio identical to the ones the guards use.

"Is it still charged?" Ariana asks. Naomi looks it over before she responds.

"Yeah, looks like it," Naomi answers.

"Well that's good at least," Ariana says. I stand below the ladder and Naomi drops the radio down to me.

"Can you get her out of there by yourself?" I ask.

"I think so," Naomi says, taking a deep breath. "Not gonna be easy. Or pretty for that matter. I think I'm gonna have to drop her down there." She pulls on Mika's legs until her knees and thighs are exposed.

"I can't look..." Ariana says, handing me the flashlight. I take it from her and she turns away from the ladder. Naomi clings to the side of the ladder, still pulling. The body is moving an inch at a time. She looks up above her and starts feeling around with one hand.

"Shine the light up here for a moment, will you?" she requests. I step closer to the ladder and shine it above her head where she's pointing. She grabs hold of a steel bar and pulls on it a few times to test it. Then she grabs it with both hands and swings her feet up to the top of the ladder. She gets a good grip on the body with her feet and pulls with all her might. The body slides out to the waist and begins teetering on the edge of the shaft. She repositions her feet and pulls the body the rest of the way out. I jump back as the body falls down toward us and lands with a crack on the pavement.

"Jesus..." I whisper, staring at the body. The sight of it is starting to make me sick to my stomach. The limbs are stiff and rigid, and her skin is deathly pale and peppered with nasty bruises and gashes. She looks like someone, or something, bludgeoned her to death. The skin in the areas that were touching the ground in the crawlspace are turning purple, and her eyes are half-open and lifeless. It's difficult to believe that this is the same person I met over a month ago.

"This can't be real..." Ariana mumbles under her breath. "This wasn't supposed to happen, she wasn't supposed to die. None of us were." She continues facing away and shifts her weight as she speaks. Naomi swings her feet back to the ladder and tries to get one of her hands close enough to grab it. She slips and lets out a yelp. I panic and look up to see her dangling from the ladder by her knees. She curses and rubs the back of her head.

"You all right up there?" I ask. The sudden disturbance prompts Ariana to turn back around and look up at Naomi.

"I'm fine," Naomi says. "Just hit my head on the rung."

"You bleeding?" Ariana asks.

"Doesn't look like it," Naomi replies. "I didn't hit it that hard." She curls up on the ladder and grabs it with both hands, then pulls her feet out and climbs back down to the bottom without incident. I drag Mika's body out of her way so she can land and she drops off the ladder seconds later. Naomi brushes her hands off and then looks down at Mika's body.

"So. Which one of us is carrying her back?" Naomi asks. Ariana shakes her head and backs away.

"Don't look at me," she says.

"I'm navigating," I reply. Naomi scowls at us both.

"That answers that question..." she mutters. "Fine, whatever. I started this, it's my fault, I should be the one to do it. Is that what you're thinking?"

"I'll do it if you want," I offer.

"No, no, it's fine, I don't mind. I asked and you gave me your answer," she grumbles, approaching the body as she speaks. She bends down and starts trying to pick the body up, but the corpse's stiff muscles are making it difficult. She lets out a frustrated groan and steps back.

"Like I said, I'll help," I offer again. She shakes her head.

"No, you're navigating for us," she answers. "Ariana, get over here."

"What? No!" Ariana protests. "Just drag her or something! She's dead, she's not gonna care." Naomi clenches her teeth, turns, and points at Ariana.

"If you end up dying next, I swear to God I'll slap your corpse around!" Naomi seethes. "Mika's one of us! Was one of us. I'm not dragging her around like a sack of fucking potatoes! Now get over here and help carry her!"

"Sarita already offered to help you!" Ariana half-shouts. Naomi lets her arm fall to her side.

"She's navigating," Naomi growls.

"Then I'll take over for her!" Ariana says.

"Like hell you will!" Naomi snaps. "You have got to be the biggest fucking coward I've ever seen! You were already suggesting we leave without even looking for Mika and right now I don't trust you to not run off with the map!"

"There's two maps, you idiot!" Ariana snarls, waving hers around. "If I run off with this one, Sarita still has the other! I get that you're upset about this, but don't go taking it out on me!"

"Upset? You think I'm upset?" Naomi snorts, pointing at herself. She lets out a derisive chuckle and shakes her head. "I am beyond upset at this point, Ariana. And it's because we are completely and totally screwed!" She throws her hands up in the air and lets them fall to her sides. "Mika was vital to this plan and now she's dead!"

"You think I haven't thought about that?" Ariana says, taking a step toward Naomi.

"I'm sure you did around the time you started wanting to leave without even looking! It's like you already knew she was dead or something!" Naomi accuses, brandishing her finger in Ariana's face. Ariana slaps it away and I step between them.

"That's enough!" I shout. The two of them glare at one another before relaxing and stepping away from each other. "I don't know what's going on, but I do know this. I want out of here and I don't want to stand around waiting for whatever attacked us to come back and finish the job." I hand Ariana the flashlight she gave me and fold up my map. Though it sticks out quite a bit, I place it in my back pocket and walk over to the body. Naomi hands my flashlight back to me, then stoops down to grab Mika's arms and I take hold of her legs.

"You know which way we're going?" Naomi asks Ariana. She nods.

"Yeah, I should be fine."

"All right. On three," Naomi says to me. "One, two, three!" We lift Mika's body up and Ariana takes the lead.

* * *

Twenty minutes pass with the three of us walking in silence. Seems like the three of us are still trying to process the discovery we made. Can't imagine what's going through Naomi and Ariana's heads right now. The sound of a door creaking somewhere down an adjacent corridor catches our attention and Ariana shines her light toward the source of the sound. She doesn't say anything and looks back at her map after a few seconds. A few minutes pass and our group stops. The sound of metal scraping along pavement is echoing down the tunnel behind us.

"We should hurry," I say, starting forward again at a quickened pace. Naomi almost trips as she struggles to match my speed. The three of us stop a second time a few minutes later.

"I think it's gone," Ariana whispers, shining her flashlight around.

"Or it's watching us," Naomi says.

"Let's keep going," Ariana says, gesturing for us to follow. We're now less than fifty feet from the next turn we need to make. We slow down as we approach, listening for anything unusual. Ariana scans the area in front of us with her flashlight. When we come to the next turn in our route, Ariana leads us around the corner. Lights flicker near the middle and end of the hallway that greets us. Halfway down the tunnel we hear something stir behind us. Ariana turns and shines her light toward the sound. There I see a figure lurking in the shadows. Her hair is long and tangled. Her skin is discolored, taking on a purple-ish tinge. Most of it is focused on her left side, apparent on her cheek, jaw, and outer arm. She's floating a few inches above the ground, her feet dangling below her. Cables cling to her neck, leg, and waist. Two glowing, dark purple irises contrast her black scleras.

"Am I the only one seeing that?" Ariana whispers, her face as pale as the moment she burst from the locker. The figure sways above the ground and disappears with the flickering of the nearby lights. The three of us freeze with bated breath as a metallic clang sounds somewhere behind us. The sound of it echoes in our direction and is soon followed by another closer one. Ariana lets out a shriek and tumbles across the pavement as a cable hanging from the ceiling strikes her across the back. It slithers back up and out of sight seconds later. Naomi and I drop Mika's body and stand motionless in the silence. Ariana gets to her feet and Naomi is pulled onto her back by another cable that snares her wrist and disappears as quickly as the first.

"Run!" Ariana screams, bolting further down the tunnel. Naomi follows after Ariana, abandoning Mika's body in the process. Before I can follow them a cable snags my ankle and pulls me to the ground. The cable begins dragging me down the hallway and the map falls out of my pocket. Naomi and Ariana race to assist me. Naomi dives forward and grabs my wrist. Her weight slows my progress enough for Ariana to latch onto the cable.

"Get it off!" I scream.

"We're trying!" Naomi shouts. Ariana strikes the cable several times with her flashlight and it begins to split apart and loosen. Before she can remove it, it violently jerks backward. I'm dragged down the hallway and around a corner, through an open door, and down through a gaping hole in the floor. The cable releases my ankle and I crash onto a desk. My flashlight falls out of my pocket and rolls somewhere nearby. I roll onto the floor and race to my feet in a panic. It's pitch black and I can't see where my flashlight landed. Moving on my hands and knees, I feel around for it in the darkness. After about a minute, my hand collides with the end of the flashlight. I swipe it up and begin shining it around the room. The room seems different than the rest of the ones I've seen so far. It's less like a storage or maintenance room and more like an office.

The walls are the same dull grayish color, parts of it still damp and some of the corners containing the same dark mold I've seen in other areas of the tunnels and in small amounts in the bunker. A pipe up along the edge of one of the walls and just below the ceiling is dripping down onto the pavement below. There some of the mold has spread along the wall. The pipe circles the room and goes through one of the walls. Old, faded papers lie across a metallic desk with an old office chair sitting behind it. I knocked some of the papers onto the floor when I fell, along with a stapler and pens. I'm just glad the pens weren't standing upright in some kind of container when I landed.

Looking up at the hole in the ceiling, I can see that several cables are still hanging down through it. I reach up to grab one and it breaks under my weight. I land on my feet and stumble backward. The cables retreat back up into the hole and disappear, leaving over ten feet of space between me and freedom. I try the rusted door nearby and find that it's jammed. I step back and kick it a few times, but it doesn't budge. I rattle the knob and try pulling on it again. After backing up several paces, I turn and run at the door, kicking it as hard as I can. All I manage to do is send a stinging pain through my foot and leg. I turn back toward the desk I landed on. Maybe I can use that. I start pulling the drawers out and setting them aside. Some are empty, others are full and heavy. Once I'm finished, I stop for a second and look up at the hole. I take a deep breath and cup my hands around my mouth.

"Naomi! Ariana! Can you hear me?" I shout. I wait a few seconds and try it again. "Hey! I'm down here! Help!" I let my hands fall to my sides and look down at the floor. No response. Did they ditch me? I look back at the desk, and with some effort, I manage to tilt it onto its side. It's about five-and-a-half feet long. If I can climb on top of it, I should be able to grab the ledge. Problem is...how do I climb up? There's nothing else to stand on. The file cabinet in the room is broken and dented. The metal I'm sure is far too thin and flimsy to support me. The chair that was near the desk is sitting on rollers and will likely slip from under me. Last thing I need is to bash my head in a fall. I'm tempted to try it anyway. Maybe if I'm careful I can get up onto the desk without any trouble. I still don't like the idea, though. I walk over to a locker and try to pull it onto its side. Whatever's inside is so heavy I can barely budge it. I try to open it to empty it out, but it's locked.

Frustrated, I walk back over to the drawers I took out of the desk and start looking through them. Maybe there's something in here I can use. Most of what I find are old dusty papers and a couple of lighters and stray cigarettes. In the final drawer I sift through, I find a stapler, a few pens, and a flat-head screwdriver with a few loose screws. The latch doesn't seem that solid. This should do just fine. I grab it and approach the locker again. I wedge the screwdriver into the locker and start prying at it. The latch comes loose and the door swings open. Inside are three stacked boxes, all full of a variety of equipment. I stand to the side and push the boxes out of the locker. Among the items that spill out are several thick binders filled with papers to the point of bursting, some bolt-cutters, a drill, and three ammo boxes. One of them opens when it hits the floor and a series of live rounds spill across the pavement. I look in the locker a second time and see two rifles leaning against the wall. Beside them on the bottom of the locker are two pistols. I pick one of the pistols up and examine it.

I'm not an expert by any means, but my dad taught me and my sister the basics a few years back. I know part of Naomi's plan to escape involved procuring weapons, but part of me doesn't want to take the two pistols with me. It's one thing if I get caught with tools. If I get caught with a weapon, especially a firearm, there's no telling what will happen to me. For all I know there might be a team of guards heading our direction. From what I saw on the map, the mouth of the tunnel isn't far from here.

Naomi never said what her plan was as far as stashing items, but I remember there being two small rooms on either side of the exit. For now I'll just plan to hide them there. I dig through the rest of the locker and find several magazines, most of them empty. The one in the pistol I picked up is full. I imagine the other one and the two rifles are as well. I'll leave the rifles behind. They're too big and clunky, unable to be concealed. I snatch up the two pistols and a few magazines for each, placing them all on the ground in front of me.

I need a better way to carry this stuff. I start digging through the other boxes and find a satchel in the bottom of one. I start placing things in it. The screwdriver, one of the pistols, and the bolt-cutters. I place two of the magazines in my pocket and set the other pistol down on the floor in front of me. I open one of the ammo boxes and load all the empty magazines I have. Once I'm finished, I stand up and sling the satchel over my shoulder. Now I just need to get out of here. I pick the pistol up, then grab the top of the locker and push it over. It lands with a deafening clatter and I drag it up alongside the desk.

"Here's hoping this works..." I mumble, climbing on top of it. It seems sturdy enough. I put the flashlight between my teeth and tuck the pistol in my waistband. I climb up onto the desk and feel my stomach drop out when it begins to wobble. I hold still with my breath held. The desk stops moving and I start trying to stand up. It wobbles a second time as I straighten up. I jump and feel the desk tilt out from under me. I grab the ledge and the desk crashes onto the floor below me. I pull myself up and place my forearm in front of me. I try to swing one of my feet up, but miss. The momentum causes my grip to loosen and I struggle to maintain it. Someone grabs my arm and I look up to see the burned girl from earlier. She's kneeling down in front of me, staring at me with two fiery orange eyes. Vesna. I scream and lose my grip. The flashlight falls from my mouth and clatters into the room below. I look back up at the girl in a panic and she gives a sinister smirk before letting go of my arm. I fall back down into the room and crash onto the desk.

The impact knocks the wind out of me. My vision briefly goes out of focus and I feel dizzy. Above me, Vesna is still staring down at me. She moves away from the hole and I start to hear scraping sounds coming from above. I force myself to sit up and hold my head in my hands. After a moment, I manage a ragged breath and look back up at the hole. The scraping sounds continue and I look up to see a locker being pushed toward the hole. I leap to my feet and bolt across the room, turning in time to see the locker crash down where I fell. I lean my back against the wall and stare in terror.

There has to be another way out of here. I start looking around the room and pushing furniture and other things out of the way. Nothing. For a moment I stop and look back up at the hole. It's quiet and I don't see any sign of Vesna anywhere. Now I'm just hoping she stays gone. I start digging through the second locker and begin pulling things out of it. Inside I find a small crowbar. It's small enough to fit in my satchel, but I can tell it'll stick out about six inches or so. Maybe with this I can get the door open. I wedge it between the door and the frame and start prying at it with all my strength. The door comes loose and I topple over as the crowbar falls to the floor in front of me.

Once back on my feet, crowbar in hand, I shine my light around the room outside. There's another door sitting ajar to the left. I make my way toward it and jump back in shock when it swings open. The door smashes into the wall with enough force to shatter the glass in the window. I back up and set my satchel on the floor, placing the crowbar in it without taking my eyes off the door. I put it back over my shoulder and take the pistol from my waistband. I approach the door a second time and find that there's a small passageway just outside.

To the right are two sets of stairs. One leading lower, the other to the upper levels. With my heart racing in my chest, I trot up them and find myself at another door. I try the knob, but it's locked. I kick the door in frustration and peer out through the window. There's not much to see. Even with the flashlight, I can only make out small slivers. I put the gun back in my waistband and set the satchel down. After removing the crowbar, I smash the end of it through the glass and reach through to unlock the door. I push it open and step out into the tunnel. I can see lights flickering nearby. I trot down the tunnel and round the corner. It's hard to tell for certain, but this looks to be near where I was before getting dragged off. I put the crowbar back in the satchel as I glance around the tunnel.

There's a wall to my right as I come out of the door. In front of me on the wall is a faded metal sign with an arrow pointing left. It says the dock entrance is that direction. I glance down the tunnel and hesitate for a moment. I follow the sign and start trotting down the tunnel, checking for other signs as I go. Moments later I slow to a halt, my flashlight trained on Mika's body. Looks like Naomi and Ariana haven't come back for her yet. I shine the light around the area and locate my map a minute later. After putting it in my back pocket, I approach Mika's remains again. Right now I'm not sure if I should drag her to the end of the tunnel or not. Naomi didn't seem thrilled with that idea and neither do I. It doesn't make sense for me to go find them and bring them back to get her, though. There's no telling where the girl with the cables went. What did Ariana say her name was? Mattie?

After about a minute of consideration, I take a look at my map and see that I just have to go straight down this tunnel and take a right. From there the exit is dead ahead. It wouldn't be much of a walk, but dragging the body along will slow me down quite a bit. I'm going to have the same issue Naomi had. I won't be able to carry her on my back. With my mind made up and dreading my task, I grab hold of Mika's feet and start dragging her down the tunnel toward the docks. Twice I have to stop and take a break, both times before I reach the bend in the tunnel. After passing the bend, I start hearing the faint sound of two voices. At first they're too far away to make out, but once I'm halfway between the bend and the exit, I can make them out much better. It's Naomi and Ariana. Whatever's going on, they sound angry. I follow the sound of the voices to their source, one of the small rooms not far from the exit. Leaving Mika's body a few feet from the door, I peer in through the cracked window to see Naomi and Ariana arguing. Ariana has the radio in her hand and Naomi keeps trying to snatch it from her.

"What's the point?" Ariana snarls, backing away with the radio behind her back. "That thing probably killed and ate her by now!"

"Yeah, like the way it ate Mika?" Naomi contends.

"Maybe it was saving her for later," Ariana replies, dodging another swipe.

"Just give me the radio!" Naomi growls. "You're not calling anyone until we go back and get Sarita!"

"Why are you so intent on finding her, anyway?" Ariana demands, walking behind a table in the center of the room. She holds the radio over her head and uses her free hand to keep Naomi at a distance.

"We already lost Mika, I'm not losing her too!" Naomi snaps. "Now hand it over!" She pushes Ariana and the two of them begin a tense stand off as Ariana tries to keep the table between her and Naomi.

"You're not getting the radio!" Ariana snarls. Naomi runs right, then left, and right again, still opposite to Ariana despite her attempts.

"Fine, screw it..." Naomi mutters. "You can call the guards if you want, but I'm gonna go look for her." Ariana lets out an exasperated sigh and her arms fall to her sides. Naomi turns for only a brief moment, then does a one-eighty and dives over the table. She grabs the radio from Ariana and falls to the floor. Ariana grabs Naomi and tries to pin her down. The two begin snarling and cursing while they fight over the radio, with Naomi struggling to both stand up and keep it away from Ariana. I push the door open and the two of them both stop and stare in alarm.

"Jesus, Sarita!" Naomi exclaims. "You scared the hell out of me!"

"You're alive," Ariana observes, a shocked expression across her face. "Good." She takes the radio back before Naomi notices.

"Yeah, no thanks to either of you," I say. "Is this what you were doing the entire time I was gone?"

"Hey, I was going to come look for you," Naomi replies. "Ariana ran off with the only working flashlight and I had no choice but to follow her. I can't exactly do anything if I'm stumbling around in the dark, now can I?" She notices that Ariana has stolen the radio and makes a few grabs for it. All of them miss as Ariana backs further away from her each time.

"Will you two quit fighting over that thing? One of you is gonna break it."

"Yeah and it'll be Naomi who does it," Ariana mutters, gesturing at her with her thumb.

"I beg to differ," Naomi murmurs, crossing her arms. The two of them glare at one another for a few tense moments.

"Will one of you just call?" I groan. "We're all here, regardless of how or why, and we need to figure out where the others are."

"We still need to get Mika's body back," Naomi says. "We had to leave her back there and Halsey's going to wonder why we have Ariana and not Mika."

"It's already taken care of, just call," I reply. "I left her outside the door." I gesture behind me and let my arm fall to my side.

"Oh...okay then..." Naomi says, looking surprised. "Well, then I guess we're ready. You gonna use that thing or what?" Naomi asks Ariana.

"Yeah, yeah, I got it," Ariana replies. "What am I supposed to say, anyway? Halsey's going to go nuts when she finds that we're using this thing. She needs to know we're serious."

"Give it here," Naomi demands, holding out her hand. Ariana mumbles something under her breath and hands it over.

"This is Naomi Beckham," Naomi says into the radio. "We're in Sector S, we've been separated from the guards who came in with us. We're attempting to locate officers Martin and Richards. Can anyone hear me? Over." The three of us wait in silence for several seconds.

"No good," Ariana says. "Try it again. There has to be someone listening."

"We are separated from Martin and Richards, can anyone hear me? Sector S. Please respond." Silence again. Then just as she's preparing to give it a third try, a voice comes over the radio.

"What the hell is going on?" Halsey snarls over the radio. "Why do you have a radio, Beckham? Explain yourself at once!"

"I'm glad you're all right, Beckham..." Naomi mocks before pressing the button again. "Something happened and we got lost. Martin and Richards are missing. We're near the dock entrance. We have both missing inmates with us."

"Who's there with you?" Halsey demands.

"It's me, Sarita, and the two missing inmates. One deceased, one alive," Naomi responds.

"Wait there for assistance," Halsey orders. The radio goes silent and I look down at the satchel slung over my shoulder.

"Crap, I need to hide this thing," I say, heading back toward the door. "Be right back, I'm going across the hall for a second."

"Why would we go anywhere else?" Naomi says with heavy sarcasm. I roll my eyes and make my way across the hall. There I find one of the rooms I remember from the map. I try the door and find that it's locked. I smash out the window with the crowbar and unlock it. Once inside, I find a locker and swing the door open. I place the map and pistol in the satchel, then switch off the flashlight and place it in with them. After placing the satchel inside, I turn to leave and let out a scream when I collide with someone.

"It's me, relax!" Ariana shouts. "Jeez! My ears are ringing." I shove her aside and storm out of the room.

"You couldn't announce yourself first?" I growl.

"Sorry, I thought you heard me behind you," she says with a shrug. "What were you hiding?"

"Some weapons," I answer, stepping into the room where Naomi is waiting. "I'll explain it all later." Naomi's now seated at the table with the radio sitting in front of her. She looks up at us and opens her mouth to say something. Before she can, a voice crackles over the radio.

"Beckham, this is Halsey. Are you there?" Halsey says. Naomi picks the radio up and presses the button down.

"I'm here, what's going on?"

"I'm sending a someone to collect you," Halsey answers. "I assume you're still in the same location?"

"Yes," Naomi replies.

"All right, good. Stay put and don't move. Any available officers near the docks, make your way to the Sector S entrance and escort the in-mates to Tower B at once. They have a body with them." The radio goes silent and Naomi gets up from the table, setting the radio down as she does so.

"Sarita, you wanna help me move Mika to the exit?" I nod and follow her outside. Ariana gets the radio from the table and joins us seconds later. Naomi takes Mika's legs and I grab her wrists. Leading up to the exit is a long ramp through a smaller tunnel. It takes us a few minutes of walking in silence before we reach the landing at the top. There Naomi sets Mika along the wall and then plops down on the floor a few feet away. Ariana and I seat ourselves near her and away from Mika's remains.

"So when do we leave?" Ariana asks.

"Hell if I know," I say with a shrug.

"No, not here," Ariana replies, shaking her head. "I meant when do we leave the island?"

"Late next week," Naomi replies. "The supply ferry is heading out then. We can't afford to sustain serious injuries, get locked up for long periods of time, none of that. We need to stay ahead of Halsey and make sure we don't attract attention to ourselves. Otherwise we risk delaying it again, just like we had to after I dealt with Parsons. That's why we don't do anything until I give the order. Got that?"

"Got it," Ariana nods. "I don't know about you two, but I'm sure I'll have hell to pay for running down here in the first place. Let's hope it doesn't hold us back too much." She's right. Halsey's going to be furious with her. From there it's out of our control. Naomi and I are both still in the midst of our own punishment, the whole reason we're down here in the first place. Somehow I'm regretting this whole thing. This plan has already gotten someone killed. How many more casualties are we going to see by the end of this? And how are we going to replace Mika? Naomi still hasn't said why she was so important to us.

The doors open a minute later and a team of guards come trotting into the tunnel. Two of them arrive with a stretcher and quickly load Mika's body onto it, before disappearing out the doors. The rest of the guards cuff us and wait for the body to be removed. After that they stand us up and pat us down. From there we're escorted outside. Naomi and Ariana are lined up behind me, single file. A transport vehicle is summoned and twenty minutes later we're back outside Tower B.

A cool breeze escapes the building as we're led inside. At the end of the hallway and beside the door, Vesna is sitting with her back against the wall. She stands up as we're closing in and holds both hands in front of her, palms facing up and together. A ball of flames erupts in her hands and she gives a sinister smile before vanishing. The door fails to open and the guards in the control room are forced to try it a second time. The door remains closed and I can hear someone moving around on the other side. One of our guards thumps his palm against the door.

"What's going on in there?" he shouts. Seconds later a muffled voice is heard on the other side.

"Hold on a second!" Halsey shouts. "The door's stuck again!" Moments later the door slides open and we're led inside. Tia and Jeff are waiting for us. The guards line us up along a wall beside Tia and step back as Halsey approaches. She glares at us all with intense frustration.

"You've all got some explaining to do!" she snarls. "Tell me...tell me why it is that one of my staff is dead! How the hell did it happen?" Silence ensues. "Well?" Who died? Wait...Laura's not here. I thought she was having her head checked out in the infirmary.

"That must have been after we got separated," Naomi says.

"Oh, how convenient," Halsey drawls, backing away a few paces. "You just happened to be somewhere else. How on earth did you even get separated in the first place?" Jeff clears his throat.

"That was partially my fault," he cuts in. "Richards and I had them looking for maps and-"

"I am not talking to you, Martin!" Halsey roars. "When I want your input, I will ask for it!"

"I'm just saying they had nothing to do with it!" Jeff insists. "None of them! Something weird is going on down there and it got my partner killed!"

"I don't have time for your ridiculous ghost stories!" Halsey growls.

"It's not a story!" Jeff insists. "Something attacked us and it killed Richards! No one here is responsible for her death!"

"Do not make excuses for the inmates!" Halsey bellows. "They're guilty as hell and your interference is inching you closer to losing your job!"

"It's not their fault!" Jeff shouts. "I would never be so adamant about something if I wasn't a hundred percent sure of it! These girls are innocent and barking at them isn't going to change what really happened! If I'd seen any of them, or even suspected for a moment that they attacked Richards, I'd be singing a different tune, but I'm not because I know what I saw down there!"

"Martin, I swear to God, if you're lying to me..." Halsey mutters, clapping a palm to her face as she speaks.

"I'm not lying about this!" he insists. "But I guess that doesn't matter in the end! All you ever want to hear is what you think is true, what you think is right, and to hell with the facts!" Halsey's eye flashes as she removes her hand. She turns and rips her pistol from its holster. Jeff's eyes widen as she points it at his head.

"You'd do well to watch your mouth, Martin," Halsey hisses. "I don't know what the hell has gotten into you, but I sure as hell don't like it."

"Okay, okay, I got a little carried away, I'm sorry," Jeff apologizes, holding his hands up in front of him.

"Too late..." Halsey growls. She points the gun at his shin and fires. Jeff howls in pain and stumbles back into the wall. He falls against it and clutches his bleeding leg. It's brief, but my eye catches the blur of the discarded rubber round tumbling across the floor. "I will not tolerate insubordination on this island! Not from any one of you! Is that clear?" Halsey barks at the other guards.

"Yes ma'am!" they chorus. She kneels down in front of Jeff, who glares at her with his teeth gritted.

"One other thing, Martin," Halsey growls. "You nearly botched this recovery effort by getting your team separated. I need to make certain you know not to do it again." She raises the pistol and fires it a second time, this time striking Jeff in the arm. He yelps and snarls in pain. "Maybe next time you'll think twice before you fuck up on my watch!" She shoves her pistol back into its holster and storms toward the door. She turns to face the rest of us just before reaching it. "Put the inmates back in their cells at once," she orders. "I need time to decide what to do with the surviving escapee. Once you're finished, take Martin to the infirmary and return to your stations. Is that understood?"

"Yes ma'am!" the guards chorus.

"Good. Now get to it!"

Chapter 11

Voices

That night I'm tossing and turning in my cell. My dreams are tearing at me again. I keep revisiting the things that happened in Sector S. The discovery of Mika's body, the unseen force that chased us through the tunnel, and the cables that dragged me away. My eyes snap open and I sit bolt upright in my bed. Screaming is coming from the cell beside mine again, cutting through the darkness like a razor. I tumble out of my bed, heart racing and sweat dripping down my face. What on earth has her screaming like that? The screaming ceases as I look out the window, trying to see if anyone else woke up. I feel a presence behind me and turn to see Helena sitting at the head of my bed.

"Trouble sleeping?" she taunts.

"Why are you here?" I demand.

"That's a good question, Sarita," she chuckles, standing up as she speaks. "Keep asking yourself that and maybe you'll find the answer." She lunges forward and shoves me backward. I fall to the ground with my back against the door. She kneels down in front of me. "Now I have a question for you. Why'd you do it, Sarita? Hmm? Why'd you kill me?"

"It was an accident."

"Liar!" she hisses. "The least you can do is be honest. Are you at least sorry for what you did?"

"No," I declare. She grabs me by the throat with both hands, slamming my head into the door.

"Why...the hell...not?" she growls, tightening her grasp.

"Because it wasn't my fault!" I choke. She loosens her grasp and tilts her head to the side.

"So, what then?" she snorts. "You and Phoebe were just playing a friendly game of catch with a rock? Let me guess, you threw it too fast, she missed it, BAM! Right in the head. It was an accident. Right?"

"I know you, Helena," I growl. "I know that if you were in the same position I was, you would've fought for your life...and that's what I did."

"Yeah, keep telling yourself that..." Helena snarls, tightening her grasp again.

"You know it's true," I choke, struggling to pull her hands off.

"Let me get one thing straight with you, Sarita," she growls, her eyes burning into mine. "You – don't – know me!" She shakes me with each syllable. "But I do know you...and this is far from over." She tightens her grasp a little more. Everything goes black and moments later I find myself lying on my bed again. I sit up and look around the room. All's quiet and it doesn't sound like anyone is awake. For a moment I think about going back to sleep, but decide against it. Instead I stare up at the ceiling and count the tallies left by former inmates. Something about it starts to creep me out and I roll over on my side. Minutes later I hear a voice down by the floor, beneath the sink and near the base of the toilet.

"Hey. Hey! Hello?" I glance down at the vent, then roll back to face the wall. The voice continues speaking and I try my best to avoid it.

"Heeeeeyy...yooouuu... Wake up! I know you're awake, so don't try to ignore me! Hey! Hey you! Say something!" The voice stops for a moment and is replaced with an unsettling cackle.

"Will you shut up!" I snap, rolling to face the vent. I yelp as I roll too far and fall off the bed with a thud. The cackling stops and her voice comes back through the vent again as I stare straight at it. This time her tone is flat and void of emotion.

"You're awake..." says the girl in the cell beside me. Something about her tone sends a shiver through me.

"Leave me alone..." I reply. "I don't want to talk."

"Then why are you?" the girl asks. She lets out a giggle and the vent goes silent.

"I fell out of bed."

"How did you manage that?" she asks, a sinister tone in her voice.

"What's it to you?" I demand. She lets out a cackle that stops as suddenly as it starts.

"Something's eating at you, isn't it?" she taunts.

"Right now it's you," I retort.

"I know a way out," she giggles. "It's risky, though. Wanna hear?"

"Sure...why not?" I grumble, rolling onto my back.

"You got your shoes, right?" she replies. "The laces. Take them out."

"Fuck you!" I snap.

"It works! I've done it! I swear, they'll take you out if they think you're gonna hang up.[14] Or you could do it for real too, that's always an option!" She lets out another crazed cackle and moments later she's moved away from the vent and begun making a racket. She slams her fists against the door and I jump in alarm. There's a brief pause and the girl erupts into a fit of hysterical laughter as she slams the door several more times. Moments later a guard comes trotting up the stairs, flashlight in hand. The beam washes over my cell as he approaches.

"Quit banging on the door!" he snarls, thumping his fist on my cell door. I sit up and look at him.

"It was the girl next to me!" I argue. "I had nothing to do with it." He goes to the cell to my left and I roll my eyes in frustration. "No, not her!" I say. "The one on my right! Other cell!" He gives me an incredulous look through the glass.

"What, you think you're funny?" he snarls. "There's no one in that cell."

"What are you talking about? I was just talking to her!" I argue.

"You wanna see for yourself?" he offers. "I'll show you. Hands through the slot. Hurry up, I don't have all night." I put my hands through the slot and he cuffs them together.

"Control, open 37 and 38," he says over the radio. The door to my cell and the one beside me opens up. He grabs me by the upper arm and shoves me in front of the cell. My eyes widen. He's right, it's empty.

"That doesn't make any sense!" I say. "I heard her! I swear I did!"

"Control, close 37." My door slides closed and I feel my heart skip a beat.

"What are you doing? You got the wrong door!" He shoves me into the cell and I try to run back out. He throws me to the ground and draws his pistol.

---

[14]Suicide by hanging.

"Close 38!" he orders. The door slides closed just as I get to my feet. I rush forward and kick the door as hard as I can. "You wanna tell me again that you didn't do it?" he snarls, putting his pistol back in its holster. "Hands in the slot, I need my cuffs back."

"Fuck you!" I shout. "Put me back in the other cell! I'm not staying in here all night!"

"Hands in the slot! Now!"

"Why don't you make me?" I snarl.

"Fine, then I'll request a cell extraction[15]," he threatens. "Is that what you want?" Part of me wants to keep this up, but if Naomi's plan is going to work I can't risk anymore trouble.

"Fine, whatever..." I mutter, shoving my hands through the slot. He takes the cuffs off and I pull my hands back through.

"I still want out of this cell!" I snarl. "Open the door!"

"Sorry, can't," he taunts, turning to leave.

"Hey! Come back! Open the door, asshole! There's something in here with me! Let me out!" I slam my fists against the door again.

"Calm down and go to sleep!" he snarls, turning to face me. "I'm sick of listening to you!" He heads back down the stairs and I'm left alone in my new cell, still fuming and scared. I glance over my shoulder and then back out the window. I turn and sit with my back against the door, watching the rest of the tiny cell. For forty-five minutes, I sit in silence, watching, and waiting...

* * *

At some point after the exchange with the guard, I doze off. Sometime later I open my eyes and I glance around the cell. I thought I heard a voice. I stand up and rub my neck. It's stiff and so is my leg. I plop down on the bed and fall onto my side. My head hits the pillow and I exhale my held breath. After a few minutes I sit up and get to my feet. Right as I turn to face the door, I see that it's blocked by someone standing in front of it. I back away two paces and blink a few times, but she's still there, standing with her back to me.

"Hello?" I whisper. My heart is racing. She ignores me and continues to stare out the window on the door. I approach her with caution and

---

[15]A procedure in which an uncooperative inmate is forcibly removed from their cell by a team of officers.

reach out toward her. She glances over her shoulder at me and I back off. She's about my height with black hair, light brown skin, and brown eyes. She turns to face me with a malicious grin on her face. She lunges toward me with an angry shriek and knocks me to the floor. I headbutt her in the nose. She yelps in pain and loosens her grasp, allowing me an opportunity to throw her off. After I do, she punches me in the cheek and I scramble to my feet. She lunges at me and I kick her in the stomach. She tumbles back against the wall and I leap on top of her. I try to hold her down and before I can restrain her, she bites my wrist. I scream and she throws me off.

Still expecting a fight, I rush to my feet to find that the girl is gone. I'm left standing in the cell, alone and more terrified than ever. Examining my wounded wrist, I find it has bruises in the shape of teeth starting to form. Outside I can hear someone trotting back up the stairs. As much as I hate that guard, I'm almost happy to see him reach the top of the stairs. Whatever was in here with me, I don't want to see it again. I need to get out of this cell, I don't want to stay here another minute. He comes up to the door and pounds his fist against it.

"The hell are you doing in there?" he shouts.

"I told you! There's something in here!" I shout back.

"Oh there's something in there all right," he snorts. "A screaming lunatic! Now go to sleep!"

"Make me!" I taunt.

"I will make you! That what you want?"

"Did I fucking stutter?" I snarl. There's no way this can end well, but right now I'm just desperate to get out of here.

"Hands through the slot!" he orders.

"What? You afraid to open the door?"

"Screw this..." he snarls, drawing his pistol. My eyes widen and he flings the slot open as I back away from the door. He fires five rounds through the slot, two of which hit me in the leg and three that miss and ricochet around the cell. The rubber pellets sting so bad my eyes begin watering and blood seeps through my clothes. Nothing went in, but there's no doubt I'll have welts.

"What the fuck is your problem?" I scream, clutching my leg on my bed.

"Control, open 38," to the guard orders through his radio. The door slides open and he storms into my cell, grabbing me by the arm and dragging me off the bed. I try to get loose and he puts the pistol to my head.

"These might not be lead, but this close and you're in for a world of hurt," he growls. "Now hold still!" He cuffs my arms behind my back and drags me to my feet. He orders the guard in the control room to close the cell door and escorts me downstairs. Once we reach the control room, he pushes me toward a wall, uncuffs my hands and points at the wall.

"Two hours," he says. "That's how long you're going to stand here with your hands on the back of your head. You so much as try to put them down in that time and I'll come out and blast you. You got that?" I remain silent. "Hey! I'm talking to you!"

"Yeah, I got it!" I snap. In the brief instance I look back at him, I catch sight of his name tag. "M. McClain." Instantly I feel a mixture of anger and dread wash over me. Rashida yelled at a Matt McClain last month for firing live rounds at us. If he's that crazy, there's no telling what he might do here where no one can stop him.

"Because I'm feeling generous, you get two hours no matter what," he continues. "So you'd better be counting your blessings! This goes down two ways. You leave at the end of two hours with some more welts, or you don't. It's that simple. Now get to it!" I put my hands on the back of my head and he storms back into the control booth behind me. After ten minutes, my arms are starting to ache. Ten more and my neck is throbbing. After a total of thirty minutes, my arms are on fire and my neck is getting stiff. I turn to face the booth and see that neither of the guards are paying attention. I let my arms fall to my sides and feel a sense of relief wash over them. Moments later, McClain takes notice and storms out of the booth with a shotgun.

"You got ninety minutes left! Hands back on your head!" he orders, pointing the weapon at me. I turn back toward the wall and put my hands back up. A beanbag slams into the wall beside me and I jump in surprise.

"The hell is wrong with you?" I shout.

"Keep your hands where they belong!" he snarls. "I won't miss again." He's back in the booth seconds later. Fifteen more minutes pass and I'm starting to feel hopeless. I can't afford to keep getting shot at, but my arms are in so much pain I can't stand it. McClain comes back out of the booth and I turn to face him.

"I didn't do anything!" I protest.

"Didn't say you did," he answers. "Put your arms down, you look like a fuckin' idiot. I have a new job for you." I let my arms fall to my sides as he speaks and feel the pain begin to subside. My neck is still so stiff it hurts to move it. "You see that door over there? The one that goes into Sector S?" He points across the room and toward one of the windows. Through it I can see the door he's referring to.

"What about it?" I ask.

"What? You don't see it?" he snorts. "It's stuck, dumbass! You're gonna go wriggle it around a bit, get it unstuck. Then you come back here and face the wall. Think you can handle that?"

"What do you mean by wriggle it around?" I ask.

"Jostle the door around, get it unstuck, it's not that hard!" he growls. "Now get going!" I look back at the window and then head for the door to the hallway. The other guard in the booth unlocks the door to the hall and I start navigating the circular hallway. Once I come to the Sector S door, I stand staring inside for several seconds. For a moment I glimpse what appears to be a shadow moving around inside and step back a pace. I jump a foot when McClain bangs on the window behind me and points at the door.

"Hurry up!" he says, his voice muffled. With a great deal of hesitation, I step closer to the door and take hold of it. I give it a sharp tug, but it doesn't move. A few more attempts and it barely manages to budge. I see the shadow a second time, but it's gone when I look up. I jostle the door and this time it moves, shifting back onto its track. It slams closed and then opens again, revealing a long black cable that appears to have been the cause of the derailment. I go to pick it up and it leaps up and snares me around the wrist. I don't even have time to react. The cable yanks me forward and drags me several feet. It lets go and before I can get up, another snares me around both ankles, binding them together and lifting me up into the air.

I scream and fall silent in terror as I'm hung upside down, where I find myself staring into the cold, malice-filled eyes of Mattie. Her expression is at first blank and soon morphs into a malicious grin. My voice is caught in my throat and body paralyzed with fear. She reeks of decay, so much so that I fear I might vomit.

Another cable leaps from the ground and fastens itself around my neck, squeezing so hard I struggle to breathe. Everything starts to go dark and I blackout after a short time. I'm unaware of how much time passes, but at some point I start to feel myself returning to consciousness. My body feels as if it's made of lead and I can barely move a muscle.

Somewhere nearby I hear the guards, the sound of a struggle, shouting and panic. Then two gunshots followed by silence. Next is the sensation of being dragged by my wrists. Soon I begin to smell gasoline. My vision starts coming back into focus and I sit up to see McClain standing over the body of the other guard, his baton clutched in his hand and coated with blood. He tosses it aside and Vesna walks up beside him. It's almost as if he's in a trance. Vesna notices me watching and catches my eye. My vision is still blurry and it's hard to make out her features. Unmistakable are those two fiery orange eyes, burning like hot coals inside her otherwise hollow eye sockets. She gives an unhinged grin and I feel myself losing consciousnesses again. Everything goes dark and I find myself lying on the floor, an intense heat around me.

I sit bolt upright to see the room filled with smoke and angry orange flames. The smell of gasoline and burning bodies fills the air. An alarm is going off, the sound of which is deafening. Leaping to my feet, I race toward the stairs and find the door engulfed in flames. Gasoline has been poured all over behind it and I can't get past. The flames spread closer to the staircase and I race to the top of the stairs, colliding with Naomi near the first landing.

"What's going on?" she shouts over the alarm.

"The building is on fire! The door's blocked, we can't get through!" Naomi grabs me by the arm and pulls me up the last few stairs. Flames spread along the walls, following after us.

"Come on, this way!" she urges.

"How did you get out?" I ask, racing up the steps behind her.

"The cell doors opened when the alarm went off," she explains. Moments later we reach the third floor to find the other inmates, all out of their cells and gathering around us. "The main entrance is blocked," Naomi informs everyone. "Does anyone know another way out? A fire exit or something?" Tia steps forward.

"I've been further up in here once before," she says. "I saw an emergency exit that goes to the roof. Everyone follow me." Tia starts up the stairs and the rest of us follow after her. We trot up two more flights of stairs and arrive at the top floor. In the corner of the room is an unlatched door with "Emergency" written across it in red lettering. Tia pulls the door open and beckons for us to follow her through. The door's latch must have opened the way our cells did after the alarm went off. The rest of us follow Tia up the steps, single file. I step out onto the roof behind Naomi and begin looking around. The others emerge from the exit and our group begins searching the edges of the roof. Tia finds something and calls to the rest of us.

"Over here!" Tia calls, waving at us. She points at the top of a ladder that leads down to the bottom of the tower.

"You're kidding! We're supposed to climb down that?" I say.

"That's idea," Tia responds as she lowers herself over the side. "That or stay up here." Once she's low enough, I follow her down. Gripping the rungs as tight as I can, I begin descending the ladder, balancing between wanting to get down soon and not wanting to fall off. Halfway down I hear a blast on the opposite side of the tower, accompanied by the sound of glass shattering. Ariana and Naomi are on the ladder with me; Naomi only a few feet above me. The ground, though much closer, still seems far away. Several feet lower, my foot slips on the rung. I cling to the ladder for a few extra seconds and look up to see Naomi's feet less than a foot above me. When I reach the bottom I look down and see a patch of grass below me. I lower myself down with my feet dangling and drop off from the bottom rung.

The landing is hard enough to sting my feet. Tia helps me up and I trot away from the tower and start heading for the footbridge. Staff are already responding. They're opening the gates up ahead and over a dozen of them are racing across the footbridge and toward the main entrance. A few of them break off from the group and race over to us. Without missing a beat, they all order us on the ground and perform a quick head count. Once they're satisfied that they have everyone, they cuff our hands behind our backs and escort us across the footbridge. I take one last look at the building and the smoke pouring from it.

Chapter 12

Aftermath

I don't want to be here. That's all I can think as I'm led closer and closer to Halsey's office with the others.

"All right, in you go," Rashida says, opening the door. Inside everyone else is waiting. Naomi, Tia, and Ariana. An empty chair on the end is waiting for me. In the corner is Jeff. If his wounds are bandaged up, they're under his uniform. Beside him is Nicole. I sit down in the empty chair, and Halsey, who's sitting behind her desk, lets out an exasperated sigh. She's leaning forward with one arm lying parallel with the length of the desk, and her head held in the other.

"I'm at a loss for words..." she murmurs, lifting her head up and laying her arm down beside the other. She leans back in her chair, her remaining eye fixated on the ceiling. The tension in the room is stifling. She looks at each of the guards, then down the row of inmates. She picks a pen up off her desk and pinches the ends between her thumbs and index fingers on both hands. "In a very short period of time, this island has begun its descent into chaos. This one's ill-conceived escape attempt," she points to Ariana with her pen. "This one stealing my keys and then gouging my fucking eye out!" She points at Naomi. "And then we have Teymouri here who just seems to be nearby for most of it. She's in Tower B when it burns, she runs off with my keys in the chow hall, she was even present when one of my guards croaked. Down in the tunnels where surveillance wasn't possible, where I have nothing but the word of criminals and a useless guard to tell me what happened."

"Ma'am, if I could just say something-" Jeff pipes up.

"You may not!" Halsey snaps. "I've heard enough out of you. You'll speak when I say so, you got that?"

"Yes, ma'am," he answers, his gaze focused on the floor. Halsey turns her attention back to me and the other inmates.

"Twenty years I've been here. I've seen escape attempts, I've seen fights, plenty of deaths, but here we are with a total of three dead guards. One in Sector S and two more in the fire! This is completely unprecedented! Do any of you girls have even the slightest idea of the colossal fucking headache you've created for me?" Nicole grits her teeth and clenches her fists. Rashida coughs into her hand and crosses her arms. Halsey takes a deep breath and exhales, shaking her head with her gaze fixated on her desk. Jeff glances at her and then back at the floor. "I take it that's a no?" Halsey mutters, her eye falling on me and the other inmates. "Really? None of you have anything at all to say about what you've done?"

"We had nothing to do with it," Naomi replies.

"Sure thing, Beckham," Halsey snorts, locking eyes with her. "You're the only one here with a prior charge of arson, so I'm sure I can trust whatever you say in this matter."

"That charge isn't even why I'm here," Naomi argues. "That was two years before I was arrested and it was dropped. I wasn't even the one that started that fire, it was some idiots I knew."

"Yeah, sure..." Halsey replies. "Whatever you say." Naomi rolls her eye and lets out a frustrated groan.

"They borrowed my lighter and that was the end of my involvement," Naomi continues. "Just because someone saw me walking away from them around the same time, they thought I had something to do with it. Those other people started the fire, not me. And this time isn't much different."

"So you're saying that one of the other inmates here started the fire, but that you had nothing to do with it?" Halsey asks.

"No, I meant that none of us started it," Naomi answers.

"Well, let's see," Halsey says, getting up from her desk and standing in front of it. "How about I tell you what I know? You four were the only inmates in that building when it caught fire. The guards stationed there are both dead. Explain that to me, will you?"

"Maybe they killed each other," Ariana suggests. "I'd go crazy if I had to work here too." Halsey glares at her for a moment before slapping her across the face.

"You'd do well to watch that smart mouth of yours," Halsey hisses, still leering at her. She turns her attention to all of us. "Moving on, let me make this clear to you all that there will be severe consequences for this. Teymouri, Beckham, Ellis, and Miller...as of now I'm putting an extension on each of your sentences by six months."

"What?" I exclaim. "Are you serious? How could we have even done anything?"

"That's what we're here to find out," Halsey replies, returning to her seat. "One thing I've learned in my time here is that you little shits can be quite crafty. Why should I think any less of you now?"

"No one here had anything to do with it," Tia declares. "There's nothing to talk about."

"I will not give you another chance to do the right thing," Halsey warns. "Come clean now and I may just lighten your punishments." Naomi clenches her fists and shakes her head.

"You always say something like that," Naomi growls, looking up at Halsey. "Everyone knows you never mean it." Halsey leans forward, buries her face in her hands, and lets out a frustrated groan before folding her arms in front of her.

"All right, fine...I guess we're doing this the hard way," Halsey sighs. "Rashida. Make yourself useful and go check the surveillance footage from the interior of the tower and do it quick. I don't want to be here all night."

"Yes ma'am," Rashida replies. She turns and leaves the room. The door creaks open and latches as she steps outside. Her footsteps fade away and the room becomes silent again.

"You sure none of you want to admit you did it?" Halsey asks. "Holding your tongues isn't how you get off this island. Keep it up and I'll keep you here till you're twenty-one. Then you can go straight to a federal prison and see how you like it there. The choice is yours."

"There's nothing in that footage," Naomi remarks.

"I'm not inclined to listen to a liar, Beckham," Halsey replies, lighting a cigarette. She blows a puff of smoke into the air, never taking her eye off of Naomi.

"Hypocrite..." Naomi mutters.

"Excuse me?" Halsey demands, leaning forward. "What did you say to me, Beckham?"

"I said you're a hypocrite," Naomi sneers. Halsey lets out a chuckle and takes another drag on her cigarette.

"I am many things, Beckham, but I am not a hypocrite," Halsey replies. "However, if it makes you feel better, you can just go on and think whatever you want about me, because at the end of the day I'm not the crook here. Insufferable little firebug. I know you did it, Beckham, just like I know you strangled that classmate of yours into cardiac arrest. Dead for two minutes, wasn't she? What was your excuse for that again? 'She made me do it?' Something of that nature?" Naomi clenches her teeth and glares at Halsey. "Funny how some things never change. No matter how many girls pass through here the story's always the same. None of you can accept responsibility for anything you've done and certain ones seem to have a harder time than others."

"I never said she made me do anything," Naomi argues. "You call us liars and here you are lying about my case."

"I am not lying about your case, but you are, Beckham," Halsey counters. "I read through everyone's files when they arrive here, I know you all quite well. I know that you were charged with attempted murder for what you did, Beckham. Ellis here sold drugs to an undercover cop, Miller beat her boyfriend with a bat. That one was especially stupid, wasn't it, Miller? Didn't you tell the police that he was cheating on you or something?"

"So what if I did?" Ariana demands.

"And then we have Teymouri," Halsey continues. "Who stabbed a girl to death-"

"She was the one trying to stab me!" I interrupt. "She fell and stabbed herself! I was trying to get the knife away from her!"

"She was stabbed in the neck," Halsey contends. "That sounds pretty intentional to me. You should consider yourself lucky you got hit with manslaughter instead of murder. Not many girls like you would have gotten off so easy."

"And what would you know about any of that?" Naomi demands. "You might've read a file on us, but you weren't there to see any of what happened. Not before, not during, not after. You have no idea what any of us have been through, you have no idea what's gone on in any of our heads or why we did what we did! So why don't you shut your whore mouth?" Naomi stands up as she finishes her sentence and Halsey's eye flashes with anger. What is Naomi thinking? I know we're already in trouble now that the tower has caught fire, but this is only making things worse. She told us not to get locked up if we could help it, to keep our heads down. I want to grab her and shake her at this point. Something about her case seems to have struck a nerve.

"What did you just say to me, Beckham?" Halsey hisses, slowly standing up. "Shut my what?"

"You heard me," Naomi growls.

"Keep talking like that, Beckham, keep pushing and you'll find yourself somewhere you don't want to be," Halsey warns.

"This entire island is already somewhere I don't want to be," Naomi snorts. "I've been locked up, maced, shot, beaten, lost an eye, took a walk through Sector S, even carried a corpse around! What else could you possibly do to me? Huh? You gonna blow me away like Eston? No, I don't think even you'd go that far! You're not that fucking stupid! It might ruin YOUR life if you did that! Right? Oh wait...no it wouldn't, cuz you're still here!"

"You have no idea what you're talking about, so why don't you listen for once in your miserable life and back off before you say something you regret?" Halsey suggests.

"How about I tell you what that stupid file of yours never said?" Naomi offers. "That report didn't tell you why I strangled that girl. I did it because she was a smug piece of trash who loved that my father died while serving overseas! By the time I got around to strangling her, my father had only been dead for two months! Care to guess why she thought it was funny? I'll give you a hint!" She waves her hand up and down in front of her face.

"Sit down, Beckham," she orders.

"Real fun suddenly having your only living parent taken away from you at fifteen!" Naomi snarls. Halsey walk up and grabs her by the shoulders. She slams her back into her chair, then crouches down in front of her. "I don't think you understand the gravity of the situation you're in," Halsey snarls. "A pitiful, worthless, little orphan like you could disappear in the blink of an eye and no one would ever find you. Now I suggest you straighten your ass up and start acting like a model prisoner before it's too late to do so!" She and Naomi glare at one another in a tense silence. It's soon interrupted by Rashida stepping back into the room. She closes the door and stands there with her hands clasped behind her back and her gaze averted. "Well, do you have it or not?" Halsey demands. She stands up and turns to face Rashida who still seems lost in thought. Halsey steps closer and waves her hand in front of Rashida's face. She comes back to reality and looks at Halsey, then at the floor in front of her.

"Umm...I..." Rashida mumbles.

"Do you have the footage or not, Rashida?" Halsey asks again. Rashida shakes her head. Halsey looks away in frustration and paces back toward her desk where she sits on the edge of it. "Rashida, I need an answer from you. What's going on?"

"We don't have it," she murmurs.

"And what does that mean?" Halsey demands.

"There must have been a malfunction," she explains, looking up from the floor. "It's just...gone." Halsey steps away from her desk, arms crossed, and head tilted.

"Pretty convenient timing," Halsey responds. "Why don't you tell me what really happened, hmm?"

"Ava, I already-"

"Never call me that again," Halsey hisses. "I'm your superior, you don't use first names with me."

"Fine, I just-"

"Don't you stand there and talk to me with that tone!" Halsey growls. "What? You think just because I've known you longer than the other staff that you get a free pass or something? To just talk to me however you wish?"

"I didn't mean it like that," Rashida insists. "I just don't appreciate you calling me a liar! I told you there was a malfunction and that's what it was! You can go down and speak with Lacey and Andrew if you want, but I swear I'm telling the truth!"

"Do you expect me to believe that all of the interior footage just happened to blink out of existence?" Halsey growls.

"It's all gone, Halsey. There's nothing I can do," Rashida replies. "Andrew and Lacey won't be able to do anything either."

"Is the exterior footage intact at least?" Halsey asks.

"Yes."

"And was there anything unusual?" Halsey inquires.

"No, just some guards trading shifts with the deceased," Rashida answers.

"And who were they?" Halsey demands.

"Peters and Brent, ma'am," Rashida answers. "They left the tower after Matt McClain and Rodgers arrived for their shift. The only explanation is that one of the deceased started the fire. Or that someone snuck in through Sector S. We checked the cameras near the dock entrance too. Nothing."

"And we're certain that only two girls escaped into Sector S prior to all of this?" Halsey asks.

"I'm positive only two escaped into Sector S," Rashida answers.

"That can't be right," Halsey declares. "Clearly there was someone else working with these brats. For the fire to get as bad as it was there had to have been accelerant splashed everywhere. Somehow I doubt they found it in their cells."

"Footage reviewed at the time that Miller and Sato escaped into Sector S showed only them fleeing into the tunnels. I realize we need to open an investigation into Tower B, but I don't believe anyone in this room had any part in what took place." Halsey rolls her eye and shakes her head.

"You frustrate me sometimes, you know that?" Halsey growls. "I'm not convinced that they aren't withholding information. Get them up and take them all to the bunker. They can all stay there for a few days, or until they feel like talking." The guards step forward as each of us get to our feet. They cuff our hands behind our backs and Halsey opens the door. Rashida takes the lead with her hand placed firmly on my arm. I'm led out into the hallway first, followed by the others.

Chapter 13

Past Transgressions

The entrance to the bunker looms in the distance. We'll arrive in less than a minute. Halsey hasn't said a word the entire time and neither has anyone else. She did give Jeff and Nicole stern looks before we left her office, but that was about it. Since I was the first one brought out of the van when we arrived, I'm in the lead behind Halsey. Rashida is to my right and the others, including Nicole and Jeff, are following behind us. The doors leading to the bunker are a short distance away now. We're led through and near the top of the stairs I snap and kick Halsey in the back. She topples forward and crashes down the stairs, landing in a heap at the bottom. Rashida stands in shock for a few seconds before racing to help. She drags me along as she goes and leads me into the cell where she removes one of the cuffs and latches it to one of the steel rings on the wall.

"You really shouldn't have done that," Rashida grumbles, pacing back out of the room. I don't care. If I have to spend time in the bunker, I'd like to at least know that I made Halsey pay for doing it. Besides, Naomi's pretty much sunk the ship at this point. Maybe this entire thing was hopeless from the start. From the wall I can see Halsey getting to her feet with Rashida's assistance. Jeff and Nicole both lead the other three inmates past Halsey and Rashida and begin placing them in the cells further down the hall.

"You all right? Anything broken?" Rashida asks Halsey.

"I don't think so," Halsey grunts. Once on her feet, she turns and scowls at me through the doorway. Rashida steps in front of her and redirects her attention.

"Head back up, I'll take care of this," Rashida says. Halsey pushes her aside and slams the cell door shut. Their voices become muffled and soon they fade into nothing.

"So tell me..." says a voice. "...was it worth it?" Helena appears beside me and begins pacing around the room.

"Why are you here?" I groan, sitting down on the floor. My arm hangs from the cuffs still latched to the wall.

"Oh, no reason. I was just in the neighborhood."

"Find someone else to bother," I growl. She chuckles and sits on her knees in front of me.

"I'm not here for anyone else," she says, tapping the end of my nose with her finger. She's got a crazed look in her eye. One that's starting to freak me out.

"Get lost," I growl. "I liked it better when I couldn't see you."

"That was then, this is now," she says, standing back up. "I guess you'll just have to deal with it." She begins pacing back and forth in front of me.

"Fine. You're not even here, anyway."

"So what do you think Halsey's going to do to you?" Helena asks, brushing her hair behind her ear as she stops to look at me. "Maybe beat you bloody? Starve you? Hey I know, maybe she'll toss you down the stairs."

"Will you just go away already!" I snap. "You're dead! I shouldn't have to deal with you anymore!"

"Why do you want me gone so badly?" Helena asks with an amused chuckle. "At least with me you have someone to talk to. That's got to count for something, doesn't it?"

"I'll take my chances..."

"Fine, have it your way," she snorts, taking a few steps back. "I can always drop in some other time." She disappears in the blink of an eye and I'm left alone in the cell. I'm not sure how much time passes, but it has to be at least a half-hour, maybe more. Even with my arm still attached to the wall I begin to doze off. I'm not out for long when I hear shouting out in the hallway. It's too muffled to make out the words, but it sounds like Halsey and Rashida. Halsey pulls the door open and their conversation becomes discernible.

"...too far with this!" Rashida protests. "You need to think of the long term here!"

"I don't pay you to argue with me!" Halsey hisses. "Now get her legs and carry her inside." Halsey walks away from the door and grabs the arms of what appears to be an unconscious inmate. Rashida stands at the inmate's feet with her arms crossed, refusing to budge.

"I'm not helping you do this," she declares. "Punishment is one thing, but torture is another."

"You know I could always have you arrested for fragging[16] Sergeant Chambers," Halsey threatens. "I'm sure the statute of limitations haven't run out yet. You're all kinds of lucky that Rose covered for you! Otherwise you'd be rotting away in prison!"

"She shot Rose for standing up to her!" Rashida argues. "Chambers was a goddamn psychopath and you know it. The only reason you were even a little mad when Rose admitted it was because Chambers was your fucked up friend!"

"I bet that's the real reason she blew her brains out that night," Halsey replies. "If it was big enough to leave in a suicide note, I'm sure it weighed heavily on her. Great job, Rashida, you feel good about yourself?"

"Chambers executed a civilian for Christ's sake! I didn't sign up for murder! She did it for fun too! The guy didn't give her the info she thought he had, so she shot him after he tried to run! Chambers deserved to die for that and more!"

"Yeah, keep on pretending you were some hero for what you did," Halsey sneers. "Rose was wrong to cover for you and it still sickens me that you were involved in that mess!"

"He was a teenager, Halsey! He couldn't have been older than sixteen! This is exactly why I know you don't care about any of the girls on this island!"

"Watch your mouth!" Halsey hisses. "You've been on the thinnest of ice imaginable ever since you were involved in Eston's death!" Rashida stares down at the floor. "Biggest goddamn P.R. nightmare this facility has ever faced!"

"I wasn't the one who pulled the trigger," Rashida argues.

"Regardless, McClain heard you give the order to fire," Halsey count-

---

[16]The deliberate act of killing or attempting to kill a fellow soldier by another soldier.

ers. "So don't pretend you're innocent!"

"I told him to HOLD his fire!" Rashida explains. "How many times do I have to tell you before you believe me?"

"I haven't trusted you since we left the war," Halsey mutters. "Now get her legs, I'm sick of standing here arguing with you." Rashida lets out a defeated sigh and takes hold of the inmate's legs. Up until now, the legs are all that I've been able to see. Once they carry the inmate into the cell, I can see that it's Mika's body. I leap to my feet and back up against the wall.

"What the hell is going on?" I demand.

"Uncuff her from the wall and attach them both by the wrist," Halsey orders, ignoring me. "I'll watch the door." She stands in the doorway and draws her pistol from her hip. Rashida gives me a concerned look and removes the cuffs from the wall. She pushes me toward the body and forces me onto my knees. I pull my arm away and she takes a firmer hold of it.

"Quit being difficult," Rashida mutters. I rip my arm away again and stumble to my feet. Before I can take even two steps, Halsey fires her weapon. The round bounces off my ribs and I fall to one knee, clutching the wound.

"Halsey!" Rashida bellows. Halsey turns to face Rashida and the two stand staring at one another for a few tense seconds.

"Do your job," Halsey growls, pointing the weapon at Rashida's head. "Chain her up!" Rashida hesitates and remains in place.

"No..." she murmurs. Halsey grits her teeth and storms over to her. She shoves Rashida against the wall and pins her there with one hand.

"I've cut you more slack than you could ever imagine!" Halsey snarls. "Your one chance to redeem yourself is to take that filthy little shit's hand and cuff it to the dead girl! Now quit complaining and do it!"

"I always thought you were different than him," Rashida murmurs. "I had hope for you, considering the life you came from. The father who raised you. You're just like that asshole. You even told me you wanted to do better than him. To be better. And yet, here we are. Are you proud of yourself, Halsey? Are you proud to be that bastard's shadow?" Halsey's eye widens and she holsters her pistol. She clenches her fist and her face starts to turn red. Halsey smashes her fist into Rashida's cheek and she falls to the ground unconscious. Halsey stands there for a moment before making her way over to me. She drags me back toward Mika and cuffs me to her wrist. She stands up without looking at me and then takes Rashida by the wrists and drags her out of the room. The door closes and everything soon grows quiet.

Chapter 14

Unhinged

My ribs are killing me. I can only hope she didn't break them. I struggle to get loose, but I'm not making any progress. The cuffs are latched tight on both ends. I pull with all my might, but it's slow going. I can feel my hand slipping loose, but only a little. After about twenty minutes, I manage to get it about halfway out. Problem is my fingers are all crammed together now. I pull harder, but it doesn't budge. My fingers are starting to ache. Each time I strain to pull my hand loose, I can feel my wrist wanting to separate. Frustrated, I let out an angry shriek and pull harder.

"Come on already!" I snarl. I clench my teeth and keep pulling. To my relief, my hand comes loose. My shoulder is aching and it feels like I pulled something. I wince and examine my hand. One look at the body and I cringe before retreating to the other side of the room. I sit down in one of the corners and pull my legs up to my chest, the same way I did the last time I was left down here. It's hard to ignore Mika lying in the center of the room; eyes open and staring straight at me. After about ten minutes I can't deal with it anymore and move to the opposite corner. There I settle in for the long haul.

There's no telling how long I'll be down here. Right now I wish there was a way for me to communicate with Naomi and the others. Time crawls by and soon I can feel myself getting drowsy. As much as I try to fight it, I end up losing. In my dreams I'm sitting in a dark room. Nearby I can hear the sound of someone humming. I crawl toward the door on the far side of the room and push it open. Sunlight blinds me and I flinch, my eyes stinging. Shielding my now watering eyes with my forearm, I stand up and step outside. The humming is a little louder now, but there's no sign of the woman doing it. Outside of the room is a massive field of flowers. Blue, purple, pink, yellow, orange, every color imaginable. The door behind me slams shut and I look back to see that I've emerged from a cabin.

Looking around at the field, I start searching for the woman. I walk around the outside of the cabin until I see her a short distance away. She's standing with a blue sundress blowing in the breeze. From here it looks like Mika. Her hair held back in a low ponytail with a beige sunhat atop her head. In front of her is a massive garden and on one arm she's holding a basket full of fruits and vegetables. Apple trees line a fence to the side, each with some lying on the ground below them. As I start toward her, the sky becomes gray and snow begins to fall. Looking up at the sky, I start to feel the snowflakes landing on my face. Mika doesn't seem to notice the sudden change and continues standing with her back to me. The plants and trees begin to wither and snow begins to pile up. She continues humming. Before I can reach her, she freezes and collapses into a pile of icy shards.

The wind picks up and snow begins to fall even harder. Soon I can't see anything but white. My eyes open and I blink several times until my vision comes into focus. How long have I been out? I can still hear the humming. It takes me a moment to realize it, but Mika's no longer in the center of the room. The humming continues as I turn my head to see her sitting a few feet away from me with her back against the wall. She stops humming and opens her eyes as she turns her head toward me.

"Sorry, am I bothering you?" she asks. I get to my feet and race to the other side of the room, my heart pounding in my chest.

"This isn't real, this isn't real, this isn't real!" I panic.

"Would have been nice if you'd shown up sooner..." Mika sighs. "You know? Back in Sector S?"

"All in my head, it's not happening," I mumble. "This isn't real, it's in my head..." With my back against the wall, I cover my eyes with both hands and slide down into a seated position. By this point the room has gone silent again. Lowering my hands, I see that she's back in the middle of the room, staring right at me. I walk over and look down at her. Her mouth is open and her eyes gazing into oblivion. I shudder and walk back to my original corner. After I sit down, she sits up and speaks again.

"You know she lied, right?" she says, turning her head toward me. Her neck cracks as she does so.

"Who?" I ask, my voice shaking.

"Ariana," she answers. "Come on, I know you put the pieces together already. I was beaten. What did Ariana have with her when you found her?"

"A flashlight," I murmur.

"A three D-cell one," Mika nods, brushing her hair out of her face. "She beat me down and left me for dead. Nothing dragged me away, she made the whole thing up."

"That doesn't make sense. You were in that crawlspace up along the wall," I answer. "Naomi had a hard time getting you down as it was. There's no way Ariana got you up there by herself."

"I crawled up there when I came to!" she hisses, getting to her feet as she speaks. "I died a short time later. I was trying to find somewhere to hide."

"Explain the ladder," I demand. "Part of it was torn from the wall, there's no way you could have gotten up there in the condition you were in."

"You know exactly why it was ripped down," she counters. "You know what sorts of things are lurking down there, you've seen it with your own two eyes and so has everyone else who's gone down there."

"With the tunnels full of the things we saw, going alone doesn't make sense. It doesn't add up. There's no clear reason for why Ariana would kill you. She told me Vesna killed people in the same way you were. Beaten with a blunt object. I know what I saw down there. That place is clearly haunted."

"You need to stop trusting your senses so much," she says tilting her head to the side. Her neck cracks again as she does so.

"I'm not trusting them right now," I argue.

"But you didn't question what you saw in the tunnels...did you?" she points out.

"I wasn't the only one who saw what happened down there," I counter.

"Doesn't mean you all saw the same thing," she says.

"You're not making sense."

"Or...maybe I'm making perfect sense," she replies. She gives me a malicious grin.

"Since all you seem to want to do is waste my time, how about you go back to being a corpse?" I growl. She takes several steps forward in quick succession. I jump to my feet and brace myself for a fight. She stops a few feet away with her fists clenched and her head bowed.

"Don't be so quick to believe what you want to believe," she warns. "That sort of thinking gets people killed...and I should know..." She raises her head and glares at me. The moment I blink she's back on the floor again, still lying there as if she's never moved.

"Keep it together...just...keep it together," I murmur, turning my gaze away from the body. The more I look at her, the more unnerved I begin to feel. The humming starts up again and I look up. Nothing. She's still lying there.

"Will you please stop doing that?" I shout. I'm at my limit. I can't stay awake any longer. My eyelids droop and I start to hear the humming again. I want to tell her to shut up, but I drift off to sleep before I can. Sometime later I find myself awakening in the middle of the cell. Something is very wrong. The door is wide open and severely damaged, looking as though someone broke in. I can only make out bits and pieces of it at a time due to the flickering bulb hanging from the other side of the room. The other bulb is completely gone, smashed to pieces. The interior of the cell has changed, but much of it remains the same. The main differences include Mika's now missing body and graffiti across some of the walls. New cracks have formed all around and the place looks like it's been abandoned for years.

I close my eyes and try hard to wake up. There's no telling what's waiting for me if I leave. No matter how hard I try I just can't do it. I'm stuck here for the time being. I must be too tired to wake up. I only need to wake up for a minute, to sort of reset everything and hope for a new dream. Pinching myself, twisting one of my ears, even pulling out a strand of hair all fail. Feeling defeated, I get to my feet and exit the cell. Maybe if I happen to run into something unpleasant, I can be scared into waking up. The hallway and stairs look much the same as the inside of the cell. Decrepit, decaying, and patches covered in graffiti. One of the doors at the top of the stairs is missing and the other is bent and twisted. Outside I tilt my head back and look up at the sky. It's pitch black with no moon or stars. My only light is from the lampposts scattered across the island; some of which are bent and twisted with bits of their shattered bulbs lying on the ground beneath them.

A mild breeze ruffles my hair as I walk further away from the bunker. Something moves near the water towers and I instead turn and head to my left, toward a small building nearby. A sign above the entrance says "Armory." The door is ajar and the window in its upper half smashed to pieces. Feeling as though I'm being watched, I turn and glance around the area. Movement near the edge of the building catches my eye, but whatever it is vanishes before I can get a good look at it. I push the door as far open as I can and start looking around inside. The first room is empty with an old counter and a few rusted and damaged metal chairs along the wall. Trash and other debris litters the room.

Behind the counter is another door that leads to a larger room with one dim light in the corner. Inside I find a series of empty racks where rifles and shotguns were once kept. One of the weapons remains; a battered old rifle, similar to the ones the guards in the watchtowers use. I don't know how much I need something like this, but right now I'd feel better having it around. My hope is that if I were to die in this dream, I would just wake up in the bunker. Something about this one seems different, though. I'm much more lucid than previous ones and because of that it feels all the more real. After retrieving the rifle, I remove the magazine and see that it's still loaded. Comparing the size of the magazine to the size of the rounds inside, it looks to hold somewhere around fifteen or so. Maybe more, maybe less.

Pulling back the bolt reveals an empty chamber and so I replace the magazine and chamber the first round. I sling the rifle over my shoulder and keep my hand gripped on the sling to hold it in place. After taking a moment to look around, I don't find any trace of extra ammo. Looks like I'll just have to work with what I have. If I'm lucky, I won't need to use it. Part of me wonders if I might find more ammo lying around elsewhere, but it doesn't seem likely. Better to not get my hopes up. I move back outside and past another nearby building. One about triple the size of the one I just left, if not larger. Peering inside, I find dozens of old rusting bunks, most of them missing their mattresses. Is this where the guards sleep?

Continuing on, I pass by the dock entrance to Sector S. The doors are gone and a chain is across the entrance. From the chain dangles a weathered sign with the word "Danger." Another sign is bolted beside the doorway, warning that the area inside is contaminated and that the air isn't safe to breathe. Turning away from the entrance, I start walking toward the docks. The fences and gates that were once along it are gone and somehow they don't appear to have ever been there. No holes where the posts once stood, nothing. The docks no longer have the ferries I'm familiar with, and instead there's one small ferry with a much different paint job that's covered in rust and sunk halfway into the dark, murky water below.

Behind me I see that the graveyard is gone and a different building is standing in the same area. Building C, just west of where the graveyard used to be, is shaped a bit different. It's smaller and doesn't have the fencing around it that it once did. Walking past it, I find that the track still remains and the metallic bleachers are replaced with wooden ones that are falling apart and rotting. Reaching C Street, I find it just like the other streets and walkways I've seen so far. Riddled with cracks and covered in puddles. The more I explore the island, the more it seems as though I've traveled through time. What I can't figure out is if it's forward or backward. I suppose it doesn't matter, though. It is just a dream, after all.

As I continue west down C Street, Tower B comes into view. The bridges are the same as they've always been, minus the fact that the fences are now topped with barbed wire. There are three signs on the front of the gate blocking access to the footbridge. Two are the same as the ones I saw at the dock entrance to Sector S. "Danger" and "Contaminated area." The third sign lists the tower as an unsafe structure and warns potential trespassers to stay out. Somewhere to my left and near Building A, where the dorms are located, I hear a door creak open. When I turn to look, I spot a figure walking inside. The door closes behind them and I stand there for a moment, wondering if I should follow them or stay put.

I decide against following after whoever, or whatever the figure might have been, and instead head south down A Street, toward Buildings A and B. When I arrive between the two buildings, I stop and stare at the entrance to the dorms for a few seconds. There's no sign of whatever walked in moments before. No movement, no anything. I pull one of the doors open at the entrance to Building B and walk inside. My foot catches something on the ground and I look down to see an old lighter in front of me. After picking it up, I flip it open and ignite it. Right after I do so, one of the doors to Building A flings open and slams against the wall. With the windows on Building B's doors boarded up, I can't see what's going on, but I can hear someone coming. I rush further into the building, trying my best to keep as quiet as possible. After ducking inside a small storage closet, I close the lighter and plunge myself into a pitch black darkness.

Footsteps approach, accompanied by the sound of wheezing and gasping. There's no door on the closet and I'm exposed. My rifle is too big to maneuver in such a cramped space and there's little I can do to prepare myself for a fight. After the noises fade out, I make my way back to the door, only to find it locked. If I try kicking or otherwise forcing it, I'll just attract attention to myself. With the lighter still in my hand, I take a deep breath and start moving down the hallway. The entire time I try my hardest to remain silent. Each time I step on something or catch my feet on debris, I cringe and prepare to douse the lighter. After a few minutes I arrive at another door and try hard to pull it open. No use. It's stuck.

Building B's one of the largest on the island. There's bound to be an exit somewhere. I'll just have to keep looking. Further inside I try a few more doors, but nothing comes of it. After I check the last one, I come to a dead end. Part of the ceiling and walls have collapsed in the hallway, forcing me to turn back the way I came. Since I haven't seen or even heard whatever walked past me near the main entrance, I decide to try going back. Maybe if whatever is walking around in here is far enough away, I can kick the door open and make a run for it. It's near the entrance that I start to hear someone shuffling around. The same sounds of wheezing and gasping for air can be heard coming from the direction of the doors the moment I come near. I'll have to turn back. Staying where I am will mean that I risk getting caught by whatever is ahead of me. I turn and catch my foot on something on the floor, sending me crashing to the ground. The lighter falls out of my hand, extinguishes, and plunges the hallway into darkness. I lie there frozen, listening. The sounds have stopped and I start to panic. Should I try to get up? Should I run? Stay put? My mind is racing and the fact that I can't hear or see anything is making it worse. I feel around for the lighter and when I find it, I place my thumb on the wheel and wait with bated breath. I'm not sure how much time goes by, but it feels like an eternity. Then, right as I'm about to try using the lighter again, something moves behind me. It sounds like something crunching underfoot.

My heart pounding in my chest, I hold my hand over my mouth to muffle the sound of my breathing. A few more minutes tick by and the sound of gasping and wheezing resumes in the background, still by the entrance. I drag myself to my feet with the lighter now lit and glance back down the hallway behind me. The light doesn't reach all the way to the entrance, but there's enough to see some of the outlines of the structure. After taking only a few steps, I catch my foot on a piece of metal and the sound echoes down the hallway. The gasping and wheezing stops for a moment, then is replaced by a shrill, blood-curdling shriek. I take off running at a dead sprint and soon find myself in the chow hall. The strong scent of gasoline catches me off guard and causes me to flinch.

Halfway through the room, something strikes me in the back and sends me crashing onto the floor. The lighter falls from my hand and ignites a trail of spilled gasoline. The flame snakes along the ground and toward a handful of containers left sitting in the corner of the room. I stand up and race behind a pillar with my hands clamped over my ears. The fuel canisters explode and send flaming pieces of debris in every direction. When I look back at the door I passed through, I see Mattie floating in the doorway. Her head is down and her gaze focused on the floor in front of her. Cables cling to her body and one extends up toward the ceiling from her neck. She looks up at me and catches my eye, sending an intense sensation of terror through me. I turn and race toward the other set of doors. Before I can reach them, a series of cables slither past me and slam them closed. The cables bind the door handles together and I turn to see the second pair slam and do the same.

Fire spreads to trash left along the walls and on the floor. Old plastic bottles, food wrappers, anything it can reach. Thick, toxic black smoke is billowing up toward the ceiling and spreading out in all directions. Mattie is nowhere to be found. I take the rifle from off my shoulder and try to stay as near to the flames as possible without choking on the smoke. One of Mattie's cables snares my ankle and pulls me to the ground. I roll and fire once at her, missing and taking out a chunk of the wall in the process. The cable tightens around my ankle and pulls me away from the fire and into the darkened parts of the chow hall. From there I'm lifted up and shaken before being cast aside. I tumble across the floor like a rag doll, losing hold of my weapon as I go.

Another cable snares the barrel of the rifle and tries to pull it away. I take hold of the stock and yank it backward. I can see Mattie's outline in front of me in the flickering light of the flames. With a great deal of effort, I manage to keep hold of the rifle and fire it again. This time the round strikes her shoulder, splattering the ground with blood. She vanishes and the cable releases. I race back toward the fire and face away from the bright orange flames. Another cable snakes toward me along the ground and I pin it down with my foot. Another strikes me across the back and I stumble and turn to see Mattie floating nearby. This time I fire three shots, two of which hit her in the chest and the third piercing her stomach. She drops to the ground for a moment and vanishes as she backs through the now bloodstained wall.

My ears are ringing from the sound of the rifle and the smoke is continuing to spread, making it harder to detect her by the minute. Another cable sneaks up behind me and wraps itself around my neck. It pulls me backward and onto the floor. The rifle falls from my hands as I attempt to pull the cable off. It takes all my strength, but I can just hold it far enough from my throat to keep from suffocating. Mattie appears in front of me, glaring at me with her two purple eyes. I hold onto the cable with one hand and reach for the rifle with the other. One of her cables snares my weapon before I can reach it and drags it off into the darkness. She gives me a malicious grin as I'm hoisted up into the air in front of her. Still fighting with the cable and losing strength, I kick her in the jaw as hard as I can, sending her stumbling and causing the cable to loosen and let go.

Before she has a chance to recover, I dart in the direction of the rifle and begin feeling around in the darkness. There's no way she'll let me escape like that again. I glance back at Mattie to see that she's vanished again. It's only a matter of time before she comes back. I need to find my weapon before she has a chance to finish me off. I run back toward the flames, coughing as I inhale some of the smoke. I snatch up a piece of burning debris and carry it to where I last saw the rifle. There it singes my fingers and I'm forced to drop it. It provides just enough light for me to see the end of the rifle along a nearby wall. Without hesitation, I race to retrieve it and dart back toward the flames, still coughing and sputtering from the increasing smoke.

My eyes are burning and watering, I'm forced to stoop down a little to see. A cable hits me across the face, slicing open my cheek. Another slashes my leg and I struggle to stay focused long enough to find Mattie. The longer this goes on, the more hopeless it starts to seem. Something moves nearby and I turn and fire the rifle twice more. Both rounds miss and Mattie vanishes yet again. Watching every corner, every visible area, I start firing at any movement I see. Five more rounds are spent that way and only one finds its mark, striking Mattie in the throat.

"Gotcha!" I snarl, lining up another shot. Blood and bone cover the floor behind her and she falls to her knees, clutching her neck as blood pours from the wound. I fire the last few rounds at her, hitting her in the chest, shoulder, face, and forehead. Some of her teeth tumble across the ground and she falls into a heap on the floor. Now empty, I toss the rifle aside and approach her with caution as blood pools around her.

Without warning, a cable wraps around my waist, picks me up and hurls me across the room. I tumble across the floor and feel my back collide with a wall. My vision goes out of focus, my entire body aches. My arms, legs, and face are scuffed, and my head is throbbing. Mattie drags herself to her feet, struggling to do so and appearing to be on her last legs. When at last she's able to stand, she sways and struggles to keep her balance. Her eyes glow in the darkness, locking with mine as she starts toward me. My vision comes back into focus and I grit my teeth as I force myself to stand. In front of me is a piece of rebar with two jagged edges. I snatch it up and start toward Mattie. One of her cables snares my free hand and I slash at the cable with the jagged end of my weapon.

The cable comes loose and I race toward Mattie as fast as I can. I'm stopped several feet away from her, halted by a pair of cables that have wrapped themselves around my waist. Another springs up and takes hold of the rebar. I struggle to maintain my hold as the cable pulls harder and harder, straight away from me and toward Mattie. Realizing the opportunity in front of me, I put all my strength into pulling on the rebar and then let go of it. It flies back at her and impales her through the chest. She stumbles backward, looks down at the wound, then back at me in a mixture of fury and disbelief. The glow in her eyes fades and she falls to the ground in a heap. The flames and smoke freeze as if time has been paused, and slowly the world begins to dissolve around me.

I sit up in alarm, terrified and glancing around the room. It takes me a moment to realize that I'm back in the bunker. I get to my feet and begin pacing around the room, scared to death and trying to calm down. It's then that I notice how much my body aches. Pain in my wrist catches my attention and I examine it to see a bruise in the shape of a cable around it. I check my waist and ankles to find the same thing. Though I can't see my neck, it feels as tender as the other areas. Looking back at my wrist, I find that the bruise is rapidly diminishing, as is the pain in the rest of my body. I look around the room to see that Mika is still lying in the center. I make my way back to my corner and sit with my back against the wall.

The entire time I sit there, my mind struggles to make sense of what just happened. The bruises and other injuries, the dream, and Mattie's appearance in it. Will she come back? Or is she gone for good? If she attacked me like that, did she also do it to Naomi and Ariana? Are they okay? What I don't understand more than anything else is how I can get hurt in a dream. Hurt in a way that follows me back to reality. Even if it only lasts a short time after waking up. There's no way I did that to myself...not the marks from the cables at the very least. What could I have possibly used that was available to me in here? I want more than anything to just forget that any of it happened. Pretend I never had the dream and hit reset; go back to the way things were before I started questioning reality.

For some time I sit staring down at the floor. After a while I turn my attention toward the door. For a moment I feel like kicking it. I can't really explain why. I just do. The feeling is there and gone as quick as it arrived. How long is it going to be before someone opens it? Last time it was a week, but after what I did to Halsey, she might leave me down here for longer. I turn my attention back toward Mika to see that she's moved again. She's now sitting on the opposite side of the room, staring at me.

"I see you," she drawls in a mocking voice. I stand up and keep my back against the wall, never taking my eyes off of her.

"Just...stay away from me...all right?" I say, bracing myself for a fight.

"I won't make any promises," she replies.

"Is that a threat?" I ask, trying to keep my cool.

"Threats are usually made toward other people," she says with a chuckle.

"I'm that other person."

"But I thought you said I wasn't real?" Mika taunts, tilting her head to the side. "If I'm not real, how can I threaten you?"

"Real or not, I don't want any trouble from you," I say. "I don't have the energy to deal with you right now."

"Oh, that's hurtful," Mika snickers, cocking her head. "Am I too much of a burden? Do you want me to go away?"

"What do you think?" I retort.

"Wow, maybe I misjudged you," she mutters, glaring at me. "Is this how you treat other people? Tell them to shut up, to go away, to leave you alone?"

"Are you finished yet?" I demand. She gets to her feet, keeping her eyes on me the entire time.

"No...not yet," she says. "But you are if you plan to ignore what I told you before. About believing what you want to believe."

"I don't what to hear this again," I grumble, looking away.

"That's exactly my point!" she shouts, taking a few steps toward me. "I spelled it out for you and you're still not listening to me! Maybe there's no solid evidence of what Ariana did to me, but-"

"She didn't do anything to you!" I shout. "Will you stop being so paranoid?" She lets out an angry snarl and pulls on her hair before brandishing her index finger at me.

"It's not being paranoid, it's being observant!" she argues. "It's being careful! You wanna die here? That's how you die here! You assume that no one else here has their own agenda and you follow them along like a good little lamb begging for slaughter!"

"I'm not going to die," I declare, gazing down at the floor in front of me. "Not here."

"Sure thing, Sarita, keep telling yourself that," Mika snorts, letting her arm fall to her side. "I told myself the same thing. I didn't listen when Naomi pointed out that any one of us could die. I thought I was an exception, that it wouldn't happen to me, that I would get off this island alive. You should know that death can reach out and touch you from anywhere it wants, any time it wants. If you only ever pay attention to what's in front of you, you'll never see it coming when someone stabs you in the back." I look away for a moment and when I look back, she's back in the middle of the room, motionless and staring at nothing. I fall to my knees and slump over onto my side. I'm exhausted and my head is spinning. When does this ever stop? It's faint, but I can hear the sound of someone approaching the door outside. Moments later the door opens and I expect Halsey to say something about how I've gotten loose. Instead it's Rashida's voice I hear from behind me.

"Hey, you alive, kid?" she asks, walking toward me. I sit up and turn to face her. She stops a few feet away with a look of concern on her face. Her cheek is bruised and a handful of stitches are visible along the corner of her mouth.

"Yeah...I'm alive..." I answer. She looks at me, the body, then back at me.

"Come on...get up," she says. "You're going back on cleaning crew today. How'd you get loose?"

"Doesn't matter," I murmur. She shakes her head and motions for me to turn around.

"Hands behind your back," she orders. I do as she asks and she latches her cuffs around my wrists. She leads me outside and into the hallway.

"What about the body?" I ask.

"I already called for someone to come get her," Rashida explains. "Don't worry about it." We reach the top of the steps and walk out into the fresh air. The sky is gray and cloudy, but the daylight is still something I'm glad to see. I glance over my shoulder and try to see if I can spot anyone else coming out of the bunker.

"Eyes forward," Rashida orders.

"Screw you..."

"I don't need attitude from you today," she grumbles.

"Yeah, cuz I'm sure your day's been so terrible," I snort.

"That's enough, Teymouri," she growls.

"It's Sarita, jackass..."

"Whatever, kid," she sighs. "Just keep your eyes forward and cut the sass. I'm not in the mood right now."

"I'm sorry, did you also spend the night with a corpse?" I sneer.

"This is exactly why I was against the idea," she grumbles. I'm led past the water towers and toward the street. There we wait for the van to arrive. From the curb I can see the graveyard. A sobering reminder of what's in store for me if I slip up somewhere along the way. What about the others? What am I going to do without Naomi around? What's Leah going to do? Is it just us for the time being?

"What about the others?" I ask.

"That's none of your concern," Rashida says as the van appears at the end of the street. We stand waiting in silence until it arrives. Once it does, she herds me into the back of it. She gets in the back with me and slaps her palm against the back of the cab to signal that we're ready. She sits down opposite me and places her hands on her knees. The van begins moving and the two of us ride together in silence. Much of the time my eyes are focused on the floor between us. When the van comes to a halt, someone steps out and the gates are opened soon afterward. After the passenger returns to their seat, the van continues down the street. Minutes pass and the van stops again. Both of us glance at the doors. The passenger in the front comes back around to unlock them. Rashida and I step out and she escorts me into Building B. Rashida leads me toward her office, just down the hall from Halsey's, and stops when approached by two other guards.

"What do you need?" Rashida demands, giving them both a withering scowl.

"We needed to speak with you about the Tower B investigation," one of them says.

"Why on earth would you need to speak with me about that?" she demands. "I'm not apart of that investigation. Fulmer is the lead, why aren't you there with him?"

"He's back at the tower waiting on us," the second guard explains. "We were actually sent to speak with Halsey."

"Then why aren't you?" Rashida asks. The two guards glance at one another, then back at Rashida who continues to scowl at them.

"It didn't seem like a good idea," the female guard admits, "Something happened..."

"And by that you mean you screwed something up, right?" Rashida deduces. The male guard nods and the female one clears her throat.

"Well, it's a little more complicated than that, but-" she says.

"I don't have time for excuses, now what happened?" Rashida interrupts.

"The gates, Halsey sent a team to go unlock them," the male guard explains. "We were with Fulmer, waiting for the others to circle back around and have a look at the fuse box. The lever on the Tower B side isn't functioning, so we can't get the gates open."

"Those gates are over five-hundred feet from the tower entrance," Rashida replies. "Why do you need them open?"

"There were traces of fuel all over, but no sign of any fuel canisters," the male guard explains. "We need the gates open so we can conduct a proper search of the area. We can't afford to send people all the way through the tunnels and back multiple times just for that. It's not feasible. Hell, the last team we sent in a few hours ago just came back and half of them are banged up like something attacked them." No fuel canisters? I'm sure saw some before the fire was set. After that I was in too much of a panic to notice.

"Something?" Rashida snorts. "What is this? Another ridiculous ghost story? No wonder you don't want to speak with Halsey."

"There's a reason that area was shut down," the female guard insists. "We all know the stories. It wasn't just inmates making things up, there were guards reporting things too, and that hasn't changed in all the time any of us have been here."

"Ghost stories aside, what are you expecting me to do about it?" Rashida demands. "Here's an idea. How about instead of coming to me and expecting your problems to disappear, you let me do my job, and you go to Halsey and do yours? I'm not your fucking babysitter, now get to it!" The other two guards nod and head back down the hall and toward Halsey's office. The male guard glares at me just before turning to follow his companion. Rashida opens the door to her office and leads me inside. I sit down in a chair in front of the desk and she closes the door behind her. She plops down behind the desk before turning to get something off the shelf behind her. She takes a thin stack of papers and plops them down in front of her, then picks up a pen beside her keyboard.

"Your last name's T-E-Y-M-O-U-R-I, right?" she asks. I nod and she looks back down at the papers in front of her, the scratching of her pen rivaling the ticking of the clock on the wall. A moment after that she asks the same about my first name, only this time asking me to spell it.

"S-A-R-I-T-A," I recite.

"Thank you," she murmurs.

"What's this for?" I ask.

"Since I took you out early I have to document it," she explains.

"Why did you?" I ask.

"Because I didn't agree with what was going on, that's all," she declares, looking up as she speaks. "Don't get any funny ideas. I'm still here to do my job." She flips to the next page and checks some things off before writing a few more things down.

"And it had nothing to do with Halsey decking you last night?" I say, giving her an incredulous look.

"What do you think, kid?" she snorts, looking up at me.

"I think I'm on the right track," I answer. She remains silent for several seconds before responding.

"Well you're right, detective," she responds. She flips to the next page and continues her work.

"What happened with Eston?" I ask. She stops and continues staring at the papers, not moving an inch. She takes a deep breath and looks up at me.

"Some things are better left in the past...where they belong..." she says. "Some of us have things we want to forget." She looks back down at the papers and continues working.

"Most people do."

"I didn't take you out of there to chat with me, Teymouri!" she growls.

"Then why did you?" I demand.

"Enough!" Rashida snaps, standing up with her hands planted on the desk. "I didn't agree with Halsey and that's all there is to it! If you keep this up I'll drag your happy ass right back down there and let you rot in there for the week you were supposed to!"

"No you won't," I declare. She looks taken aback, her eyes open wide in surprise for a split second.

"Don't test me, Teymouri," she warns, sitting back down in her chair.

"Something's going on and I want to know what it is," I say. She places her elbows on the desk and buries her face in her hands. She lets out a frustrated groan then lets her hands drop onto her knees, her head tilted back and eyes fixated on the ceiling. After a moment she picks her pen up again and taps it on the papers in front of her.

"It's a long story," she explains. "All of it. Me and Halsey, Eston...and right now I'm not sure I'm up for telling it. Okay? So can you please just do me a favor and quit asking questions?" She picks up the forms in front of her and begins straightening them. The door opens and the male guard from earlier steps into the room. Rashida lets out a frustrated groan and slaps the papers down on her desk.

"Goddammit, what do you want, McClain?" Rashida demands.

"I'm sorry to interrupt, but Halsey wants you in her office," McClain answers. McClain? Is he related to the one who died in the tower?

"Why on earth would she need to see me?" Rashida demands.

"All I know is she wants to see you," McClain replies, looking at me, then Rashida.

"Just what I want to deal with," Rashida mutters, getting to her feet. "More of that screeching harpy." She pushes her chair back and makes her way toward the doorway. "Stand outside the door and make sure she doesn't run off. You think you two can handle that?"

"Yes ma'am," McClain answers as Rashida starts down the hallway. McClain sneers at me and closes the door behind him. For about a minute there's silence. McClain coughs outside the door and I turn my head. Before long I can hear the other guard speaking with McClain, but I can't make out what's being said. The door cracks open and I look back at it. It shuts again and I start to feel a little uneasy. What are they doing out there? Seconds later the door opens all the way.

"Get up. You're coming with us," McClain orders.

"What? Why?"

"Just do it!" he growls.

"I'm not going anywhere," I declare. He grabs me by the arm and yanks me up out of the chair. After we exit the room, the female guard closes the door to the office and grabs my opposite arm.

"The hell are you doing?" I snarl.

"Stow it!" the female guard growls. I'm led down the hallway and around a corner. Moments later I'm shoved into an empty restroom and

McClain throws me into a wall. He grips his baton and grabs me by the front of my jacket.

"It was you, wasn't it?" he snarls. "That traitor is covering for you, isn't she?"

"What are you even talking about?"

"The surveillance footage! It's gone!" he shouts. "Sayed's protecting you! You had a hand in this, didn't you? The fire, you set it! You and Beckham!"

"I didn't set any fire!" I insist.

"Don't lie to me!" he snarls, slamming me into the wall again. "Do you have any idea who died? Whose bodies they removed?"

"I don't know anything about it!"

"My brother was one of them," he growls. "Charred beyond recognition, like someone doused him in gasoline!"

"Where would I even get gasoline?" I snarl.

"Don't play dumb with me, I've seen inmates siphon it out of the vehicles. I know how crafty you little shits can be."

"I had nothing to do with the fire!" I insist. He throws me to the ground and kicks me twice before pacing around the room, seething and gripping his baton with both hands.

"You remember the kind of things that would go on between them, Tess?" he asks the other guard. "My brother and Sayed?"

"You mean how they were at each other's throats twenty-four seven?" Tess responds. "I'm sure everyone who saw it remembers." On the yard over a month ago. That was this guy's brother, Matt McClain, who shot at us. Rashida was furious with him and after it happened there was mention of some kind of feud between them. Rashida had said something about how it was already out in the open.

"Makes perfect sense, doesn't it?" McClain seethes. "Inmate happens to kill the one guy she's held a grudge against for the past five years and now she's thanking this brat for it! Taking her out of the bunker and only God knows what else. Well guess what, missy?" he continues, looking down at me. "You're not getting away with it!" He raises his foot to stomp on my head and I clench my teeth, bracing for the impact. It never comes. The door swings open and Tess stumbles away from it. The door strikes the wall and Rashida stands glaring at McClain with one hand pinning the door open.

"Did I interrupt something?" Rashida hisses. McClain grips his baton and clenches his teeth.

"No. Nothing..." he answers.

"Get her off the floor," Rashida orders. "Now!"

"And if I refuse?" McClain snorts.

"Then you'll be dealing with me and Halsey together," Rashida answers.

"Fine! Bring her on down!" McClain taunts. "We know what you're up to! Why you're giving this degenerate special treatment! Let Halsey come down here and we can have a nice little chat all about that."

"Get...Teymouri...off...the floor," Rashida hisses, placing her free hand on her pistol. McClain eyes it before stooping down to help me. He pulls me to my feet and gives me a rough shove toward Rashida. She grabs me by the arm and pulls me over to the wall beside her. From there I watch the rest of the scene unfold.

"There, she's up," McClain growls.

"I appreciate that, McClain," Rashida sneers. "Now, care to explain what it is you were just gassing on about? Special treatment and the like?"

"Everyone remembers what you said to Matt," Tess cuts in. "Everyone except you, it seems."

"Matt McClain?" Rashida asks. "No...no I didn't forget. Not what I said to him, not what he did the night I said it."

"What did you say to him again? Something about plenty of water to lose a body in around here?" McClain asks.

"I was angry, Rick, what does it matter?" Rashida argues. "Are you really gonna get hung up on something I said five years ago? I had nothing to do with the fire and as soon as I heard this morning that your brother was dead, I had a feeling you were going to start spreading rumors about my alleged involvement. Your brother was a crook and with any luck he's roasting in Hell right about now."

"Don't you dare talk about him like that," McClain growls, taking a step forward.

"You might not like it, Rick, but your brother was a murderer!" Rashida snarls. "I told that prick to hold his fire and he disobeyed me!"

"His radio cut out! Eston was going for a weapon! What did you expect him to do?" McClain half-shouts.

"I expected him to follow orders!" Rashida snarls, brandishing her finger in McClain's face. "But no! He was so bad at his job that he couldn't even do that! That night was far from the first time he disobeyed me and it certainly wasn't the last. He was an obnoxious clown, just like you! If I'd have been in charge of the hiring process on this island I would have told him to turn right the fuck around and never come back. It's a damn shame I didn't have that authority too because if I did, then maybe that girl would still be alive! I don't like liars, Rick, so I'll tell you the truth right here and now. I had nothing to do with your brother's death, but it is one hell of a relief to know that I don't have to deal with him anymore!"

"And there's your motive, right there," McClain argues. Rashida steps closer and pushes him up against the wall.

"You listen to me, asshole," Rashida hisses. "I went to war. I cut a guy in half with a fifty cal, I got blown up and shot, I lost friends, and I damn near lost my mind! And let me tell you something, Rick, coming home doesn't make it any better!" She slams him into the wall and shakes him violently. "Hear a car backfire and you're back in the war, go to sleep at night and you're back in the fucking war!" she rages, hurling him to the ground. "Does anyone care, Rick? Hell no!" She stomps on his legs. "They tell you what a hero you are so they can feel better about letting you rot in the gutter, and that's as far as it goes!" She stomps on him twice more and stares down at him. "Any problems your brother ever caused me were nothing compared to what I've dealt with, and I would never have killed him over rampant disobedience... but what he did to Eston was unforgivable and anyone with a brain stem could see that. I didn't kill your brother, but I will kill you if I ever catch you beating the piss out of any inmate ever again!" Rashida starts to walk away and Tess clenches her fists and follows her.

"Must be nice being the boss's pet!" Tess snarls. "Do whatever you want and get away with it!" Rashida spins to face her.

"I don't know if you've noticed, Tess, but I have some fresh stitches and a nice new bruise," Rashida snarls, walking toward her. Tess matches her pace and backs away until they both stop in the center of the room. "How do you think I got them, huh? Take a wild guess!"

"Sounds to me like there's even more reason to drag Halsey down here; tell her all about what you just did!" Tess growls, gesturing at the door as she speaks.

"You think that's smart, Tess? Huh? Do you?" Rashida taunts, giving Tess a quick and rough shove. Tess stumbles, but retains her balance. "I'm sure Halsey would love to know about how you've been mistreating her inmates! Need I remind you that that crazy ass woman has a method to her madness! Punishment is one thing, but maltreatment is another! So fine! You go on and tell her what I did! Hell, I dare you to try it! See what happens, Tess!" Rashida turns and storms out of the restroom, gesturing for me to follow as she does so.

"You all right, Teymouri?" she asks once we're out of earshot.

"Yeah...I guess."

"That doesn't sound reassuring," she says. "Come on. Let's get you down to the infirmary."

"What was that all about?" I ask. "Back there. Eston, that guy's brother..."

"The past catching up with me, that's what," she mutters. "Nothing you need to worry about." I clench my teeth and trot in front of her, stopping in place and forcing her to do the same.

"Nothing I need to worry about?" I rage. "Are you kidding me? If you hadn't walked in when you did I might have had a busted neck! Whatever you did it's affecting me now and I think I have a right to know about it."

"You wanna go back in the bunker? Cuz I'm three seconds from taking you back," she growls.

"Yeah, that'll solve the problem!" I snarl. "No cameras or anything down there and all it'll take is one of those lunatics we just left in the restroom coming down to pay me a private visit."

"Not my problem."

"You made this your problem by taking me out of the bunker, and then you made it my problem by threatening those guards! You're not taking me back to the bunker. You're one of the few people on this island who seems to have a conscience and I doubt it'll let you put me back down there."

"You're wearing on my last nerve, Teymouri," Rashida warns.

"Just tell me what's going on and why it made two guards wanna bash my brains out!" I demand. "You've been here a lot longer than me and you know what kind of threat I'm facing, and again, that threat is your fault! I'm only asking for information. I don't think that's unreasonable." Rashida shakes her head and looks away for a moment. She takes about a minute to consider what I've said before looking at me again.

"I'll make a deal with you," she offers. "You keep your mouth shut until you're looked over at the infirmary and I'll tell you what you want to know. Sound good?"

"Seems fair."

"Good," Rashida says, stepping around me. "Come on. I need to go speak with Halsey once I drop you off, so stay there until I come back for you. I have a feeling she might want to see you too."

* * *

Rashida and I make our way to the infirmary in silence. The entire way there my mind is racing. I know for certain that I need to avoid those two guards who attacked me, but who knows how many others are going to come after me now that they'll likely hear that I'm linked to Rashida in the death of that McClain guy's brother. The medical staff look me over and make sure I'm not bleeding internally. I have a nasty bruise where I was kicked, but not much else. From there I wait for about twenty minutes before Rashida returns to the infirmary. When she does, she seems rattled and angry.

"Come on, Teymouri, I need you for something," she says the moment she finds me. She gestures for me to come out into the hall and I do so. Once out of earshot of the medical staff, we continue speaking.

"What's going on?" I ask. "Halsey want to see me or something?"

"No, but she has a job for the two of us," Rashida answers.

"What sort of job?"

"You happen to remember what those other guards were discussing with me by my office?" she asks.

"Yeah, they mentioned something about the gates being stuck closed." She nods.

"And we get to go open them," she says. For a moment I fall silent. Going back into Sector S is the last thing I want to do. Part of me even feels that going back to the bunker would be a safer option.

"And why does she want us to go?" I ask.

"She's not happy about me taking you out of the bunker and she said

145

something along the lines of "if she's out, she's gonna be put to work" and then said something about how she's not planning on letting you off easy. As if spending the night with a corpse wasn't enough."

"So it's about getting back at me for the fire."

"That and kicking her down the stairs, I'm sure," Rashida adds. "But that part aside, I need someone about your size to reach the fuse box."

"Why can't you?" I ask.

"As you may have already noticed the last time you were in Sector S, the place has fallen into disrepair in the years it's been abandoned. The usual access to the fuse box is obstructed and the doors won't open. Some piping and parts of the ceiling broke off and blocked the doors."

"If it's a problem, then why not fix it?"

"Because the attempts we've made over the years to renovate the place have always come up short," Rashida explains as we exit the building and start down the street. "Started back around 2010 when we began seeing a series of accidents and attacks, some of which were fatal. There were escape attempts, like whatever those girls you searched for were up to, along with some of the guards taking advantage of the lack of cameras in a myriad of ways."

"I don't want to know..."

"You really don't," Rashida continues. "Sometime around December that same year, one of the inmates was electrocuted while she was working down there. And that's where things started to take an unusual turn."

"What do you mean?" I inquire.

"It's like Tess was saying earlier outside my office," Rashida says. "I know I told her I don't believe her, that the whole ghost story thing is nonsense, but...well...sometimes things happen that I have a hard time explaining."

"Is that why the footage from Tower B was "lost" last night?"

"I suppose anything's possible at this point, but I'm not ready to say it was something...well...otherworldly," Rashida answers. "It just wasn't there. The cameras went offline before the fire.

I wish I had an explanation, but I don't. It could've been a simple malfunction for all I know, but the timing just seems off. Missing footage aside, I've seen some odd things in Sector S ever since that girl died. Things get launched at the walls, doors slam when no one is there, and sometimes you...it's like I hear voices, but not like in my head or anything. Just like...in some of the rooms, further down the tunnel. It's like they're conversations that happened years ago, echoing in the tunnels. If that makes any sense."

"I think I know what you mean."

"Voices, maybe someone's there that I don't see, doors slamming, maybe it's the same thing," she continues. "But what I can't explain is seeing shadows cast against walls with no one to create them. And you only see them for a split second. It's like whatever is down there, it knows you're questioning your sanity. Like it wants you to do it. I know that sounds deranged at best, but that's the best way I can describe it."

Chapter 15

Return Trip

Rashida and I stop near the end of the street and she radios for a van to meet us. Meanwhile I'm still thinking about everything that led up to this point, starting with the fire in Tower B. If Vesna and Mattie are capable of that much, then what will they do while we're in Sector S? I wish there was something I could say, something I could do to get out of going back down there. It was bad enough the first time. Rashida notices I've been silent and gives me a nudge.

"You doing all right?" she asks. I nod.

"Yeah...just fine," I murmur. "Not looking forward to going back is all."

"I'm not either," she admits. "Neither of us have much choice, though."

"Yep." There's a pause in the conversation that lasts close to a minute. Now that Tower B has burned and two guards have been added to the body count, I have to wonder how much more this plan could spiral out of control. That's assuming the plan is still active.

"All right..." Rashida says. "How about we change the subject? You wanted to hear about Eston, now seems like as good a time as any." I take a deep breath and exhale.

"What happened?" I ask, locking eyes with her. "And how were you involved?" She clears her throat and takes a moment to think before she speaks.

"Well, you heard some of it already," she begins. "That McClain brother, the living one, Rick. His younger brother was named Matt.

I know you heard some of that too, but I suppose repeating it for the sake of clarity doesn't hurt. There's a lot of little pieces to this story, so pay attention. Matt was one of the worst guards this island has ever seen. Or at least since Halsey and I took over. Halsey likes to think she hires people who'll be tough on the inmates, but what she doesn't see is that half of them go beyond that. I'd be lying if I said I don't still have nightmares about that night. Almost every day I think about what I could have done to prevent Eston's death. It was so brazen and needless. I failed her. I failed most of the inmates who've passed through here, maybe even all of them. The system fails them. I should've run up to the watchtower and snatched the rifle out of Matt's hand that night, he had no business being up there. What he got was too good for him, but that's beside the point. Eston was one of the inmates who Matt regularly targeted. He threatened her, he tried to control her, and Eston didn't like it. So of course she got fed up with him and he ended up regretting it."

"How so?"

"One day she got into an argument with him and he tried to cuff her," Rashida explains. "She took off with his baton and hid. When he found her she cracked him across the face with it and knocked out two of his teeth, busted his nose, just mangled his face with it. He was in the hospital for a while and he returned a week before Eston tried to escape. Halsey's become increasingly careless ever since she started running this place, but back when Eston was still alive, and after Matt came back from the hospital, she at least had the common sense to put him on the graveyard shift in one of the watchtowers, to give him some time to cool down. The one problem I had with that was that the watchtower guards are the only ones allowed to have live rounds in their weapons at any given time. I didn't like the idea of him toting live ammo around, but there wasn't much I could say about it."

"So it took Eston beating Matt's face in to get Halsey to separate them?" I ask.

"Halsey's excuse was that she had her hands full running the place. That she didn't have time to notice what was going on between them," Rashida explains. "I never bought it. She knew about the problems Eston was having with Matt. She has that 'tough on crime' mentality and it's been perverted into the twisted belief that overlooking abuse will somehow teach the inmates a lesson. Fine, be tough on crime, but maybe try going after dirtbags like Matt McClain too. She only cared when Matt shot Eston in the back and that was only because of the P.R. nightmare it became. Not that a fifteen-year-old girl got shot by an out of control guard who she never bothered to fire or turn over to the authorities. No, she defended him and she did it because she knew what a coward he was. If he'd been arrested, and he narrowly escaped that, she knew as well as I did that he'd plead guilty and start spilling his guts about this place to try and lessen his sentence. I know Matt shot her because of what she did and he found a flimsy excuse to do it. I could've cared less if they were commandeering a ferry. I mean, yeah, granted we have an obligation to do something about that, but shooting a fleeing and unarmed inmate isn't the way I was taught to go about it."

"I remember hearing about Eston's death when it hit the media," I recall. "There was a dispute over whether or not she was running away or going for a weapon. I take it that's what you and Rick were talking about earlier?" Rashida nods.

"She was going for the railing, it was obvious to anyone," Rashida declares. "I saw the whole thing and so did dozens of others who didn't dare say anything for weeks afterward."

"Why didn't you say something to the media when all that was happening?" I ask. "Shed some light on the case, lend some credibility to the two inmates who spoke up?"

"Halsey threatened me with the same thing she used last night," Rashida explains. "It's her trump card. She's afraid of what will happen to her if what really goes on here is ever proven, she knows she's in over her head, and since I'm one of the few people with enough credibility to testify against her, she holds my past over my head any time I step out of line. If I'm being honest, I've long contemplated killing her. I just don't know how to do it without getting caught." The van pulls up in front of us a few moments later and the two of us climb into the back. Seconds later the van takes off and we're on our way to Sector S. About a minute after the van pulls away, I've resigned myself to the possibility that we'll both be sitting in silence for the remainder of the ride. Instead Rashida clears her throat and moves us on to another subject.

"What did you guys see down there, anyway?" she inquires. "Back while you were in Sector S." I'm not sure how to answer the question at first. There was quite a bit that we saw and some of it was only heard.

"A mixture of things," I reply. "Why do you want to know?"

"You know who Jeff Martin is?" she asks. I nod.

"Yeah, he was one of the guards who escorted us through the tunnels. Him and Laura or whatever her name was."

"The one that died, yeah," Rashida nods. "First in a while. The reason I asked is because of Jeff."

"What happened? Did Halsey do something?" I don't know why, but as much as I still dislike Jeff for leaving me behind in the tunnels, I feel bad for the way Halsey went off on him for sticking up for us.

"Oh, she did something all right," Rashida snorts. "Laid into him for putting in his two weeks just before I got you out of the bunker. I know Jeff's been considering quitting for a long time. He's been bellyaching about it for years. Still, I don't think I've ever heard of him sticking up for inmates, even if he didn't think they deserved whatever they were in for. Very unusual. On top of that I've heard he's clammed up about Laura's death. There's been threats to turn him over to the police if he doesn't start talking. I don't think Halsey will do that just yet, but the point is that they're trying to get him to crack."

"Why make those kinds of threats?"

"Because Laura was strangled with some kind of ligature," Rashida explains. "They think he knows who was responsible and that he's covering for you, Naomi, and the other girls."

"We had nothing to do with it," I say, shaking my head. "I wasn't anywhere near Laura when that happened. Neither was Naomi. I didn't even know Laura was dead until we got to Tower B. Me and Naomi got separated because Jeff and Laura ditched us while we were looking for a map so we could find the exit."

"Ditched you? Wait, if you needed a map to find the exit, then why leave you behind?" I shrug and let my arms fall back to my sides.

"He was trying to use it as incentive to hurry up," I explain. "That's all I know. It sounded like Laura had a good idea of where to go already, but they wanted the map just to be sure." She crosses her arms and leans back against the wall.

"So you and Naomi got separated and then what?"

"I found Ariana, then I ran into Naomi, and then something we couldn't see attacked us." Her expression morphs into a confused gaze.

"Something you couldn't see?"

"It chased us through the tunnels, rattled them too. We got away and then we ran into...Mattie."

"Who's Mattie?"

"Ariana and Naomi mentioned that there was an inmate who got lost in Sector S sometime last year," I explain. "Someone named Mattie. They said the guards found her after she'd been missing for a while."

"And you saw this girl in Sector S?" Rashida asks.

"I did," I nod. "She had cables wrapped around her. If Laura was strangled, my guess is that Mattie was responsible. Which sounds crazy, I know..." Rashida remains silent as the van continues onward. When the van comes to a stop at its destination, one of the guards at the front comes back to unlock the doors. Rashida escorts me to the dock entrance of Sector S after the van departs moments later. Standing before the large steel doors, I feel a sense of dread as Rashida pries one of them open. She takes her flashlight from her belt and shines it around inside. Part of me wonders if Mattie is gone for good after that dream. Another part of me doesn't want to find out. Rashida backs away from the door and tosses me her smaller spare flashlight. I catch it, switch it on, and she gestures for me to follow her inside.

"Come on. Let's get this over with..."

* * *

For thirty minutes the two of us walk through the tunnels with few words spoken. Every now and again we stop for a moment to listen, but nothing seems out of the ordinary. Despite this, I'm on edge the entire time. Rashida knows most of the main tunnels, having been down here more than most guards; the result of repeated threats by Halsey to turn her in for the fragging incident. She clenched her fists and took on a sinister tone when she mentioned it. I wasn't sure how to respond and so elected to remain silent. All I know is that Rashida is someone who's bad side I'm sure I would never want to be on. After a few minutes pass and she's had some time to cool down, I decide to change the subject.

"So, is anyone meeting us by the gates?" I ask.

"Yeah, Fulmer and Halsey's favorite sycophant," she responds.

"And who would that be?"

"Callie Fenton," she says. "You might've seen her around a few times. Blonde, braided hair, looks like she hasn't seen the sun in several months. Arrogant, obnoxious. She's a lot like Halsey in some ways, but unlike her, she's reckless. Doesn't always think ahead. She's one of two captains. One rank below me. What makes her a problem is that she's got something I don't have, and that's the respect of most of the guards here. After Eston died, after I threatened Matt McClain, any respect those same guards had for me started to fade. Not just with the people below me, but Halsey as well. Callie saw an opportunity there and she's been gunning for my job ever since. Halsey appears to have just about the same degree of trust in her as she does me. Stupid decision if you ask me. She's playing Halsey for a fool. Callie's involved in shady dealings around the island. Extortion, smuggling, abuse that even Halsey wouldn't allow. The list goes on."

"How is it you know about that stuff, but not Halsey?" I ask.

"Because she doesn't have the same mindset as me," she answers. "I look for the dirt on everyone here. Halsey only acknowledges it if she happens to see it." The two of us continue on through the tunnels, shining our lights around at the doors, piping, and other structures as we pass. Something clangs in the distance and the two of us pause for a moment. Whatever it was, it sounded like a wrench striking a pipe. The story Ariana told me about Vesna and the wrench she wielded in her mania comes to mind.

"You don't suppose they got the gates open without us, do you?" I ask. Rashida shakes her head.

"I doubt it. Wouldn't know if they did anyway. Reception in this area is hard to come by. Especially in the middle of the tunnels." We continue forward and moments later we hear a scraping sound coming from somewhere behind us. I turn and shine my light down the tunnel and Rashida does the same. We wait for about a minute, listening for anything further.

"Let's keep moving," Rashida urges, heading down the tunnel at a quickened pace. "I don't know about you, but I'd rather spend as little time down here as possible." I follow her and after several minutes I start to smell something revolting. An acrid scent, almost like a mixture of sulfur and charred meat. I feel a sense of dread in the pit of my stomach. I've smelled it before. It was back when Tower B was burning. The charred bodies, that must've been what it was. Ariana mentioned she smelled burnt flesh while she was down here. For a moment I consider asking Rashida if she smells it too, but after giving her a few glances as we go, it's clear she doesn't. From further down the tunnel and near the gates, the sound of a man screaming echoes toward us. Rashida pauses and takes a step back. From the beam of her flashlight I can tell that her hand is shaking. Against my better judgment, I walk past her and toward the screaming. Whoever it is, they sound as if they're in agony. I stop and look back to see that Rashida has started following after me.

As I turn with the flashlight, the beam washes over one of the nearby doors and catches something unusual. I didn't get a good look at it, but it appeared to be the top of someone's head ducking out of sight from the window. I stop and keep the light trained on the door as Rashida approaches. She looks at me, then shines her own light at the door and the area around it. The screaming stops and we both turn to face the direction it came from. Seconds after our lights move away from the door, it bangs open and I turn my light in time to catch someone's leg disappearing down a nearby corridor.

"You saw that, right?" Rashida asks, a subtle unease present in her voice. While she appears composed, she seems about as on edge as I am. I nod and she mutters something under her breath. For the next minute or so, I start to feel as though someone is watching me. Twice I look over my shoulder, but never do I see anything. Seconds after I finish looking the second time, I hear a voice in my ear.

"Guess who?" Helena whispers. My heart skips a beat.

"Go away," I mumble, trying to retain my composure.

"Did you say something?" Rashida asks.

"Just thinking out loud," I lie, continuing down the tunnel.

"I suppose that was at least part true," Helena says as she follows behind me. "I'd say you've been doing quite a bit of thinking lately. Sort of like how you're wondering whether or not you can trust this woman." My eyes widen for a moment and I clench my teeth.

"How much further to the fuse box?" I ask Rashida. "Do you know?"

"Another twenty minutes maybe," Rashida shrugs. "I can't say for sure."

"Not fast enough," I say, quickening my pace.

"You sure you're okay, kid?" Rashida asks. "You're starting to freak me out."

"I'm fine," I reply.

"You haven't been fine since you got here," Helena argues. "You know that and now she's starting to pick up on it." I stop in my tracks and feel Helena bump into me. She snickers and I keep walking. Rashida's attention is focused on the opposite side of the tunnel.

Glancing over my shoulder, I find that Helena has vanished.

* * *

Fifteen minutes pass and the gates are now in sight. There haven't been many disturbances since the incident with the door swinging open. Twice we heard something fall over in one of the rooms, but nothing else. Regardless I'm still on guard and so is Rashida. She points to a pair of doors not far from the gates and we start toward them.

"This is where you'd normally go to get back there," she explains as we approach. "See what I mean about a collapse?" She shines her light through the windows on the doors, illuminating the debris lodged behind it.

"So where do we get in from?" I ask. She points to a nearby corridor to my left.

"Down this way," she says, leading me toward it. The two of us walk down the corridor and near the end of it we come to a stop. Instead of going through the doors at the end, Rashida examines a broken window leading into an adjacent hallway. On the other side is a pile of equipment and other objects, shrinking the hole down a considerable amount.

"Here we are," she says, gesturing at the window. "It's just you from this point on." Glancing through the broken window, I shine my light into the hallway and pause for a moment, thinking, or rather worrying about what it is I might find. Taking a step back from the window, I take a deep breath, pocket my flashlight, and climb through. Rashida stands close by, waiting to assist if need be. On the other side I switch the flashlight on and shine it around the hallway. Unlike elsewhere, this part of Sector S has no lingering lights to illuminate any of it.

"Get moving, kid," Rashida urges, glancing down the corridor and looking more anxious than before. "It's straight down to the end, then through a door to your right. Fuse box is in that room. Just pop one of the spare fuses in and hit the lever on the side. That's all there is to it."

"Got it," I nod. "Be back soon." I turn and trot off down the hallway, my thoughts consumed with images of that figure I saw creeping around the tunnels. As I move further down the hallway I find myself stepping over tools and debris. Wiring dangles from the ceiling and walls, putting me further on edge. No telling how much of this has power running to it or will once I'm finished. A familiar odor reaches my nose and I stop in my tracks near the end of the hall. My heart is pounding, my palms beginning to sweat. Before when I smelled burnt flesh, I worried that Vesna might be nearby. Now after what I saw in the tunnels a short time ago, it's clear she might not be the only one down here. With caution, I inch along the wall, creeping closer to the room ahead of me.

After reaching the end of the wall, I take a deep breath and peer out into the room with my light shaking in my hand. Nothing. Just old machines and other equipment. I bump into something sticking off of a shelf and it falls to the floor with a deafening clatter. I jump in alarm and shine the light on the object. A crowbar. I don't know how much it will help, if any, but I reach down and pick it up anyway. Holding it ready, I proceed through the rest of the room, coming closer and closer to the door leading to the fuse box.

"You sure like taking your time, don't you?" Helena says from behind me. I spin to face her and find her with a malicious grin. Blood soaks some of her hair and stains the upper portion of her clothes; her face deathly pale. "What's the matter? Don't you want to get this done quick? No telling what might be lurking down here."

"You follow me everywhere I go, so what's the difference?" I retort, turning away from her. As soon as I do so, she's reappeared right in front of me.

"You're wrong, you know," she taunts.

"Wrong about what?" I demand, taking a step back and gripping the crowbar. She takes a step toward me.

"I can hurt you," she says. "You're thinking I can't."

"Move aside," I growl. She eyes the crowbar and lets out an amused chuckle.

"You should put that down before you hurt yourself," she warns, pointing at it.

"I know what I'm doing."

"Do you, though?" she taunts. She's gone the moment I blink. I shake my head and look down at the floor. Each time she's around I try my best to stay calm, to never show that she's getting to me, but the more she's around the harder it gets. With my heart thudding in my chest, I scan the room with my flashlight to make sure she's gone before moving toward the door. With some hesitation, I push the door open and stand ready with the crowbar. She's not here, but the smell of burnt flesh is still lingering. Stepping inside the room, I use the crowbar to smash the doorknob off the door and pin it open with a small crate full of tools.

Last thing I need is her trapping me in here. Halfway to the fuse box, an ear piercing scream reaches my ears. It rattles me to my core as I muster the courage to turn and face the doorway. The screaming stops just before I do so. The doorway is untouched with no sign of the person who screamed. Seconds pass and I turn and race toward the fuse box, wrenching it open as I approach. Inside are a handful of unused fuses. I drop the crowbar on the floor and pin it under my foot. Moans emanate from somewhere behind me as I work to swap out the fuse. I look over my shoulder, scan the room with the flashlight, and see that burns in the shape of hand prints have appeared all over the walls.

Almost dropping the flashlight at the sight before me, I spin back around to finish my task, swapping the fuse and hitting the lever inside. As soon as I throw the switch, sparks fly from the fuse box and I gasp in surprise. I stumble backward into a shelf behind me. My back slams into it and it begins teetering. Within seconds I'm back on my feet. I slam the fuse box closed and race out of the room as another earsplitting scream erupts somewhere nearby. Outside the door, I dodge the debris scattered across parts of the floor and make my way to the corridor. Behind me I can hear footsteps, the screams getting louder and the smell of seared flesh wafting through the air. When I glance over my shoulder, I don't see anything following me, but it doesn't make me want to slow down. I arrive at the window moments later, panting and out of breath.

"All right, I'm back," I say. "Can you give me a hand? Hurry, there's something back here with me!" No response. I poke my head through the window and glance down the hall. "Rashida? Rashida!" I shout.

Again, no response. That bitch! She left me here, didn't she? A scream echos down the hall behind me and when I look back I spot a figure stumbling toward me, grabbing at the walls and clutching at its face and neck. In the darkness I see that the figure appears as if it's burning from the inside, orange vein-like lines covering its face, neck, and hands. Sparks fly from it as it walks. I scramble through the window, nicking my ear on some of the glass as I go. Crawling through headfirst, I land on my arms and pull my legs through, scratching the end of my jeans on the glass and scrambling to my feet.

Without looking back I race down the corridor and toward the gates. When they come into view I see that they've been opened. I clench my fists and search for any sign of Rashida. Part of me knows I shouldn't be surprised. Rashida may seem like she has her head on straight, but she's still one of Halsey's guards. Something like this was bound to happen. I never heard anything from the fuse box room, but I suppose I didn't have to. My guess right now is that she freaked out and abandoned me after the screaming started. How did she get the gates open? The lever on this side doesn't work. Maybe she radioed the people waiting for us. Speaking of which, where are they? Shouldn't they still be here? I have a hard time believing they all ran off. Someone's got to be here somewhere.

"Hello?" I shout, cupping my hands around my mouth. "Anyone?" I let my hands drop to my sides and continue walking toward the gates. Stepping onto the bridge that spans the piping, I feel a sense of apprehension as I remember what happened to Laura when she walked across it. I keep my eyes on my feet the entire time I'm walking across. When I reach the end, I look back. Something was just shuffling around in the shadows. I heard it. Seconds pass and I brace myself for another ghostly shriek, but it never comes. "Screw this," I murmur, turning and trotting through the gates.

I call for Rashida a few more times, but at this point there doesn't seem to be any reason to continue. It's clear that I'm the only one here. Sort of. It's then that I realize I left my crowbar down by the fuse box. No way am I going back to get it. I'll have to find something else. Something thuds back the way I came, the sound of which echoes throughout the tunnel. I don't care about logic anymore. I'm finding a weapon, regardless of whether or not I can hit a ghost with it. I'll feel better if I at least feel like I can defend myself. I walk into one of the rooms not far from the gates and begin looking around. After a minute or two, I find an old steel pipe lying under a workbench.

"I suppose this will have to do," I mumble, examining it in my hands. It's about three feet in length, heavy enough to do some damage, and light enough to carry. I just hope it proves useful. Right as I start toward the door, I start smelling burnt flesh again. That guard, or what used to be a guard, must be nearby. I switch my flashlight off and pocket it before crouching down along the wall near one of the doors. My heart pounds as I wait with bated breath. Just go away, just leave. The exit isn't much further.

Footsteps pierce the silence. They begin just beyond the gates, near the grated bridge, and continue toward me. The footsteps stop and silence returns once more. Still crouched, I creep closer to the doorway and peer out into the tunnel. There are few lights in this area and it's difficult to see. There's no sign of movement, no noise, nothing. I stand up and lean back against the wall again, trying my best to keep myself together before taking another look out into the tunnel. Still nothing.

Right as I go to take a step through the doorway, someone grabs me around the waist and claps their other hand over my mouth. My scream is muffled as I struggle to get loose. The smell of burnt flesh is so strong now that it's disorienting. I jam the end of the pipe into the ribs of my attacker and dart out into the tunnel when they let go. When I turn back, I can see Vesna's orange irises glowing in the darkness. I race closer to the Tower B entrance and she follows me. I spin and slam the pipe into the side of her head. For a moment I stand shocked as she stumbles and falls to the ground, her pipe wrench clattering on the floor as she goes. Part of me is surprised I was able to hit her.

Vesna wastes no time getting to her feet. She swipes up the wrench and takes several vicious swings at me. I manage to deflect two of the swings and dodge the others. The impact of the wrench rattles the pipe and transfers to my hands, stinging them each time. She swings again and I raise the pipe in the air, bringing it down toward her head. She sidesteps the blow and swings at me again. I duck and feel the wrench skim the top of my head just before cracking her in the ribs. She stumbles and charges at me. I trip her and she tumbles across the floor. She's back up in seconds. I race toward her and swing at her shoulder. My pipe impacts her shoulder at the same moment her wrench slams into my side.

I yelp and she stumbles. I back away, clutching my ribs and gritting my teeth. She regains her footing and grips her wrench with both hands before racing toward me. She makes three attempts to strike me, one of which comes too close for comfort. I trip over my own feet as I backpedal and fall onto my back. She leaps on top of me and raises the wrench over her head. The pipe still clutched in one hand, I raise it up and block the swing. The impact stings my hands and I fumble the pipe. She goes for a second swing and I grab hold of her arm. I manage to slow the swing enough to avoid smashing my skull, but not enough to keep her from striking my nose. Blood drips into my hair and down my cheeks and neck.

I hurl her arm backward and smash the wrench into her face. It stuns her long enough for me to throw her off. I retrieve the pipe and turn back to face her. She forms a ball of fire in her free hand and hurls it straight at me. I'm only just able to dodge it. The flames singe my hair and the fireball collides with a nearby wall, charring it black. Some of the flames stick to the wall and continue to burn. She throws another and I dive out of the way. The flames catch my jacket and I race to put them out as I leap to my feet. While I'm distracted with the flames, she rushes me and takes a vicious swing at me with her wrench. She misses, but it's close enough to feel the wind. I strike her across the face with the pipe and retreat while she's recovering.

She hurls another fireball and I duck to avoid it. When another one comes for me, I use my pipe to bat it away, sending it back at her in a shower of embers. She sidesteps the returned fireball and readies another. Flames cling to the end of my pipe and she hurls another ball of fire at me. I bat it away and charge straight at her through the resulting shower of embers. I swing the pipe at her with all my strength and feel it collide with the side of her head. She spins and falls away from me. She tries to get up and I slam the pipe into her back, knocking her back to the ground.

When she tries again to get up, I smash the pipe over her head. Once, twice, three times. Blood splatters across the concrete and covers the pipe, seeping down between my fingers. After several blows, I back away and stare down at her motionless form. Her body erupts into flames and I step back, watching as she burns to ashes within seconds. Embers within the ash remain for little more than a moment before every trace of flame vanishes altogether. I back away from the pile of ash and turn toward the exit. I wince and grab at my side. Pain shoots down from my ribs and into my thigh. My leg gives out and I fall to one knee. As soon as my knee hits the ground, the smell of burnt flesh, gone for only a moment, returns in full. The faint sound of wheezing echoes behind me. My eyes widen in terror and I stumble to my feet. When I turn, I glimpse the charred phantom of Matt McClain. Uniform singed and smoldering, flesh seared and bone and muscle exposed along his face, neck, and arms. I hold the pipe ready and take a few steps back. He starts toward me, slowly at first, and within seconds he breaks into a full blown sprint. Right as he's about to grab me I close my eyes and slam my weapon into the side of his head. The sound of the pipe clanging against something metallic pierces the air. My eyes snap open and I find myself standing near the fuse box again. The sound I heard was the pipe hitting the side of the shelf near it. The pain in my nose and side are gone and I'm left standing there glancing around the room in confusion. I toss the pipe aside and snatch up my dropped flashlight before moving back to the fuse box. The fuses are still swapped, but the lever hasn't been flipped. Rashida is calling me from the window.

"Teymouri! Teymouri, answer me!" I focus my attention on the fuse box and this time I hit the lever without any problems. Shining the flashlight around the room, I find no sign of McClain or Vesna. I'd better leave before that changes. After exiting the first room I continue down the hallway as Rashida calls to me again. "Teymouri!" she shouts, the sound of which echoes around me. She spots my flashlight and calls again. "Hey! You all right?"

"Yeah, fine," I answer, quickening my pace.

"What happened back there?" she demands. "Could you not hear me or something?"

"Something like that," I answer, looking back down the hall. I trot up to the window and pocket my flashlight. I start crawling back through the hole in the window, taking care to refrain from cutting myself on the glass. Rashida helps pull me through and I set both feet on the floor. For a moment I glance back at the hallway on the other side, making certain that I wasn't followed. Rashida notices me looking and puts her hand on my shoulder.

"You sure you're all right?" she asks. I nod.

"The fuses are swapped, the gates are ready to go, I'm fine," I answer. "I don't know about you, but I don't want to hang around here anymore." She glances through the window and then looks back at me.

"Come on...let's go." I resist the urge to look back through the window and follow her out to the main tunnel, lagging behind as I go. When we reach it I start toward the gates. I've never wanted to escape from somewhere so much in my life. We turn the corner and move toward the grated bridge. Rashida, walking ahead of me the entire time, stops near the bridge and stares at the lever. I slow to a halt and watch her. For a moment I start to wonder if she's going to try and use it.

"You're not thinking of using that, are you?" I ask. She turns to face me and shakes her head. She then looks back at the lever.

"No, of course not," she responds. "I take it you know it's faulty too?"

"Yeah, one of the guards said something about it when I was last down here," I say. "They mentioned the electrocution it caused."

"I assume that's why you asked if we were meeting someone on the other side?" she asks.

"Yeah, I thought that's why you had them stay there."

"That's part of it. That and Fulmer is just adamant about doing his job," Rashida answers. "He caught some guards snooping around in the tower when they shouldn't have been. He stays over there as long as he can because he's paranoid that someone's gonna tamper with evidence. As for Callie, she's just there because she's part of the investigation and wants to poke around when she can. Replaced someone who lost their nerve from the sound of it. The incident with the lever happened long before either of them were here." She starts to walk away from the lever and pauses, first looking down at the floor, then back at the lever.

"What is it?" I ask. She remains silent for a moment, then looks at me.

"Just thinking," she says.

"What about?"

"About how it'd be a shame if someone were to try using it," she answers.

"What are you saying?" I ask.

"How good are you at keeping secrets, kid?" she inquires.

"Better than most," I reply with a shrug. She looks me over and then takes the radio from her belt, clutching it in her hand.

"Good to know," she says. "Sergeant Fulmer, are you still at the gates?" A pause and a voice responds.

"Standing by, ma'am," Fulmer answers.

"You mind trying the lever on your side?" Rashida asks. "We've got a slight problem on our end."

"Understood, wait one moment," Fulmer responds. Around a minute ticks by as the two of us stand in silence. Movement further down the tunnel catches my eye and I tense up. I shine my light around, but I don't see anything else. Behind us the gates groan and begin to open. When they're far enough apart, I can see Fulmer walking toward us, his flashlight beam washing over us and then focusing on our feet as he approaches.

"What sort of problem were you having?" he asks. He's about five-ten with a thick mustache, salt and pepper hair, and an average build with a beige complexion. My first impression is that he seems like an old security guard you might find wandering a museum in the middle of the night. He has a relaxed demeanor that gives off a slight sense of apathy. Our eyes meet for only a brief moment, but it's enough to see that he's got plenty of fire behind them.

"Lever wasn't working, that's all," Rashida lies. "I think there's something loose. Gave me a mild shock when I touched it."

"Noted," he replies, shining his light around the area. "The wiring around here's pretty old. Just as long as the gates stay open I could care less about either of the levers. Come on, let's get you two out of here." Before I take even a few steps across the grated bridge, I get the feeling that we're being watched. When I turn around, my beam catches a hand clutching the wall of the nearby corner. The fingers drag along the wall and the hand disappears. I continue across the bridge at a quickened pace and the three of us make our way up through the tunnel.

"I heard Callie was supposed to be over here with you," Rashida says once we're about halfway to Tower B. "Where's she at?"

"She left to go meet someone outside the tower," Fulmer answers. "She should be back in a few minutes."

"I see," Rashida replies. "Thought maybe she chickened out like half the others so far."

"Not yet," Fulmer replies. "I'll be impressed if she's still here in two days. Hate to admit it, but even I'm starting to get a little uncomfortable down here." We make our way through the doors into Tower B and Fulmer stays behind as we circle around the hall on the edge of the tower's interior. Most of it's cordoned off with yellow tape. The windows around the hall and remains of the control room are melted and the floors and walls charred.

"You wanna tell me what you were getting at back there?" I ask as we near the exit.

"One second, kid," she answers. "Callie's still lurking around here somewhere." The moment we exit the building, I spot a blonde woman with her hair in a single braid down her back, walking toward us. This must be Callie.

"Hey, you made it," Callie says with a grin and a hint of sarcasm. "Good to know there's fewer cowards around here than I thought."

"Investigation's far from over," Rashida counters. "Sector S gets to the best of people. Don't make the mistake of thinking you're immune."

"If you say so," Callie chuckles, stopping a few feet away.

"What brought you out here?" Rashida asks. "I thought for a moment you'd fled the coop." Callie's expression shifts and she appears annoyed with the question.

"Nothing you need to worry about, Rashida. I just needed to speak with someone, that's all," she says walking past us.

"I don't recall being on a first name basis with you," Rashida says, turning to face her.

"After thirteen years? Really?" Callie chuckles, shrugging as she walks backward toward the entrance. "Wow Rashida, I thought we were friends."

"Colleagues, Fenton," Rashida answers.

"Eh, you're too serious," Callie says with a dismissive wave as she turns away and continues toward the doors. "See you around...colleague." Once she's inside, Rashida snorts in disgust.

"Fewer cowards, huh?" she mutters. "Where was she when the gates needed opening?" She turns and walks off, gesturing for me to follow. "Come on, let's go Teymouri." We continue to the end of the path and step onto the bridge that connects the small speck of land Tower B is seated upon to the rest of the island.

"Well, now what?" I ask. "What did you mean when you asked about keeping secrets earlier?" She glances around and then looks at me.

"What did you think I was saying?" she asks. I look down at my feet and shake my head.

"No...no, you can't be serious," I say. She crosses her arms and takes a step back.

"I know what you're trying to do and I can tell you right now that it's not going to succeed," she says. "Not without my help." The hairs on the back of my neck begin to stand up.

"I...what?" I ask, caught off guard and trying to feign ignorance.

"Halsey and I have been here for a long time, Teymouri," Rashida says. "We've seen it all. She knows as well as I do that something shady is taking place here. All the signs are there, just like they were five years ago." Do I continue feigning ignorance or do I take another route? Crap, I cannot let myself be the reason this gets screwed up. I didn't see something like this coming. What am I supposed to do?

"I don't know what you're expecting me to say here," I begin, choosing my words carefully. "And more importantly, why are you trying to drag me into what sounds like a murder plot?"

"I'm suggesting a pact between the two of us, and anyone else involved," she explains. "I need your help, you need mine, and therefore neither of us have any reason to backstab the other."

"I don't think it's that simple for either side," I respond. "Assuming I am involved in anything shady. You realize we're on two separate sides, right? Guard, inmate. Your job is to make sure I stay in line, to prevent escapes. You see why I'm not sold on this? How do I know that you're not working for Halsey?"

"I am working for Halsey, kid," Rashida chuckles, shifting her weight as she speaks. I roll my eyes and shake my head as I step back a pace. My eyes focus on the ground for little more than a second before I glare at Rashida.

"This isn't the time to be facetious," I snarl. "Yeah, you seem different than the other guards, but in the end that doesn't mean much."

"You seemed pretty sure of yourself earlier when you declared that I wasn't about to put you back in the bunker," she argues. "What's changed since then?"

"Nothing at all," I respond. "I was risking time in the bunker when I said that, not admitting to an escape attempt."

"Will you at least hear me out?" she asks. Silence ensues as I take a moment to think about it. Doesn't seem like it would matter either way, but maybe I can learn something if I let her speak.

"You know why I was sent here, right?" I ask. "You know the charge?"

"Manslaughter," she nods.

"You sure you don't want to take a page out of Halsey's book?" I snort. "Call it murder?" She lets out another chuckle and looks away for a moment, an amused grin across her face.

"The first thing you gotta stop doing is placing Halsey and me in the same box," she says, looking back at me. "We don't think the same way and we never have."

"Maybe that's true, maybe it isn't," I shrug. "But the point is that I already killed someone and it's been bothering me since I got here. Before that even. I'm not sure I want to be responsible for another death."

"Not even if they deserve it?" she asks. I clench my teeth and pause for a moment. I want so badly just to scream at her. She doesn't seem to grasp that I'm not thinking the same way she is. Yeah, Halsey's a monster, but I'm more focused on getting far away from her than killing her. If it came to blows then sure, I'd do whatever I needed to survive, but standing here thinking about killing her just doesn't feel right. Halsey doesn't need to die for me to escape and that's the problem. This is about what Rashida wants, what she needs to leave the island...and I'll need her to make this work. I don't have a choice. If I blow her off she might just rat me out in retaliation.

"Fine...I'll help," I grumble, holding out my hand. She shakes it and I let my arm fall to my side.

"Smart decision," she replies.

"Maybe so," I say with a shrug. "Doesn't mean I'm gonna like it."

"Liking it is the least of your worries," she replies. "When you leave this place alive, you'll thank me."

"If you say so," I mutter, looking away for a moment. "How's this going to work, anyway? Lure her down to the lever?"

"Something like that," she replies. "Were those two inmates you went to search for in on this plan?"

"So what if they are?"

"I'm asking if you have any plans to go back through Sector S," she explains. "Right now there aren't a lot of options." The bag. The bag by the dock entrance. That could work. But that seems like a huge risk. I'd have to tell Rashida where it is and right now that's not something I'm eager to do. Even worse than that, Halsey would have to know about it too. She'd have to be with us when we retrieve it. I suppose I don't have to be there. That way I wouldn't have to witness an electrocution. But that's putting a lot of trust in Rashida to do what she says she wants to do. Even so, it's not like I'd be able to do much if I was there with them. There's no cameras or anything down there. No cameras, no rules. There's no telling what Halsey might do.

"Something on your mind?" she asks.

"Just thinking," I answer.

"You have an idea? Let's hear it."

"Were you not listening to me earlier? I don't trust you."

"You and I have a deal, kid," Rashida growls. "Don't think you can back out now." Now what do I do? Tell her? Make something up?

"I'm not backing out," I declare.

"Then tell me what you're thinking," she demands.

"It's not my call to make," I explain. "It would be an enormous gamble. I could screw this entire thing up."

"This whole thing is a gamble, kid," she argues. "Just spit it out. If you've got a good idea, I want to hear it."

"You said Halsey's aware, right? She knows something is going on. What if we trick her? Make her think she's won?"

"And how do you propose we do that?" she inquires. I pause again, uncertain of what to say next.

"Before I get to that, I want to ask you something about that lever. About Sector S," I say.

"Sure. What do you want to know?"

"An inmate died when she tried to use that lever," I say. "I would assume Halsey would remember something like that. What's the story behind that, do you know?" She nods.

"It was back in 2010, shortly before Halsey called for Sector S to close," she answers. "Inmate tried to use the lever at the order of one of the guards. She was part of a crew that was performing maintenance down there. Something went wrong and she was electrocuted."

"I take it the maintenance crews were similar to what I do with the custodial staff?" I ask. Rashida nods.

"You got it," she says. "The idea was to teach kids a trade, teach them discipline and focus their energy on something productive. Do you remember that classroom just inside Sector S? Right after you leave Tower B?" Images of that haunting scene flash through my mind. The overturned desks, flickering lights, and scattered papers.

"I remember it."

"Probably seems like an odd place for a classroom, doesn't it?" she continues. "Well, even that place had a purpose, back before Halsey decided to cut the program. Much of the training was on the job, but other aspects took place there in that room. Mostly written exams, tests to see which inmates were falling behind, which were ready to take over and do the more dangerous tasks. The day that girl died, Halsey wasn't on the island. It was about three days after she'd left, leaving me in charge of the place. She was gone for about two weeks. Her father had died and she was off dealing with the funeral and his estate. The death was unexpected, so she had her hands full those two weeks. I mentioned to her that there had been a death, but didn't give her the details. I wrote up a report and that was the end of it. Sector S was shut down a few months later in early 2011 after rumors started spreading about alleged sightings of the dead girl among other things. Fewer and fewer guards would stay down there to supervise inmates. Inmates rebelled, refused to work down there, it was a mess."

"So it's been abandoned for seventeen years?" I ask. "How's that possible? Half the machinery down there is still functioning and there's plenty of lights on."

"Halsey tried to reopen the area again in 2015, then in 2019, and then again in 2024. Never stayed open more than a week. During that time and up until now, she's periodically hired outside contractors to tend to the vital machinery. They struggle to get anything done down there and things barely remain running. The island's power plant is down there. Protected from bombings and the like. Had to be back then. Back when it was a military base. Makes maintenance a pain in the ass for us, but other than that there's not much to say."

"So Halsey likely doesn't know what happened with that lever?" I ask.

"Very unlikely," Rashida assures me. "She tries to stay on top of things, but she was so distracted around the time it happened that it's doubtful she remembers it. Now that this whole mess with Tower B is playing out she's got her attention elsewhere."

"Good to know," I say. "Sounds like we have a better shot than I thought."

"We'll have a better one if we can figure out how to lure her down there," Rashida adds. "Now are you gonna tell me what you were thinking about or not?"

"Not yet," I say. "Just give me some time to mull it over. Can you deal with that?"

"How long do you need?" she asks.

"A day, maybe two," I answer. "Sound good?" She shakes her head in frustration.

"All right...fine," she says at last. "But I don't have all the time in the world. If you come up with anything else, any ideas you aren't as... protective of...then you come find me. Agreed?"

"Agreed." Now I just have to figure out what I'm going to do about Rashida's proposal. Regardless, Halsey's going to be keeping an eye on us all if she's as aware as Rashida claims. Even if Rashida can help keep Halsey at bay, I'm certain there are limits to that ability. The path forward is going to be difficult at best. An uphill battle.

After everything I saw in the bunker last night, there's no doubt that Rashida and Halsey's relationship is at the very least frayed. Her trust in Rashida is likely to have eroded along with it. There's no telling whether or not that trust can be repaired, but Rashida seems sure of herself. I need to find Leah before I do anything else. She's the only one still in general population[17] who's been working on this plan since the beginning. She's got to know what to do next. Inside the residential building, I start making my way toward my dorm. Along the way I pass several dozen inmates, most of whom are heading to the chow hall. I keep hoping to run into Rochelle or Savannah, but I never see them, even when I step into the dorm. Standing by my bunk, I find a kite stuck in one of the slots of my locker. Pulling it out I find that it's from Leah:

---

[17]The section of a facility that houses the main population of inmates.

Same place you met with Mika, same time tonight. I imagine you know why.

Even though I'm certain I know what she wants and where she's referring to, the message still seems ominous. Here's hoping she isn't mad at me. Looking up from the kite I find that the dorm is now empty. Everyone's gone except one girl sitting on a bottom bunk near the exit. She's facing away from me, hunched over with her elbows on her knees. I make my way toward the door, kite in my pocket. Passing by the girl I jump in alarm when she reaches out and grabs my wrist. When I turn to face her, I find that she's drenched in blood. Her throat is slit and her eyes are sunken and void of life. I let out a shriek and pull my arm loose. She disappears and I'm in such shock that I trip over my own feet and tumble through the double doors.

I'm back on my feet in seconds and I race down the hall and out of the building. Whoever, or whatever that was, I don't want to stick around to see it again. After exiting the building I slow my pace and continue at a brisk walk toward Building B. After heading inside I start toward the chow hall, all the while feeling rattled by what I just witnessed. It seems like I'm seeing those sorts of things more often. After reaching the chow hall, I go about my usual routine with the exception of scanning the room for Leah. She's nowhere in sight. I suppose I'll just have to wait till tonight to see what she wants. I spot Rochelle and Savannah sitting at one of the tables and go to join them. Rochelle is the first to spot me. She nudges Savannah in the ribs and points me out just before I sit down. Savannah chokes on her food and gives a slight wave in lieu of staying hello.

"How did you get out of there so soon?" Rochelle asks. "We thought for sure you'd be gone another week."

"What, does the whole place know about it?" I ask, clacking my tray down on the table.

"I doubt it," Savannah replies. "We heard it from that one girl. Leah, I think?"

"Yeah, that's her," I nod. "She spoke to you guys?"

"She did about two hours ago, but she didn't say much about what was going on," Rochelle explains. "Just that she was looking for you and that she'd overheard some of the staff talking about you getting let out early. She said Rashida was involved. What was that all about?"

"She's been acting weird, I don't know what her deal is," I answer, taking a bite of food. "Rashida, that is. She had a fight with Halsey last night."

"She did?" Savannah asks. "I'm guessing that's why Halsey's so pissy today?"

"That and I kicked Halsey down the stairs at the bunker," I add.

"Nice one," Rochelle chuckles, swirling some of the food around on her tray. "Wish I could have seen it."

"What about the fight with Rashida?" Savannah asks. "What's up with that? I thought those two were friends or something."

"They are, but something gave way while they were down in the bunker," I explain. "Did you hear about what they made me and Naomi do the other night?"

"No, nothing," Rochelle says. "All we've heard was something about Tower B burning down. Other than that we've been cut off."

"Long story short we got herded into Sector S, that system of tunnels underneath the island," I explain. "We were supposed to be searching for two inmates who went missing in there. Those two from the day we all got in that fight on the yard. The ones with Leah."

"Yeah, the red-haired girl and the other one," Savannah says.

"What exactly is that group cooking up?" Rochelle asks. "I saw your little stunt in the chow hall. You stole Halsey's keys and almost started a riot. I take it that's why you were put down in the bunker?"

"That it was," I confirm.

"What have they been asking you to do?" Rochelle inquires. "It must be something you want pretty bad if you're willing to risk ending up in the bunker over it."

"I can't talk about that right now," I answer. "I have to run some things by Leah and then we'll see."

"You sure they aren't using you?" Rochelle asks, giving me a stern look as she speaks.

"I doubt it," I say, shaking my head. "Look, it's complicated, but... well, something happened and now things are a bit shaky. Just trust me when I say that I know what I'm doing. But know that Halsey might be paying closer attention to you from now on."

"What?" Savannah exclaims. "Seriously? What did you do?"

"I said might, I didn't guarantee anything," I point out.

"I like you, Sarita, but you'd better not be dragging us into your business," Rochelle warns.

"It's nothing bad, it's...ugh...look, just wait till tomorrow and I'll figure out by then if I can say anything," I groan. "Just try to fly under the radar for now, it's no big deal."

"Getting tossed in ad-seg and then having it burn down a short time later is a pretty big deal, Sarita," Rochelle counters. "I don't want to wake up dead because you did something to piss Halsey off."

"It will all make sense in time, just let me explain what I can, all right?" I say.

"Fine, but I'm with Rochelle on this one, Sarita," Savannah says. "You'd better have a good reason for all of this."

"I swear I do," I reply. "Now, as for the Sector S thing, that leads up to why Rashida and Halsey were fighting last night. Like I said, we were supposed to find those two inmates who ran in there. We found them both, but...well, only one was alive."

"Jesus..." Savannah whispers.

"After that they took us back to ad-seg, then the next thing I know it's in the middle of the night and the tower is on fire. And Rochelle was apparently telling the truth when she mentioned ghosts."

"Wait, you saw something down there?" Rochelle asks.

"Yeah and it damn near killed us," I grumble. "And...um...I think one of them burned down the tower."

"One of what?" Savannah asks.

"One of the...things, the ghosts...I ran into one on the way here, it's like-"

"You're losing your mind?" Rochelle interrupts, an amused grin on her face.

"It's not funny!" I hiss through gritted teeth. "I know what I saw down there and I wasn't the only one who did. I thought it was all in my head, but...I don't know, some of it might be, but maybe some of it isn't?"

"Christ, you sound like my sister," Rochelle sighs. "Look, I just said that thing about ghosts because I was messing with you, Sarita, I didn't mean this place was actually haunted."

"Well it is!" I insist. What am I doing? This isn't making things any better. They're both looking at me like I'm losing it.

"What makes you so sure?" Rochelle argues. "None of the staff ever talk about seeing anything unusual. It's just the inmates and it's because they're trapped here."

"First off, that is bullshit, and second, are you telling me you don't believe anything your sister has said about this place?" I ask.

"I told you before that she's not right in the head anymore, Sarita," Rochelle contends. "I hate to say it, but maybe this place is getting to you too."

"You know what? Screw this," I growl, getting up from the table. I glare at them both and move to another table. There I finish my food and leave without them.

* * *

Back in the dorm, I climb up onto my bunk and sprawl out on my back. For a moment I start to doubt everything I said to the others. What if Rochelle's right? What if this place really has gotten to me?

I start thinking back to what I saw in the bunker with Mika's body lying nearby. The way I kept seeing her moving around. Could "Mika" have been right? Ariana was indeed carrying a heavy flashlight with her. It would have been easy to use it as an effective weapon. Did she tell me that whole story about Vesna beating people to death just to throw me off? Even Naomi was suspicious of her in the tunnels, calling her a coward and pointing out that she wanted to leave without Mika. I could drive myself crazy going over everything again and again, but Savannah's arrival at the foot of my bunk interrupts my thoughts.

"Hey, Sarita, you got a minute?" she asks. I sit up and see her hand sticking up over the end of the bunk, waving back and forth at me. With a heavy sigh, I climb down and stand with my arms crossed in front of me.

"What is it?" I ask. "Did you come to poke some fun at me?"

"No, I just...look, Rochelle was being an asshole," she begins. "I just came by to see how you were doing."

"Still as insane as I was back in the chow hall," I retort.

"You're not insane, Sarita," Savannah contends, shaking her head with with her eyes closed.

"No?" I snort. "How do you know that? How do I know that? How does anyone know that?"

"I'm just saying you don't seem-"

"Crazy?" I interrupt. "Is that what you were going to say?"

"No, I just think Rochelle is wrong," Savannah insists.

"This isn't helping anything," I mutter, climbing back up onto my bunk as I speak. "You're just here to kiss my ass and lie to me."

"Why would I lie to you?" she asks.

"You tell me, liar," I reply, looking over the side of the bunk at her. She buries her face in her hands and lets out a groan before letting them fall back to her sides.

"Rochelle's been acting weird since you left for the bunker," she says. "I can't say for certain what's going on with her, just that she seems like she's seeing things."

"What makes you say that?" I inquire, tilting my head to the side.

"I woke up two nights ago to her screaming bloody murder in here," Savannah explains. "I don't know if what she saw was real or imagined, but whatever it was it scared the hell out of her. My first thought was that it was a nightmare or something, but this seemed different somehow. My guess is that's why she was acting the way she was. So when you started talking about ghosts and whatnot, she was probably remembering what she saw." I turn my gaze toward the ground and take a deep breath. My thoughts return to the apparition that appeared by the doors here in the dorm. Is that what she saw?

"So, what happened with Halsey and Rashida?" Savannah inquires, "You never told us about it."

"Right," I say, clutching the elbow of my free arm in front of me. "Remember when I mentioned that one of the inmates we found in Sector S wasn't alive?"

"Yeah, I remember that," she nods, averting her gaze for a moment. "And I don't like where this is going."

"You'll like it even less as I go," I warn. "What caused the fight was Rashida disagreeing with Halsey about my punishment. Remember when I said I kicked Halsey down the stairs?"

"Yeah, I do" she confirms, shifting her weight. "What of it?"

"It just got her all riled up," I answer. "So she locked me in the cell and came back a short time later with the body of the inmate we found."

"You're kidding me..." I shake my head.

"I wish I was," I say. "They dragged the body down to the cell, Halsey and Rashida. Then Rashida started refusing to be apart of it, saying it wasn't right. Then Halsey started threatening to go to the authorities over something that happened in the war. Sounded like Rashida killed a fellow soldier."

"Seriously? What for?"

"Rashida mentioned that the person she killed shot someone else for dissenting over the murder of a civilian. I don't know how she killed the other soldier, just that Halsey said she "fragged" her. I don't know much else about it, just that Halsey vehemently disagreed with the murder."

"And so Halsey's blackmailing her with it?" Savannah surmises.

"It looks that way," I nod. "Right at the end of the argument, Rashida said something that got under Halsey's skin and she decked Rashida for it. Knocked her out cold."

"So I'm guessing since Rashida didn't like what was going on, and got punched in the process, that's why you got out early?"

"Yep."

* * *

Our conversation wrapped up soon after that. Now it was just a matter of time before I'd have to explain everything to Leah. I dozed off for a little while, dreaming of the day I would get out of this place. Go back home and just try to forget that any of this ever happened. In the dream it was easy to do. Brush everything off and move forward unhindered. I awoke again at around 11:30pm. My eyes met the clock and stayed there for over fifteen minutes.

Another minute passes and I begin making my way down the side of the bunk and toward the door. In the hallway I can feel myself tensing up a little. I can't help but get the feeling that she's going to be all kinds of frustrated with me. I know I would be. Here's hoping she doesn't ask me to do something stupid as a way of making up for it. That stunt with the keys was bad enough. I push the door open and lean against the wall just inside. Less than a minute later, Leah steps into the room and jumps in alarm when she notices me.

"Jesus! What are you doing waiting there like you're ready to ambush me? Did you forget where you are or something?" she growls.

"I'm sorry, relax," I sigh, stepping away from the wall.

"When you've taken a shiv to the gut just for stepping into the restroom at night, THEN you can tell me to relax!" She brandishes her finger at me as she speaks, letting both arms fall to her sides right as she finishes.

"Fine, fine, I won't do it again, all right?" I reply. "Now what's going on? What did you need to see me for?"

"Hey, I'm the one asking the questions here," she snaps. "Which one of you morons burned the tower down? Huh? Who thought that was a good idea? Ariana? Mika? Or was it Naomi?" She throws her hands up in the air in frustration.

"No, we don't know who did it," I explain. "And didn't you hear about what happened to Mika?"

"How would I know anything about all that?" she demands. "Tia was our intel line, without her I've got next to nothing. All I hear lately are worthless rumors about the tower thanks to you idiots!"

"You think I'm not upset about it?" I half-shout. "Come on, Leah, I think we all know what this means for us. Let me explain what happened, I promise you'll love what I have for you."

"The sarcasm isn't promising," she grumbles, looking away from me with her arms crossed. "But whatever, just catch me up. How long are the others locked up?"

"I heard they're supposed to be there for a week," I answer. She grabs her hair and pulls on it with her teeth clenched.

"Are you kidding me? A week?" she exclaims. "We already delayed this a month! We can't keep doing this, we're going to get caught!" She kicks the stall hard enough to rattle it and turns to face me again.

"We might have a way around that, but I can't guarantee anything," I say.

"Well don't keep me in suspense, what is it?" she demands.

"It's Rashida," I answer. "Rashida's requesting that we do something for her in exchange for her help. She might be able to help us get them out of the bunker sooner, but it's sort of a long shot." Leah stares at me for a moment, her expression blank at first. After a few seconds it contorts into a withering scowl. She turns and makes her way to one of the sinks and turns the faucet on, letting the water run over her hands. "Leah?" I say. She holds up her index finger and then splashes some of the water on her face. She stands with both hands gripping the sink, staring down at the drain for over a minute. Water slides down her cheeks and drips off her chin. After stepping away from the sink, she runs her hands over her face a few times and flicks the water from the ends of her fingers.

"Okay...so...Rashida...right?" she says, locking eyes with me.

"Yeah."

"I take it she knows what we're doing? She knows we're trying to escape?"

"She does," I confirm, glancing down at the floor.

"And if I know anything about guards, I know she's blackmailing us. Right?" Leah continues. "What does she want?"

"She wants Halsey dead." For several seconds I wait for Leah to reply. She just stands there, staring at the ground. Then she lets out a chuckle that turns into a full blown cackle. She sits down with her back against the wall, one hand clasped over her eyes as she continues to laugh. This keeps up for almost a minute straight before she at last takes a deep breath and lets her hand drop to her side.

"Sarita, I swear to God you'd better be screwing with me," she says, slowly turning her head toward me.

"And what if I say I'm serious?" I ask, leaning my back against the wall.

"Then I'd ask why," she answers, pulling her legs up to her chest. "How did it come to this?"

"She and Halsey got into a fight last night," I explain, dreading having to go over the details yet again. "And...before I forget, Mika's dead."

"What? Are you kidding me?" she exclaims, leaping to her feet. "What in the world happened? What does this have to do with Rashida? Did she have a hand in it?"

"No, no, it's nothing like that," I explain. "Something happened in Sector S."

"And what was that?" she demands.

"I don't know," I admit. "Me, Naomi, and Tia were placed on an impromptu search party to look for Ariana and Mika. We found Ariana first. She told us that she and Mika got separated. Sounded like Mika was acting weird along the way; hearing voices and whatnot. We found Mika later on, stuffed up in a crawlspace at the top of a ladder."

"And what killed her? Do you know?"

"Looked to me like someone beat her to death," I answer. "You don't happen to think Ariana had something to do with it, do you?" She looks away for a moment, lost in thought.

"No...no, I don't think so," Leah replies. "I mean, she got in a couple of fights before we recruited her, but those didn't involve Mika. So I know she'll fight when she needs to, despite that she's a little timid at times. She seemed to get along with Mika pretty well. No bad blood or anything that I saw. They seemed on great terms with one another. My only guess would be that something happened before they went down to Sector S, but even that seems like a hell of a stretch. Why do you think she had something to do with Mika's death?"

"Sector S messed with my head," I answer. "It was hard to understand how Mika could end up beaten to a pulp in a place that only the two of them were supposed to be. Stay down there long enough and it starts to get to you." I probably should leave out some of the details. The things I'm not sure were real. If Leah even begins to suspect that I'm starting to lose it, I imagine she'll question my ability to function. I could lose my chance to escape. There's no way I'm putting that on the line. Not after everything I've been through so far.

"Can you give me some kind of example?" she asks, raising an eyebrow.

"It's a whole story in itself and I have no idea how much longer we'll be alone in here," I explain. "Let's just move on."

"All right, fine, whatever," she says with a shrug. "Why did you go off and start talking about this anyway?"

"Because it was important to note that we're down a member and it also ties into why Rashida and Halsey were fighting with each other," I explain. "After the tower caught fire, Halsey dragged us all into her office. Me, Naomi, Tia, and Ariana. One of the guards escorting us in the tunnels ended up dead under strange circumstances. I got separated from the group and they ended up ahead of us after they ordered me to search one of the rooms. They just kept on walking. The point is that Halsey wasn't too happy about the whole thing. She interrogated us and gave up when she couldn't get anything useful. So she decided to soften us up by tossing us in the bunker. I wasn't happy about it and I kicked Halsey down the stairs."

"Great..." Leah sighs, shifting her weight. "And how did that work out?"

"She decided to chain Mika's corpse to me," I say. "And that's where it all started. They got her body to the bottom of the stairs and then Rashida started objecting to it. She said it was crossing a line and that she wasn't going to help her do it. Then Halsey mentioned something that happened in the war, a crime that Rashida committed, something Halsey threatened to go public with. She taunted her, said she could always have her carted off to prison. Then Rashida said something about Halsey's father, Halsey didn't like it, and she punched her in the face. Knocked her out cold."

"Wow..." Leah murmurs. "Never thought Halsey would go that far with her. I mean...as long as I've been here it's been difficult for me to get a bead on Rashida. One minute she's neutral, doesn't care what's going on, then a week later she's a raging lunatic, pretty much always toward fellow guards, and then other days she seems almost protective of the inmates. Sort of like Nicole, but different."

"That's been my experience with her so far. Like I said, she knows what we're up to and she's certain that Halsey's picked up on it as well."

"Normally I'd run this by Naomi, but..." Leah begins. Her voice trails off and we're left standing in silence for a few moments.

"But what?"

"But I wasn't expecting something like this to happen," she groans, tilting her head back and staring at the ceiling. "This thing with Rashida. I had to call the shots while Naomi was locked up after the thing with Parsons, so that's not much trouble. Until she gets back, whether that's soon or right at the last minute, I'm in charge. And the first thing I'm going to do is ask you what you said to Rashida. Did you agree to anything?"

"I told her we'd help, but I didn't name any of you," I say, shaking my head. "I didn't feel like I had much of a choice. If I'd told her I wasn't interested, I was worried she'd just go and rat us out for the hell of it."

"Understandable," Leah admits. "Still not a good position for us to be in. Unless it turns out she really can be of use to us."

"What should we do next?"

"I'm not sure," she says, crossing her arms and looking down at the floor.

"I know this is my fault and I'm sorry," I apologize. "I didn't mean for things to end up like this." She looks back up at me.

"Why do you think this is your fault?" she asks. "Sounds to me like Rashida had you cornered." I shake my head.

"No, before that. The other day in the chow hall, I picked up the keys after Naomi dropped them," I explain. "I brought attention to what was going on. I imagine that just fueled any suspicions Halsey had before that. Now because of that I put this whole thing in jeopardy."

"If anyone is to bear the blame for that, it should be Naomi for being such a klutz," she replies. "Can't imagine she isn't still kicking herself for it. If anything, you saved it by taking the initiative to bring them to me. So don't worry about it. It's not gonna solve anything. Right now we need to figure out how we're going to move forward. Rashida wants Halsey out of the picture...so now we need to decide if she's trustworthy or not."

"What harm could it do?" I say with a shrug. "Seems like there's a great deal of risk either way. If we refuse to follow her demands she could snitch on us. If we do help her and she snitches anyway, it's the same result, right?"

"I suppose that's true," she admits. "You've talked with her a bit. What do you think?"

"I know she saved me from a couple of guards earlier," I answer. "She left her office to talk with Halsey and they snuck in and dragged me into one of the restrooms, started freaking out, claiming Rashida was giving me special treatment and that it lined up perfect with the death of one of the guards in the tower. I guess Rashida didn't get along with one of them. Rashida stormed in a few minutes later and threw one of them on the floor. Chewed them both out and warned them not to pull something like that again. On top of her fight with Halsey, threatening those two guards is a huge risk for her. It seems like we could trust her, but I need to talk with her more."

"Then that's for you to deal with," Leah replies. "Talk with her again soon, go along with whatever she asks...within reason of course. Let's just hope this doesn't backfire. I know from experience that when guards want something, they're usually sincere. So long as they get it, we shouldn't have too many problems. Now we just have to work that into the plan somehow. The idea was to leave quietly, not stir up any trouble, that sort of thing. Last time someone did cause a spectacle they ended up dead."

"You got the key made, right?" She nods.

"That I did," she confirms. "It's stashed away with the note from the bus. Before we get into the rest of this, did you or anyone else locate any weapons in Sector S?"

"I found a few and some ammo," I answer. "Bolt cutters too. They're stashed away just inside the secondary entrance to Sector S. Right near the docks."

"And you're sure we can get into those doors?" she asks. "They didn't bolt them up?"

"They open from the outside and I don't think I saw a lock on them, but I'm not a hundred percent on that," I answer. "I'll talk to Rashida about it, maybe she can make sure it's open for us."

"Sounds good," Leah says. "Keep me posted, all right? You bring any new information to me."

"Got it," I nod.

"I don't know if Naomi filled you on the rest of the plan, but it involves obtaining copies of the footage of something that took place in Tower A before you came here. You know what a cell extraction is?"

"One of the guards said something to me about it while I was over there," I explain. "I assume it has something to do with forcing an inmate out of their cell?"

"Pretty much," she nods. "They tape each one they perform for legal reasons. They always find a way to spin whatever content is on each tape, and they don't have to try hard; cuz let's face it, no one believes what any inmate says about anything. If we get maced then we should have complied, we get shot it's good riddance, we get sick we're not worth medical attention or we're just making it up, and the same thing goes if we file a complaint against a guard. We're just mad that we got what we deserved, right? You can't take human rights away from someone society doesn't even consider human. That was the case back while Naomi was over there last year. We need a specific tape of the cell extractions that took place. Naomi convinced the others to fight back, to resist. It ended with ten injured inmates, two of whom had to be flown off the island. Our hope is to take that tape public, show everyone what they really do here. If I'm being honest, Naomi and I don't have a lot of faith in the public at this point. You've lived through this mess, the courts and whatnot. Fairness? What fairness? If it had been the other way around and that girl had killed you, I doubt she'd have gotten anything as severe."

"Or nothing at all considering her father got nothing for assaulting mine last year," I mutter. "Sucker punched him in a store parking lot."

"And I bet the prosecution would have used that against you," she sighs. "If you'd gone to trial, that is. Try to make that the motive. Bad blood between families, that sort of thing."

"That's just what my attorney warned me might happen if I turned down the plea deal," I reply. "I know what I was told on the bus ride here, but I'm having doubts about Randall Adams. He's not exactly looked upon the same way he was ten years ago. If we take any tapes to him, is there even a chance he can help?"

"Hell if I know," she says with a shrug. "All I know is he's our best bet right now. We have to at least try." She glances at the door and pauses for moment, placing her index finger on her lips.

"What?" I ask.

"I think I hear someone outside," she answers. "Get going, I'll hang back for a little bit. I'll catch up with you later." I nod and push the door open. An inmate I don't recognize is coming down the hallway; half asleep with her eyes focused on the ground. We pass by each other without a word or even a glance. When I get back to my bunk, I curl up and fall asleep within minutes.

Chapter 16

Think It Over

The next morning, the guards storm in and begin conducting a surprise shakedown.[18] They tear everything off the beds, dump everything out of the lockers, and search each of us as they go. As usual they pick a few people to single out. Thirty minutes pass while I watch the clock in frustration. They came in early, so at least there's that. The other dorms are supposed to be heading into the chow hall soon. Assuming they aren't dealing with the same situation as us. Two of the girls are dragged out in handcuffs over contraband[19] discovered hidden under their mattresses. After what seems like an eternity, the guards let us leave the room and start toward the main building.

The shakedown has me wondering just how Leah's been able to hide everything from the guards so far. Part of me wants to ask, but at the same time I don't want to know. If Halsey decides to try interrogating me again I'd rather I not know anything. Just as I'm halfway across the street, Halsey steps out of the main building and starts heading in my direction. My chest tightens. She seems calmer than the last time I saw her, but that doesn't mean much. She eyes me as she walks past and I continue toward the building.

Stepping inside I start searching for any sign of Leah. A few stares from inmates cause me to avert my gaze. Something about those looks feels threatening. I never did ask Savannah or Rochelle about any attacks in the dorm since I've been away. That girl with the slit throat has

---

[18] A thorough search of a cell or dorm with the intent of locating and removing contraband items.

[19] Prohibited items. i.e. cell phones, weapons, drugs, etc.

been on my mind since I saw her. While I slept last night I kept seeing her in my dreams. Now doesn't seem like a good time to ask about any recent attacks, now that Rochelle seems anxious to avoid discussing such things.

Waiting in line with my tray, I'm about to give up looking for Leah. I'm starting to wonder if maybe her dorm took a hit as well. Guards are probably rifling through their things as I stand here. What if the reason I don't see her isn't because her dorm was shaken down, but rather because her part of the plan was uncovered? The key and the napkin with Adams' contact info. I push the thought out of my mind almost as soon as it appears. The reality is that I don't know what's going on and I need to just stay calm and remember that. As I'm heading toward a table, I hear Leah behind me.

"Hey! Sarita!" she says. I turn to face her and she gives me a quick nod. I sit down at the far end of a mostly empty table. Minutes later she joins me, sitting down on the opposite side. She clacks her tray down in front of her and glances at the nearest inmates, none of whom appear to be paying attention to us.

"What's going on?" I ask, swallowing a bite of food.

"What's going on is we're down a few people and we never discussed what to do about that last night," she answers.

"We never discussed why Mika was so important either," I point out. She holds up her index finger and finishes chewing.

"All right," she begins, clearing her throat. "First thing we're going to start with is recruiting people. That's top priority. We need a team for this to work. Just because everyone else is locked up doesn't mean we stop. We're hitting our deadline no matter what. Resupply is once a month and we are not staying until next month."

"And what happens if the time comes for us to leave and they're still in the bunker?" I ask.

"It means we leave without them," Leah answers. A tense silence ensues. I don't feel right about leaving anyone behind, but if it comes down to it, I won't have a choice. We all knew the risks when we joined. I'll just have to hope it doesn't come down to that.

"I see," I mumble, taking another bite. Leah looks up at me with a confused expression.

"Something wrong with that?" she asks.

"Yeah, I just...don't feel right about leaving without them," I admit.

"You don't strike me as the naive type, Sarita," Leah replies. "Come on. You must have realized that was the case. It's not that I want to leave anyone behind either, it's just that it's too risky to play hero. You know what I mean?"

"Yeah, I get it," I say. "Just sucks is all."

"Try not to worry about it. Right now we need to focus on our next move or else none of us are going anywhere." She sets her fork down on the tray and places her folded arms on the table before her.

"What about Rochelle and Savannah?" I ask. She takes a minute to think about it, biting her lip and gazing down at the table.

"I'm kind of fifty-fifty on those two," she answers. "I know Naomi and I considered them and that Mika said something to you about it. I'm not sold on the idea that they'll do what I ask of them. You know from experience the sort of things this plan demands. On top of that I won't tolerate snitching and each time we bring someone new onboard it creates uncertainty. How am I to know they won't turn on us out of desperation? You've been on the receiving end of Halsey's wrath, you know how bad it can get. Parsons cracked under those sort of circumstances and I was convinced she was solid from the start. Boy was I wrong."

"What did she do?" I ask.

"She made nice with one of the guards and agreed to spill the beans in exchange for gain time," Leah explains. "Fucking idiot, they were never going to give it to her. I told her to get a grip on herself and just follow along, but she tried to stab us in the back instead. No faith in us at all. She started talking about how the whole thing was doomed, we were all gonna die, and then she starts talking about Eston's escape attempt and how that one went all to hell even though it was well thought out. Then Naomi confronted her, she lied to her face, and Naomi attacked her. It's unfortunate, yeah...but this isn't a game. We get one shot, there is no reset button, no do-overs, the dice stay where they land and that's just how it is."

"All about survival, huh?" I murmur, brushing some loose hairs away from my face.

"All about survival," she nods. "Gotta do what you gotta do. Fight or die, that's all we have. Well...other than sit quietly and be good little girls. Do our time, leave, let this place keep running, let the machine keep grinding people to dust. People don't always do so well after they leave a place like this. They fall apart. They kill themselves or they get brought back on parole violations and the system kills them. That's why I'm willing to leave people behind. If it means we put an end to this place, it's worth it."

"If we did leave people behind..." I begin, my voice getting caught in my throat. "If...do you think we'd be able to get them out? Save them? After we make our case?" She shrugs.

"I dunno, maybe," she says. "Depends on a lot of things. Are we believed? Do enough people care? Do the people in power make the right decisions? Cuz we sure as hell wouldn't be the ones coming back here; launching some crazy ass rescue mission. It's up to fate at that point. It's all a gamble, Sarita. Every step of the way. That's why I try to live in the present. Cuz sometimes there are things in the future, things that might happen, that I don't want to think about. And I don't get an ounce of comfort out the possibility that they also might not happen. You said they're in the bunker up until just before the escape. There's still time, we still have another chance to make this work. So that's why I'm gonna ask you what you think about Rochelle and Savannah."

"What do you mean?"

"Exactly that," she chuckles, giving a rare smile. "You know them pretty well. Do you think they can be of use?" I take a moment to think about it. Both Savannah and Rochelle seem iffy at best. I know they both have my back, but that doesn't necessarily mean they'll be up for something as dangerous as an escape attempt. They've both been keeping their heads down this whole time. They both got upset with me when I told them that Halsey might be watching them because of something I was involved in.

"It seems like a coin toss on those two," I say. "I know that they can be trusted, I know they can keep their mouths shut, that they won't go ratting us out for anything...but..."

"But what?"

"They both seem to prefer keeping their heads down, you know?" I continue. "I know they hate it here, but I don't know if either of them are willing to put their lives on the line for something like this. Rochelle seems like she'd be a little more reluctant than Savannah."

"I can't do anything with a maybe, Sarita," she sighs. "Do you want to take a chance on them or what? Cuz if not, we need to try something else."

"I'm sure I can at least convince Savannah," I reply. "I'll do what I can with Rochelle, but I won't make any promises."

"None of us really can make promises," she says. "About anything. Even if it's just Savannah, that's still better than just us two. Once we're through here, go talk with them and tell them to meet us out at the track."

"Got it."

"Now on to Mika," Leah says. "She's gone, we need a replacement. Do either Savannah or Rochelle work in medical?" I shake my head.

"No, they don't," I answer. Leah places her elbows on the table and buries her face in her hands.

"Of course not..." she groans. She stays still for a moment before removing her hands and setting them in front of her.

"I do know someone who does," I say.

"Well? Who is it?" she demands, leaning forward a little.

"Her name's Jackie, she came in on the same bus with me," I explain. "Problem is I don't really know her. We were both held at the same facility for a while, just before we were bused here."

"So, what then? You kind of know her?" Leah snorts. "Whatever. Anyone else?"

"No, that's all I have," I say with a shrug. Leah stares down at her tray for a moment before lifting her head back up and looking me in the eye.

"That's a huge risk from the sound of it," she says, giving me a stern look. "Hold off on talking to her for now."

"What? I thought we were on a time limit here?"

"Relax, I just want a second opinion on this," she says with a dismissive wave. "You said Rashida's involved now, right? Well, how about you go and ask her for a favor? Get Naomi out of the bunker."

"I can try, but that doesn't seem likely," I say.

"All I'm asking is that you try," she responds. "If you can't get to Naomi, then we'll go ahead with your suggestion. Talk to Rashida, then let me know what you find out." She stands up with her tray.

"Where are you going?" I ask.

"I'll meet you at the track, make sure you get Rochelle and Savannah to follow you," she says, walking away. I'm left sitting alone for a few minutes while I finish up. Now I just have to sit down with Savannah and Rochelle, which is going to be a little awkward after my spat with Rochelle. Whatever...that's minimal compared to dying here. I can see them both from where I'm sitting. As soon as they both stand up, I discard my tray and follow them out into the hallway. Savannah notices me approaching, prompting Rochelle to turn her head toward me.

"I need you two to follow me," I say right as Savannah opens her mouth.

"What? Why?" Rochelle demands.

"Just follow me to the track, all right?" I insist.

"I told you yesterday that I don't want anything to do with whatever it is you're doing," Rochelle growls. "Why are you leading with that instead of apologizing for yesterday?"

"You were the one being a jerk yesterday, not me," I argue, rolling my eyes. "Look, you don't have to do anything but listen, okay? Nothing happens unless you want it to. I promise you'll want to hear it."

"What? You find a ghost or something?" Rochelle snorts.

"Rochelle, knock it off," Savannah grumbles, nudging her in the ribs.

"Now you're siding with her all of a sudden?" Rochelle snaps at Savannah.

"I know that you saw something the other night and I know you don't want to be here anymore," I say. Rochelle's eyes widen just before her expression contorts into a scowl. She glares at Savannah.

"What did you tell her about that?" Rochelle demands.

"Just that you were acting weird ever since it happened," Savannah says with a shrug. "I was just trying to give her an explanation for why you got upset."

"Well, thanks for that," Rochelle mutters.

"And am I wrong that you don't want to stay here?" I ask. Rochelle crosses her arms in front of her and looks away for a moment.

"So what if that's the case?" she asks, looking back at me. "Doesn't mean anything. Everyone wants out of here, but I also don't want to end up in the bunker. Or like that girl your new partner carved up."

"It's not going to happen," I assure her. "Just come with me and listen to what Leah has to say to you." Rochelle takes a moment to think about it before taking a few steps closer to me.

"You sure about this?" she asks. "Sure it's not gonna backfire on us for some reason?" I nod.

"One hundred percent," I answer.

"I want to trust you, Sarita, but I also know that stirring up trouble in a place like this can't end well," Rochelle continues. "After what happened to you, you should know that as well as anyone."

"Just hear her out, that's all I'm asking," I say. She takes a moment to think and lets her arms fall to her sides.

"All right. Fine. I'll listen, but I'm not committing to anything, you got that?" she says. "That means you don't pressure me, you don't try anything to influence my decision. If I end up saying no to whatever it is, then you gotta respect that. And that goes for both of you," she continues, pointing at us both. "Right now my top priority is getting out of here in one piece." She strides past me and I turn and watch her walk a short distance before turning to face us. She beckons for us to follow and I turn to face Savannah.

"I hope you know what you're doing," she says, heaving a sigh as she speaks. She brushes past me and I follow after her.

* * *

Out at the track, we find Leah circling back toward us as we make our way to her. She gives a subtle nod and we wait for her to approach before walking alongside her.

"Nice to see you two again," Leah says, looking at Rochelle, then Savannah. "Did Sarita tell you anything?"

"Just that you wanted to see us," Savannah answers.

"Before I say anything, I need you both to understand that what's said here, stays here," Leah warns. "Can I trust you two to do that?"

"No problem," Rochelle answers.

"Got it," Savannah says.

"All right, since I don't want to beat around the bush here, the gist of it is that this is an escape attempt," Leah says. "It's not just about getting out of here, though. It's about shutting this place down. Are either of you on board for that?" Savannah is the first to respond.

"You know there's never been an escape from this island, right?" she points out.

"No one's ever tried what we're doing," Leah responds.

"I'm sure everyone else who tried said the same thing," Savannah contends.

"And how do you plan to shut this place down?" Rochelle asks.

"By taking things further than any other inmate has before," Leah explains. "You're both familiar with the Eston incident, right?"

"Yeah, who isn't?" Rochelle responds.

"And you remember the two inmates that spoke out about this place?" Leah continues.

"Clear as day," Savannah replies. "I also remember that they got hammered into silence after a few months. Them speaking out did literally nothing to change this. Eston was murdered and no one cared. How are you planning to take this further than them?"

"The only thing the public had to go on was the word of a couple of inmates," Leah says. "They had no evidence to back up anything they said, so naturally the public questioned what they were saying. We're going further by taking solid evidence of what Halsey does here with us when we leave. We're going to make sure that people can't just dismiss us or anything we tell them."

"What evidence?" Rochelle asks.

"The first part of it is the note we put together on the bus ride here," I explain. "We're going to call those people to testify about Rachel Caine's death on the bus and anything else we've seen here. The more people speaking out the better."

"And what's the second part?" Rochelle inquires.

"Video footage," Leah says. "Halsey keeps records, recordings of things like cell extractions and other incidents and procedures for legal purposes. We're going to bring some of the more damning ones off the island and release them to the public. Halsey's never had video footage leak from the island, she's very careful about that. Leaking some of it would be a major blow to both her and McGinley's."

"And walking off the island isn't an option, I'm sure of that," Rochelle sighs. "They searched us top to bottom when we first got here. No way we're sneaking anything out of here once our sentences are up."

"Exactly," Leah nods. "That's why it needs to be done this way."

"What happens to us if and when we leave?" Savannah asks. "I mean, yeah, we can show the world what this place does to people, but none of us have finished our sentences. I have to wonder if the courts will just move us somewhere else to serve the remainder of our time."

"They might," Leah admits. "But do either of you feel comfortable with the idea of letting this place continue to exist? Of letting Halsey continue to get away with murder?"

"Not at all," Rochelle replies, staring at the ground in front of her as she walks.

"Me either," Savannah says.

"So are you in or out?" Leah asks. "I need an answer from you both."

"What if we say no?" Rochelle asks. I clench my teeth and hold my breath. Come on, Rochelle, don't walk away from this.

"Then you forget what you heard and go back to serving your sentence," Leah answers. "Simple as that...assuming you both keep quiet about this. Loose lips sink ships."

"I'm not planning to snitch on anyone," Rochelle answers.

"So is that a no?" Leah inquires.

"It's not a no, but it's not a yes either," Rochelle admits, watching her feet as she walks. "I'm just not sure. What's been done so far? How are we going to make it out of here alive? I mean, what are you planning to ask of us?"

"Good question," Savannah adds.

"You'll be taking over the roles of two of our original team," Leah answers. "They're both stuck in the bunker for the time being."

"So why are you asking us to fill in?" Rochelle inquires. "They'll be out of there eventually. Why not just put everything on hold until then?"

"It's because the length of time they're set to stay down there puts their release right on the day before we're set to leave," Leah explains. "That's assuming what we know about their sentences is true. It could be longer for all we know. Halsey's known to leave people down there for months."

"So you're saying you'll just leave them behind if they don't get out in time?" Rochelle asks. Leah nods.

"That's right," Leah confirms. Rochelle takes a moment to think as our group continues down the track. I imagine she's thinking the same thing I was just a short time ago. Something about her expression tells me she doesn't like it any more than I do.

"What were the other two doing before today?" Savannah asks.

"One was gathering intel, the other was more or less on standby at the moment," Leah responds.

"Sitting around doing nothing doesn't sound all that difficult," Rochelle snorts. "I still don't see why I'm here. It sounds like you need one person."

"When it comes time for us to leave, we'll need you both," Leah replies. "You won't be sitting on your hands the entire time, I can promise you that much."

"Even if that's the case, I still haven't heard you say how we're planning to get out of here," Rochelle says.

"I need to know that you're in before I tell you anything else," Leah answers. "So...what will it be?" Rochelle and Savannah both remain silent for over a minute as we continue along the track.

"I'm in," Savannah says at last.

"Glad to hear it," Leah says with a nod. "What about you?" she asks Rochelle. Rochelle shakes her head and lets out a sigh.

"I need some time to think," she says. Leah rolls her eyes and clenches her teeth.

"You have until this time tomorrow," Leah says, leading us all off the track and toward the bleachers. "I can't afford you any longer than that. Sound good?" Rochelle nods and the two of them shake hands. "Meet me here tomorrow, all right?" Leah says.

"Got it," Rochelle says. "Come on. We're gonna need to get back to work pretty soon." She gestures for me and Savannah to follow. Leah stops Savannah for a moment.

"That means you too," she says to Savannah. "Back here at the same time tomorrow. I need to fill you in on everything."

"Got it," Savannah nods. She follows after Rochelle and they both stop about fifty feet away, waiting for me to follow.

"Whatever you need to do to get her on board with us, you do it," Leah says, turning to me. "I don't care if you have to bullshit your way through it, just make sure she's in. All right?"

"I'll take care of it," I assure her. She remains beside the bleachers while I catch up to the others. As we're walking back toward the main building, I glance over my shoulder to see Leah now sitting on the bottom seat of the bleachers, leaning forward with her elbows on her knees and chin resting on her palms. Twenty-four hours to change Rochelle's mind. I know I told Leah I'd take care of it, but I have more than my share of doubts. Whatever Rochelle decides, I promised her I would respect it.

Chapter 17

Favors

Back on cleaning crew, Rochelle and Savannah are both quieter than usual. The guard watching us is someone we haven't seen before. Someone who keeps glaring at me every chance he gets. It's difficult to figure out why with everything that's been happening. My guess is the Tower B incident has something to do with it. Or it could be that the stunt Rashida pulled with me is having some sort of ripple effect. I can only hope that that's not the case.

"Get the edges too," the guard orders, pointing at the edges of the sink I just finished with.

"Are you serious? It's fine, I got every inch of it," I protest. He takes his cigarette out of his mouth, taps it on the faucet, and spills ashes all over the area between the knobs. He turns the water on and gets some of it on the ashes before smearing them around the edge and backing away.

"Looks to me like you missed a spot," he says with a smirk, returning to his place by the door. Jackass. Half of me wants to throw the rag at his face. Can't imagine he'd be smirking after that. My ribs are still sore from the other day and I'm not about to take any chances this close to our escape. Right as I start cleaning up the sink again, someone can be heard coming down the hall toward us. Rashida steps into the room moments later.

"Teymouri, I need you to follow me," she says, beckoning me forward.

"She'll go once she's finished in here," the other guard declares.

"I'm sorry, is your name Halsey?" Rashida asks, glaring at him.

"Course not," he snorts.

"Then you're attempting to interfere with my ability to do my job?" Rashida continues.

"I didn't say I wasn't going to hand her over, just that she needs to finish before she goes," the guard answers, crossing his arms in front of him. Rashida walks past him and yanks me away from the sink. I toss the rag back in the bucket and she lets go of me as I follow her toward the door. Right as we step out into the hall the guard speaks again.

"Watch yourself, Sayed," he warns. "You might outrank us, but we outnumber you." Rashida stands silent for a few seconds, head bowed and fists clenched. She doesn't say anything and instead continues down the hallway. We round a corner and she stops and slams her fist into a door. Still silent and gaze focused on the floor, she looks as though she wants to go back and strangle the other guard. She lets her arm fall to her side and takes a deep breath before proceeding down the hall.

"Sorry about that," she apologizes. "Day's half over and I'm already regretting getting up."

"Why'd you bring me along?" I ask.

"Halsey wants to see you in her office," she explains. "It's about the investigation. She's got nothing on you and now she's just looking for any excuse she can to send you back to the bunker. So be on guard and watch what you say to her."

"Great," I sigh. "I take it you can't bail me out a second time?"

"Nope, not a second time," she answers.

"What was that guy saying a minute ago? About you being outnumbered?" I inquire. She shakes her head and runs her fingers through her hair.

"Nothing you need to worry about," she answers. "Staff related bullshit. Nothing else."

"Considering the fact that that guard was hassling me just now, I would say I have reason to be worried," I argue. "Does this have something to do with yesterday? Those two guards you threatened?"

"What I did with those two is never a good thing," she says. "I'm in a unique position, though. Halsey favors me more than the others, even if she does make my life hell, and that's why I abuse that favoritism every chance I get. Otherwise guards like Matt McClain and his idiot brother get away with things they shouldn't...and inmates like Iris Eston get killed. Inmates have their own unwritten rules and so do guards. When you violate those rules, things start getting messy."

"Sounds like what Nicole told us about her old job," I say.

"It's a lot like that. Those two I threatened yesterday are supposed to be my comrades, you know?" she explains. "Us guards, we're supposed all be on the same side. Have each other's backs, not get in anyone's business, ruin anyone's good time. If something shady is going on they expect that any do-gooders who come along will keep their traps shut and their heads down. I violated that. So now they're warning me that I'd better get back in line." We turn another corner and step out of Building A. A gust of wind throws me off balance for a moment.

"Does this mean I shouldn't bother asking you for any help?" I ask.

"Depends on what sort of help it is," she answers.

"Naomi. I want her out of the bunker," I declare. She stops and leads me off to the side and between two of the buildings.

"What did I just say to you, kid?" she demands. "I'm not a magician, I can't just go and drag your partners out of the bunker on a whim. Like I said, if you go back, I won't be able to get you out."

"I didn't expect it to happen at the snap of my fingers," I respond. "Could you at least try?"

"Halsey's already on my back over your release," she says, shaking her head. "There's no way."

"What about a visit?" I ask. "Just bring me down there to talk to her for five minutes, that's all I need." She claps a hand to her face and lets out a groan before removing it.

"Fine, five minutes," she says. "I can take you down there tonight, provided that Halsey doesn't flip her lid here in a second. Look, if you don't end up in the bunker over this, meet me outside your dorm at 1am tonight. Got it?"

"Got it," I nod.

"Five minutes," she says, holding up her palm with her fingers splayed. "That's all I can give you. The longer we're there, the more suspicious it looks. Now come on. Let's not keep Halsey waiting any longer. She was already miffed when I came to get you." She and I walk back around the side of the building and enter Building B. From there we start heading for Halsey's office, dodging guards and inmates alike as we move through the halls. Arriving at the door, I can feel a sense of dread wash over me. My get out of jail free card has been used up. If I screw this up somehow, I'm stuck down there until Halsey decides I've had enough. And that means I could end up being left behind. Rashida opens the door and I step inside and take a seat in one of the chairs in front of the desk. As soon as I walk in, Halsey looks up from her computer.

"Having a nice afternoon, Teymouri?" she asks, her tone dripping with sarcasm. My knee-jerk response is to give some kind of retort, but instead I clench my teeth and hold back.

"It's been fine," I answer. She paces around to the front of the desk and stands with her arms crossed, staring at me.

"Do you know why you're here?" she asks, glancing at Rashida and then back at me. Rashida clears her throat and stands by the door.

"No," I lie. "Just that you wanted to talk to me."

"I'm certain the Tower B fire is still fresh in your mind?" she asks.

"It is."

"Traces of accelerant were found inside the remains of the building," she continues. "Some of it even goes all the way to the gates in Sector S and vanishes a short distance after that...as if someone was carrying a leaky fuel canister. Do you see why this is a problem?"

"Because you sent us into Sector S," I answer.

"Officer Martin says he lost sight of you and Beckham early on in your search for the missing inmates," Halsey continues. "That sounds to me like one of you could have gone back and left the fuel canisters by the doors without either him or Richards noticing you."

"We couldn't even get back to the entrance, the gates were locked," I argue. "There was some kind of electrical issue or something. They just closed on us and we couldn't get them open again." Halsey leans back against her desk, still eyeing me.

"I'm well aware that they were closed, Teymouri," Halsey sighs. "The problem is that gates don't just magically close and given what happened, I'm willing to bet that there was someone else involved. An inmate I don't yet know about. Officer Martin happened to tell me about a voice he heard over the radio. He was making an attempt to call for backup after the gates closed and an unidentified female spoke to him instead. Do you know anything about that?"

"I was there when it happened," I confirm. "Nothing else."

"You're sure?" Halsey asks, leaning forward.

"I'm certain I heard someone speaking with him," I answer. "He didn't seem to know who it was. He seemed a little put off by it."

"Given what a coward he is, I'm sure getting trapped down there by a few crafty inmates wasn't his idea of a good time," Halsey says. "So... we know there were canisters moved up to the gates and likely back since they weren't found at the scene of the fire, and now we appear to have a mystery inmate working in your favor. Who is it? I want a name and don't you dare lie to me!"

"I don't know anything!" I insist. "I was just as surprised as anyone to see the tower burn! What would even be the point of doing that? We were already in trouble as it was! Why go to such insane lengths to make it worse?"

"Normally I would be thinking the same thing," Halsey admits. "But since Beckham took to gouging out my eye over something she brought on herself, I have to wonder if something like setting fire to a building was done for the same reason."

"And what reason is that?"

"Spite perhaps?" Halsey suggests. "Or maybe it goes deeper than that. Maybe those two guards had something on you. Maybe you needed them dead for some reason. Beckham already went out of her way to stab another inmate within an inch of her life...despite that from what I understand she was quite chummy with her for a long time prior to that. That tells me that, at least in Parsons' case, something was being covered up. I wonder...was it the same thing in this case?"

"That seems a little extreme, doesn't it?" I reply.

"Not if you're desperate to escape, it isn't." Her words catch me off guard. I can only hope that nothing suspicious is showing on my face. Seems Rashida was right about Halsey knowing. "It's not just coincidence that I called you in here alone, Teymouri," Halsey continues, crouching down in front of me as she speaks. "I know the other three inmates in the bunker right now are part of this misguided endeavor... and that is why they will stay in the bunker just a little longer...until I decide what to do with them. But you, Teymouri...you're here because I think there's still a chance for you. Beckham and the others are lost causes, you don't have to be like them. You could walk away from this right now and I'll remove the six-month extension on your sentence. Hell, I could even go further than that. I have a lot of pull outside of this facility and I could even expunge the charges from your record. You could have a chance to go back to your normal life and live it however you wish. But that doesn't come cheap, kid."

"I'm not helping you do anything," I declare.

"Don't be so quick to brush such an offer aside," she continues. "Just hear me out, will you? I don't believe for one second that you and the three inmates in the bunker are all there is. Eston had quite a pack of inmates following her lead. There are still some gaps that need to be filled and if you can tell me who else is involved in this, I'll hold up my end of the bargain...provided that once you provide me the information, you keep your nose clean until the end of your sentence. Sound good?" She's lying. There's no way she'd do anything she says. Keep my nose clean until the end of my sentence? I'm willing to bet that that means she'll find some sort of excuse to make sure she doesn't have to fulfill her end of the bargain before my time's up. Maybe get one of the guards to plant contraband in my locker or something similar. Then she could say I didn't do what she asked and walk away from the deal with what she'd see as a valid excuse.

"You have my answer," I say. She snorts and stands up.

"Sleep on it if you have to," Halsey says with a dismissive wave as she returns to her seat. "You're free to go." She plops back down in her chair and I stand up from mine. I glare at Halsey then turn and walk out of the room with Rashida right behind me. The door closes behind us and we start down the hallway.

* * *

Later that evening I find myself lying awake yet again. This whole process of sneaking around at night is starting to wear on me. I'm not getting enough sleep and each day I feel as though I have less and less energy. Rashida said to meet her at 1am, but right now I'm worried that if I fall asleep I'll sleep right on into morning without even realizing it. It's not quite 11pm as of now. My eyes keep opening and closing. They get heavier and heavier each time. I do end up falling asleep despite attempting to avoid it. My eyes snap open again fifteen minutes before Rashida is set to arrive.

Another troubling dream is fresh in my memory as I climb out of the bunk and start heading toward the restroom. This time it was about what Halsey told me; that phony deal she offered me. I dreamed that I for some reason accepted it and that my release date had arrived. I was free. The moment I boarded the ferry, however, I heard a gunshot and felt a searing pain in my back. Someone in one of the watchtowers had shot me dead. Less than three seconds after the round struck me I awoke. What bothers me more than the dream is the way I failed to react much to it. It feels like this is just part of the routine here, like I'm becoming numb to it.

In the restroom, I find another inmate coming out of one of the stalls. She looks half-asleep and doesn't bother to give me so much as a glance as she heads to the sink. I step into one of the stalls for a moment and wait for her to leave. After she's gone I go back out and stand at one of the sinks, splashing water on my face and rubbing at my eyes. I thought getting up and moving around might wake me up, but it's not helping much. I start back toward the dorm and right as I'm crossing the intersecting halls, Rashida calls to me.

"That you, Teymouri?" I blink a few times and turn to face her as she approaches.

"Yeah, it's me," I answer.

"You still looking to speak with Beckham?" I nod and rub my eyes.

"Yeah...yeah, let's go," I say, following her down the hallway. We exit the building and step out into the street. I glance around for a moment, looking for any sign of an approaching van.

"We're not walking all the way over there, are we?" I ask.

"No, I arranged for someone to meet us," she replies. "Just keep walking." Further down the street I hear the gates opening and see the headlights of a van approaching us. The two of us wait on the curb as it pulls up alongside us. Rashida opens the back and I step inside, sitting down on one of the benches along the interior. She shuts the doors and I'm left alone with a dim light illuminating the interior. The van does its usual stop at the gates and continues forward. Minutes tick by and it stops a second time. Rashida comes to the back of the van and opens the doors. I step out and she shuts them behind me. She approaches the driver side of the van and the driver rolls down the window.

"Take this thing over to the lot and wait there for eight minutes, then come back. Got it?" she says to the driver.

"Got it," the driver responds. It's difficult to hear, but it sounds like Fulmer, the guy we met up with after we reopened the gates in Sector S. The window rolls back up and Rashida rejoins me. She nods in the direction of the water towers and we start down the path. Something moves near the base of one of them. When I turn my head to look there's nothing there. Rashida notices me looking and shines her flashlight in the same direction.

"Did you see it too?" I ask, feeling a sense of relief.

"No, but I heard something rattle the fence," she answers, turning her light back onto the path in front of us. I glance over my shoulder for a moment and glimpse the graveyard across the street behind us. The edges of it are lit up by a series of streetlamps, but it's difficult to see much else.

"So...what did you think about Halsey's offer?" Rashida asks.

"I thought it sounded fake," I answer.

"I'm sure you don't need me to tell you it is."

"Unless you're just hellbent on getting me to help you kill her," I reply. She lets out an amused chuckle.

"Well at the very least you got to see first-hand that I was telling you the truth about her," she says.

"True..." I reply. "You sure we can pull this off? I don't know Halsey as well as you, but she sure didn't seem like she was messing around."

"Just keep doing what you're doing and leave the rest to me," she assures me. "Anything this risky has a chance of failing, but this is far from over." We walk in silence for another few minutes, until we arrive at the entrance to the bunker.

"Here we are," she says, shining her light along the doors. She unlocks them and pushes them open. I pause for a moment, staring down at the bottom of the stairs, thinking about what took place the last time I was here.

"Something wrong?" Rashida inquires.

"The body's not down there anymore, is it?" I ask. Rashida looks down the stairs and then at me.

"I doubt it. I let medical know that she was down there," Rashida says, shaking her head. "They were pretty peeved about us taking her out of the morgue in the first place. I'm sure they were eager to bring her back." With some slight hesitation, I follow her downstairs and down the hall to the cells. She unlocks the door to Naomi's cell and yanks it open. The creaking of its hinges echo throughout the hall. Inside we find Naomi sitting against the far wall. She looks up at us as we step inside. A spark of intense anger flashes in her eye and she jumps to her feet. Her eye is bloodshot and her hair is down around her shoulders. Some stray hairs are plastered to her cheek and forehead. I start toward Naomi right as she begins walking toward Rashida. She stops little more than a foot from her, staring daggers and clenching her teeth.

"Naomi, relax," I say. "I just need to talk to you for a minute." Naomi looks at my wrists, sees they aren't cuffed, and then looks back up at me.

"What's going on here?" she asks.

"I got out early," I explain. "Rashida came down to get me after about a day."

"And why would she do that?" Naomi demands, looking at Rashida, then back at me.

"She's with us," I answer. "That's why."

"Excuse me? What did you just say?" Naomi asks.

"She knows all about it," I explain. "It's a long story."

"What did I tell you about squealing, Sarita?" Naomi snarls.

"It's not like that!" I argue. "Halsey's hot on our trail, we won't get out of here without Rashida's help. We have a deal, I promise this isn't as bad as it looks."

"I don't know, Sarita, this looks pretty bad to me," Naomi snorts.

"Halsey tried to make a deal with me earlier today," I explain. "She knows that you, Tia, and Ariana are plotting an escape, but she doesn't have any other details. She wants me to give her names and other information. That's how serious this is. We need all the help we can get."

"I sure hope you said no to Halsey," Naomi replies.

"Of course I did! I'm not going to throw anyone under the bus for anything she promises!" I say.

"How do you know this one here isn't spying for her?" Naomi demands, pointing at Rashida. "Maybe this is part of Halsey's little game to get what she wants, regardless of whether or not you cooperate with her."

"Halsey and I haven't been on friendly terms for many years," Rashida cuts in. "Like I told Teymouri, I want off this island too and working with Halsey would only jeopardize that."

"Yeah, like I'm gonna believe you!" Naomi retorts.

"It's true, Naomi, I saw them come to blows over something that happened in my cell," I insist. "Leah's onboard with this arrangement, she had a similar reaction when I first told her too."

"I would've expected her to use better judgment," Naomi mutters. "Great...fine, I guess this is what we're doing now. Did Leah finish... well...did she do what I asked of her?"

"She has everything taken care of," I nod. Naomi glances at Rashida, then back at me.

"You tell Leah that she'd better be watching what she does out there," she growls. "If this all turns out to be for nothing, I swear to God I'll carve her up worse than Parsons. One chance is all we get. You know that and so does she. I still don't like the idea of discussing this in front of...well, her..." She gestures at Rashida as she finishes speaking. "Let alone her being apart of it. But if she's aware of everything, then I guess there's no backing out."

"If Rashida wasn't around to help we'd be screwed anyway," I reply. "Just trust me on this. Trust Leah. We have it all under control."

"Besides agreeing to bring a guard into this, what else has Leah agreed to?" she asks. "Anything I should be aware of?"

"Since Tia and Ariana are down here with you, we brought Rochelle and Savannah on board," I explain. "Savannah's with us on this, but Rochelle's still thinking it over for about twelve more hours."

"What's holding her back?" Naomi asks.

"She's scared," I reply. "Scared of what will happen if this doesn't work, of what will happen if it does. I think she knows as well as anyone that life as fugitives won't be easy."

"It won't be," Naomi agrees, shaking her head. "Just do whatever you can to try and get her to join up with us. It'll be too difficult to find someone else in such a short span of time."

"I'll do what I can," I answer. "One other thing. Since Mika's dead there's another member we're looking to take on, but Leah wanted a second opinion first."

"You're joking, right?" Naomi snorts. "Seriously? She just gives the go-ahead on a guard, but when she wants a replacement for Mika, that's when she wants a second opinion? Unbelievable. Whatever...who is it?"

"Jackie. She's not someone I know very well. We rode here on the same bus, we were held in the same facility for a while, that sort of thing. Other than that we've barely spoken."

"Sounds promising," Naomi snorts, looking away for a moment.

"She's the best chance we have and she's where we need her to be, same as Mika," I respond.

"There's no one else in the same location?" Naomi asks. "No one at all? You can't think of any names?"

"No, none," I say, shaking my head. "Jackie and I may not have much of a history, but it seems better than trying to start from scratch when we're in a hurry."

"Wrap it up, you two," Rashida cuts in. "Can't be here much longer."

"Well then try talking to her, see what she says," Naomi answers. "I hope you know what you're doing, because if that girl can't be trusted it...wait...why can't she do it?" Naomi asks, gesturing at Rashida.

"Do what?" Rashida asks.

"Records, we need to get into the records building," I answer. "We need a few discs out of there."

"Halsey's the only one allowed in that room," Rashida answers. "She doesn't even trust me to be in there. Good luck getting in, though. Only key that opens that door is Halsey's skeleton key. Somehow I think you both know she keeps it on her person at all times."

"We have it covered," I reply.

"Could be a good way to prove you're on our side," Naomi suggests. Rashida shakes her head.

"It's a little more complicated than that," Rashida says. "Assuming you do have a way to get around the problem of opening the door, and I trust you do, there are still other factors at play that could jeopardize the plan."

"Great, so we recruited a useless guard," Naomi mutters.

"I would do it if it were possible," Rashida insists. "Unfortunately I've become a potential target for the other guards and I'm being watched closer than usual. I broke away from them a few years ago and things have only gotten worse after pulling a few strings to assist you. If I'm seen going into the records building, and trust me someone will see it, it will get back to Halsey, and whatever you want removed would be noticed within a short period of time."

"Can't you get the surveillance footage erased or something?" I ask. "Just walk in, get it, erase the footage, no one has to know." She shakes her head.

"The building is closely monitored all hours of the day and night and there are two watchtowers near the building, both of which are tasked with keeping a close eye on that building. The towers are equipped with spotlights and the area in front of the entrance is well lit. Only medical staff are allowed in there," Rashida explains. "Before anyone goes inside, medical radios the watchtowers near the building to let them know who to expect and when. If the towers spot someone going in without a heads-up, they'll report it to medical and if they don't know anything about it, Halsey gets involved."

"Great, I guess we're doing this the hard way," Naomi groans. "Sarita, when you leave you need to make sure you get this Jackie gal to help out and if you can't for some reason, you bust your ass to find someone else and you do whatever you can to make this work, because we cannot leave without the discs we need."

"I'll make sure it happens," I say. "One way or another."

"Come on, Teymouri. Your time's up," Rashida says. She beckons for me to follow her. We step out into the hallway and Naomi approaches the door.

"So, what then?" Naomi asks. "I'm just getting left down here?"

"Sorry, kid," Rashida replies, turning to face her in the doorway. "Nothing I can do at the moment."

"Can you at least try to do something?" I ask. "They've all been down here long enough." Rashida looks back at Naomi. Her gaze moves to the floor and then back at her.

"Come here, Beckham. I have an idea," she says. Naomi steps out into the hallway and stands next to me.

"What's your idea?" Naomi asks. Rashida closes Naomi's cell and moves to another one. She opens it up and the three of us glimpse Ariana lying on the floor. She grunts and sits up, blinking several times.

"We getting out?" she asks, spotting me and Naomi.

"Not yet," Rashida answers. "Come on, get up. Get out here." Ariana stands up with a confused expression and stumbles out the door.

"If we're not getting out, then what's happening?" Naomi asks.

"Since I can't take you out of here, I'm going to put you three in the same cell," Rashida explains. "I've got a few other guards I can convince to help cover this up. I'll have one of them take over with bringing food down here. I'll have them deliver it to the one cell. Hopefully that'll make it a little easier on you. I'll arrange for the same person bringing you your food to come let you out when it's time." She opens Tia's cell and finds her just behind the door, appearing to have been listening.

"What's going on?" Tia asks.

"Moving you all to one cell," Rashida answers. "Down the hall to the larger one." She unlocks the cell I was in a short time ago and directs the others to step inside. Once they're all in, she starts closing the door.

"One sec," Naomi says, rushing up to the door. Rashida opens it up a bit and Naomi pokes her head out. "Sarita...good luck out there. We're trusting you and Leah to make this work."

"Thanks. We won't let you down," I say. She nods and steps back into the cell. The door closes and Rashida and I head back up the stairs.

Chapter 18

Living with a Ghost

Back in the dorm I lie awake thinking about what took place a short time before. 6am arrives in what feels like record time. It seems as though I've only just closed my eyes when the guards charge in and start shouting for us to get up and stand at attention. I notice Rochelle standing several bunks down. I'm running out of time to speak with her and I haven't even tried to do so yet. The guards finish their usual routine for the day and we're released to the chow hall. In the chaos of the crowd I end up losing sight of Rochelle. While still searching for her, Savannah approaches from behind.

"Morning," she says, giving a small wave as she catches up with me.

"Morning," I reply. "Did you happen to see which way Rochelle went?"

"Yeah, toward the chow hall," she says with a mischievous grin.

"This is serious. I need to talk to her as soon as possible," I say. "She hasn't said whether she's in or out yet."

"I talked to her a little after dinner last night," she says. "She's still thinking things over, but she hasn't said much else."

"Well she did say she didn't want either of us trying to influence her decision," I point out as we reach the opposite side of the street.

"Then why are you?" she asks.

"Why were you?"

"I wasn't trying to influence anything, I was just listening to what she had to say," she argues.

"And how do you know that wasn't my intention?" I counter. She shrugs.

"Because you seem like there's a sense of urgency, like you feel like you need to sway her or something. It's just the way you said you were looking for her."

"I asked you where she was going," I counter.

"You know what I mean," she groans. "I'm just reminding you not to push her. Fine, sit and chat with her a bit, but don't pressure her into this."

"Maybe that's what she needs, though," I argue. "I was scared at first too. I still am. I imagine I will be for a long time, but...the idea of dying here, of staying here long enough to allow it to ruin me...that scares me more than anything. I just don't want her to be left behind."

"Neither do I, but there's no denying the seriousness of this," Savannah says. "It's not just that we might get caught, but everything that follows if this succeeds." She's right. Getting caught will also increase the amount of time we're stuck here. We'll be put under lockdown, we'll be seen as high risk and stuck down in the bunker for only God knows how long. Regardless of anything Halsey might do, someone is going to report us missing from the island. They'll figure it out, they'll know we left. Then what? Live the rest of our lives on the run?

"You know...the more I think about this whole thing, the crazier it seems," I say, stepping through the doors of the main building. "I mean...even if we do get out, even if the rest of this goes the way we want...we can't just go straight home and act like nothing happened."

"I've been thinking about that too," Savannah replies, rubbing one of her eyes. "It's a lot to consider." I can just imagine it. Me hitching a bus back to California, dropping in on my family and then having the cops break the door down ten minutes later, dragging us all outside.

"I don't know about you, but my home's a long way from here," I say, cracking a few knuckles out of nerves. "It'd take me days to get back. Maybe a week, I don't know. I never thought I'd have to do something like this. When you think about it, it seems pretty terrifying."

"Rochelle's likely thinking the same thing," Savannah says as we enter the chow hall. "This doesn't end with an escape." Standing in line a few moments later, I take some time to mull things over. Savannah's right. This doesn't end until McGinley's is shut down, until we expose this place for what it is, and even beyond that. I'm starting to see why it might be tempting to just try and ride this place out, even with as terrible as it is. Finishing a sentence here at least means you get to go home and move on with your life. Still...what's the point of going back home if you're not yourself anymore? If that happens then I might as well be dead.

And what about all the other inmates here? It just doesn't feel fair that we have to be the trailblazers, the ones to stand up against what feels like impossible odds, and when all is said and done, it could all be for nothing. Atrocities have taken place all over this country for decades, centuries. The routine is always the same. A brief moment of outrage followed by damage control and another tragedy swept under the rug, lost to time and the truth twisted to diminish what took place. We could end up as another forgotten story that fades from the mind of the public over the course of a few years.

Minutes later I'm sitting at a table with Rochelle and Savannah. Rochelle has a somber expression on her face, staring down at her tray with her cheek resting on her fist. Savannah gives me a look that seems to warn me not to cross a line with Rochelle. She then turns her attention to the food in front of her while I sit in silence, wondering how I should start things off. Rochelle notices me looking at her and I avert my gaze. She takes a deep breath and lets her arm rest on the table in front of her. When I look back at her, I see that her eyes are still on me.

"Something on your mind, Sarita?" she asks. I look down at my tray and take a bite of food. An awkward silence hangs between us.

"It's just about been a day," I say. "Just wasn't sure what was going on with you." She lets out a sigh and starts eating.

"I said I didn't want anyone trying to push me," Rochelle reminds me, swallowing a piece of bread. "And to be honest, I still haven't decided."

"Well Leah's gonna want an answer soon," I point out. She rolls her eyes.

"I don't give a damn what Leah wants," she groans. "I'm thinking about what I want. And if I'm being honest, I don't want to be here anymore. Something's...something's not right." She continues eating, staring down at her tray while Savannah and I glance at one another.

"Care to explain?" I ask. Rochelle looks up at me for a moment, then back down at her tray.

"It doesn't matter, I just...I don't like it here," she says. "No one does. That's all it is. I want to go home."

"We can't go home, though," Savannah contends. "We'll be fugitives."

"You know what I mean," Rochelle sighs. "I just thought I was immune...because I was naive and didn't listen to her."

"To who?" I ask.

"My sister," Rochelle replies. "She tried to escape less than a month after she got here. It screwed up the rest of her sentence. She talked about everything they did to her and I just thought that that was the real reason she wasn't right when she came back. I thought if I just listened to her, kept my head down, then nothing could touch me. Yeah, I knew I'd be homesick, that's not surprising, but what does surprise me is waking up to headless inmates stumbling around near my bed. She told me this place was haunted, but I just thought it was in her head! Now I'm sitting here wondering if maybe I'm losing my mind. I mean...when that happens do you even know it?"

"Hard to say," Savannah shrugs.

"I looked this place up before I came here, before I was even in trouble," Rochelle continues. "I just have a morbid curiosity, you know? I wanted to see what I could find. I wanted to know why Tanisha was holding conversations with herself in the middle of the night, and why she tried three times to kill herself. First she tries to overdose, next she tries hanging herself and the belt snaps, and the third one she just left for me to find. After the first attempt I started checking on her during the night. So one night, when she tried the third time, I come into her room and she's lying there on the floor with a knife in her hand and a gash in her neck. Didn't cut deep enough and lived, but still...had to wait there with her until the ambulance arrived, blood all over the place, scared to death the entire time. You see what I mean? I don't want this plan to go south and have all of that happen to me."

"More than understandable," Savannah says. "Sounds terrible."

"Terrible is an understatement," Rochelle says. "As for looking this place up, never once did I see anything about anyone getting decapitated. But even though I didn't find any record of something like that, I just...I keep thinking...they didn't release everything to the public, we don't even know what happened to half the inmates who died here over the years. My sister is pretty much one of them. It's like she never came home. When I spoke to her, I could tell there was still some of her in there, but...she just wasn't the same person anymore. It's like living with a ghost. They're gone, but you still see them around. And the bottom line here is that I'm scared. But even more than that, I'd like to watch this place go down. I'd like to see Halsey and her accomplices get what they deserve." Rochelle picks at her food and takes a deep breath. She exhales and looks me in the eye.

"So what do you want to do?" I ask.

"Count me in," she says.

* * *

During the time that I'm in the chow hall I never once catch sight of Leah anywhere. Savannah, Rochelle, and I all make our way out to the track and spot Leah sitting on the bleachers. She notices us approaching and gives a subtle nod to her left. It takes me a minute, but I realize she's telling us to sit nearby. There must be guards watching. The three of us sit down behind her and she buries her face in her hands.

"Sarita, stand up and face the other two," she instructs. "That jackass in the watchtower's been more attentive than usual today. Just make it look like you're ignoring me and talking to them. I'm going to get up and start around the track. Count to one-hundred and follow me onto the track with the other two. Stay a few feet behind me, none of you talk until we round the bend and have our backs to the tower." She stands up and walks toward the track without so much as glancing at any of us. Ten seconds in, I stand up and face the others with my back to the tower.

"Now what?" Rochelle asks. "We just sit here and wait?"

"Something like that," I answer, trying my best to keep track of the seconds. Fifteen, sixteen, seventeen, eighteen.

"I hope she's not just screwing with us," Rochelle continues, leaning forward with her chin resting on her palms, elbows on her knees.

"She knows what she's doing," I assure them. Twenty-three, twenty-four, twenty-five... "Rochelle, are you sure you want to do this? There's no backing out once you give Leah your answer." She nods.

"I'm sure," she answers. Thirty-five, thirty-six... I keep counting in my head up until Savannah interrupts me at eighty-eight.

"Should be just about time to head onto the track, right?" Savannah asks. From her position she should be able to see Leah without creating any suspicion.

"She almost back?" I ask Savannah.

"Yeah, not much longer," she replies. Rochelle stands up and I turn and walk toward the track. The three of us follow after Leah and maintain the distance she instructed us to give. After we turn the corner and start heading away from the tower, Leah speaks up.

"All right, straight to the point, let's make this quick," Leah says, clearing her throat. "Rochelle are you in or out?"

"I'm in," she answers.

"Sarita, did you speak with Naomi?" Leah continues.

"Yes, I ran the whole thing with Jackie by her," I reply. "We're to move forward with that right away. I told her about Rashida and that she's working with us. Wasn't too thrilled, but she's more or less on board with it."

"Good," Leah says. "Find Jackie as soon as you can and have a word with her. Report back to me as soon as you have an answer, whether it's a yes or a no."

"Got it," I reply.

"Good," Leah replies. "Now walk a couple more laps. Do whatever you want from there. Savannah and Rochelle, I'll speak with you at lunch. I'll fill you in on what you need to do. Don't forget." We come around the curve in the track and Leah walks off toward the bleachers.

Chapter 19

New Recruit

When the lunch hour arrives, a similar process that took place during the breakfast hour begins to unfold. Rochelle and Savannah break off to find Leah while I keep an eye out for Jackie. I spot her in line and go about my usual routine with my tray in hand. Once she leaves the line, I watch where she goes and see her plop down at one of the tables near the far wall. As soon as I reach the end of the line, I start toward her. She looks up at me as I approach and I sit down across from her.

"Hey, you got a minute?" I ask. She gives me a confused look.

"Yeah, I guess..." she murmurs. "Um...I know you, but I don't know your name."

"Sarita," I answer.

"Jackie," she replies.

"I remember," I say.

"Well now I feel like an asshole," she chuckles. "Never been good with names. I almost called you 'Rita'."

"It's not a big deal," I assure her. "Rita's fine if you want. I won't complain."

"I'll keep that in mind," she says, taking a bite of food. "What brings you here? Haven't spoken to you since before we got on the bus. I thought you didn't want to talk to me or something."

"And now it's my turn to feel like an asshole," I reply with a weak smile. "Let's just say I didn't come by just to chat." She swallows her food and looks me in the eye.

"So you want something from me, don't you?" she surmises. I give a nervous smile and nod.

"Yeah..." I murmur.

"I've seen you with that Naomi girl a few times," she continues. "Watched that whole stunt with Halsey's keys play out in here the other day."

"I'm just gonna come out and say it," I say. "Do you want to get out of here? That's what the thing with the keys was the other day." She snorts and lets out a derisive laugh.

"Yeah, sure, I'll run down the hall and play keep away with a key ring, that sounds great," she mocks. "Are you serious?"

"It's more complicated than that," I explain. "I can't tell you what was going on with the keys just yet, but it wasn't a pitiful attempt at escaping."

"Sure looked like it."

"It was suppose to look like that, there was...just forget it, do you want out of here or not?"

"Are you serious about this?" she asks. "You guys are really going to do it?"

"Yes and that stays between you and me whether you join us or not, understand?"

"Whoa, relax, I'm not going to tell anyone," she assures me. "Honestly you came by at a good time. I'm sick of being forced to work in the infirmary. I don't know what's wrong with me, maybe hypochondria or something? You know what I mean? Sick inmates come in there and then I start freaking out about getting what they have and now we have something the guards are calling "gladiator fights"[20] coming up and that means a ton of inmates showing up with only God knows what kinds of injuries. I can't deal with it anymore."

"Can you deal with it long enough to help out?" I ask.

"I suppose," she shrugs. "I'm kind of irritated, though. Complete radio silence from you for months and then you just pop in and ask for my help out of nowhere."

"Yeah, I know, it's...kinda-"

"Messed up?" Jackie finishes. "Look, I'll help, but only because I

---

[20]Inmates and correctional staff in various U.S. prisons have come forward in the past to report that guards have sometimes forced inmates into "gladiator-style" fights with one another. The guards have reportedly placed bets and even cheered the combatants on. Some of these fights have allegedly involved fatalities.

want out out of here. Now what do you need?"

"We need you to access the records room," I explain. "Do you know where that is?"

"Yeah, it's by the morgue," she replies. "Staff gave me and the rest of the medical assistants a tour that includes that. They mentioned something about the possibility of having to wheel dead bodies down there if anyone happens to croak while I'm here. Not looking forward to that. Especially with what's happening here soon."

"You mean those "gladiator fights" you mentioned?" I inquire. She nods.

"You know what that is?" she asks.

"No," I say, shaking my head.

"I heard some of the guards talking about it while I was working about a week ago," she explains. "All I know is that it's some thing where they force inmates to fight one another, the guards place bets on the inmates, and it's going to be in the middle of the night. If I were you I'd keep on your guard in the dorm. I have no idea how they decide who they force to fight."

"So you think I might be targeted for this?" I ask. "Why?"

"I could be way off, but I'm just warning you since you pulled that stunt with Halsey's keys. That alone labels you a fighter to some extent. If I was looking for people to force into a fight, you and Naomi would be two potential candidates."

"Great...that's comforting," I murmur. I hope she's not serious. I've never considered myself to be much of a fighter. To this day I'm still surprised that I lived through the one that sent me here. I'm always terrified in each one I get dragged into.

"So...how are you expecting me to get into the records room?" she asks. "It's locked up tight and I have no reason to be over there. Well... for now at least."

"Wait, do people die in these gladiator things?"

"I have no idea," she says with a shrug. "There is a graveyard here, so maybe that's how some of them died. They made it sound like it was something they do every so often. Once a month I think. But they'd want the inmates to live, right? Bet on them again?" She's right. Having inmates die in fights would just attract attention that Halsey doesn't want. Come to think of it...how is Leah planning to give Jackie an excuse to go down to records?

"I see," I say. "Just keep your head down for the time being, don't do anything to call attention to yourself. I need to go speak with one of the others and let her know that you're with us. Either me or Leah will come find you soon and give you further instructions."

"And who's Leah?" she asks.

"She's about my height, brown complexion, matching eyes, black wavy hair."

"That doesn't really narrow it down much," she sighs. "Can you give me anything else?"

"She's sort of got this perma-scowl thing going on," I answer. "She has a low raspy voice, bushy eyebrows, and there's a spot on one eyebrow where it looks like she got cut or something. Sort of an oval shaped face, ears that stick out a little. She's missing the nail on her left thumb too."

"That helps," she says. "I'll keep an eye out for her."

* * *

Later that same day I pass on what I've learned about Jackie. Leah's happy to hear it, but took to warning me a second time that I'd better be certain that Jackie is trustworthy. Seems like the closer we get to the date of the actual escape, the more on edge she becomes. I would hear soon after that that she instructed Savannah on what to do in order to take over Tia's duties. She didn't go into too much detail, and when I asked her about the gladiator fights, she told me not to worry about it and refused to answer any questions. It's obvious to anyone that she's planning something and it has to involve the fights. Frustrates me to no end when she clams up about what she's planning. She must be expecting that someone might die in the fights, but that seems to go against what Jackie said about it. Maybe it depends on who's involved?

Later that night I find myself having trouble sleeping again. It's something I've grown used to. For one fleeting moment I think of how nice it will be to go home and sleep in my own bed when we get out. The thought quickly evaporates as I come to terms with the reality of the situation. After what feels like an eternity, I manage to doze off. My dreams are strange at best. I'm walking along the street somewhere in my hometown. The color is drained from both the people and the landscape. It's as if I've stepped into an old photograph. Next the world melts away and I'm pulled back to reality by the sensation of the bunk trembling.

I sit upright and look down the sides and over the end of the bunk, seeing no sign that anyone is nearby. My first thought is that the girl below me must be moving around in her sleep. I lie back down and before I have a chance to drift off I feel the bunk move for a second time. This time it feels like someone deliberately shook the end of it and that's where I look first. Again there's no sign of anyone. I know I felt the bunk move, but part of me is beginning to wonder if I'm imagining it. As I'm turning to lie back down I spot Helena sitting just behind me, smiling maliciously. Before I can react she grabs me and hurls me off the end of the bed. I let out a yelp and land on the floor with a thud. It's difficult to see her in the darkness, but Helena is standing over me. Her eyes burning into mine. I blink a few times and she fades away in front of me. My fall woke a few people up and now they're sitting up and looking around. I curse a few times and get to my feet, holding my shoulder as I do so.

"What happened?" my bunk-mate mumbles, sitting up and looking at me.

"I think she fell," someone behind me says.

"Sarita?" says a familiar voice. I turn to see Jackie walking toward me. Half asleep and squinting. The lights flick on and two guards come into the room. Everyone who's awake by this point groans and clamps their eyes shut.

"What's going on in here?" the first guard demands. "What are you doing out of bed?"

"Someone fell out of their bunk," someone says.

"Was it you?" the same guard inquires, pointing at me. I nod.

"And how did you manage that?" the second guard demands, glaring at me.

"I was moving around in my sleep," I explain.

"You look fine to me," the second guard says. "Get back in your bunk and go to sleep."

"Hold still for a sec," Jackie orders, examining my shoulder. She asks me what I'm feeling and I tell her everything.

"I broke something, didn't I?" I say. Jackie shakes her head.

"I don't think so," she answers. "They'll have to x-ray it to be sure. It's most likely just bruised."

"All right, that's enough chitchat you two," the first guard cuts in. "Now get back in your bunks."

"She needs to go to the infirmary," Jackie argues. "She injured her shoulder."

"Sounds like a personal problem," the second guard replies. "Now get back in bed." He uses his baton to point at the nearest bunk.

"She needs medical attention," Jackie persists.

"I'm not walking some brat all the way down there over something so minor, now do what I tell you to and go back to sleep! That goes for everyone in this room!" He points at several inmates all standing around watching.

"I'll take her," Jackie says. "It'll just be a quick walk there and back."

"Quit arguing and get back in bed!" the first guard growls.

"It's my job," Jackie insists. "I'm a medical assistant. Part of my job is escorting inmates to the infirmary and it doesn't matter what time of day."

"You expect us to believe that?" the first guard snorts, starting toward Jackie. The second guard holds out his arm to stop him.

"Hold on a minute. I've seen her in there a few times," he says. "She's telling the truth."

"I don't care if she's telling the truth or not, she needs to listen and not argue with us!" the first guard snarls.

"I don't need the medical staff giving me grief," the second guard cuts in. "Just let her go or else I'll never hear the end of it." The first guard glares at Jackie and then nods in the direction of the door.

"Fine...get moving before I change my mind," he says. "And stay out of trouble. I'll be letting the medical staff know you're coming." Jackie gives him a frustrated look and leads me past him. Both of us remain silent until we step out into the hallway. Once we're out of earshot Jackie turns to me.

"What happened in there?" she asks.

"Nothing...sleepwalking..." I murmur, keeping my eyes forward.

"You sure that's all it was?" she inquires.

"It was nothing, okay?" I insist. She shakes her head and looks away for a moment. A sense of guilt washes over me and I glance at her, then back down at my feet.

"I'm sorry..." I apologize. "I just have a lot on my mind."

"It's fine...I get it," she says, still avoiding eye contact.

"I didn't mean to-"

"No, really, it's fine," she interrupts. "I'm not doing so great myself. Can't sleep to save my life ever since that fight broke out. I keep waking up thinking I heard something. Like someone's gonna jump me again if I'm not on guard. Tons of fun."

"I'm not trying to use you," I declare. "Just so you know."

"I know, Sarita," she sighs. "Look...I don't have anyone here I can rely on. You got those other two you're always with. It's hard to get through this kind of thing on your own and it's starting to take a toll on me. I'm glad you're asking me to help out, but I just hate it when people come to me for something, they take whatever it is, and then they run off, like I'm just some soulless vending machine. Starts to get old after a while. It's the whole reason I came here in the first place."

"What happened?" I ask.

"Lot of things," she responds. "Lot of fakers and takers. Users. And my idiot cousin was no different. I don't understand why I do the things I do. I help people with something and I get the short end of the stick... and it better not happen this time."

"We're not exactly a group of friends," I say. "We're just inmates with a common interest."

"Like I said, it's not about friends, friends are for the outside. It's about people looking at other human beings as tools, things to use and discard," she continues. "And that's the kind of person my cousin Eirlys is. A user."

"What happened?" I ask.

"A lot of little things that led to something bigger," she replies. "I used to look up to her. When I was little she seemed almost like the cool big sis I never had. You know? I'm an only child, but Eirlys and I were together all the time since we lived in the same neighborhood. She was the one person I could always depend on. Then one day she asks me for a favor and I said sure, whatever you want. I never should have done it. I didn't even know she had a gun. I mean...I suspected it, but I never saw it."

"What did she do?" I ask.

"Eirlys started out a good person...or at least I thought she was," Jackie says. "But somewhere along the way the Eirlys I knew disappeared. Instead I had this version of her I barely recognized. Things in her life were always rocky, especially at home, but she took a turn for the worse after her parents got divorced. It was this big pile of drama that'd been building up for years. Caused her a ton of stress. I didn't see her for a while. Left town with her father, her mother went only God knows where, I never asked. It was three years before I saw her again, and about six months before we both got arrested."

"What for?"

"It's a long story," she says. "The gist of it is that she had some friend who stole something from her, a family heirloom, and wouldn't give it back. It was something her grandmother gave her, a ring. Meant a lot to her. She'd been over at this friend's house and left there the same night they got into this big fight. Turns out her "friend" was a pretty shady character. Part of a group of people she'd gotten caught up with. Drug deals and use were involved. The so-called friend stole the ring and Eirlys had confronted her about it before she got run out by one of the other people living there. He brandished a gun at her. She didn't tell me anything about these people, didn't tell me anything except that her ring had been stolen. Somehow she talked me into helping her break into the house on a night the friend was supposed to be out of town, so we could get the ring back. Turned out the friend's roommate, the one who threatened to shoot her, was still there. He shot at us and Eirlys fired back, killed him. And the next day we were both arrested for murder. She went to prison, I got sent here."

"That's messed up," I say.

"What's messed up is the way I let her manipulate me into doing it," she mutters. "I knew it was stupid, I had better judgment than that. So yeah...she used me to get what she wanted, and what she sure as hell lost now that she's in prison...and I never got an apology or anything. We were held in the same facility for a while. She avoided me like the plague."

"I see..." I say. "I'm sorry."

"It's not your fault," she says with a dismissive wave. "People are terrible. And sometimes those people are family. We're here, by the way." She gestures at the doors and I walk up to them. She remains standing a few feet away and I look back at her.

"Thanks," I say. "I appreciate it. Sticking up for me and walking me down here." She gives a weak smile.

"You're welcome," she murmurs. "I'm gonna get back before they decide I've been gone too long. See ya around, I guess." She gives a half-hearted wave and starts walking away. I turn back toward the doors and something to my left catches my eye. Watching me from beneath a nearby streetlight is Helena...

Chapter 20

Fight Night

My time in the infirmary was short-lived. An x-ray of my shoulder showed that nothing was broken. After that I was released and sent back to my dorm. When it comes time for breakfast, I lag behind the other inmates as they make their way to the chow hall. Instead of following everyone else, I start toward the restroom and run into Rashida halfway there.

"There you are," she says, leading me back toward a room I just passed. "Come on, we need to talk."

"What? What's going on?" I ask as she leads me through the doorway. She closes the door behind us and stands in front of it. She takes something from her pocket and tosses it to me. It's a key. A roughly cut one. It must be the one Leah made in the shop.

"Where did you get this?" I demand. "Why do you have it?"

"I found it in the shop," she says. "There was a search conducted in there this morning. I don't know if it had anything to do with Halsey's suspicions, but it was sheer luck that I happened to find it. Be sure to hide that thing and make sure this doesn't happen again. There's no way I'll be that lucky twice." She turns and exits the room before I have a chance to say anything else. I pocket the key, head to the restroom, and then start toward the chow hall. I need to find Leah as soon as I can and let her know what just happened. To say we dodged a bullet would be a huge understatement.

Right as I enter the chow hall I spot Leah in line at the counter and watch to see where she sits down. Once I have my tray I make my way to meet her. When I tell her about the key, as well as who found it, her eyes widen in surprise and I pass it back to her under the table. She thanks me and tells me she's surprised it was discovered. Before she leaves, Leah explains she's got a new place in mind for hiding the key and that she's heading there. Later that evening, just after the dinner rush, Savannah, Rochelle, and I find ourselves cleaning the floors and tables in the chow hall. I felt relieved to find out that Nicole was supervising us for the first time in a while.

"Wait...what happened?" I ask. We're all about ten minutes into a conversation with Nicole. Up until now it's been a lot of minor things. Rumors, checking up on us, the usual. Now she's dropped something unexpected on me.

"You heard me," she says, folding her newspaper. "Your judge is under investigation."

"Why?" I ask.

"Bribes, kickbacks, that sort of thing," she answers. "Been going on for years, the judges and other officials tied to this and all the other places like it. I'm amazed someone finally caught one of them."

"What do you mean?" I ask.

"I mean that there's more than just McGinley's and this guy was taking kickbacks related to some of the cases at other facilities."

"I think I've heard something about that before," Rochelle says. "Something about how there were a few reform schools like this one where they've been sending people off for trivial reasons."

"What do you mean by trivial?" Savannah asks, dunking her mop in its bucket. Rochelle sits down at one of the tables, facing away from it.

"Incorrigibility, getting into fights with their parents, school pranks, just stupid stuff like that," Rochelle explains.

"Where was this happening?" Savannah asks.

"I don't remember," Rochelle admits with a shrug. "It was like five states where they were doing it. Do you remember, Nicole?" Nicole shakes her head.

"Just that three of them were east of the Mississippi," she says. "They're all owned by the same company that runs this place. Part of a network of such places, originally built to provide an alternative to prison for minors. Or so they said. Didn't take them long to start gutting everything."

"Like how this place used to have classrooms?" I ask.

"Exactly," Nicole nods. "McGinley's is supposed to be where the worst of the worst are kept, so to speak. But I dunno...you three don't seem like vicious demons to me."

"I imagine the public sees us that way," I snort. "Media made damn sure to paint me in a negative light. The murderous, knife-wielding refugee! Hide your kids, she's coming for you next! I don't even want to think about it..."

"And that's how they placate the public," Nicole says with a sigh. "All that law and order shit. Yeah, there needs to be order for a society to function, but this...this is just wrong." She holds out both arms, gesturing at the entire room. "This isn't how you rehabilitate people. Instead the public is led to believe that evil lives here, they happily vote against helpful measures, and support legislation that doesn't help anyone in any of these reform schools. Yeah, let's ruin the minds of kids, send them back out into society, expect them to function without giving them the tools they need for it, and then drag them on back when they can't get their footing. That'll fix everything."

"So what happened with the judge?" I ask.

"Same thing that happens when any rich, powerful person gets arrested," Nicole snorts. "He's out on bail, which I'm sure was a drop in the bucket after all the money he took. Looks like he's in for a hell of a ride, though. Some pretty damning evidence from the sound of it. We'll see what happens, but I'm not holding my breath. With an attorney like yours, Sarita, I'm surprised she didn't have you go to trial. You might've stood a pretty good chance."

"Wait, my attorney was apart of this?" I ask, walking toward her. Nicole shows me the article in the paper. I snatch it up and read through it. Sure enough, my attorney is mentioned a handful of times. I wrinkle my nose at the mention of her name.

"Wow...that useless bitch surprised me," I mutter, handing the paper back to Nicole.

"Your attorney?" Rochelle asks.

"Yeah, she was no help at all back when I was sitting in jail," I answer. "All she did was keep trying to convince me to take the plea deal until I finally felt like I didn't have a choice."

"Mine did the same thing," Savannah says, ringing out her mop.

"How about you, Rochelle?"

"Yep. I got the same thing," Rochelle sighs. "I guess in the grand scheme of things it made some legal sense...but I never felt right about it."

"Neither did I," I add. "I was just afraid of what would happen if I lost."

"I think we all were," Rochelle says.

"Two years here or a hell of a lot more in prison," Savannah adds. "It's enough to scare a lot of people into just taking the plea deal." After our shift ends, Rochelle, Savannah, and I all start packing things up and getting ready to head back to the dorm for the night. Nicole walks back to the storage closet and watches to make sure everything gets put back. After walking into the dorm, I tell Rochelle and Savannah that I need to lay down for a minute. The day's been a long one and I feel dead on my feet. As soon as I climb up on my bunk, I sprawl out on my back as usual. Despite feeling as tired as I do, I don't feel like I'll fall asleep anytime soon. My eyes have that tired, itchy feel to them, but that's about it. Minutes later I'm surprised by an impromptu visit from Leah. Right as she approaches my bunk, she slaps the side of it and calls up to me. "Wake up, Sarita," she orders. "I'll be by the door." I just want to relax for once on this miserable island. I'm exhausted, why does she have to show up now? I crawl down the side of the bunk, grumbling under my breath. I walk over to the doorway and see Leah standing with Rochelle and Savannah. She sees me coming and catches my eye, followed by a subtle nod.

"What's going on?" I murmur, rubbing one of my eyes as I speak.

"We're having some issues with Savannah's role in this," Leah explains. "Ginoza doesn't trust her as much as Tia."

"And Ginoza is...?" I ask, my voice trailing off.

"She's one of the inmates here who's more in the know than others," Leah explains. "She's not apart of the plan, but she does have connections. It took some time for Tia to build up her trust to get more valuable info out of her, but at the moment she's limiting what she's telling Savannah."

"So our intel line is shot?" I ask.

"Not shot, but it is hindered at the moment," Leah answers. "The main problem, other than Ginoza's trust level, is that we're having trouble confirming something. She doesn't like me at all, so I can't just ask her myself, and it's too late in the day to keep prying."

"What about?" I ask.

"The gladiator fights," Leah says. "They're fights that-"

"Yeah, Jackie told me about it," I interrupt.

"Good, that makes this easier," Leah replies. "The guards are going to be making their rounds tonight around midnight, looking for participants to force into the ring. Sarita, I want you to be outside the dorm no later than eleven forty-five. You need to go find somewhere to hide and be sure you don't get caught."

"And where am I supposed to go?" I ask. "The restroom down the hall's pretty much the only place I can get to."

"There are storage rooms around here too, some of them should be unlocked," Leah explains, handing me a kite. "Look this over and make sure you know where everything is. Destroy it once you're done with it."

"How long are they going to be looking for me?" I ask, taking the kite from her. "Fifteen minutes? Thirty? More?"

"Don't go back into the dorm until at least twelve-thirty," Leah answers. "Things should settle down by then. They'll have moved on and started making their way over to the fight on the other side of the island. The fight should be at the intake center as usual. They'll need time to get there and back, on top of however long the fights go on for."

"What about us?" Rochelle asks. "Should Savannah and I be concerned?" Leah shakes her head.

"I don't think either of you need to worry," she answers, "Neither of you have been in any fights or anything, right?"

"No, never," Savannah says. "Not here, anyway."

"That's generally what they're looking for," Leah says. "Inmates with reputations for fighting. If you aren't one of them, it's unlikely that they'll drag you along."

"Good to know," Savannah says, sounding relieved.

"Doesn't mean I'll sleep any easier," Rochelle says, looking away for a moment.

"It would be best to be on guard tonight regardless," Leah warns. "Your affiliation with Sarita might be a reason to take you along, but that's a bit of a stretch. They want people they've seen fight, people they know they can make money off of."

"Is there anything we can do to help her out?" Rochelle asks, nodding in my direction.

"Not unless it's dire," Leah answers. "Even then you could be inviting disaster. Tonight isn't to be taken lightly. Just try to stay out of it." For a moment I consider discussing the idea of having Rashida alert Halsey to the bag down at the end of Sector S. I haven't said anything to Rashida about it yet, so Leah can't get too mad at me, can she? I'll need to start from the beginning, maybe cushion the blow a little.

"Something on your mind, Sarita?" Leah asks, reading my expression.

"Yeah...something..." I murmur, crossing my arms. Maybe I should just forget about it.

"Whatever it is, spit it out," Leah says, growing impatient. "It's just about time for me to head back to my dorm."

"You remember the bag I told you about?" I begin, taking a deep breath. "The one by the dock entrance of Sector S?"

"I don't remember you telling me anything about a bag," Leah replies.

"The weapons, the tools, you know?" I whisper.

"So they're in a bag down there or something?" Leah asks. I nod.

"Yeah, they are, but the point is that I was talking with Rashida recently," I explain. "We know how we're going to...you know...get rid of our problem. We need to lure her down to Sector S for it to work, though." Right away she picks up on what I'm suggesting and claps a hand to her face. She lets her hand fall to her side and glares at me.

"How much harder do you plan to make this? Huh?"

"There's no other way, it has to be done," I protest.

"You don't think that maybe we've made enough gambles in this mess already?" Leah growls. "This is just...I don't know what to say to you. You're insane, you know that?"

"I take it that's a no?" I sigh.

"That's me needing time to think about it," Leah replies. "Tell me you didn't go behind my back and say something to Rashida."

"I didn't, I swear," I say, shaking my head. "I felt it was better to run it by you first." She takes a minute to think about it and looks up when guards start walking into the room, shouting for visitors from other dorms to leave and ordering the rest of us to settle down for the night. Leah heaves a sigh and runs her fingers through her hair. She looks down at the floor, then up at me with a stern gaze.

"We'll talk tomorrow morning," she says, turning to leave. "Just concentrate on what I told you to do tonight." She walks off and leaves me and the others to move back into the dorm.

* * *

After the lights go out, I can barely keep myself from leaping out of bed and running down the halls. Leah, you'd better be right about this. The minutes tick by at a snail's pace. Ten-thirty...ten-fifty...eleven-ten. With my departure time closing in, I'm having mini-heart attacks over every sound I hear. Twice I sit up in a panic and look around the room. Nothing. Just the occasional snore or clearing of someone's throat. I keep looking at each of the sets of doors, keeping an eye out for any guards who might be checking in on us more than usual. Nothing there either. I know someone is walking around. At least one guard. I can hear the footsteps every now and again. Rolling to check on the other exit, I'm again met with silence.

Fifteen minutes remain. Come on...just a little longer and then I can run clear of here. Part of me wants to just leave early. What harm could it do? No...I have to trust Leah...but what if she's wrong, what if going early is what saves my skin? I take a deep breath and exhale. Worrying isn't helping. All it's doing is distracting me and that's the one thing I can't afford to do right now. I look back at the doors on each side of the dorm. First one and then the other. Still no sign of anything unusual. That is until someone grabs the end of my covers.

My blankets jerk toward the end of the bed and I struggle to hold onto them. It's difficult to see, but I can make out the hand that's holding onto them. Whoever it is lets go and I sit there for a moment, trying to decide what to do next. The last thing I want is to fall out of the bunk again. With a deep breath I start crawling toward the end of the bed. When I reach the end, my hand lands in something wet and I pull it away in revulsion. It's too dark to see what it is. Movement behind some of the far bunks catches my eye. Is someone else awake? My pillow is yanked onto the floor behind me and before I give it any thought, I race down the ladder with my heart thudding against my ribs.

It's eleven-thirty. Close enough. I'm not staying here a second longer. Out in the hallway I stop and turn to face the dorm. There's an inmate standing at the end of my bed. Her head is tilted back and she's looking up at the foot of my mattress. She reaches up and pulls on the sheets again, then steps back and continues staring at the bed. Is she sleepwalking? My fear immediately turns to intense anger. Part of me wants to deck her for scaring me like that. I'll just keep an eye on her in case she isn't sleepwalking. Shaking my head, I start toward the restroom. Inside I find that I have blood smeared on my hand. Taken aback, I turn and glance out the door for a moment. The girl has followed me down the hall and is now standing motionless in the shadows.

"Hey! Hello?" I call to her, waving as I do so. No response. She just stands there. It's too dark to make out her eyes, but I can see her nose and chin. I pull my head back into the restroom, rinse the blood from my hand, and hide in one of the stalls. I stand against the wall with my arms crossed and breathing shallow. The door swings open seconds later. The girl stops near one of the sinks and water begins to flow. I start to reach for the door of the stall and stop for a moment. Even if that girl is sleepwalking, she's still giving me the creeps. It has to be her who walked in a second ago. I'll just wait for now. Maybe if I'm lucky she'll go away or wake up.

Minutes later I step out of the stall to find the girl staring blankly into the mirror. I avoid eye contact and make my way toward the door. Before I can get far, I slip in blood and come close to losing my balance. I stop and look back at the girl. A shiv is sitting on the edge of the sink and she's washing blood off her hands. What's more alarming is the lifeless look in her eyes. Something about it isn't right. She notices me staring and turns to face me. Blood is dripping from one of her ears and seeping from a nasty gash on her neck. How she's still standing up is beyond me. My heart skips a beat as she swipes the shiv off the sink without breaking eye contact. She takes a step toward me and I step back.

She hasn't blinked once since she turned to face me. She raises the shiv and begins coming toward me with it. I turn and bolt out of the restroom only to feel a hand grab me by the back of my shirt. I anticipate the shiv sinking into my neck, but it never happens. Instead I'm hurled to the ground by two guards. One holds me down while another cuffs my hands behind my back.

"Scream and you'll regret it..." the guard holding me down hisses.

"How much you betting on this one?" a second guards asks.

"I'm putting fifty down on her for the first fight," a third answers. "Kid's tougher than she looks."

"Hurry up and get her to the van," the first guard orders. "We don't have all night." I'm pulled up off the floor by two guards on either side of me. As soon as my feet touch the ground I try to run, only to be held in place. Even so I continue to struggle as I'm led down the hallway.

"All right, that's enough of that," one of the guards growls. He picks me up and throws me over his shoulder while the other continues alongside him. I continue thrashing about until the second guard thumps me across my back with his baton.

"Knock it off!" he snarls. "Next time it'll be your head."

"Like hell it will!" the guard holding me growls.

"What's it matter?" the other guard demands. "She's gonna get clocked at least a few times anyway."

"Do it before the fight and I'll consider it cheating." I'm brought through a pair of double doors and carried down the street. The guards both break into a trot. Moments later I'm set down on my feet and I try again to flee. This time I'm dragged to the ground a second time and one of the guards sits on my legs until a van pulls up. The sound of the engine gives it away as it comes toward us. With my head turned the other direction there's little I can see. I hear the van stop and the guards talking with someone else. I'm picked up and shoved into the back of the van with about fifteen other inmates. I crash onto the floor and slide forward. Someone's foot touches the back of my head and I try to sit up as the doors are closed.

"What the hell are you doing here?" I turn to see Leah sitting on the bench beside me. Her expression is comprised of both shock and anger. "One job..." she continues. "You had one job!"

"I did what you told me to!" I insist.

"If you had you wouldn't be here!" she contends.

"Or maybe you just fucked up! You ever think of that?" I snap.

"Me? What about you?"

"It's a team effort, Leah!" I growl. "I followed your instructions and it failed. So don't pin this on me!" I teeter over and thump my cheek on the floor of the van as it pulls forward, much to the amusement of several other inmates whose snickers only fuel my anger.

"Whatever..." Leah growls. "Just keep your mouth shut and follow along. You'd better know how to fight, I swear to God..."

"She killed someone didn't she?" one of the girls chimes in.

"No one asked you!" Leah snarls.

"Yeah, she stabbed that one chick to death," another says.

"See what you started?" Leah growls at me. I scowl at her and scoot backward until my back is against the wall that separates the front and back.

"I've been in plenty of fights," I mutter, glancing at Leah for a moment. "Don't worry about it." Easier said than done. Things I'm sure are much different here.

"I think I will worry about it since this wasn't supposed to happen," Leah hisses.

"Why are you even here?" I demand, still keeping my voice low while the others continue talking. "You're sitting here bitching at me because I got caught and here you are, just as captured as I am!"

"I have my reasons!" she snarls. "Unlike a certain someone, I know what I'm doing."

"This is apart of the...thing...right?" I deduce. "Why didn't you tell me? I would've come along on purpose."

"Shut up and quit asking questions," she growls. I glare at her and look away. That's when I notice Tala sitting nearby. The girl who threatened Mika with a shiv several weeks ago. To her left are Leilani and Kelly, the other two girls involved in that same incident.

"She's why you're here, isn't she?" I whisper to Leah. "Jackie needs a reason to go to the morgue."

"Aren't you clever..." Leah mumbles.

"And you still didn't think to ask for help?" I snort. "You're unbelievable."

"And you're wearing on my last nerve, now shut up," Leah growls. The van stops a short time later. When it does, we're led out and lined up along the sidewalk. The guards then lead us toward the intake building and have us stand along one of the walls. The tables and other furniture have been moved out of the way in preparation. Three guards, two men and a woman, whom I recognize as Callie, stand near the only table still left out. Dozens of other guards stand around the edges of the room, most of them watching us and chatting with one another. The two guards with Callie are both taking cash from those participating.

"All right ladies!" Callie says as she steps away from her companions. "Enjoy your last moments on the sidelines! Every one of you is going in the ring, no exceptions. We had two attempted runners last month. We won't tolerate any beyond that, you understand?"

"Yes ma'am!" the line choruses.

"Now I see we have a few rookies here this evening," she continues. "I'll be going over the rules just like always, so you damn well better pay attention! Number one I already said. Everyone goes into the ring without exception. Two is that you follow all orders given to you by any of us. Same as a typical day on this island. Sounds simple, doesn't it? Number three, don't go killing your opponent. Hard to bet on dead inmates..." Callie then steps back and turns to face the other guards in the room. "Everyone gather 'round! The show's about to begin! You have one minute to finish placing your bets, no ifs, ands, or buts!"

The guards start to gather around the edges of the ring marked at four corners by red tape. Glancing down the line I can see Leah, but she doesn't notice me. For a moment I consider trying to get her attention, but think better of it. Here I have an ally a few feet away and she's of no use to me. Fantastic. Soon the other guards are all ready and the room has fallen silent with Callie moving to the center of the ring. The side on which I stand is the only clear one, allowing me and the others to see everything that goes on. In Callie's hand is a hat full of scraps of paper. She smirks as she holds up the hat while guards all around her egg her on with shouts and cheers. She takes two slips of paper out of the hat and looks down at them.

"Thirteen and seven!" she shouts. She holds the slips of paper over her head while her two assistants from earlier start down the line, starting from my right. They count each inmate as they go and when one of them reaches me, I'm grabbed by the arm and shoved out into the ring. There I find myself staring down Kelly. Callie remains in the center of the ring as we enter, watching us with her cold blue eyes. She holds one arm in the air with the thumb and middle finger of her other hand in her mouth. She whistles loud enough to make my ears ring and swings her other arm downward before quickly backing out of the ring.

The guards surrounding the ring start cheering, and before I know what's happening, Kelly's fist collides with my cheek. The crowd groans and cheers as I stumble backward. I dodge a second swipe and back away long enough to gather myself. She charges at me and I trip her as she goes. She tumbles across the floor and I waste no time in leaping on top of her. I grab her by the hair and punch her twice in the face. She throws me off and I stumble to my feet. No way am I letting her get her bearings. I try to kick her in the stomach, but she catches my foot and pulls me onto my back. She jumps on me and pins me down on my back. Before she can do anything I spit in her eyes and she recoils in disgust. It buys me just enough time to get one arm loose while she's wiping her face. I can't let her pin me like that again, I won't be lucky enough to get away twice. Without hesitation I pin her down and clamp my hands around her throat. She struggles to get free as she flails about. I maintain my hold, despite her attempts to escape. The next thing I know, Kelly's lost consciousness and Callie is running toward me.

"That's enough!" Callie shouts, hurling me off of Kelly. Her two assistants come up behind me and grab me by both arms as they drag me to my feet. Callie kneels down and checks Kelly's pulse before motioning for two other guards to carry her out of the ring. Once's she's been moved, Callie stands in the center of the ring, pinching the bridge of her nose with her thumb and index finger. A look of immense frustration across her face. She composes herself and throws her arms out to her sides.

"Looks like we have our first winner of the night!" she exclaims. "I don't know about you guys, but I'm betting someone in line would love a little payback! What do you guys think?" The crowd roars and the two men holding my arms let go, but remain beside me. Over on the sidelines I can see Leah watching me. Her expression shows a mixture of concern and relief. I imagine she thought I was a goner when I got pinned. "I think we should do something special for this next round, what do you guys think?" Callie continues, her words met with cheers. "I see two eager looking young women standing there in line. I'm guessing they want revenge! Well I say we let 'em have it!"

"What?" Leah shrieks from the sideline. "That's bullshit!" The two men beside me walk off and escort Tala and Leilani into the ring. I'm left standing alone with my heart pounding and my palms sweating. I glance back at Leah who takes a step forward. She's stopped by one of the two men, both of whom stand guard in front of the line. Behind me I can hear Callie speaking to someone along the sidelines.

"...fine, she's just unconscious. Not a big deal. I'll make sure to stop them if they get too serious, same as always. Just relax, okay?" she says to another woman. The woman nods and disappears into the crowd again. Callie then turns and walks over to me. She slaps me on the back hard enough to make my eyes water, then grabs my arm and holds my hand up in the air by my wrist. "Those of you placing bets, I hope you picked this one!" She lets go of my arm and grabs my shoulders and glares at me. "All right you little brat, let me tell you something about these fights," she snarls. "They're fights, not murders. It ain't easy for me to explain dead inmates and if I find myself having to do so, you'll pay for inconveniencing me." She walks away and stands with her arm raised in the air. Tala and Leilani are glaring at me, both looking as if they want to tear my head off. Callie repeats the same process of whistling with one hand and swinging her other hand downward before exiting the ring.

"This is bullshit! That ain't a fair fight!" Leah screams from the sidelines. As quick as I can I steal a glance of her. She's fighting with one of Callie's assistants, trying hard to get loose. Right now I'm really hoping that she does, but I can't count on that happening. Even if she does, they might just drag her back out of the ring. If I'm going to fight them alone, I'll have to take care of Tala first.

Tala is the first to charge straight at me. I dodge two punches and a third catches me in the ribs. It's enough to stun me long enough for her to land a fourth on my cheek. The blow spins me to the side and sends me crashing down onto the floor. Tala goes to grab me and I roll away in time to get to my feet. I need to put some distance between the two of us. I'm too close to one side of the ring and Leilani is waiting to catch me if I try to circle around. Meanwhile Leah is still struggling to get loose on the sidelines. She gives me a frustrated look, one lined with a hint of determination. A guard holds her back when she makes another attempt to enter the ring. She bites the guard's wrist and throws him off as he yelps in pain. She's at my side for less than three seconds before the second of Callie's assistants drags her back. A welcome distraction for Leilani.

I catch sight of her in time to lessen the blow. She aims for my nose and her knuckles instead scrape my ear. I slug her in the stomach and she doubles over right as Tala comes charging toward me. She lunges forward and misses me as I jump aside. She instead crashes into Leilani and the two of them tumble across the floor. The crowd boos and several near the edge of the ring are looking at me with their thumbs pointed at the floor. I'm not about to take any chances. Right as Leilani is getting to her feet, I race up alongside her and kick her hard in the ribs. She screams in pain and falls back onto the floor in a heap, clutching her chest and struggling to get up. Tala shoves me to the ground and I try to get back up. Tala dives for me and wraps her arms around my ankles.

"Get the hell off!" I scream, struggling to get loose.

"Get up, you idiot!" Tala shrieks at Leilani who's now on her knees. She takes one staggering step and falls back on one knee. She looks at me with her face contorted in intense rage and tries a second time. Once she's halfway toward me, I manage to free one of my feet and begin kicking at Tala. She lets go after I land two solid kicks to her shoulder and forehead. Leilani lunges for me as soon as I start to get up, bowling me over and ripping some of my hair out in the process. Pain shoots through my scalp as I elbow her in the ribs. She curses and catches me as I get to my feet. She circles behind me and hooks her arms around mine, keeping them pinned behind me.

"Your turn to get up!" Leilani taunts Tala as the two of us struggle. Back on the sidelines, Leah now has an unexpected ally helping her. I can't hear what they're saying and I'm not paying much attention, but it looks like one of the other guards is arguing with the man Leah bit. He's brandishing his index finger in the guy's face and pointing at me with his other hand. My guess is he's one of the ones betting on me, and I doubt he's happy that I'm being ganged up on. I smash the back of my head into Leilani's face, but she holds steady as Tala gets to her feet. She storms over to me and never makes it. Leah comes running into the ring and jumps on her back. She puts Tala in a choke-hold and drags her down.

I stomp on Leilani's foot and she loosens her grasp enough for me to escape. I spin around, take a swipe at her and miss. She ducks just low enough for my fist to miss and kicks me to the floor. Right as I'm getting back up she runs toward me and makes a vicious effort to kick me in the jaw. Her foot misses by mere inches. Right as I have my first foot planted, she jumps on my back and drags me back down with her arm looped around my neck. I roll onto my side and struggle to get her off. While this is taking place, Leah and Tala have both gotten to their feet with Tala's face still red as a tomato. Leah's at a bit of a disadvantage due to her smaller stature. Even so, she continues baiting Tala and hitting hard whenever she can. She makes the mistake of spotting me struggling to get loose and takes a heavy blow to the cheek.

Leah stumbles and makes the split-second decision to run toward me. In doing so she dodges another vicious swipe. Leilani sees her coming and lets go, but not in time to avoid a swift kick from Leah. Her foot collides with the side of Leilani's head, knocking her out cold. Tala kicks Leah in the small of her back and sends her crashing to the floor. Coughing and struggling to catch my breath, I drag myself to my feet with sweat dripping into my eyes. Leah managed to get up and get away, but is now trying hard to stay away from Tala who's attempting to corner her. I stumble to my feet and run toward them. Leah and Tala trade several blows and Leah ducks the final one, managing to sprint past. Right as Tala turns to go after her I slam my fist into her jaw with all my strength. Blood spatters across the floor and two of her teeth quickly follow.

She stumbles backward and catches herself before she falls, stunned by the blow. Pain surges through my knuckles as I clutch them and grit my teeth. Her teeth ripped open the skin around them. Leah takes advantage of the moment and rams into her, sending her tumbling to the ground. Right as Tala is getting up, Leah kicks her in the jaw and Tala collapses. This time she doesn't get back up. The crowd erupts with a mixture of cheers, boos, and shouts. Callie is standing on the sidelines, her expression that of both dismay and fury. She glares at us both and shakes her head before walking toward us. I take a step back and Leah averts her gaze. Callie walks right past us with two other guards, the same ones who removed Kelly from the ring. They spread out and assess our opponents and then motion for others to carry them off. Both Tala and Leilani are motionless as they're removed. Callie confronts Leah and slaps her across the face.

"What the hell was that all about? Jumping in the ring like you own it! I never said this was your fight! Did you not hear what I said about killing? What, do you not speak English or something? Or did you just not care when you kicked that last one?"

"Who said I was trying to kill her?" Leah demands, glaring up at Callie from her lesser height. "It was an accident!" Callie balls her hand into a fist and draws her arm back. Before she can hit Leah, two men and a woman come racing up behind her. Callie stops and turns to face them.

"That was low, Callie!" the woman barks, giving her a rough shove.

"We agreed that there would be even teams, it was unfair for the gamblers! You just about cost me with that crap!" the first man snarls.

"It was an impromptu grudge match, we've had gang-ups before!" Callie argues, brushing a few strands of hair away from her face.

"We put a stop to them because people were getting ripped off!" the second man replies. "Your job is to run these things, not change the rules midway through."

"I saw you arguing with my assistants," Callie growls, pointing at the first man. "Who do you think you are?"

"Me? What about you?" he shoots back.

"I never called her into the ring! This was about giving the crowd what they want! To hell with the gamblers! That's just a side thing, no one says you have to put money down! You never know what's going to happen when you come here! It's gamble at your own risk!"

"Are you serious?" the woman bellows. "Easy for you to sit there and say that! You never put anything down on anyone!"

"What a load!" Callie counters. "I did before I started running these things!"

"I meant that you can't now because you're running it, you moron!" the woman hisses. "Maybe next time you can remember that before you go and try to ruin it for the rest of us!" Callie remains silent while the others leave the ring. She shakes her head and glances over her shoulder at us. She looks away, takes a deep breath and one of her assistants whispers something in her ear before moving back to the edge of the ring. Callie turns and walks over to us.

"Stand here and here," she orders, pointing to her left and right sides. Leah and I flank her on both sides and she grabs our wrists. "All right everyone!" Callie shouts. "What'd you think of that last round?" The crowd cheers with a few boos peppered in. She shoots the three guards she was just speaking to a dirty look. She then raises our arms into the air and some of the boos grow a bit louder. "We have our winners for this round! I don't know about you guys, but I think we'll have to bring them back next time!" The cheers grow louder and she lets go of our wrists and then orders us back over to the wall. One of her assistants then guides us to the other end of the room and places us both in one of the holding cells. As soon as he's out of earshot, Leah turns to face me. She gives me an approving grin and then turns to sit down on one of the benches along the walls. I sit down across from her with my back against the cold brick wall.

"I thought you were mad at me," I say.

"I was," she says. "Still am, but I'm also impressed. You did a lot better out there than I would've expected. How did you get caught, anyway? What did you do wrong?"

"It's not what I did wrong, it's..." My voice trails off as I remember what I saw in the restroom.

"It's what?" she asks, making a beckoning motion with her hand, as if to say "out with it."

"It's nothing, just forget it," I murmur, turning my gaze toward the bars.

"Fine, don't tell me," she sighs, crossing her arms and looking away. What am I supposed to say to her? I got caught because a ghost chased me out of the restroom? There doesn't seem to be a good way to explain that. While I'm trying to come up with a lie, I think back to where our conversation in the van ended.

"I know it was part of the plan, but how do you think this is going to effect us?" I ask.

"Because of what I did to Tala?" she asks.

"What else would I be talking about?"

"The guards do this under Halsey's nose," she replies. "I doubt anything will come of it. Trust me, I thought this over quite a bit before doing it."

"Why come here alone?" I ask. "You really expected to get through this by yourself? You accuse me of taking risks, of making this whole thing more complicated than it needs to be, and then you run off and do all of this?"

"Two reasons," she says, holding up two fingers. "The first is that Naomi was supposed to be the one doing this. Obviously she's locked up, so it fell to me to take her place. The second reason is that having two of us here complicates things. Yeah, it worked out for us in the end, but did you ask yourself how it would work if we'd been forced to fight each other? Cuz it could've happened that way."

"No...no, I didn't think of that," I admit. "I guess that would have been difficult to figure out. Do you go with it and just try pulling punches or...I don't know, I'm just glad it didn't turn out that way."

"You and me both."

"You think maybe now you'll listen to what I was saying about the bag earlier?" I ask.

"Nope. Not happening."

"It's the best option we have right now, think about it!" I urge. "Halsey's always giving us that same line over and over again about coming clean. Admit something and she'll go easy on us, right? Pretend we're admitting to something and lure her right where we need her."

"Lure her where?" she asks.

"It's a faulty lever by the gates just before Tower B," I explain. "An inmate was killed there years ago with that same faulty lever and it was never repaired. The area was shut down right after and when I was in Sector S one of the guards mentioned that the lever is still broken. The death happened when Halsey was away, Rashida is certain she doesn't remember it. All we'd have to do is lure Halsey to that lever, get her to use it, and she'd be electrocuted. Once we do that she's out of our hair, Rashida's happy, we can make our way to the docks and do our thing." Leah opens her mouth to say something and then thinks better of it. She takes a moment to think and begins pacing back and forth.

"When would this take place?" she asks. "If we don't time it right someone will notice she's missing. Are you expecting to go down there with Halsey by yourself?"

"It will be the night of the escape," I say. "And no, not by myself. Rashida will go too, and if I give Halsey a convincing enough story, I can get her to take Naomi along too. Rashida's one of the few guards Halsey could get to go with us into Sector S, considering that most of them are too scared to go near the place."

"Hmm. Let me think about it a little," Leah replies. "I know we don't have much time, but we can't be too cautious with this. We should both be going over it in our heads until breakfast tomorrow, all right? Make sure it's air tight, that we don't miss anything. Sound good?"

"Works for me."

"Then it's settled," she says. "I'll meet you outside the dorm tomorrow...er...later today, I mean." My thoughts circle back to the day Naomi and I first spoke on the track. "From this point on, your time here is about survival and nothing else." Survival. It's all about survival...

Chapter 21

Restricted Area

Leah and I sat in that holding cell for two hours after that. We were joined by a few others as the night went on. A fight broke out between two of the inmates and a guard had to stand and watch us for the remainder of our time there. Some of the inmates in the cell seemed afraid of me and Leah. Two others were giving us nasty looks. If the guard wasn't there I have no doubts that they would have tried something. When we were taken back to the van, it just got even more awkward in the much more cramped space. It was a major relief to be let out. Those of us with more urgent injuries were taken to the infirmary before being returned to our dorms. My hand was cleaned and bandaged, but it continued to throb. Back at my bunk I fell straight to sleep despite the pain.

My dreams the remainder of the night were brief, but no less jarring. I kept seeing the ring, the people surrounding me. They morphed into demonic creatures and the building changed to match. It was as if I'd been tossed into Hell itself. When the time comes for us to get up, I'm nothing short of exhausted. I feel dead on my feet, like just one frustrating thing will sap me of what energy I have left and I'll keel over and lapse into a coma. I lag behind the other inmates as we vacate the dorm. I'm so out of it that when I walk right past Leah it takes her three attempts to get my attention.

"Hey! Sarita! Hello? You awake?" she asks, waving her hand in front of my face. I slap it away and rub my eyes.

"Yeah...yeah I'm awake," I yawn.

"You look half-dead," she observes as I follow her down the hallway.

"I wonder why?" I grumble.

"If it makes you feel any better, I didn't sleep well either," she says. "Everything aches."

"I hear that," I reply. Leah's face is bruised, as are parts of her arms. When we pass by a window, I can see that not only do I have bags under my eyes, but my cheek is swollen and bruises are visible. Somehow I feel like six months have been punched out of my lifespan. My hand still aches where my knuckles caught that other girl's teeth. Spots of blood are visible through the bandages. "How's your whole 'mulling the plan over' thing coming along?" I ask. She shakes her head and yawns.

"Not well," she admits as we step into the main building. "I was so tired that I just zonked out the second my head hit the pillow."

"I thought you said you didn't sleep well?" I inquire.

"Yeah, I had an endless parade of nightmares, one after the other until I woke up to guards bellowing for us to get up," Leah answers, rolling her eyes. "I woke up four times before staying up. Just wait until dinner, all right? I need a little more time. I might come to you sooner than that, so keep an eye out for me. In the meantime, take this with you." She hands me a kite and I pocket it without so much as a glance at it.

"What is it?" I ask.

"It's for Jackie," she answers. "I don't know if you forgot or not, but today's the day she needs to fetch the items from records. It's now or never."

"Are you sure they didn't take the body to the morgue yet?"

"Since you were taking your sweet time this morning, I had a chance to speak with Jackie outside the door before you showed up," Leah explains. "She was certain it's still there since standard procedure is for an autopsy to be done. She took off to the infirmary right after that. When she gets back to the chow hall here soon, she should know when they plan to do the autopsy, if they haven't done it already. Keep an eye out for her in the chow hall, pass that kite to her, and then find Rashida ASAP."

"I thought you wanted me to hold off on talking with her?" I ask.

"No, not that," she says, shaking her head. "There's more than likely a couple of cameras watching the entrance to records. If we have a guard on our side we might as well take advantage and have her make sure no one catches Jackie. Just ask her if there's anything she can do to make sure this goes off without a hitch."

"I'll find her and see what she says," I reply. "That and I'll make sure Jackie gets the kite. Do we have a time limit on how long before I need to find them?"

"I'd say try and find Rashida by the end of the breakfast rush," Leah answers as we approach the chow hall. "Shit happens, I know, so if you can't find her that quick, make certain that you find her by lunch and let Jackie know what you're planning to do. Oh, and take this and give it to her too." She hands me the copy of Halsey's key and I pocket it.

"Anything else?" I ask.

"Come find me at the restroom tonight around midnight," she says. "I'll have made my mind up about your plan by then."

"Got it," I nod. I fall behind her and she disappears into the crowd. In the chow hall, I go straight to the line and stand there with a tray, keeping an eye out for Jackie and Rashida. Jackie is the first to be spotted. She heads to the back of the line just after catching my eye and giving a nod. No sign of Rashida anywhere. Once I have my food, I start toward the table Jackie usually sits at and plop down with my tray. Jackie joins me moments later.

"Is it still there?" I ask. She nods and sits down across from me.

"Yeah, they're doing the autopsy now and then sometime after lunch I'm supposed to take her down to the morgue. The time I'm supposed to go to the morgue could get delayed, though. Depends on what they find. It's not exactly a murder mystery and most of the medical staff are in Halsey's pocket. I don't expect them to be all that thorough, but you never know. Mostly just document everything, photograph the body, record the injuries, make sure everything's on record. How'd she die, anyway? Did you see what happened?"

"Leah kicked her in the face when she was trying to get up," I answer. "Whipped her head back pretty good."

"Probably a busted neck from the sound of it," Jackie says. "I doubt that'll take long. I think they just have to note that it was an unnatural death, time of death, record basic information like hair and eye color, etc, and I don't know if they'll need to take samples or anything. Might check for brain damage or something too, I dunno. I'm not usually there for things like that."

"Great, they're gonna find some of my blood around her mouth," I mumble, showing her my bandaged hand.

"Hit her in the teeth, did you?" she asks. I nod.

"Yep."

"Someone I used to know did the same thing," she answers. "Anyway...that girl died in the fights, so that'll effect what they do. They'd have to get a blood sample from you to tell if it's your blood, I think... but beyond that, her death was linked to illegal activity on the part of the guards. They could try to say it was you or whoever, but that creates a complicated mess they probably won't want to deal with."

"I suppose," I say. "Halsey didn't take Eston's death well, I doubt they'd try to throw something else out there that could jeopardize McGinley's."

"Exactly. I wouldn't worry about it. Is there anything else you want to know?"

"No, but I do have something for you," I reply, removing the kite from my pocket. "It's from Leah. It should tell you what we're looking for in records." She takes it from me and sets it down beside her tray.

"I'll look at it when I leave," she says. I nod and she takes a few bites of her food.

"You'll need this too," I add, passing her the key under the table. "Make sure you don't lose it. It's the key to the records room. Don't get caught with it either." She takes it and pockets it before doing the same with the kite.

"I've heard there's a couple cameras watching the door," she says. "How's that going to be covered?"

"I've got someone who can take care of that," I assure her. "Just go about your business as usual."

"And where do I bring the items once I have them?" she asks.

"Just bring them to me and I'll take care of the rest," I answer. "The key too."

"Got it."

* * *

When breakfast ends, I make my way out into the hall and start looking for Rashida. Savannah and Rochelle catch up to me soon after and start asking what happened to me as we're heading to retrieve our tools. Both of them seem a little put off by what happened. For a moment Rochelle fell silent. When she spoke again, she asked if I was sure this was all going to work. I told her that things appeared to be moving in the right direction. Her question was somewhat concerning, given the way that she seemed uncertain about this from the start, but it didn't seem like she was considering backing out.

For the first half of our shift, there's little said between us. A guard we're not familiar with has taken to watching us. He doesn't seem to care if we talk, but none of us are willing to risk it. I don't see Rashida at all as we move from room to room, and with the clock ticking, I'm starting to become both worried and frustrated. I had hoped that maybe I could catch her attention somehow, make it clear that we needed to speak, but right now it looks like that isn't going to happen. The guard looks out into the hall for a moment and then steps outside. Rashida's voice echoes into the room and with it, a sense of relief washes over me.

"Cooper needs you over at intake," she says to the guard. "Better get going before he pitches a fit."

"No need to tell me twice," he says. "I'll go see what he wants." Rashida steps into the room seconds later. She looks first at us, then glances out into the hall again. She then leans her back against the wall with her arms crossed in front of her. After a few moments she clears her throat and catches my eye.

"Do I need to take you outside, Teymouri?" she asks, nodding toward the door. I shake my head and she looks outside one more time before closing the door.

"I've been trying to find you all morning," I say, walking up to her. "What's going on? You're usually around more."

"I do have a job, kid," she replies. "Got my own list of things to do each day. Probably doesn't help that Halsey's up in arms over the Tower B investigation again."

"What happened?" I ask.

"Earlier today, I was sitting in her office while she cursed out two other guards who just abandoned the Tower B investigation. Too scared to remain part of it," she explains. "Nothing any of us need to worry about. Just a typical day. Anyway, what do you need to talk to me about?”

“We have one of the inmates, part of the medical staff, sneaking into the records room pretty soon,” I say. “That’s what the key you returned to me was for. We’ve had a lot of slip-ups in the past and we can’t have this go wrong, so I want to know if you can help us keep an eye on her. Make sure she gets in and out without any problems.”

“What, like escort her or something?” Rashida asks. “I already told you and Beckham why I can’t.”

“No, not that,” I say, shaking my head. “The surveillance system, is there anyone who can keep watch on her while she goes?” She thinks about it for a moment.

“Hmm...well, there are a couple of folks I could talk to,” she replies. “Yeah...yeah I think we can do that. When’s this happening?”

“After lunch from the sound of it,” I answer. “She said that’s the staff’s plan, but that it could get delayed.”

“They’re usually pretty punctual over in medical,” she says. “If they say they’ll do something at a certain time, they usually do. I take it you’re looking for evidence in records?”

“That’s the idea,” I nod. “We’re trying to get our hands on a certain disc that shows the cell extractions that Naomi was involved in. Do you know of any others we should grab too?”

“Yeah, a handful come to mind,” she says. “I’ll write the dates down for you in a minute,” she answers. “The more evidence you have the better. There’s a good chance that if this works, Halsey might try to destroy evidence.”

“How many discs are we talking?” I inquire.

“I have three I’d like you guys to get,” she says. “The most damning ones I know of. That’s four on top of the one you’re looking for, and there is a possibility of a fifth, but we won’t know until whoever you’re sending is in there to look for it.”

“Fifth?” I ask. She nods.

“Back after Eston’s death, about two months passed before Halsey began to panic,” she explains. “There were calls for an investigation to take place, one that never happened of course. But for things like cell extractions, escape attempts, anything that we need documentation of, we send guards to record it. It’s supposed to prove that the staff did their job as required, but Eston’s case was unique. Someone, Matt Mc-

Clain, acted out of line. A murder was committed and Halsey knew it. She kept the discs for a while, same with anything that'd been recorded before, but after the legal battle ended and she and McGinley's weren't going to be forced to hand them over, she ordered that the recordings be destroyed."

"And someone didn't agree with that decision?" I deduce.

"Exactly," she nods. "Now, I've never seen it, I can't prove it's real or anything, but Halsey put the current lock on the records room, made it so only she could get in and out with her skeleton key, after the disc was hidden in there somewhere. So we're operating on a rumor here. One Jeff passed on to me a little while ago."

"And what did he say?" I ask.

"Six months after Eston died, there was a guard, Carl Brown, who left the island," Rashida explains. "He was one of the three guards who taped the incident. He and Jeff were about as close as you can get to friends in this place. He told Jeff about the tape and that it was hidden in one of the vents in records. Apparently he stuffed it there because of how every other building gets searched for contraband on a regular basis. After he supposedly hid it, he said he was leaving...and he did. None of us ever saw him again. Knowing Halsey, I'm sure she made his life hell for doing it. I've tried looking him up a few times, thought maybe I could find out if there was a way he found to survive out in the world with his reputation no doubt trashed. My guess is that's why he left the disc here instead of just take it himself. He knew he was in hot water as it was and he was probably too scared to take the risk of releasing it. The two inmates who spoke up about Eston's death were harassed, threatened, and that was nothing compared to what I'm sure would happen if Brown had gone and released that tape to the public. Even then McGinley's might've survived that scandal. Video doesn't mean much these days when people are quick to claim it's fake or twist the truth of what's on it. Planting the seeds of doubt in the minds of the public can be a dangerous thing."

"And you think that's going to happen to us?" I ask. "The threats, the harassment?"

"I don't think it'll happen, I know it will," Rashida says, shifting her weight. I've been thinking about that ever since I knew what the plan around the records room was. Nicole's life was destroyed for speaking up about a wrongful death. Brown sounds like he's missing. What kind of future is in store for us? "It's a heavy burden, isn't it?" Rashida says, her words bringing me back to reality.

"It's a lot to think about," I admit.

"Let's not focus too far ahead," Rashida says. "Right now we need to think about what's happening next."

"Is there a way I can be there to observe?" I ask. She gives me a confused look.

"Observe?"

"Don't take this the wrong way, but you don't have my complete trust yet," I say. "I would feel better if I could see what's going on."

"I think that can be arranged," she says.

"Good."

"All right, here's what we'll do," she says. "Take this to whoever you're sending into records." She takes a notepad out of her back pocket and jots down the dates before handing it to me.

"All right, then what?" I ask, putting the note in my pocket.

"Sit down, eat as usual, then head to the track and I'll find you there," she answers.

"Got it," I nod.

"One other thing. Beckham and the others are set to get out of the bunker in a few hours," Rashida says.

"What, really?" I ask. "I thought they'd be in there till tomorrow?"

"There's been some fights today and Halsey's itching to lock the participants up," Rashida explains. "Some of the inmates in Dorm A from the sound of it. Since Tower B's not around anymore, she's got fewer cells to use."

"When you say a few hours, do you mean around dinner or...?" I ask.

"Yes, they'll be out by then," she nods.

* * *

After my shift ends, Savannah, Rochelle, and I start making our way to the chow hall. When we arrive, I'm relieved to see that I've lucked out as far as timing. Jackie is right in front of me in line and all it takes is a quick tap on the shoulder to get her attention and pass off the note with a quick explanation of what to do. She nods and tells me she understands. After that I let her know that I've arranged to make sure she's covered during her time in the records room. Our brief chat ends and twenty minutes later I'm returning my tray to the counter and starting out toward the track. Savannah and Rochelle wish me luck and lag behind. I have to walk about halfway to the track before I run into Rashida. From there we make our way to the security room in Building B.

"Did you pass off the info I gave you?" Rashida asks as we approach our destination. The hallway is deserted, something I'm happy to see. The less people around to see me with her, the less chance of problems coming my way.

"I did, but I don't know where she's at with transporting the body at the moment," I reply.

"I've got eyes out in the field. We'll know once she's near the records room."

"Eyes in the field?" I ask.

"Jeff and Nicole are keeping an eye out for her," Rashida explains as we arrive at the security room. "In here." She opens the door and I step inside to find two other guards, a man and a woman, sitting at the control panel. They both swivel in their chairs to face me as I enter the room. Rashida closes the door and locks it before standing beside me. The woman has short, curly red hair with a dusting of freckles across her nose and cheeks. She wears a pair of black, horn-rimmed glasses, has deep brown eyes, and beige skin. It's hard to tell since she's seated, but she looks like she's around five-three or four. The man beside her has green eyes, light brown skin, and looks to be about five-ten. He has a scruffy beard and tattoos on his hands, wrists, and presumably further up his arms, hidden by the sleeves of his uniform.

"Sarita, these two are Lacey Flokhart and Andrew Gray," Rashida says, introducing us. "Andrew, Lacey, this is Sarita." Each of them give me a nod and a quick hello. I return their nods and remain silent.

"All right, let's get to it," Rashida says, walking over to the panel. I follow after her, keeping a couple of feet between the two of us. "Have either of you seen her yet?"

"Not yet," Lacey answers. "We haven't heard from Jeff or Nicole either."

"Should be any minute now, shouldn't it?" Andrew asks, glancing at Rashida, then me.

"Yeah, she's supposed to be leaving the infirmary soon," I nod. He turns back to the panel.

"Okay, let's get eyes on the infirmary," he says, working the controls. One of the screens flickers and changes to something new several times before I can see a room with a series of gurneys lined up along a wall. One near the end has a sheet over a motionless body. I feel a shudder go through me. It's one thing to see something like that, it's something else entirely to know that you're part of the reason it's there.

"Check the exterior too. Look for any sign of her at the end of the street," Rashida orders.

"On it," Lacey nods. She pulls up two screens showing both locations. Again there's no sign of Jackie. Seconds later, I notice someone walking into the room in the infirmary.

"Is that her?" Andrew asks me and Rashida, pointing to the monitor. Jackie enters the room and pulls the gurney with the body away from the wall. From there she begins turning it toward the door.

"That's her," I confirm. The four of us watch as she leaves the room and disappears from view. Minutes pass and we see her on the second monitor, exiting the infirmary and parking the gurney along the building. She's now with a guard I don't recognize. The two of them speak with one another and the guard goes back into the infirmary. Around five minutes pass and a transport van arrives outside the infirmary. Soon Jackie has the gurney loaded up in the back and the doors have been closed. The van does a u-turn and heads back toward Tower B. At the end of the road, it turns right and starts toward the records building. Lacey and Andrew shift the images on the monitors to match new locations each time the van leaves the screen. The van makes a stop at the gates and drives through moments later. A short time after that, Nicole's voice comes over the radio.

"Halsey's on the move," she reports. "Just got out of a van near the water towers. Looks like she's got a couple of inmates with her. Callie too."

"Keep your eye on them," Rashida replies. I'm tempted to ask, but I'm sure I already know the answer. They must be communicating on a different frequency. "Must be the inmates I heard she was taking to the bunker. They should be out of there and gone soon."

"Here's hoping she stays out of our hair," Lacey says, watching the monitors. "Are either of them close to our target?"

"Are either of you near the target?" Rashida asks. A moment passes and Jeff replies.

"I just saw her walk by with the gurney," he reports. On the monitors I can see that Jackie is heading down the walkway toward Building G; the morgue and records building. She's just passed the water towers and reached the fork in the path.

"Lacey, Andrew, can you guys get a camera on the bunker entrance?" Rashida asks.

"There's just the one behind the armory, but it should do," Andrew replies. He pulls up the feed for the aforementioned camera and each of us pays close attention to both screens as Jackie enters Building G. Lacey shifts the feed to the hallway inside and we watch Jackie move toward the morgue in the back of the building. She passes by a red steel door on the way to her destination.

"There it is," Rashida murmurs, glancing at me before returning her gaze to the screen.

"The records room, I take it?" I ask. Rashida nods. The screen flickers and swaps to a new feed, this time in the morgue. Jackie parks the gurney near the cold chambers along the wall and opens one of them. Moments later she's slid the gurney inside and closed it back up. She turns and hurries out the door, stopping down the hallway in front of the red door. Jackie removes the copy of the skeleton key from her pocket and unlocks the door.

"Halsey's back," Nicole reports. Sure enough, the feed behind the armory shows Halsey coming up out of the bunker with Callie.

"We've got eyes on her," Rashida answers. Meanwhile in the records room, Jackie appears to be struggling to find the second disc. She already has one in her hand. Halsey and Callie start toward their own van, still parked across from one of the water towers and less than two hundred feet behind the van Jackie arrived in. Jackie finds the second disc and starts looking for the third. By the time she locates it, Callie and Halsey have both returned to the van and begun conversing with one another.

"Come on Jackie, hurry it up," I murmur. She finds the fourth one and sets the stack of discs on one of the shelves, then begins searching the room for the final one. She checks two of the vents on the ceiling, staring up at them and squinting, looking for anything unusual. Something catches her eye and she starts climbing up one of the shelves. Everyone in the security room holds their breath in anticipation. Jackie reaches up and pulls on the vent cover. The force of her actions causes the shelf to tremble each time she pulls. Halsey steps away from the vehicle and starts toward the records room.

"You guys still watching her?" Jeff asks.

"We are," Rashida confirms. "Be ready to stall her."

"Understood," Jeff responds. Jackie pulls the vent cover off and the fifth disc falls to the floor. The case opens and the disc begins rolling around the room. She hops off the shelf and snatches it up before stuffing it back in its case. Halsey is closing in on the building.

"Now Jeff!" Rashida orders. The feed switches to a camera on the front of Building G and we see Jeff head Halsey off. He calls to her and Halsey slows just feet from the door. Jackie snatches up the other four discs and comes close to fumbling them as she moves toward the door. She presses her ear against it as Halsey attempts to sidestep Jeff.

"Just get out of there!" I panic, pulling on my hair.

"Nicole, are you close by?" Rashida asks.

"I'm already on it," Nicole replies. Jackie races down the hallway and stops at the door right as Halsey puts her hand on the handle. Her eyes still focused on Jeff who now stands to her left, Halsey cracks the door open and then lets it shut again. Jackie takes notice and bolts back down the hallway. She races into the morgue and closes the door behind her. Halsey wrenches the door open with one hand, using the other to brandish her index finger at Jeff who backs away with his hands up in front of him. Nicole trots up behind them and Halsey takes one look at her before shaking her head and walking into the building. For one brief moment I feel we might be in the clear. Jackie remains by the door with her ear pressed against it. She's crouched down with the discs cradled in her arms. Nicole and Jeff remain outside the door as Halsey begins walking straight toward the morgue.

"Oh no..." Lacey whispers.

Rashida curses under her breath and Jackie flees from the door. She wrenches one of the cold chamber doors open and climbs in with the discs in hand. She pulls the door closed, leaving it cracked and almost unnoticeable. Halsey enters the room seconds later and makes her way over to one of two file cabinets in the corner of the room. She sifts through it and spends about five minutes pulling out folders and reading through them. After she finds what she's looking for, she turns and starts toward the door, stopping when she notices that one of the cold chamber doors is ajar.

"Shit...no, no, no..." Andrew murmurs. Halsey walks up to the door, pushes it closed, and locks it in place before turning and walking out the door.

"Go into Building F and await further orders," Rashida orders Jeff and Nicole. On the monitor we see them both trot toward the building right next door and step inside. Halsey exits Building G moments later and starts back toward the transport van where Callie is still waiting. The two of them climb in and drive off. Back in the morgue, one of the cold chamber doors further down the row rattles twice and flings open, revealing Jackie's legs. She rolls onto her stomach and backs out of the cold chamber, then retrieves the discs, looking over her shoulder multiple times as she does so.

"Oh thank God..." Lacey says with a heavy exhale, tilting her head back as she does so. Jackie finishes collecting the discs and hides them in her jacket before approaching the door and pressing her ear against it. She waits a moment, cautiously opens the door, peers outside, then hurries out of the building. The rest of us continue to watch the monitors as she makes her way back to her van and climbs in. Right as it leaves, Jeff's voice comes over the radio.

"Did she make it back out?" he asks.

"The inmate's away," Rashida answers. "We're done here."

"Understood," Nicole replies. Rashida places her radio back on her belt and turns to me.

"What did you tell her to do with the discs?" Rashida asks.

"To pass them off to me," I reply, feeling a slight hint of suspicion at Rashida's question.

"You've got a place to hide something like that?" she asks. I nod.

"The usual places," I answer. "Why?"

"Just making sure you know what you're doing, that's all," she answers. "All that aside, we need to talk about our next move. You never told me how you're planning to get off the island in the first place. I'm gonna take a wild guess and say it has something to do with the supply run.”

“How’d you figure?”

“Just seemed like the most logical option,” she says. “You’ve only got a few days if that’s the case. I’m still waiting to hear what you have planned for Halsey.”

“Sorry, there’s not much I can do right now,” I say, shaking my head. “I have to be certain that the others on my end are okay with me sharing that information.”

“Still don’t trust me I see,” she snorts.

“Something wrong, you two?” Andrew asks. Rashida and I both turn to face them. They appear to have been listening to us the entire time. Rashida and I trade glances.

“Do they know?” I ask, keeping my voice low. Rashida nods.

“Of course they do,” she replies. “They helped you with this part, didn’t they?” The moment she says that I feel my face get hot. I should have realized that was the case.

“Rashida told us everything before you got here,” Lacey says.

“All except whatever it is you’re still holding back on,” Rashida says. “We need some kind of idea of what to expect in the next few days. You and the other inmates aren’t the only ones who plan to leave. Even if it’s just bare bones, we need something to work with. If we’re planning to do this the night the island’s due for resupply, then we don’t have much time left.” She’s starting to get on my nerves with the way that she wants me to bend the rules. Leah or Naomi need to sign off on my suggestion first and I’m not doing it any other way. Our lives are hanging in the balance and frankly I could care less about any of the guards right now. I just want to get home. Maybe there’s a way I can give her an idea of what’s going on without specifically saying what it is.

“Fine...” I sigh. “I’ll tell you what I can, but I will not go into detail. What I can tell you is that I might have left something Halsey would find interesting down in Sector S somewhere. My guess is that if I give her a false confession, we could lead her to the alleged item to convince her that I’m telling the truth...and along the way we can lure her to the lever. She’d be under the impression that I’m taking her up on the offer she gave me regarding gain time.” Andrew and Lacey take a moment to consider what I’ve said. Lacey is the first to respond.

“Might just work,” she says.

"Where's the item located?" Andrew asks.

"Somewhere I could get to it easily," I reply.

"Tower B's under watch, so I'm gonna guess that means the dock entrance. We'll need her to walk further than that," Rashida points out. "It's a long way to the gates from there."

"There is something further back from the docks that would be relevant," I say. "Connected to the original item. Something I'm certain that Halsey would want to see."

"And what would that be?"

"Let's just say it's contraband," I say. "Trust me, it's gonna piss her off to find it. There's no way she won't want to know where it came from." The rifles and ammunition left in the basement. Halsey likely will want to know where I got the pistol from. If there are weapons lying around where inmates can get them, I have no doubts that she'll want to remove them.

"Sounds like either drugs or weapons," Andrew says, leaning back in his chair.

"My money's on weapons," Lacey says.

"Moving on," Rashida says, clearing her throat. "We need something else to make sure she continues all the way through the area. We've got a long way for everyone to walk."

"About that," I say. "There was a shortcut we found that cut our time down there in half. Naomi and I both know where it is, it won't be hard to find it again. It should work just fine. The shortcut isn't far from the room where I found the contraband items. As for luring her through there, she's convinced that fuel canisters were removed from Tower B after the fire was set. Can we maybe find some and throw them back near the gates somewhere? Make it look like Naomi and I dumped them or something?"

"That should work," Andrew says. "It's believable and I'm sure we can find some down there somewhere. We can have Fulmer take care of that since he's down there a lot. Maybe have him do it in the middle of the night so no one else on the investigation notices."

"I'll go with him," Rashida volunteers. "I'd rather we have a team of at least two down there in case something goes wrong. I doubt anyone will find it strange if I head over there to help." Everyone goes silent for a moment and Andrew is the first to speak again.

"Now we just have to hope this works," he says. "If she tries to head back to the docks for any reason...it's game over. We lose our chance to act."

"Well, not exactly," Lacey says. "We could just cap her or something if we have to. Leave the body somewhere. Almost no one is brave enough to search those tunnels. If we leave the body somewhere down there, it would at least buy some time. Hell, we could even burn it or something, destroy evidence."

"It's too risky," Rashida counters. "It would arouse suspicion from the other staff. If Halsey dies by what looks to be an accident, that's one thing, but if she straight up disappears with no explanation, that's another. What you're suggesting would mean we'd have to leave the same night she dies."

"Hey, I'm all for running away," Lacey declares, raising her hand for a moment and then setting it on her knee. "We'll have to at some point anyway."

"Yes, but if we do it right and we let the investigation take place without interference, we can leave over time and avoid suspicion," Rashida argues. "Taking off right after Halsey croaks? We might as well walk right up to the cops and tell them we did it."

"True," Lacey admits with a sigh.

"I don't know about you two, but I'd like to be able to support myself when I leave," Andrew says. "Hard to do if all signs point to us. We'd have to watch our backs the rest of our lives."

"Exactly," Rashida nods. "Even just being suspected of murder could hurt our chance to have somewhat normal lives when we leave. I don't want to take that chance."

"We should be thinking about what happens if this does blow up in our faces," Lacey continues. "There's no guarantee that it won't. If Halsey doesn't try the lever, what do we do?"

"Exactly," Andrew says. "We should be prepared to off Halsey another way and leave the island the same night as the inmates. I mean, that's worst case scenario, but still..."

"And how are we supposed to do that?" Rashida demands. "It's going to be difficult enough to hide the inmates on the supply ferry, not to mention the fact that they'll need to sneak off without getting caught."

"If worse comes to worse, we can commandeer the smaller ferry,"

Lacey says. "I know how to operate it, I used to run the thing before I ended up working in here. The smaller one is a great deal faster, so if the other one is still here at the time we leave, then good luck catching us. We'll have a major head start."

"Not if someone alerts the cops before we dock," Andrew points out. "We'll have to disable the communication system somehow."

"And how do we do that?" Rashida inquires.

"We could disable the power plant down in Sector S," Andrew suggests.

"What about cell phone usage?" I ask.

"Reception here is so bad that a cell phone wouldn't be of much use," Rashida explains. "On top of that, Halsey has sensors around the island that can detect the presence of any phone being used. She has a hand-held device on her person that can alert her to such activity in seconds. No one's expecting Halsey to croak, there's no reason for anyone to have a cell phone if they know they can't even use it without getting fired within the hour."

"How about the radios?" I ask.

"The radios only reach one mile," Lacey answers. "By design, of course. We can't do anything about those, they'll operate as long as their power supplies hold out. But that leaves a small window where they could potentially alert guards on the supply ferry. They could in turn alert authorities, but that's only if they're close enough to get the message. It's three miles to shore."

"True, but it's something we'll have to be aware of," Rashida admits. "If we take the smaller ferry we still need a place for it to dock. We can't go to the usual spot. The other ferry will be either waiting or near-by, depending on when we disembark. Inmates are never picked up in the middle of the night, they'll know something is wrong."

"I have an idea," Andrew says, holding up his hand with his index finger aimed at the ceiling. "I know of an abandoned dock east of here. It's old, falling apart, but it's better than nothing. We can take the ferry and ditch it there."

"Okay, so that covers transportation, communications, and now we just need to make sure the gates are shut so Halsey has a reason to bother with the lever," Lacey says.

"Fulmer can take care of that just before we set things into motion,"

Rashida says. "It's best we keep them open until that point. Make sure Callie or someone else on the investigation team doesn't notice it."

"Sounds like a plan," Andrew says, stretching his arms over his head. "Seems we're set."

"For now," Rashida says. "With that out of the way, I suggest you delete the footage from today. Make sure nothing of it remains." Andrew and Lacey both nod in unison.

"Consider it done," Andrew nods.

"Good. I think it's time I took this one back to where she needs to be," Rashida says, clamping her hand onto my shoulder and giving me a light shake.

"Sounds good," Lacey replies. "We'll start deleting the footage." Rashida nods and grabs me by the upper arm and leads me out the door. Right as we exit, the familiar sound of Callie Fenton's voice echoes down the hall.

"Sayed? What are you doing?" she asks. Rashida and I freeze in place. Rashida grits her teeth and turns to face Callie who stops a short distance away. She looks at Rashida and then at me with a suspicious gaze.

"Something wrong, Fenton?" Rashida inquires. Callie gives her a confused look then lets out an irritated snort. Her expression shifts back to one of suspicion.

"Yeah, I'm wondering why you just brought an inmate out of the security room," Callie answers. "There a reason you did that?"

"Is there a reason you feel compelled to interrogate your superior?" Rashida shoots back. The two of them glare at one another for a moment.

"It's not an interrogation, just a question. I'm curious, that's all," Callie insists. "Inmates generally aren't allowed in there."

"The brat was arguing with me about something she did," Rashida replies, giving me a rough shake. "Rotten little thief. Stole a knife out of the kitchen and then lied about it." The look of suspicion fades from Callie's face and her lips curl into a smug smirk. She eyes me for a moment, then focuses her gaze on Rashida.

"So since she lied about stealing it you decided to show her, right?" Callie deduces. Rashida nods.

"Something like that," she answers, glaring at me for a moment. Callie crosses one arm in front of her and rests her elbow atop the other, her free hand curled into a fist and her chin resting atop it. She takes a few steps toward us, keeping her eyes on me the entire time. She uncurls her fist and points at me.

"This the same inmate you took out of the bunker?" she asks. "The one who got out early?"

"I fail to see why that matters," Rashida replies. Callie ignores her and crosses both arms in front of her. She bends down until her eyes are level with mine and less than a foot away.

"Teymouri, right?" Callie asks me.

"Yeah..." I murmur. "How'd you know?"

"You're pretty well known around here," Callie replies with a smirk. "Keep that in mind the next time you consider stepping out of line. Solitary's not the worst thing that can happen to you. But I'm sure you know that already." She straightens back up and locks eyes with Rashida.

"You finished, Fenton?" Rashida demands, leering at her. Callie smiles and steps back a few paces.

"For now," she replies, giving Callie a lazy, mocking salute as she turns and begins to walk away. "See you around, Sayed." The two of us watch her until she disappears around a corner. Rashida gives my arm a light tug and lets go.

"Come on, let's get going," she murmurs. I nod and follow after her, taking one last look over my shoulder.

Chapter 22

Wrongful Death

When dinner rolls around, Rochelle, Savannah, and I pack up our tools and start making our way to the chow hall. Near the entrance I spot Jackie walking toward us. She sees me and gives a nod before walking into the chow hall with the rest of the crowd. Once I have my tray, I split off from Rochelle and Savannah to find Jackie. I sit down across from her and she looks up from her food.

"Where did you leave the discs?" I ask.

"Dropped them in your locker," she answers. "Key's in there too. Seemed like the best option since I could barely carry all of that stuff with me."

"Good, I'll go check on them when I can," I reply with an approving nod. "I watched the whole thing from the security room. We were keeping an eye on the cameras. Had my heart pounding."

"Yours?" she snorts. "What about mine? Thought I was screwed when I had to crawl into one of those drawer things. There were two bodies in there with me. To say it gave me the creeps would be a huge understatement. I just hope it was all worth it."

"It will be in the end," I assure her. Behind Jackie I spot Naomi coming into the chow hall with Tia and Ariana behind her. Each of them look as bad as I feel. Every one of them looks exhausted. Naomi's scowl vanishes the moment she notices me. She gives an acknowledging nod and continues with the others to the line. None of them speak to me the rest of the night. For a moment I wonder what Naomi would think of the suggested plan. Letting Halsey find that bag in Sector S. If she was upset about Rashida, I'm sure explaining this will be no easy task.

* * *

After dinner, I make my way back to the dorm before most of the others return and check in the locker by my bunk. Sure enough, Jackie delivered. I should ask Rashida if I can take a look at these and make sure they have what we need. Especially the one that's supposed to have Eston's death recorded on it. I close the locker up and climb up onto the bunk. I'm so exhausted that I have to give it everything I have to stay awake. I know that if I fall asleep now I won't wake up in time to meet Leah. The lights go out sometime later and I'm left staring up at the ceiling.

Despite my best efforts, I doze off and find myself snapping awake a short time later, relieved that I didn't sleep too long. Glancing at the clock, I see that I still have an hour until I need to meet up with Leah. My head hits the pillow once more and this time I feel even more determined to stay awake. I was only out for about forty minutes. Here's hoping that it's enough of a boost to carry me through to midnight.

It's now quarter after eleven and I don't know how much longer I can keep my eyes open. Maybe it would be better to just walk down there and stay there till she shows up. My eyes close again, but not for long. Voices across the room catch my attention. Whoever it is, they sound angry. The voices are quiet at first, and soon they grow louder. My heart starts to pound. If they start a fight, if someone has a weapon, the guards will storm in and check every inch of this place. I sit bolt upright and drop down beside the bunk. As soon as my feet hit the floor, I fling my locker open and start rounding up the discs and the copy of Halsey's key. I'll just have to leave now and hope for the best.

When I have everything I need, I start trotting past the other bunks, racing for the door. The two girls start shouting and soon others are joining in and hopping out of their bunks. Right as I reach the end of the bunks, three guards come trotting into the room and start shouting for order. I drop down behind the nearest bunk, empty thanks to both occupants having gotten up. I crawl along it and poke my head out for a moment, seeing that each of the guards have their backs turned. It's now or never. I dart out from behind the bunk and sprint toward the restroom. The entire way I'm dreading the moment one of the guards notices me. None of them do and I burst into the restroom moments later.

The door comes close to striking the wall as I race to the far stall and push it open with my shoulder. I set the items on the top of the toilet paper dispenser and then use the toilet and one of the railings to climb up to the top of the stall. The roof is supported with I-beams and the discs are small enough that I should be able to hide them on the ledge where they won't be seen; each one about half the size of an average dvd. I kneel down on the railing with one hand on the top of the stall and stand back up with one of the discs in my hand. I reach up and set the first disc on the edge of the I-beam.

I'm relieved to see that the disc, case and all, is just small enough to keep from hanging over the ledge. I kneel down and grab the key and the rest of the discs, then do the same with them. The key topples off the ledge and clatters on the floor and I start back down to retrieve it. Outside the restroom I can hear voices and footsteps approaching. I swipe the key up off the floor and close the stall door right as the restroom door swings open. Knowing I won't be able to hide it, I toss the key in the toilet and flush it as someone approaches the stall. A guard bangs on the door.

"Get out here! Now!" she barks, thumping her fist against the stall a few more times. It's Callie again. The stalls rattle with the force of each strike.

"Will you give me a second?" I shout back, flushing the toilet a second time. The key, still stuck, at last comes loose and vanishes. "You ever heard of privacy?"

"You don't get privacy here!" Callie snarls. I unlock the stall and she grabs me by the arm. Without a word she drags me out of the stall and pushes me against the wall. "Don't move, Teymouri. One second, Carter! I think the brat tried flushing something!" She looks down at the toilet and then back at me. My heart's thudding against my ribs. "What'd you throw in there? Huh?"

"Nothing, I was just using it," I answer.

"I don't buy it," she growls, seizing me by the arm again. She drags me out of the restroom and past the guard in the hall, who I assume is "Carter." She escorts me back to the dorm where I find that two inmates are missing and spots of blood are in the middle of the floor. Beside them is a shiv. Callie orders me to stand at the side of my bunk.

Seconds later the guards are searching our lockers, beds, even parts of the room where someone might stow something away. The search lasts over thirty minutes. Part of me wonders how they knew I was down in the restroom. My first concern is that someone might have saw me running down the hallway, but if they had everyone line up, it would have been easy to see that I was missing. Seems like common sense to check the restrooms first.

Even so, I look around at the others in the room. I'll have to be more cautious. No telling how many potential snitches are in here. Some of them might already be feeding info to guards. I might have been lucky to have been forced to flush that key now that I think about it. Callie was so focused on that that she didn't look anywhere else. I just hope we didn't still need that key. Even if we did, it seemed better to lose it than get caught with it. After the search wraps up, Callie and the other guards order us back to our bunks. They linger for several minutes before departing and returning to their patrols. I'm dead asleep soon afterward.

* * *

When it comes time to get up, I hang back behind the crowd and sneak off to the restroom. Halfway there, I hear Leah shouting from behind me.

"Hey! Sarita!" she calls, trotting after me through the crowd. I stop and turn to face her. "What happened to you last night? You never showed up."

"There was a fight and someone got stabbed," I explain. "Guards started searching the dorm and they dragged me out of the restroom." Leah takes two steps forward and grabs me by the collar of my shirt.

"Tell me you didn't lose them!" she demands, her expression that of great concern. "You got them out of the dorm before they searched it, right? Tell me you did!"

"Yes, all of it's out of the dorm, but..." I say, my voice trailing off. She lets go and takes a step back.

"But what?" she asks.

"I lost the key," I admit.

"But no guards found it?" she asks. I shake my head.

"No, no guards found it," I answer. "One of the guards walked in right as I tossed the key in the toilet. She didn't see it in there, she didn't see me flush it, but she's suspicious nonetheless." Leah looks like she's about to have an aneurysm. She clenches her teeth and fists, then walks past me in a huff, grabbing my arm as she goes. Without a word, she leads me to the restroom and upon seeing that someone is at the sink, storms into one of the stalls. I follow suit and walk into the one furthest from hers. I'm relieved that the other inmate is in here. It'll give Leah a minute to cool off. After the inmate is gone, Leah flings her stall door open and throws open the door to the one between ours. Then she walks over to mine and stands outside.

"Where did you hide the discs?" she demands, her voice a mumbling monotone. I open the door and see that she seems a little more relaxed, but not by much.

"I thought you were pissed off about the key?"

"What are you talking about, Sarita?" she mocks. "I'm totally fine! There's nothing to be mad about! I mean, all you did was flush a vital item we still needed!" The door opens and I grab her and pull her into the stall with me. I close the door and lean my back against it. For five tense and awkward minutes, we wait while the inmate in the stall beside us does their business and walks to the sink. In that time, Leah paces back and forth in the stall in front of me, her eyes focused on the floor as she does so. At one point she stops, looks at the toilet, then looks at me as she points to it.

"Was it this one?" she mouths to me. I nod and she stands over it for a moment. As soon as the inmate leaves the room, she turns back to face me.

"You're not thinking of reaching down there to look for it, are you?" I ask.

"I'd be lying if I said it hadn't crossed my mind," she admits with a sigh.

"We already have the discs, we got into records, what else could we still need it for?" I inquire.

"Locks, dummy! Any doors and gates we might encounter," she explains. "Which, just a reminder, there's a few of them between us and getting the hell out of here."

"I found some bolt-cutters down in Sector S, they're stashed inside the dock entrance. We can just use those to lop off any padlocks or cut through fences."

"Okay, I'll admit I feel a little better knowing that, but a key was still a better option," Leah says. "Plus I assume those are in that bag you've mentioned. That puts them at risk of getting discarded or smashed or something. Halsey might do that, you know."

"Why can't we just take the original key off Halsey after she kicks the bucket?" I ask. She stops for a moment, giving it some thought before responding.

"Well...maybe..." she says. "It would be a huge pain in the ass, though. We'd have to have Rashida or someone else return it to Halsey's body before anyone notices it's missing. Otherwise it looks like we killed her for the key instead of it appearing as an accident. And for it to look like a proper accident, she'd have to alert the other staff to Halsey's death quickly to avoid suspicion. No, that won't work. How did you even end up flushing it? That's what I want to know."

"After the fight broke out I grabbed everything out of the locker and ran down here with it," I explain. "I put everything else up there." I point to the beam above me. "The key was up there too, but it fell right when Callie came storming in. I couldn't hide it so I flushed it instead."

"And Callie found it suspicious?" she asks.

"Right, but like I said, she didn't see what got flushed."

"That's a relief," Leah says, looking up at the ceiling. "If she's looking around here for any reason, then you can bet that she'll check the I-beams at some point. Now get up there and get them down before someone else comes in here. I'll move them somewhere safe." While she's talking, I start climbing up to the ceiling. To my relief, the discs are still there.

"Did you happen to run into Naomi yet?" I ask, removing the discs. Leah catches them as I drop them down to her. "Saw her last night in the chow hall, but we didn't talk."

"No, not yet," Leah replies, examining one of the discs. "Also, what is this?" She's examining the only unlabeled disk.

"Rashida mentioned that another guard told her that one might be hidden in the records room," I explain. "If it's what he told her it was, it's a recording from the night Eston was killed." She gives me a stunned look, then stares down at the disc again.

"Holy shit..." she murmurs. "And Rashida gave you that tip?" I nod.

"Yeah, she said Jeff Martin, I don't know if you know which one he is, is the one who told her about it," I answer.

"Wow...I guess having Rashida around really paid off," she says. "That is, assuming it has what she says is on it."

"I'm going to ask her if we can look them over today," I say. "Just make sure they have what they say they have."

"Good thinking."

"Did you make a decision about the bag in Sector S?" I ask. "We were supposed to discuss that last night."

"Well since Naomi is out of the bunker, it's up to her now," Leah answers. "I was going to tell you yes, but only because it seems like our best option. Rashida gets what she wants and so do we. I still don't like it, though. And I'm sure Naomi won't either." I climb back down as she's speaking and Leah follows me out of the stall, hiding the discs in her jacket as we go.

"So who's breaking the news to her?" I ask. "You or me?"

"I'll talk to her about it," Leah says as we leave the restroom. "If it's coming from me I'm sure she'll take it a little easier. Hang back a little, all right? I'll get to the chow hall sooner and talk to her before you arrive. Meet us out on the track afterward. It'll give her some time to process the news. Sound good?"

"Yeah, all right," I murmur with a shrug.

"See you in a little while," she says, trotting off. "I'm stopping off at my dorm first, so just sit in yours for a few minutes, then get going." I nod and the two of us split up. Walking back into the dorm I feel a sense of unease. The puddles of blood are long gone, but the memory still remains. I take a seat on my bunk and stare down at the floor. A pair of feet walk past and someone sits on the bunk in front of me. When I look up, the pit of my stomach drop out.

"You seem nervous," Helena says, smirking at me.

"What do you care?" I snarl.

"Well screwing up is what you do best, that's all," she chuckles. "Take me for example. Killing me was your biggest mistake, wasn't it?"

"What happened was something you started and something I wanted no part of," I growl. "You made the mistake, not me!" I clench my fists and look away from her. She lets out a chuckle that slowly becomes a drawn out cackle. "What the hell are you laughing at?" I demand. She stops and pretends to wipe a tear from her eye. Her expression goes blank as she stands and stares at me with an eerie calmness that quickly becomes unsettling.

"What's the matter?" she asks, still staring at me. "Don't tell me you've lost your sense of humor."

"There's nothing funny about any of this."

"I disagree," she replies with an amused grin. "Watching you flail about has been very funny."

"If I have to sit here and wait I'd rather do it alone," I growl. "I'm done with you, now get lost." She leans over with her hands clasped behind her back, her eyes burning into mine.

"You'll never be done with me," she taunts, her lips curling into a crazed grin. It's the sort of smile that only insanity could hope to create, and it's enough to push me over the edge. I give her a rough shove and hurry out of the room. When I look over my shoulder, she's gone.

* * *

In the chow hall, I sit down with Savannah and Rochelle, both of whom note that I seem agitated. I explain that Leah wants me to come meet her and Naomi out on the track soon, that Naomi is going to hear what I have in mind before I get there, and how I'm not looking forward to it. From there it's off to the yard. Near the track I notice Rashida standing with her back against the wall of one of the buildings. She's holding a cigarette between the fingers of one hand with the other folded across her stomach. Good, I won't have to hunt her down. Rashida turns her head, spots me, and takes one final drag on her cigarette before discarding it as she walks toward me.

"You got a minute?" I ask as she stops along the edge of the grass.

"Yeah, what's going on?" she inquires.

"What's going on is I'm going to need another favor and it has to be sometime either today or tomorrow," I explain. "The sooner the better, though."

"And what's the favor?"

"The favor is that I need to review the discs Jackie took from the records room," I explain. "The one with Eston's death supposedly on it is top priority." Rashida nods along and pauses for a moment.

"Makes sense," she says. "Tell you what...we'll knock that out before you head back to work."

"Do we have everything ready for the night we leave?" I ask. "Is everything set up for the trip to Sector S?" She nods.

"It's all ready to go," she says. "Fulmer is set to close the gates on my signal. Lacey and Andrew are ready to disable the power plant, and Jeff and Fulmer are ready to meet us on the other side of the gates. Nicole will come get you shortly after dinner begins that night, so everyone needs to eat quick. Hard to say when you'll eat again after that."

"Right, I've been thinking about that," I reply. "I'm on my way to talk with Naomi, I'll make sure we've taken care of that. We have someone driving us, right? To the dock entrance?"

"Jeff will take care of that before he heads over to meet up with Fulmer," Rashida explains. "It's all covered."

"All right, good," I say, taking a step back and crossing my arms in front of me. "Do we have the fuel canisters set in place?"

"Fulmer and I already planted them," she confirms. "They're tossed in the drainage area near the gates. You sure you know what you're doing as far as this contraband you've talked about?"

"Of course," I assure her. She looks at her watch, then at the track behind her.

"If you're still planning on talking with Naomi, you'd better get to it. Break's almost over. We'll need to go by my office soon."

"Got it," I nod, walking past her. She turns and walks off, disappearing around the side of a nearby building. Over at the track, Leah and Naomi are coming around to where I am as I approach. They both catch my eye as I join them.

"Stand by Leah," Naomi instructs. "It's hard for me to see you on that side." I move between the two of them and we continue down the track. "Leah told me what you proposed...and before we go any further, I just want to say that I don't know if you're crazy, smart, or both." She shakes her head in frustration as she finishes speaking.

"She's still cooling down," Leah assures me. "Don't take it too personally."

"I'll keep that in mind," I say.

"What else is going on?" Naomi asks.

"We've got a few other guards in on the plan and don't freak out over it, okay? Their help will make this work better in the long run," I say.

"And what exactly does that mean?" Naomi inquires.

"We have two guards set to disable the power plant," I explain. "Of course it won't stop radio communication, but it will plunge this place into darkness, making it that much easier for us to sneak onto the ship. The communications system will go down with it and that will give us time to get to the mainland and skip town before anyone has a chance to alert the authorities. It'll buy us time we otherwise wouldn't have." For a moment I wait with bated breath as Naomi and Leah consider what I've told them. It feels like an eternity before either of them respond. Naomi nods and gives me an approving look.

"Are you sure this will work?" she asks.

"I don't think any of us can be sure of anything at this point," Leah says. "I like the idea, but I'm not going to get excited about it until I see it work."

"I'm just still hung up on the idea of outing the entire plan," Naomi says. "Just telling Halsey that we're trying to escape, even if it is to trick her."

"It's going to work," I assure her. "It's not just the bag we're going to show her. We have some fuel canisters planted near the gates for good measure. Just to be sure she walks all the way there."

"So we're lying to her about the fire too?" Naomi asks. I nod.

"That we are," I reply. "Before any of that happens, I'm going with Rashida to check on the discs we recovered. Make sure they work, especially the one that supposedly has Eston's death on it."

"Is it just me or does anyone else find that disc to be all kinds of suspicious?" Naomi asks. "Why wouldn't the person who left it there take it off the island? Why hide something like that?"

"I have no idea what they do when they discharge a guard on this island," Leah says with a shrug. "Maybe they search them or something, make sure they can't compromise the operation they have here? They could've been worried they'd be a target if it got out. The inmates who went to the press after Eston's death had their lives destroyed for daring to speak out."

"I suppose," Naomi says, crossing her arms and looking down at the ground. "Still...just kinda pisses me off, you know? Like hey, here's an opportunity to shut this shitshow down once and for all. But no... instead the moron just hides it in records like a fucking coward. Why does it have to be us who blows this open? Why is that our responsibility? Doesn't that seem unfair to any of you?"

"Glad I'm not the only one who's thought about that," I say. "If the inmates who spoke out suffered for it...what do you think is going to happen to us when we leak the video?"

"Nothing good, I'm sure," Naomi admits. "You remember how one of the inmates ended up dead after the media calmed down? Lying on the floor of her apartment with pills scattered beside her. No known history of suicide attempts, no addictions to speak of, nothing." I shiver a little at Naomi's words. It's true, one of the inmates was found dead, the other went missing several months after that. The first was ruled a suicide and the missing girl...her case went cold and was soon forgotten.

"The people running this place and others like it...the ones above even Halsey," Leah says. "They shut them up, didn't they?"

"That's what I think it was," Naomi answers. "We release that tape and we'll be looking over our shoulders the rest of our lives."

"We don't have a choice," Leah says. "McGinley's can't continue to exist."

* * *

Our conversation on the track wrapped up soon after that. I asked Leah about bringing food rations with us and she tells me it's covered. Savannah and Rochelle are set to work with Ariana on that soon since Ariana works in the kitchen. Leah, Ariana, Tia, and Naomi are also set to come by my dorm the night before we're set to leave, to explain to everyone what their roles are. Leah also tells me that the discs are in her dorm and that she'll wait there for Rashida to come get them so we can review them. After she and Naomi are both gone, I find Rashida outside the main building waiting for me. We pass by other inmates and guards on the way to her office, most of whom fail to give us even a second glance.

"So where are the discs at?" she asks.

"They're in Leah's dorm," I answer. "She's waiting for you to come by Dorm C." We arrive at her office and she opens the door for me.

"Wait in here, I'll go retrieve them," she says.

"Got it," I nod.

"Be back in a few minutes." She leaves the room and I settle in. It doesn't take long before the sound of the clock ticking on the wall starts to get to me. The memories of what happened the last time I was here are starting to return. I stand up and start pacing, feeling winded as I do so. Minutes later Rashida returns with the discs and sets them on her desk. She doesn't say a word to me and sits down in her chair. She pops the first disc in the drive and motions for me to stand up and trade seats with her. She stays beside the desk until the video begins to play; after which she sits down in the chair opposite the desk. On screen is an image of a man with brown eyes and black hair. The screen pixelates a few times, but the audio remains intact.

"Hurry up, Brown!" a male guard in the shot shouts at the cameraman. "Quit messing with that thing and let's go!" The camera swings downward at the feet of the officer holding it and he follows the man out the door and hops into the passenger seat of a waiting van. The light in the cab goes out and the van begins moving forward at a rapid pace. Chatter comes over the radios of both men in the cab, some of it garbled, still more of it code I don't understand. The van speeds through the gates and takes a sharp right toward the docks. Moments later they make a left and arrive in a parking lot across from one of the ferries. Brown races out of the cab and trots over toward the edge of the lot while guards behind him race through the gate with rifles in hand, half of whom are dressed head-to-toe in riot gear.

I glance past the monitor at Rashida as the video cuts out a few times. She's leaning forward with her elbows on her knees and her hands over her ears. Her gaze is focused on the floor and she doesn't notice that I'm looking at her. I turn my attention back to the screen and see the camera zoom in on three girls on the deck of one of the ferries as spotlights from nearby watchtowers focus in on them. One of the girls races out of sight while Eston stands with a rifle in a blinding beam of light. She backs toward the railing, struggling to see. Approaching guards hurl two stun grenades at her. Someone's voice comes over Brown's radio.

"Tower two, standing by," the man says, his voice peppered with static. Rashida's voice replies to him.

"Keep watch and await orders." Eston panics and kicks one of the stun grenades back at the officers. It detonates before it hits them, but several are still struck with the airborne pellets. Eston tries to flee the second grenade at the same time and stumbles as it goes off. Blood is visible in multiple areas where she's been struck. The rifle falls from her hands amidst shouts for her to do so and clatters onto the deck. It's unclear if she can hear them or not considering the deafening blasts that just took place around her. The guards start boarding the ferry and the voice of Matt McClain can be heard over Brown's radio.

"She's going for the rifle," McClain says. "I'm taking the shot."

"Negative! Tower two, hold your fire! Hold your fire!" Rashida orders. Eston does move toward the rifle, but she instead avoids it, racing closer to the railing. In that time she doesn't even glance at the rifle, much less try to pick it up. She vaults over the railing and right as her feet swing over the side, a gunshot rings out. The round tears through her back and she tumbles down into the inky black water below.

"Jesus Christ..." Brown whispers from behind the camera. Feeling rattled from what I just saw, I glance over at Rashida, then back at the screen. Her voice is again heard over Brown's radio.

"Tower two!" she roars. "I told you to hold your fire! Christ! Someone get her out of the water! Get medical over here! Now, now, now!" The camera swings away from the scene and the video ends. I look over at Rashida again.

"Hey...it's over," I say, waving my hand. She looks up at me and uncovers her ears.

"Is it her? In the video?" she asks. I nod and she lets out a sigh as she leans back in the chair. "So now you know. Now the whole world's gonna know."

"You make it sound like that's a bad thing." She shakes her head and stands up from the chair.

"Never should've happened on my watch," she continues. "I knew Matt McClain shouldn't have been working here. I tried telling Halsey to fire him, but she never listened. What Halsey's about to get is too good for her." She pushes the second disc toward me and sits back in her chair.

"That Naomi's disc?" I ask, placing the first disc back in its case. She nods.

"Yep," she confirms. "Hurry up and get to it. Can't be here all day." After placing the second disc in the tray, the video begins just outside the main entrance to Tower A. Inside the guards start marching up the stairs. Angry shouts can be heard above. Skipping ahead, I find Halsey standing in front of the cells, calmly talking with some of the other guards while the inmates around them bang on the doors of their cells, screaming and cursing.

Skipping ahead again, the screen is lit up by flashbang and stun grenades. The screaming and shouting is unintelligible and few words can be made out. Halsey is now back near the stairs, barking orders while inmates, some of them unconscious, are dragged from their cells amidst the clouds of smoke. Naomi is one of the last to be removed and when she is, I don't recognize her. She's different. Not as hardened as the Naomi I know. Her eyes are filled with fear as she struggles to get loose. Two guards slam her against the wall and she hits her head, losing consciousness and falling limp almost at once. One of the guards steps back and doesn't bother to try catching her, the other barely slows her down. Once she's on the floor, they each take her by the arms and drag her past the camera operator.

"I can't do this anymore, I'm done, it's what we need, I'm done," I say, pausing the video and standing up. I pace to the other side of the room and Rashida watches me. There I stand for a few minutes while she removes the disc from the drive and places it back in its case.

"You all right, Sarita?" she asks. Tears roll down my cheeks as I recall what Nicole first said about Naomi. Back before any of this had started. "She wasn't like that at all when she first came in. Timid and shy..." Naomi's been here for about eighteen months. The timestamp on the video showed that it was taken almost a year ago. I can't help but wonder...what would she have been like if she'd never come here in the first place? On top of that, what would Iris Eston have been like? Who would she have been today?

"I wish other people would react that way," Rashida says, leaning back in her chair. "People on the outside, even me when I was a kid...I thought, "Who cares what happens to them? They're crooks. They deserve it...for whatever they did." Never occurs to us to think of them as human." After drying my eyes, I turn back around and approach the desk again.

"Why is this place even here?" I ask. "I saw the remnants of the classrooms, I've lived through the punishments. Ariana pointed out the way this place or someone else is profiting off our labor. Why? Why keep it open? Nicole said there's tons of places like this all over the country! What's this really about? Who's behind it?" Rashida sits back in her chair and focuses her gaze up on the ceiling.

"Roth-Stein Industries," she says, catching my eye.

"RSI?" I ask. She nods.

"You know who they are, right?"

"Sort of," I say. "The name's come up quite a bit the past few years. Aren't they some family owned corporation? Been around since the late 1800's or something?"

"Yep," she says with a nod. She leans forward and places her elbows on her knees. "They're owned by the richest family in the country. If they don't own something, you can bet they probably have a share in it. Somewhere along the way they felt the prison industry was something they wanted in on. And why not? Sure makes a great deal of money for folks. They bought out two of the three companies providing video and phone calls to inmates in every American prison, they're about to take the third, and from there they'll start hiking the rates of people desperate to communicate with friends and family. They own some of the companies who make the ankle bracelets that suck money out of people when they're paroled, the system stacks other barriers against them to keep them locked up so companies like RSI can keep making a perpetual profit. Tell me, what do you think will happen to you if you finish your sentence and leave?"

"I'll have to get my GED somehow since there's no way I'm gonna graduate now," I say. "I'm sure that'll slow me down quite a bit. And I'm sure having been locked up isn't going to look good when I get a job."

"If you get a job," Rashida says. "You're here on a manslaughter conviction, and that plea deal they forced you into just helped that along. Most places aren't going to hire a felon, especially for a violent crime. That doesn't bode well for folks when finding employment is part of the terms of their parole. Then they get locked up again and the cycle repeats. Add to that one of those insane three-strikes laws, and people end up unable to escape the system."

"Sounds like one big conspiracy," I say.

"One with a long, twisted history," Rashida replies. "But the point I'm making is that RSI makes money off the backs of you and all the other inmates in this place and the other facilities like it. That's where the money goes to."

"How many other places are there?" I ask.

"Something like seventy-six now," she answers. "As for the class-rooms you mentioned earlier, I'll say this. It's not always about how much money they make, but rather how much they save by cutting costs."

"Yeah, I figured that was the case when Ariana called it slave labor," I reply.

"Don't let RSI hear you call it that," she snorts. "They don't pay you guys for that stuff here, but there was a time where they used to. A measly fifteen cents per hour, but that was eventually ended. But hey, you're building character, right? And it's not like you have any bills to pay, so why does RSI have to pay you if you're incarcerated for a serious crime? You're here to be punished, not rewarded. That's how they see it, anyway. It's not like they paid inmates that much. 15 cents an hour which isn't much better than what they do here now. Have you ever looked carefully at the thirteenth amendment?" I give her a con-fused look.

"What? No. Why?"

"Except as a punishment for crime," she recites.

"What?" I ask.

"Neither slavery nor involuntary servitude, except as a punishment for crime whereof the party shall have been duly convicted, shall exist within the United States, or any place subject to their jurisdiction," she continues. "And companies like RSI love that exception and they've been loving it for a long time now. On top of that, RSI has such mas-sive influence in this country that it's part of why guards are afraid to leave this place and look for employment elsewhere. Unless RSI likes you, unless they see you as harmless, unless Halsey signs off on that...they'll come after you and they'll silence you. They're terrified of their empire falling apart and they'll do anything to prevent it. Since Halsey's involved in their scheme, taking their filthy money and seeing nothing wrong with it, I need her dead in order to have a chance to leave safely."

"So this is what we're up against when we leave..." I say. "We're screwed either way, aren't we?"

"It's going to be an uphill battle no matter what happens," she says, looking at the clock.

"I suppose that's true," I admit. "So um...I know those cell extractions were in Tower A, so...why hasn't Halsey used that place to isolate inmates lately?"

"There was an earthquake last year and it suffered some damage," Rashida replies. "Halsey's not too keen on having to spend the money to fix it right now, so repairs are on hold at the moment. Also, I'm sure you noticed the blocked off hallway in Tower B right as you came in? That's why. Earthquake damaged that area too."

"How 'bout the discs?" I ask. "You gonna run those back to Leah?"

"Once I'm done checking the other ones, yes," she nods. "Should be fine where she had them, but I'll give her a heads up if I hear of anything concerning. Any planned searches or anything. You should get going, though."

"All right," I say, turning toward the door. "I guess I'll start heading back, catch up with whatever is left of my shift. Thanks for helping out with the discs. I appreciate it."

"No problem, kid."

"I'll see you later." I step out of the room and close the door behind me.

Chapter 23

Desperate Gambit

Another day passes without much talk about the plan. For now I seem to be on stand-by, which if I'm being honest, is kind of nice. Closest I'll get to a vacation. Rochelle, Ariana, and Savannah managed to gather up some food from the kitchen, but I never saw what they did with it. All I know is that Leah and Naomi have it stashed somewhere safe. Somewhere we can get to it quickly and easily. At the end of that day, Leah, Naomi, Tia, and Ariana met up with us just outside the dorm to finalize everything. Rochelle, Savannah, and I were walking into the dorm after dinner at the time. Jackie was already speaking with them as we joined everyone; Naomi waving us over after seeing us.

"Tomorrow's the big night," Naomi says, keeping her voice low. "We've got everything ready, now let's make sure everyone here knows what's going on. Jackie, have you been filled in yet?" Jackie nods.

"I know the gist of it," she answers. "Something about a false confession and Halsey getting snuffed and that I'm in Group B. We're heading to the docks with Group A joining us later."

"Exactly," Naomi nods. "Me, Tia, Sarita, and Ariana are Group A, and our group splits off in Halsey's office if this works right."

"That's encouraging," Tia sighs. "If it works."

"I don't need any attitude from anyone right now," Naomi growls. "Getting back to what I was saying, Group A splits when me and Sarita are taken to Sector S. From there we have a short amount of time to work with. Roughly ninety minutes. We lead Halsey to the locations Sarita and I have agreed upon, and we join Group B at the ferry soon afterward, with the second half of our group going ahead of us with Nicole."

"And just so we're clear, there's a back-up plan in place in the event something goes wrong," Leah adds. "The one area we need to focus on is getting Halsey to go deep into Sector S and she needs to be dealt with before anyone leaves there. If we can't do that, this turns into a mess that could get us killed."

"What's the plan if we don't get Halsey to do what we want?" Jackie asks.

"Assuming we get her where we want or close and she is dealt with, and anything before or after that compromises the rest of the plan, the guards come with us," Naomi replies. "There's several of them from what Sarita has told me and at least one can operate the smaller ferry. From there it gets a little tricky in one of two ways, assuming we all make it on board."

"How so?" Rochelle asks.

"If the supply ferry is able to get away from the island and leave radio range, then it buys us a few hours at least to get as far away as possible," Leah says. "The communications system will be down and if they don't know before they reach shore, they'll have to come back into radio range before they know what's happening. If it doesn't leave radio range in time and something arouses the guards' suspicions, it means risking the island guards contacting the guards on the supply ferry, cutting down our time to get away. They'll know what's going on and the cops will be out searching for us much sooner."

"Unfortunately, some of that is out of our control," Naomi admits. "The original plan didn't have this side-stop into Sector S, but since we have to do it now, the best thing we can do to make this work is for me and Sarita to do whatever it takes for us to keep Halsey contained in Sector S until we've done what we need to do."

"No pressure, right?" I say with sarcasm.

"And it's going to be me and Tia who are getting called to Halsey's office after you and Sarita, is that right?" Ariana asks Naomi. Naomi nods.

"Right, and I'll discuss what to say with you two tomorrow," Naomi says, gesturing at both Ariana and Tia. "We need to make sure our story is consistent or else this won't work. Moving on, Group B is also in charge of moving the food, the discs, and anything else out and onto the ferry. Nicole will help you sneak on board. This starts at dinner tomorrow and the moment me and Sarita are taken out of the chow hall, that's when the rest of you are to act; while the dorms are still empty. Everyone clear on what to do?" Everyone nods.

"Good, now everyone make sure you get some rest tonight," Leah says. "Tomorrow night's gonna be a long one." She and Naomi dismiss everyone and our group splits off into our dorms. After the lights go out, I fall asleep a lot quicker than I expected to. I was starting to feel on the verge of shaking from nerves. The pressure for this go right is enormous. I know I'm not the only one who has to play their part right, but all it's going to take is one of us falling out of line and messing up to bring this whole thing crashing down.

* * *

The entire next day I'm focusing on my work more than usual. My goal is to just not think about what lies ahead, to make sure I don't stress myself out to the point of freaking out over it. I run into Nicole and Rashida at different times and speak with them briefly about the plan and check to make sure everything is still in place. I'm relieved to hear that nothing has changed and that everything is still ready for us to move forward. I'm so involved in my work that it seems as if dinner arrives early. In the chow hall, I sit down with Jackie, Savannah, and Rochelle, and stare down at my tray.

"You gonna eat something?" Rochelle asks. I nod and continue looking down at my tray. It takes me another minute to start eating. Looking around the room, I see Leah, Naomi, Tia, and Ariana at a nearby table. The four of them are talking, but it's anyone's guess as to what about.

"You doing all right, Sarita?" Jackie asks.

"Yeah, you seem a little off today," Savannah observes.

"Just nerves," I reply, taking a bite of food.

"I hear that," Jackie replies. "Was feeling it all day."

"Same here," says Savannah.

"Me too," Rochelle adds. "There's a lot riding on this."

"Like our heads," Jackie says.

"No matter what happens too," I add. "Deal with Halsey if we get brought back, deal with the people on the outside if we don't. Lose-lose situation."

"It will be if no one cares about those videos we're planning to leak," Jackie says.

"Eston's case got under peoples' skin in a unique way," Savannah says. "That video might end up being our trump card."

"Too bad she didn't do what we're planning to do for us," Jackie says.

"And if not her, maybe someone else," I add.

"Or maybe this crapfest of an island could've never been built," Rochelle says. "Then we wouldn't be here and Eston wouldn't be dead."

"Yep, and we'd all be locked up in some other place," Savannah says. "I wonder how that would've played out?"

"Not well, I'm sure," Jackie says. "I have a feeling I'd be dead. Might've died if I didn't join up with you guys...and that's the only reason I did if I'm being honest. I just don't wanna die. I'm not cut out for this shit, I wasn't some hardened criminal, I'm still not."

"We'd become that way if we stayed here long enough, I'm sure," Rochelle says. "Naomi's living proof of that. She's probably the most hard-hearted of us."

"And Leah's not far behind," Savannah points out. "I dunno, what do you think, Sarita? You've spent more time with them."

"If I had to rate them on a scale of one to five, like how far along they are, with five being the worst," I reply. "I'd say Naomi's at three-and-a-half and Leah's at about three."

"And my sister's a full blown five," Rochelle adds. "It'll take a miracle to get her to a place where she's functioning again. Assuming she doesn't manage to kill herself first. Her mind's just gone at this point. She might've had enough in her to give me some pointers about this place, but...well, let's just say I had to filter out the sense from the nonsense."

"I take back what I said about not wanting to die," Jackie says, holding her hand up for a moment. "Going crazy sounds worse. If you're dead, you're dead. If you're not even in your right mind, that sounds like a whole new brand of hell I don't want to deal with."

"It's not fun watching it happen to someone you care about either," Rochelle says with a sigh. "Wish I could go back and check on her when we leave."

"Anyone seen Nicole around?" Savannah asks. "She's supposed to be coming by soon, isn't she?" I look up from my tray and glance around the room. No sign of Nicole or Rashida for that matter.

"Yeah, she shouldn't be much longer," I say. "The dorms have to be empty for us to get in and out with the least amount of trouble."

"Wait, there she is," Rochelle says, using her eyes to gesture toward the doors. "Better get ready to go."

"Good luck, Sarita," Jackie says.

"And don't go dying on us," Savannah adds. I turn to see Nicole approaching and look back at the others as I prepare to leave.

"I'll see you guys in a couple of hours." They all nod and Jackie gives me a nervous look.

"Get up, you're coming with me," Nicole orders. I glance at her, then back at the others before standing up. Nicole grabs me by the arm and leads me out of the chow hall. Out in the hallway, Nicole's expression relaxes and she loosens her grasp on my arm.

"Do you have to hold onto me?" I ask.

"Gotta play the part," Nicole answers. "Rashida told me to let you know that we plan to help you even after you leave. She's sorry it took this long for it to come up, but Jeff mentioned a little bit ago that his cousin is an attorney in New York. We're going to help you get in contact with him and he'll help you out from there. I already brought Naomi down to Halsey's office, I gave her a kite with directions on where to go once you reach the mainland. Don't lose it. It will tell you where to go and you need to go straight there as soon as you can. Friend of mine lives at the address inside," Nicole explains. "She can give you some cash, help you get to New York before news of the escape spreads. You'll be hitching a ride out of the state, so be ready for that. Your night's far from over." I nod as we approach Halsey's office and she places a finger over her lips. We step through the door and I find Rashida standing along the wall with Callie. Halsey is seated behind her desk and Naomi is sitting in one of two chairs in front the desk. I take a seat in the empty chair and Nicole closes the door behind us.

Halsey has a subtle smirk on her face, looking almost as though she's bursting to rub what she knows in our faces. Aside from looking particularly smug, she looks more haggard than I've ever seen her before. Her remaining eye is bloodshot and her hair, though pulled back in her usual bun, has several stray hairs falling out. Perched on the edge of an ashtray to her right is a cigarette, half gone and smoldering, a thin stream of smoke rising from the tip. Beside the ashtray is a nearly empty pack of cigarettes with two spilling out the end.

"Teymouri...Beckham..." Halsey begins, as I sit down. "It's come to my attention that you're both claiming knowledge of stolen tools and weapons, stashed away near the docks in Sector S. Is that true?"

"It is," I answer.

"Now, why would you need to hoard such things?" Halsey continues.

"Because we were attempting to escape," Naomi answers. Callie stands nearby scowling at us, hanging on to every word.

"I'm glad to see you took my advice, Teymouri. It was a wise decision, coming forward before you took this any further." Halsey continues. "I would hate to see more casualties." Images of Eston's death flash through my mind and I clench my fists.

"Got us in a whole whirlwind of trouble," Callie adds.

"Now there's just the matter of what your intent was after escaping," Halsey says, leaning back in her chair. "I don't think I need either of you to tell me. Judging by the napkin I plucked off that other girl some time ago, my guess is that you were going to go to the media. A very unwise decision. It's clear to me that you have little understanding of what you would have brought upon yourselves." She yanks open a drawer on her desk as she speaks and pulls out one of the napkins from the bus. The ones containing the information we needed to reach Randall Adams.

"Yeah...that about sums it up," Naomi admits with an averted gaze.

"What were you going to tell him? Hmm?" Halsey demands, leaning forward. "Think carefully girls."

"What does that even matter?" Naomi demands.

"No reason, I'm just curious," Halsey replies, a subtle, sinister tone in her voice. "This whole thing is rather disappointing, I'll say that much. It could have been avoided if you'd just done your time, but no... that wasn't possible for a bunch of degenerates like you. Instead you cooked up this crazy plan and added murder, assault, theft, and arson to your records! And after that you had the audacity to try planning this stupid media stunt? Make me look like the bad guy after everything you did? It's outrageous!" The room falls silent for a moment before

Halsey continues. "Where's the other note?"

"Hell if I know," Naomi replies with a shrug.

"How about you, Teymouri? Do you know where it is?" Halsey asks, glaring at me.

"I flushed it," I answer. Callie smirks.

"You did, huh?" Halsey snorts. "And you expect me to believe that loathsome pile of garbage?"

"I caught her flushing something the other night," Callie cuts in. "Didn't see what it was, but I guess now we know." Halsey looks at Callie, then at me.

"Is that so?" Halsey says, her eyes burning into mine. "Be that as it may, I find it strange that I only have two girls sitting in this room. Past experience tells me there are others." Halsey scowls at us both and snatches a notepad and pen off her desk. She clicks the tip of the pen into place and holds it at the ready. She already told me she suspects that Ariana and Tia are involved. Why doesn't she just say it? I'm guessing she's just trying to see how truthful we'll be with her. "What are their names?" Halsey demands. "Who's been helping you with this?" Naomi catches my eye and clears her throat.

"Tia Ellis and Ariana Miller," Naomi says. "They're in Dorm C with me." Halsey writes them down and looks at us both.

"Are you certain there are only two?" Halsey asks, giving us both a stern look. Naomi and I both nod. Halsey sets her pen down and moves to her computer. Moments later she tears the note off the pad and stands up to hand it to Callie.

"Come back here for a moment first," she instructs Callie as she takes the paper from her. Callie steps behind the desk. Once she's where she can see, Halsey points at the monitor. "These two," Halsey informs her. "Find them and bring them back here." Callie nods and makes her way out the door. Her footsteps fade out and the rest of us all sit in an uncomfortable silence. Halsey leans back in her chair and continues to puff on the remainder of her cigarette. The entire time she does so she rarely takes her eye off us; a piercing gaze filled with anger and hatred. Callie returns and Tia and Ariana are herded in first while Callie brings up the rear. She closes the door behind her and Ariana and Tia are instructed to stand to my left. Ariana looks nervous, contrasting Tia's cool composure.

"So...the gang's all here, I assume?" Halsey says, eyeing each of us.

"That's everyone," Naomi nods.

"I see," Halsey begins, looking at each of us with disdain. She stands up and moves to the front of her desk. "So it all started with Caine, did it not? The girl who died before she got here?"

"It did," I answer.

"And you, Teymouri, you were on the bus with her," Halsey continues, crossing her arms in front of her. "So am I to assume that you're the mastermind behind all of this?"

"Something like that," I answer.

"It's a yes or no question, you stubborn little shit, now which is it?" Halsey growls.

"Fine! Yes!" I snap. "There! You happy? It was me! I started this whole thing!"

"Thank you, now we have a point to start from," Halsey continues. "So, correct me if I'm wrong...Teymouri and another girl take copies of the notes, upset over Caine's death. Teymouri and Beckham spoke with one another at some point and the two of you began working together. Let me guess, you stole my keys because you were trying to obtain a way to get through any locked doors. You wanted my skeleton key, didn't you? But you didn't get it...or did you? Maybe someone here made a copy? Tried to?" My chest tightens and my breathing becomes shallow. "One problem with that, though. You, Miller, where do you work?" She points at Ariana.

"Kitchen duty," she answers.

"And how about you, Ellis?" Halsey asks, tilting her head to the side.

"Groundskeeping," Tia answers.

"Teymouri?" Halsey asks, eyeing me.

"Custodial staff," I answer.

"And Beckham?" Halsey continues, catching Naomi's eye.

"Laundry," Naomi answers.

"Hmm...funny...not a single one of you works in the shop," Halsey observes. "Beckham, Teymouri, I've wondered since you two led me and my staff on that fantastic little romp around the chow hall exactly why you did it. Leah Reyes. She's been a model inmate, but...I have seen her with some of you. Are you certain there was no one else helping you?"

"No, just us," Naomi replies.

"You'd better be telling the truth" Halsey warns. "If I find out you're lying, I won't give you another chance. There will be no negotiations, no begging, no pleading to change my mind. If you are to expect any degree of leniency from me, then I implore you to tell me the truth now. Miller, why did I have to send a team to find you? What was the reason you went down to Sector S?"

"To arm ourselves," Ariana answers. "We'd heard rumors that there might still be weapons in the basement. Old firearms and ammunition."

"Is that so?" Halsey murmurs. "Operating on a rumor? Seems like quite a risk. Just about everyone on this island would rather make a mad attempt to swim to shore than go willingly into Sector S. Yet you're telling me that you did so even knowing that what you sought might well be imaginary? Regardless, I suppose this links up with the bag Teymouri confessed to knowing the whereabouts of?"

"It does," I answer. Halsey looks down at me and takes a step forward. I look away from her and she taps my foot with the toe of her boot, causing me to look back at her.

"How about you show me where you found the weapons?" she suggests. Her expression has become less harsh, but her eye is still burning with a tranquil fury.

"Fine..." I reply. She smirks and takes a step back, her eye still focused on me.

"Then let's go," Halsey says, beckoning for me to stand up. "Outside, all of you." Callie opens the door and Rashida steps away from the wall.

"Wait, Halsey," Rashida says. "Let's not give them a chance to pull something down in Sector S, the way they did with Richards and Martin. Beckham and Teymouri are the key players in this, let's minimize the risk and just take them." Halsey takes a moment to consider what Rashida has said.

"Hmm...I suppose that makes sense," Halsey admits. "Fine...Fenton, Meadows. Stay here and watch Ellis and Miller. No one leaves this room for any reason. Understood?"

"Yes ma'am," Nicole and Callie chorus. Callie steps forward while Nicole remains near the wall.

"Actually, ma'am, I need to speak with you first," Callie says. "In private. It's important that I do." Halsey takes a moment to think before gesturing for her to follow her out the door. She stops after Callie exits the room and turns her attention to the rest of us.

"All of you wait here until I return," Halsey orders. She closes the door and the rest of us wait for Halsey and Callie's footsteps to fade as they move down the hallway and out of earshot. Rashida approaches the door and puts her ear up against it.

"Can you hear anything?" Nicole asks. Rashida looks back at her and shakes her head.

"Not really," she answers. "It's muffled." She carefully turns the knob and the rest of us wait with bated breath as she peers through the crack in the door.

"How about now?" Nicole asks. Rashida steps back and closes the door. She shakes her head again.

"They're too far away, I can't make out what they're saying," she says. "If I open the door any wider they'll notice."

"What do you think they're talking about?" Nicole inquires. She appears very tense. A bead of sweat rolls down her temple.

"Considering the timing of it, we have to assume Callie's got something on us," Rashida replies. "We're going to Plan B."

"You think we should?" Nicole asks.

"We don't have a choice. We have to assume Halsey knows what's going on," Rashida answers. "We're gonna have to leave tonight with the inmates or else we won't have a chance at all."

"You sure about this?" Nicole asks. "No turning back if we set this into motion. It could get messy."

"Take the group set to board the ship, put them on the passenger ferry, and go warn Lacey, Andrew, and everyone else," Rashida replies. "Worst case scenario, we say the inmates were armed and forced us onto the ferry. If it turns out Callie has nothing, we'll disable the ferry's communications, say the inmates did it, come back, and we'll buy them some time. Pretend we didn't know the system here was gonna go down. Someone will have to go back to shore from there."

"That's not gonna help our case," Tia points out.

"Yeah, they'll just see us as kidnappers," Ariana adds.

"It's our best bet," Rashida counters. "It's either that or stay here and face the consequences. I can't hear their conversation down there, but I know something is up. It might be nothing, it might not, but we need to be prepared." Approaching footsteps signal Halsey and Callie's return. Everyone looks at the door and Rashida looks back at Nicole.

"You'd better not be wrong about this," Nicole warns Rashida. Halsey opens the office door and beckons us outside.

"Hurry up, let's not drag this out," she says. Rashida leads me and Naomi out of the room and into the hallway. Outside I see that Callie is nowhere to be found.

Chapter 24

The Walls Have Eyes

The four of us exit the building and wait along the street for a transport van to pick us up. The cool air whips against my face and within minutes I'm on the verge of shivering. In the silence I can hear the sound of waves breaking against the shore. When the van arrives, Naomi and I are herded into the back and Rashida steps in behind us. Halsey circles around and gets into the passenger seat. The van pulls away from the curb moments later.

When the van comes to a stop minutes later, Halsey exits the vehicle and opens the back. The three of us step outside and Halsey closes the doors. She leads us toward the dock entrance of Sector S and across the grass. Halsey steps toward the double doors and wrenches the lock open. The bolt scrapes across the metal, the sound of which is carried off by the wind. She and Rashida each heave open the doors, creaking as they swing apart. Rashida takes her flashlight from her belt and Halsey does the same. They switch them both on and shine them inside, illuminating the cold cement floor and walls.

"Well don't just stand there, get moving," Halsey orders, motioning for me and Naomi to follow her and Rashida. Naomi and I trade glances and step inside. A gust of wind kicks up behind us, aiding in pushing us forward. Down at the end of the ramp and in the first part of the tunnel, our group stops and Halsey turns to me.

"Where's the bag at?" she demands.

"It's this way," I say, pointing to the room where I left it.

"Lead the way, Teymouri," Halsey orders, gesturing toward the room with her flashlight. Heart racing, I push the door to the room open and walk toward the locker I stashed the bag in. There I reach in and retrieve it. Halsey snatches the bag from me and plops it down on a nearby table. She begins rifling through it, removing the bolt cutters and other tools, along with the firearms and ammunition. She holds up one of the pistols, the loaded one I carried for a short while, and leers at me.

"Seems the rumors were true," she observes. "Where did you find this?"

"It was in a storage locker in the basement," I explain. She nods and examines the weapon.

"Looks like I'll be having a talk with my staff soon," she grumbles. "Clearly someone lied to me when they said they'd cleared everything out of here." She turns her head back toward me. "Since you seem braver than the cowards in my employ, you get to lead me to where you found it. Is that understood?"

"Yes ma'am." She gives a forced smile of approval, then starts packing everything up. When she's finished, she points at the door and waits for me to exit first. Outside I find Rashida and Naomi standing near the end of the ramp.

"Quit standing around," Halsey growls at the others. "We need to keep moving." Without a word, Naomi and Rashida step away from the ramp and start toward us. Helena appears from behind Naomi and smiles maliciously. Halsey notices me staring and waves to get my attention.

"What are you looking at, Teymouri? Hurry up!" she says. I glance at her, then look back at Helena. She turns and walks straight through the wall behind her and disappears. I turn away to see Halsey waiting for me to catch up. As I pass by Halsey I see that the pistol she removed from the bag is still clutched in her hand. She gestures down the tunnel with it and walks behind us with Rashida in the lead. Several minutes pass with silence kept at bay by the echos of our footsteps. Down the tunnel I can see the stairs I came up from the basement. Instead of alerting Halsey to them, I decide to try locating the hole in the floor further on. The one Mattie dragged me into. It'll force us to walk further from the entrance.

"How far do you plan to take us, Teymouri?" Halsey demands.

"It's just a little further," I answer. We loop around a room marked

"S56", taking the only passageway near it that isn't blocked. Once around it we follow the signs to S53, the room with the hole in it. Inside I point toward the damaged section of floor. Our group walks over to it and I point down at the room below. Rashida and Halsey both shine their lights down into it.

"It was right here," I say. "They were in a locker down there."

"I see," Halsey replies. "And how did you get back out?"

"I took a nearby staircase," I answer. Halsey looks at me, then back at the room below.

"I'll be sure to come back and look through it tomorrow," Halsey says. "Which means I'd better find what you described down there. Understand?"

"Yes ma'am."

"Good. I don't owe you gain time and I won't give it if your story doesn't add up," she continues, motioning for the rest of us to follow. Our group continues through the tunnels, passing by various rooms and pitch black hallways. Footsteps somewhere behind me catch my attention. I glance in the direction they came from, but it's too dark to see much. Just a few open doors and ladders leading to crawlspaces. Something crashes in one of the rooms behind us and everyone turns to face the room it came from. Rashida and Halsey both shine their lights in its direction, each of us waiting in a tense silence.

"Not this again..." Naomi whispers.

"Rashida, go check it out," Halsey orders. Rashida nods and makes her way toward the door. She approaches it with caution, her baton drawn and at the ready. She reaches out to grab the handle, swiping at it and missing once before her fingers make contact. She pulls it open and tightens her grasp on the baton before walking inside.

"Miss me?" a voice whispers in my ear. The hairs on the back of my neck stand on end. "What's the matter, Sarita? Now not a good time?" Helena walks past me and stands beside Halsey. I can't see her expression in the darkness, but when she looks back at me over her shoulder, she lets out a chuckle. Seconds later she disappears. Rashida steps back out of the room and starts toward us.

"Find anyone?" Halsey asks. Rashida shakes her head.

"No, nothing," she replies, retaking her position at the head of the group.

"Keep an ear out for anything else," Halsey orders. "Seems we have another inmate on the loose." Our group continues forward with our footsteps echoing through the otherwise quiet tunnel. Rashida stops for a minute to ask me where the shortcut is and Halsey stands nearby, listening and glaring at the two of us. I point down the tunnel and explain where to find it. After a short walk to the main tunnel, we take a right, and then another before we begin to close in on the area where the shortcut is located. Rashida and Halsey both shine their lights around the area and soon both beams converge on the crumbled section of wall we're searching for. Halsey approaches it from the left, making certain to keep the rest of us in her line of sight. She taps the bottom of the wall with her boot and steps back, shining her light through the hole. Judging by her expression, she seems very displeased by the damage.

"I should have some of you girls fixing this place up," Halsey says. "Place is falling apart even more than I thought. Never should have put a stop to...wait a minute..." She shines her light past us and the rest of us turn our heads.

"What's going-?" Rashida begins.

"Shh!" Halsey interrupts. The four of us wait while Halsey listens. "I hear someone." She shines her light around the tunnel, but nothing turns up. Just aging concrete and old rusting pipes.

"What did you hear?" Rashida asks.

"Sounded like voices," Halsey answers, still shining her light around the tunnel.

"I didn't hear anything," Rashida says.

"Well I did," Halsey mutters. "Whatever, just keep moving." Rashida nods and Naomi and I are sent through the crumbled wall first. The two of us wait for Halsey and Rashida to follow us and in that time I start to remember what happened the last time we were here. To say that being in this room is unsettling is an understatement. After everyone is through the wall, Halsey takes one final look at it before shaking her head in frustration. She orders the rest of us out to the main tunnel and we stop again, this time to discuss the location of the fuel canisters. Halsey doesn't seem fazed when it's brought up. Rashida must have mentioned it before we went into the office.

"We threw them in the drainage area," I lie. "I know the way from here, it's not too far."

"As with the weapons in the basement, I expect to see evidence of this when we arrive." I nod and she orders our group to continue through the tunnels. This time Rashida has me walk beside her in order to show her the way. We round the first corner, taking a left, and start toward the fork in the path near where I split from Naomi and the others the first time I was here. As we approach, I hear a faint voice somewhere behind us. Halsey does too and she orders us to stop a second time.

"This is getting ridiculous," Halsey grumbles. "Get out here!" Her shout echoes through the tunnel and is met with no response.

"Are you sure you heard something?" Rashida inquires.

"I know I did," Halsey replies without looking back at her.

"I heard it too," I add.

"Then you get to go look," Halsey says, grabbing my arm and shoving me forward. I look back at her over my shoulder. "Go on. Get moving."

"Why am I going?" I demand.

"Because I said so!" Halsey answers. "Consider this the start of your punishment. Now go check the nearby rooms."

"I can't do that without a flashlight," I protest.

"Jesus Christ...Rashida give her one of yours!" Halsey orders. Rashida walks past her and gives me her smaller spare light.

"Now hurry up and go. Clock's ticking," Rashida orders, pointing down the hall behind me. She winks and I turn and start down the tunnel without another word. The first room I go to has a jammed door. Halsey accuses me of faking it until I grasp the handle with both hands and lean backward. She shakes her head in frustration and orders me to move to the next one.

"Make sure you check any potential hiding places, Teymouri!" Halsey calls to me. "Whoever is down here, I want them found." Stepping through the door of the second room, I find that it's about the same size as the one I found Ariana in. Similar lockers are lined up along part of one of the walls with two of them tipped over and lying open.

"Calls her employees cowards and here she is making you do all the dirty work," Helena says from nearby. I turn my light to see that she's sitting on the edge of an old table, swinging her feet back and forth and resting her palms beside her thighs. She tilts her head to the side and gives an eerie grin.

"I don't need this right now..." I mutter, walking past her. "Go away."

"I go away all the time," she replies, hopping off the table and following behind me. "Maybe you should enjoy the moments when I'm away. Like it or not, we're stuck with one another." She giggles and I slam the locker closed as I move to the next one.

"It's you making noises around here, isn't it?" I accuse, closing the second locker and turning to face her.

"Or maybe Mika never left," she replies, her expression going blank as she speaks. "Did you ever think of that?" It's as if she's staring through me. Put off by this, I turn back toward the lockers and check the last one. When I turn around she's gone again.

"Let's hurry it up, Teymouri!" Halsey calls from outside the room. I take one last look around the room before leaving. I check a third, fourth, and fifth room before Halsey grows tired of waiting and calls me back over. Who or whatever we've been hearing never materializes.

"If I hear anything else, I'm going to assume you're covering for whoever it is," Halsey warns me.

"What? How is that fair? I didn't see anyone!"

"Don't argue with me, Teymouri!" Halsey snarls. I grit my teeth and walk past her, taking my place back in line. We turn right at the fork and I push on the door. The objects Ariana used to barricade it are still there, but they've now all been tossed around. I push past the door and wait for the others to follow. On the wall is the same sign I saw before, one side pointing to "Plant Drainage."

Halsey's flashlight beam catches the sign as we approach. Light reflects off of it and gets in my eyes. The tunnel starts to curve off to the left as we approach. A room marked as "S12" comes into view, along with another sign showing that the drainage area is still further down the tunnel. As we get closer to the opening, I start to see an open area with pipes in a trench similar to the ones by the gates. Considering where we are, this seems like it might be on the other side of that wall. To the right as we exit the tunnel is a wide platform that stops at the wall. Approaching the ledge, I can see two canisters along the pipes. Both of them are barely visible. Rashida shines her light over the pipes and it becomes clear that still more canisters have been hidden further down. Halsey joins her by the ledge and uses her own light to examine the area below. Satisfied with what she's seen, she steps back and turns to Rashida.

"We'll come back for them later," she says. "Need to be sure we don't smudge any fingerprints." She turns to face me and Naomi. "So you two admit it, then? You set fire to my tower?" Naomi nods and Halsey steps closer to us. She gives us a forced smile and slugs Naomi in the stomach. Naomi doubles over and falls to her knees. The moment I take a step toward Naomi, Halsey punches me in the cheek, sending me crashing to the ground.

"Halsey, what are you-?" Rashida begins. Halsey points the pistol at her and she stops talking the moment she sees it.

"You two disgust me...you know that?" Halsey growls at me and Naomi as she stares down at us. "What the hell was going through your stupid little heads? Huh? Hopeless! Both of you! I should blow you both away right now! God knows I'd be doing this country a favor...and in more ways than one..." I glance up to see her pointing the pistol at my forehead. Rashida steps forward and pushes Halsey's arm away.

"Halsey, don't even joke about-" Rashida begins.

"Shut it!" Halsey roars, her words echoing throughout the room. "I don't need your whole voice-of-reason spiel! Get Teymouri up, I'll take the other one." Halsey yanks Naomi to her feet and Rashida holds out her hand. I take it and she pulls me to my feet. I continue clutching my cheek as I take a few steps forward. "Now get moving," Halsey orders, glaring at us. "All of you." Rashida takes the lead again and Naomi and I start back down the way we came. After what she just did I'm even more nervous to be walking ahead of her. What's to stop her from shooting all three of us before we know what's happening?

Chapter 25

Escape

Several minutes pass before we reach the gates. The moment they come into view, Halsey is furious.

"What the hell is this?" Halsey demands as we approach the grated bridge. "Rashida!" Rashida turns to face her.

"What?" she asks.

"I sent you and Teymouri to open the gates back up, did I not?" Halsey inquires, gesturing at the gates. Rashida looks over her shoulder at them, then back at Halsey.

"We did," Rashida replies.

"Then why are they closed?" Halsey demands. My palms are starting to sweat.

"My guess is that Fulmer had something to do with it," Rashida answers. "He's down here more than anyone else. He was dealing with curious guards right after it happened. I'm guessing someone started looking around again. Probably wanted to make sure no one tampered with evidence."

"Are you sure you even came down here?" Halsey asks, brushing past her and heading toward the gates.

"I'm certain we did," Rashida says, turning toward her as she passes. "Teymouri and I should be on camera walking in through the dock entrance and coming out this side." Halsey shines her light up and down the gates before walking back toward us.

"I need to seriously rethink my hiring practices," Halsey mutters. "Twenty years of working with incompetent employees has been very draining. We'll sort this out after we get the gates open. Now where's the lever? It's around here somewhere, isn't it?" Rashida points to the lever and Halsey starts toward it. She places her hand on it and pauses for a moment. The rest of us wait for several tense seconds.

"Halsey?" Rashida asks. She ignores Rashida and lets go of the lever before turning and walking back across the bridge.

"I don't think I know you anymore, Rashida," Halsey says, stopping in the center of the bridge. "I hoped Callie was wrong, I really did." She turns to face Rashida and grips the pistol in her hand. "And yet... here we are."

"What are you talking about?" Rashida asks. Naomi and I trade anxious glances.

"How stupid do you think I am?" Halsey demands. "That lever's a faulty deathtrap, isn't it? If it weren't for Callie noticing that something was off, I daresay your plan might've worked. I should kill all three of you right now." She glares at all three of us. After several tense seconds, she crosses the remainder of the bridge and pounds her fist on the gates three times. She turns back toward us and the gates begin opening.

"You see, Rashida..." Halsey continues. "This whole thing began after Callie noticed something odd following a trip I took to the records building...but we'll get to that in a moment. I knew early on that the inmates were trying to escape, and throughout most of this, that's where my attention was focused. Unfortunately for you, it didn't stay that way." With the gates now open, it's revealed to us that Jeff, Fulmer, and Nicole have been captured. Several guards stand around them, holding them all at gunpoint. Rashida places her hand on the grip of her pistol and takes a single step backward.

"No, no, no..." Rashida whispers, her mouth barely moving.

"I knew something was wrong when one of my inmates showed up with one of those two napkins," Halsey continues. "After that I went after Teymouri, but I never did find that other napkin. I wonder why that is? Maybe it was one of you?" She turns toward the three captured guards, then back toward us. "Or maybe it was you, Rashida. You filthy, backstabbing traitor, how dare you try to kill me!" Halsey roars. "I saved your life after the blast! I protected you from prosecution after you killed Chambers! And I expected the same from you when we started running this place together! You were supposed to have my back, and for a while I guess you did. But something changed...something five years ago, am I wrong?"

"You're not..." Rashida answers. Halsey switches off her flashlight and puts it back on her belt. She racks the slide on her pistol and glares at Rashida.

"I should have known better than to bring you here," Halsey snarls. "After you fragged Chambers that should have been my cue. That should have been the moment I severed ties with you. But I stood by you as my friend, the one I grew up alongside of, the sister I never had. That meant nothing to you? Nothing I said ever meant anything at all?"

"Back when you said it, it did," Rashida replies. "Things have changed, Ava. You've changed."

"And so have you, Rashida," Halsey chuckles. "Well then...as I was saying..." She crosses the rest of the bridge and the three of us back away from her. She stops at the end and looks at the lever, then at us. "...the note. The note with that famous peddler of lies, Mr. Randall Adams, the king of false stories, the goddamn bastard who once wrote multiple scathing articles about my facility...his contact information on two napkins, and meanwhile we have Beckham stabbing an inmate half to death and then a month passes with nothing. I didn't think much of any of it until one of the girls, Teymouri, who was on the same bus as the other girl with the same information...suddenly decided to lead me on a nice little chase around the chow hall. Thought at first maybe Beckham had something on her. I tried to give her the benefit of the doubt, I really did, but it was very odd, nonetheless.

"Then came Mika Sato and Ariana Miller, running off into Sector S. Clearly they were up to something. This wasn't the first time something like that had happened. I had no evidence at the time to bind the two groups of inmates together, no way to prove they were together on this, but all the signs were there, yes indeed. And then something rather strange happened...something that hasn't happened since Rashida flipped out five years ago." She turns and points at Jeff with her free hand. "Jeff over there," she continues, letting her hand fall to her side. "Officer Jeff Martin...decided to stick up for Beckham, Ellis, and Teymouri...after Officer Laura Richards was somehow killed! That set off a series of alarm bells and so did the fire that consumed Tower B a short time later. Suddenly all the inmates I had my eye on were together in one location.

"And then my favorite part of this fun little story took place right after that!" Halsey sneers, pointing the pistol at Rashida. "My Deputy Headmistress, the one I once trusted above all others, comes back from the surveillance room and has nothing to show for it!" She lowers the pistol and continues glaring at Rashida. "The footage is somehow gone, and yes, I'll admit at first that I didn't suspect that it was your fault, Rashida. Why would I think that? Like I said, I trusted you. But that trust began to erode after you started making a fuss about Teymouri's punishment, and from there it got even worse when you decided to remove her early from the bunker. I played along, I let you have your fun, I thought maybe if I just let you do that one stupid little thing that maybe you'd shut the hell up and get back in line, but no...I was wrong and I was a fool to believe you would. Oh, but here's the best part of it," Halsey chuckles, pointing briefly at Fulmer. "Rashida tells Fulmer there about the faulty lever, and then he tells Callie who's working with him at the time." Callie, standing near Fulmer, gives an insufferable smirk and chuckles as Halsey continues speaking. "Now that you're soon to be out of the picture, Rashida, it looks like Callie will be taking over for you. I have a feeling she'll do much better than you. I expect loyalty above all else. She understands that...unlike you..."

"That's not loyalty, that's subservience," Rashida replies.

"Call it whatever you want," Halsey snorts with a dismissive wave. "Your opinion doesn't matter. Getting back to what I was saying, Fulmer didn't have to say anything specific, just that there was something wrong and even Callie has admitted that she didn't think much of it at that point. Who would? Machines break, wiring becomes faulty, it's just the way the world works. Order to chaos. But then I find Jeff and Nicole outside of the records building while on my way to find the autopsy report for Richards. Of course I thought it was odd, but after Callie spotted you, Rashida, coming out of the surveillance room with Teymouri in tow, only a short time later, she brought it up with me...and after that Nicole and Jeff's behavior started to make sense. They were stalling me. I don't know what the hell happened in there, but considering Teymouri and Beckham tried to steal my key, and Leah Reyes, who knows and speaks with them both on a regular basis, works in the shop, I would have to assume that you stole something from records, and that you managed to do that by creating a copy of my key. Because why else would you try to steal it? I bet that's all Reyes needed, just to see it so she could make a copy. How am I doing, am I in the ballpark, Rashida?"

"I'm not admitting anything," Rashida declares.

"Oh, that's fine, you don't need to," Halsey laughs. "Take the fifth for all I care, it's not going to matter in the end. How about we wrap this up? Sound good? Well...the final piece of the puzzle fell into place when Callie spoke with me just before we left my office earlier. That's when she mentioned the faulty lever. The same one that killed an inmate so long ago. That combined with the fact that she'd noticed beforehand that Fulmer closed the gates. The timing seemed off. Suddenly Teymouri wanted to confess and Rashida's telling me that there's something in Sector S that I need to come see. Hmm...a faulty lever... closed gates...and a trail of bread crumbs for me to follow. It was pretty creative, I will give you that, but I'm afraid the fun is over." Halsey raises her pistol and shoots Rashida in the chest. She falls to the ground in a heap and lies there motionless. Halsey then turns the pistol on me and Naomi.

"This way girls..." Halsey beckons, gesturing for us to cross the bridge. Naomi and I trade glances and look back at Halsey. The two of us hesitate for a moment and start over the bridge. Once across it, Halsey tells us to stop and to stand off to the side.

"I think you both know where this is leading, right?" Halsey taunts Nicole, Jeff, and Fulmer, pacing back and forth in front of them. "Now that you've picked your side, the wrong one I might add, I see no reason for any of you to continue working here. Consider yourselves fired." She raises her pistol and points it at Nicole's head. Much to my surprise, as well as confusion, Rashida sits up and fires her weapon at Halsey. Halsey lets out an angry shout as a rubber bullet strikes her in the cheek. Her pistol goes off and the bullet misses Nicole and strikes a guard behind her. From further back in the corridor the commotion is followed by two loud blasts. Two stun grenades have detonated behind the group of guards, sending three crashing to the ground and incapacitating two others. Several gunshots follow and everyone begins to scatter. Rashida fires twice more at Halsey, only one of which makes contact, striking her in the chest. Halsey fires a single round at Rashida and hits her in the stomach. She flinches and shrugs it off, implying the presence of a ballistic vest. Callie turns to fire at Rashida and is struck by two rounds in the back. Blood spatters on the ground around her and she collapses; dead before she hits the ground.

Rashida's weapon jams, and after a failed attempt to clear it fast enough, turns and bolts further into Sector S as Halsey races after her. Jeff, Fulmer, and Nicole have used the commotion to their advantage and are fighting with the other guards. Halsey drops the bag as she races after Rashida and the second pistol spills out and slides across the pavement. I snatch it up along with a spare magazine before tearing off after Halsey and Rashida. My ears are ringing as I race down the corridor. Halsey fires at Rashida again and misses. The two of them soon disappear into the darkness. It's next to impossible to navigate the darkened corridors with what few lights are still on. I consider using the flashlight I borrowed from Rashida, but it will just give me away. My foot catches something and I trip and crash to the ground. I leap to my feet, searching for the pistol. After a few seconds, I find it and continue down the tunnel.

Moments later I catch up to Halsey and Rashida, spotting them over a hundred feet away, both fighting for control of the pistol. Halsey twists Rashida's arm and the pistol goes off. The round whizzes past me and strikes the wall somewhere behind me. I trot off to the side before either of them notice me and aim my weapon at Halsey. Rashida swings Halsey into a wall and rips the gun from her grasp. Before she can attempt to fire it, Halsey punches her in the stomach and takes it back. Rashida stumbles backward and looks up to see Halsey pointing the gun at her. She pulls the trigger and I panic. Her gun doesn't go off and instead there's a metallic click.

Rashida takes advantage, knocking the gun away and punching Halsey twice in the face. The gun clatters on the floor and Rashida takes a swipe at Halsey with her baton. Halsey dodges it and I line up another shot. My finger freezes on the trigger and I can't bring myself to pull it. There's too much chance that I might hit Rashida instead. I need to wait for an opening. Halsey gains control over the baton and tosses it away. Rashida sprints away and Halsey chases her into one of the rooms. I rush toward the room in time to see Halsey tackle Rashida and begin punching her repeatedly. She grabs Rashida by the front of her uniform and hits her several more times, pushing her to the edge of unconsciousness. Her face, hair, and portions of her clothing are soaked in blood, as is the case with Halsey. I raise my weapon and point it at Halsey.

"Get away from her!" I order. "Now!" Halsey looks up at me, her fist still drawn back and ready to strike Rashida again. Her other hand gripping the collar of Rashida's uniform. She lets go and lowers her fist, locking eyes with me as she gets to her feet. Rashida lets out a groan and rolls onto her side. She spits blood onto the pavement and Halsey looks down at her with disgust before turning her attention back to me. Her expression changes from disgust to anger.

"Well? What are you waiting for, Teymouri?" she asks, taking two steps forward as she speaks. "Go on. Do it! Shoot me! Prove to the world that you're exactly what they think you are!" She takes two more steps and I take one back as the pistol trembles in my hands. "A filthy, disgusting, evil creature who deserves to be locked away!" She continues walking toward me as she speaks. "You think it's bad out there now? Oh, you just wait till you pull that trigger."

"Stay where you are," I growl, trying to keep my voice steady.

"You're not going to do it, Teymouri," she declares. "Even you're smarter than that. What happens if I die? You might be prepared for the consequences, but are you willing to make your family a target too? Do you really want to go back to find that your parents and that sister of yours have been slaughtered in their beds?"

"Shut up! Just shut up and stay where you are! I swear to God I'll do it!" I back away, matching her footsteps until I'm back out in the tunnel.

"Think about it, Teymouri," Halsey continues, her expression contorting into an evil sneer. "What would it be like to come home and find that you've lost your entire family?"

"I'm not giving you another warning," I hiss.

"The world isn't going to see things from your perspective," Halsey continues, ignoring me. "They're too caught up in the spin for that! They'll just flip the TV on like good little boys and girls and believe whatever they hear! Including whatever I tell them! Whatever the people above me tell them! You'll be the villain no matter what you say, no matter what you do. There's no way out of this, kid. So you can go ahead and pull that trigger if you think you have the guts, because you've already lost!" My back hits the wall and Halsey continues toward me. She snatches the gun away from me and throws me to the ground. When I look up she's pointing the weapon right at my forehead. A gunshot rings out and my heart skips a beat as I close my eyes. When I open them, Halsey is backing away, clutching a wound in her shoulder. The pistol falls from her hand and clatters on the pavement as she collapses onto one knee. Blood seeps through her fingers and she looks up at the shooter. I turn my head to see Naomi standing nearby. She's holding one of the rifles I saw the guards with at the gates.

"A pitiful, worthless woman like you could disappear in the blink of an eye..." she growls at Halsey. "...and no one would ever find you." Naomi pulls the trigger a second time and the round pierces Halsey's heart. She topples over onto her side and blood begins to pool around her. Naomi lowers her weapon and trots over to me. Her expression changes to that of relief as she helps me to my feet.

"You all right?" she asks.

"Yeah, I'm good," I grunt. "Rashida's pretty banged up, though."

"Where is she?" I point toward the room she's in and Naomi trots ahead of me. She looks over her shoulder at me as I follow after her.

"We need to hurry," she says, stopping for a moment to toss me the bag. "Things weren't looking so good when I left. I couldn't tell who it was, but there's at least a few bodies over there." Inside the room we find Rashida sitting on her knees. She looks up at us as we approach and Naomi helps her to her feet.

"Can you walk? Run?" Naomi asks. Rashida grunts as she stands up.

"I'm fine, I'm fine," she insists. "Let's get out of here. What's going on back at the gates, do either of you know?"

"Just that people are dead," Naomi says, letting go of Rashida who wipes blood away from her eyes and trots out the door. She snatches up her baton before giving one look at Halsey's body and hurrying down the tunnel. Halfway back to the gates, Rashida's radio starts picking something up, but it's difficult to hear through the static. Whoever it is the message sounds urgent.

"Dammit..." Rashida grumbles. "Beckham, do you know if anyone radioed for backup?"

"I wasn't paying attention," Naomi admits. "It looked pretty bad over there, it wouldn't surprise me." Rashida grits her teeth and continues running.

"Rashida!" someone shouts from near the gates. Up ahead we see Nicole standing beside Lacey with Andrew nearby. Lacey and Nicole are both urgently waving us forward. Lacey is holding a rifle that she's in the process of reloading. She and Nicole are both bruised and battered with blood smeared on their faces, hands, and uniforms. Lacey is squinting through one eye that's beginning to swell. Her glasses are lopsided and one of the lenses is cracked.

"What's going on?" Rashida demands. "Are we clear to head to the ferry?"

"For now," Andrew says, beckoning us to follow.

"One of the other guards tried to call in backup, but we're not sure if he got through. You know how spotty the reception is down here," Nicole explains. "That was about five minutes ago. We've got casualties on our side."

"Nicole tipped us off and told us something might go down," Lacey explains. "We picked up a few weapons at the armory, but we had to skip disabling the power plant at the time we intended. We still need to do that."

"Then get to it!" Rashida orders. "Head straight there. The rest of us are going to make our way to the ferry." Lacey nods, turns, and races back toward the gates. Near the gates we find Jeff sitting with his back against the wall looking dazed. He's clutching his baton in one hand. It's stained with blood and the body of the guard he appears to have beaten with it is lying nearby, the face almost unrecognizable. Beyond the gates lie the bodies of the guards that sided with Halsey. All of them scattered about, bloodied, and a motionless. Rashida snatches up a rifle and inspects it.

"Come on, get up!" Nicole urges Jeff as she takes his hand and starts pulling him up. He winces in pain and lets go. He plops back down in his seated position, clutching his shoulder.

"I think that son of a bitch broke something," he grumbles, nodding in the direction of the deceased guard.

"Well suck it up or else you're gonna get a lot more than that," Nicole grunts, pulling him to his feet. He winces and grits his teeth, standing slightly hunched as he shuffles along with Nicole's assistance. Lacey and Andrew break from the rest of the group and take off down the tunnel at a dead sprint. One of the dead guards' radios goes off and someone's voice comes over it.

"Someone get a team over to Sector S, I just got a call from someone down there," the man says. "I couldn't make it out, but it sounded urgent." Other voices respond and Rashida starts ordering everyone back on our side of the gates.

"Bring the bodies back! Get them in here! Now!" Rashida orders. Naomi sets her rifle down and the rest of the guards, with the exception of Jeff, all begin dragging the handful of wounded and dead guards back near the grated bridge. I help Rashida carry the last one over and she races back to the lever on the Tower B side. She flips it and then tries to wrench it apart as the gates close. She manages to bend it, but she's too weak from her injuries to do much more. She trots back through the gates and they close seconds later. She notices me watching and points behind me.

"Quit standing there and go disconnect the fuse for the gate!" she orders. "Hurry! Go, go, go! They're gonna be here any minute!" I nod and take off running down the tunnel and into the passageway where I found the fuse box. "I'll meet you over there!" she calls after me. I don't respond and continue running. When I reach the window, I start to hesitate. I glance through the broken section and take a deep breath before dropping the bag by the window. I crawl through so quickly that I topple onto the floor, and when I get to my feet, Helena grabs me by the arm.

"Where do you think you're going?" she sneers, trying her best to hold me back.

"Let go of me!" I scream. I throw her off and race to the end of the hallway where she appears again. This time she grabs me and throws me to the ground. I tumble across the floor and race to my feet. She rams into me and sends me crashing into a shelf. Tools and other items fall from it and she kicks me in the stomach.

"You're not supposed to win! You're a failure, a loser, you deserve to die here!" Helena shrieks, her eyes wild and teeth bared. I stumble to my feet and she grabs hold of my arm. I spin and hurl her to the ground before racing into the next room and toward the fuse box. Helena catches up to me and tackles me right before I reach the fuse box. I elbow her in the nose and drag myself from beneath her. She grabs at my face and hair and I punch her twice in the cheek before hurling her off. I get back up and fling the fuse box open. After locating the fuse, I pull it out and race back to the door to find Helena blocking my exit.

Helena lunges forward, clamping her hands around my throat and sending me stumbling backward into the shelves near the fuse box. Her grasp loosens for a brief moment as we both land, giving me just enough time to escape. She grabs my hair as I try to stand and pulls me back down, knocking us both over in the process. I'm the first to get to my feet, slugging her once in the cheek before doing so and racing out the door immediately afterward. Helena shouts after me in a rage.

"Run all you want, Teymouri!" she screams. "It doesn't matter where you go, I will always find you!" Her words cut through me as I race down the hallway. Waiting at the window is Naomi and Rashida. They help pull me through the window and we hurry back to the main tunnel.

"You cut it close there, kid," Rashida says as we reach the main tunnel. "I just heard them announce their arrival at Tower B a second ago."

"I take it Andrew and Lacey haven't made it to the power plant yet?" I ask, noticing that the lights are still on. Rashida shakes her head as I pick up my bag and sling it over my shoulder.

"They should be done soon," she explains. "Come on, let's get moving. We have to get to the docks while we still have time." We stop back in the tunnel near the gates and Rashida orders everyone to follow her. Nicole and Jeff join us and Fulmer, now holding one of the discarded rifles, brings up the rear.

"Anyone have any ideas on where to go?" Fulmer asks. "They're likely going to cover the dock entrance before we get there. Once they find the gates closed they'll know something is wrong."

"We can try the tunnel to Tower A," Nicole suggests. "We'll be above ground and exposed for longer, but it'll at least give us an out."

"How do we know they aren't going to cover that too?" Jeff asks.

"They won't bother," Nicole replies. "It's been shut down for months and they locked the doors from the other side."

"Then how do we get through them?" Rashida inquires as our group makes the first right and starts toward the tunnel where I found Ariana. The sign I saw in there must've meant Tower A when it read "Eastern

Tunnel Access."

"I don't know how effective it'll be, but I have a crowbar in my bag," I say, slowing a little to search for it. I pull it out and hold it up.

"We might be able to pry one of the doors off the hinges," Rashida says as we reach the first set of doors. Our group files through them and turns right. We race down the tunnel and come out near the sign pointing to the drainage area and Tower A. We pass two more rooms before at last reaching the doors. Right as we do, the power goes out, plunging us into near darkness; our flashlight beams the only source of light remaining.

"Looks like the others found the power plant," Fulmer remarks. "How long should we expect to wait for them?" Rashida takes the crowbar from me.

"Up to ten minutes, maybe a little longer," Nicole answers. Rashida hands Naomi her flashlight and has her hold it while she wedges the crowbar into the side of the door. She pulls as hard as she can, but she's not making much progress.

"Dammit!" Rashida snarls. "Someone give me a hand! Everyone else, go look in the rooms for a wrench or something; anything that can give us some extra leverage!" Fulmer assists Rashida while the rest of us split off and start searching. Nicole and I take the nearest room and the two of us sift through drawers, lockers, and anywhere else we might find something. When she doesn't find anything, she trots out of the room and I follow her to the next room. There she finds a large wrench and the two of us race back to the others. Nicole passes off the wrench to Fulmer and Nicole. They attach the loop to the crowbar and start pulling. The door begins to give way. Rashida and Fulmer start working on the lower part of the door and soon it begins to become unstable. They remove the tools and start kicking at the door.

"Get the top one too!" Rashida says, pointing at the top hinge. They struggle to hold the two tools steady as they pull with all their strength. Bits of concrete come loose around the frame and soon the hinge is pulled away enough to try again. They both start kicking at the door again and this time it falls and scrapes across the floor, still clinging to the padlock on the other side.

"Should we risk getting in touch with the others?" Jeff asks. "They don't know we decided to take this route."

"No," Rashida grunts, helping Fulmer move the door out of the way. "We have to assume the other guards know we turned traitor. They might be scanning the comm channels for us." She and Fulmer finish moving the door out of the way and turn to face the rest of us.

"I'll stay behind to direct the others," Fulmer volunteers, starting back down the tunnel with his flashlight in hand. "Wait for us at the tower if you can, we'll meet you there soon."

"Got it," Rashida replies. "All right, everyone else get moving." She gestures for us to head through the door and Rashida takes the lead after snatching her rifle back up. I place the crowbar and wrench in the bag and follow after her. Fulmer disappears down the tunnel and the rest of us make our way to Tower A. Once there, Rashida borrows the crowbar again and uses it to pry open the sliding door. She hands it back to me and pulls the door open while the rest of us file through. We pass by the control room and circle around a hallway similar to Tower B before reaching the only exit. There Rashida pushes the doors open and looks out at the rest of the island. If not for the moon overhead, it would be pitch black. She pulls her head back inside and looks at us.

"Teymouri, what else is in that bag?" Rashida inquires.

"A few tools, some ammo, things like that," I reply. "The wrench and crowbar from earlier and some bolt cutters too."

"Perfect," Rashida says. "Take them and go cut the chain off the gates up ahead. Try not to attract any attention. There's a watchtower behind this building." I nod and brush past Rashida. Naomi holds the door while Rashida sneaks out with her rifle in hand, crouched by the corner of the building and ready to fire on the watchtower if needed. Keeping as low as I can, I hurry toward the gates. There I cut the chain off and wave for the others to follow.

Rashida goes back to the door and squeezes past the others, aiming her rifle down the hall. Someone must've heard something from the looks of it. She turns to face the others and points at me, gesturing for them to move toward me. I glance up at the watchtower as they all start toward me. There doesn't appear to be any movement, but it's difficult to see much. Rashida remains by the door, soon joined by Andrew, Fulmer, and Lacey. Naomi and I push the gates open and Rashida takes the lead again. We head down the path until we come to the tool shed near some of the farmland. From here it's a game of follow the leader with Rashida still in front. Headlights coming up the road signal the approach of a van. It stops at the gates and our group waits behind the shed until it passes. Once it's gone, we follow Rashida to the records building and walk along the front. She leads us between the records building and the one next door to it. Halfway to the back of the buildings, alarms begin sounding across the island.

"Shit!" Rashida snarls. "Teymouri, Beckham, stay here! Do not move!" She races past us and nearly collides with the others as they catch up. "Andrew! Lacey! Guard the inmates! The rest of you follow me!" Lacey and Andrew trot up alongside me and Naomi, both clutching their rifles. Rashida leads Fulmer and Nicole to the parking lot beside the barracks. Jeff hangs back behind us, clutching his wounded shoulder. Rashida, Fulmer, and Nicole race up alongside a parked van and start climbing into it. Gunshots ring out from the barracks and they quickly abandon their efforts and hide behind the van as multiple rounds tear through the air. Other guards begin shouting as Rashida and the others return fire. Andrew steps forward and fires three rounds at two guards attempting to sneak up on Rashida. They fall to the ground and Rashida stands up and climbs into the driver seat. She ducks as two rounds shatter the passenger window and leave holes in the windshield.

Fulmer and Nicole kill off the guard firing at Rashida right as the engine roars to life. It's difficult to hear what's being said, but Rashida begins shouting and waving us over. Andrew motions for us to follow as he darts toward the van. There are more shouts from near the docks as we reach the van. Jeff grunts in pain as he rushes into the back of the van. Naomi and I hop in behind him and are soon joined by everyone but Fulmer, who takes the passenger seat. Once the doors are closed, Nicole pounds on the wall separating us from the cab and Rashida spins the van around, sending us crashing to the floor and flinging others into the wall. The van speeds down the road and two rounds pierce the walls, one of which comes within inches of both me and Jeff.

The van tears across a section of grass and moments later our ears are met with the deafening sound of metal scraping against the sides of the van. The vehicle slows abruptly in the same instance, signaling that Rashida's driven it straight through the gate by the docks. The van hits a few more rough areas before rapidly coming to a halt. Rashida spins it around and starts backing it up and at last it comes to a complete stop. Andrew throws the doors open and Rashida stumbles out of the driver seat. I hop out of the van and Rashida grabs me and drags me to the ground. Several rounds sail overhead and pierce the wall beside us. Andrew returns fire and Rashida drags me to my feet. She pushes me around a corner right as Lacey races past me. Naomi is right behind me.

"Get below deck!" Rashida orders. "Lacey, get this thing moving, now! They're right on top of us!" I look back in time to see Fulmer shoot one of the guards out of a nearby watchtower. Naomi grabs me by the arm and pulls me along.

"Quit staring and let's go!" Naomi shouts over the gunfire. Guards are closing in on the ferry. Lacey and Andrew sprint to the bow of the vessel while Rashida and Fulmer take cover behind the railing and alongside the van. They fire on the approaching guards, forcing them to retreat to cover. Naomi and I race to the front of the ferry and locate the stairway. Right at the foot of the stairs, Naomi slips and crashes onto the floor. My foot catches on her leg and I'm sent tumbling after her. I drag myself onto my hands and knees in time to see Leah and the others trotting toward us.

"Hey! You guys all right?" Leah asks as she helps Naomi to her feet.

"We've been listening to the commotion upstairs," Jackie says, coming up alongside Leah. "What's going on out there?"

"A shootout," Naomi grunts, getting to her feet. "Alarms started going off and people started shooting at us." The engine roars to life moments later. Soon after that we all turn our heads as the door at the top of the stairs opens and Rashida and the other guards begin descending the stairs. Nicole and Jeff seem shaken, contrasting Fulmer and Rashida's composure. They join us at the base of the stairs and Nicole helps Jeff seat himself against a wall.

"It's over..." Rashida says, glancing at everyone. "We're away from the island. You got about thirty minutes till we disembark, so don't go falling asleep on us."

"Did everyone make it?" Savannah asks.

"Yeah, barely," Rashida answers, seating herself against the wall. "I about got my head taken off back there."

"Where's Andrew at?" Jeff asks.

"He went to help Lacey" Fulmer answers.

"Right, got it," Jeff grunts, adjusting his back against the wall. "I lost sight of him up there."

"My head is still spinning," Nicole says, leaning her head back against the wall. "Thought we were dead for sure."

"Would've been if it hadn't been for Fulmer and the others," Rashida says. "We owe you guys one." Fulmer gives a weak grin that disappears as fast as it appeared.

"Just doing my part," he says.

"So...now what do we do?" Jeff asks. "It should be a while before the cops are after us, but...after that...?"

"Let's just focus on right now," Rashida says. "Hard part's over. We made it out alive. We'll figure the rest out as we go."

* * *

Over the next twenty minutes, Naomi and I fill the others in on what took place while we were in Sector S. The others are riveted the entire time. I never mention Helena to any of the others. Each time I think about her and what she said to me the last time I saw her, I start to feel a sense of dread building up in my stomach. In the chaos of our escape, I didn't think to keep an eye out for her. Part of me is left to wonder if she was ever real and if I'll ever have to see her again. When it's time for us to leave, Rashida stands up and has everyone follow her up onto the deck.

The others and I get to our feet and follow her upstairs. When we reach the deck, I make my way to the railing and peer over the side. The water is calm and the moonlight is reflecting off the glassy surface. I look back and see that the island has disappeared into the darkness. In that brief moment I feel a sense of relief. Mixed in there somewhere is a strange sense of hope. I know what lies ahead and what it will mean for all of us, but right now I just want to live here, in this moment, for as long as I can. The dock is closing in and we'll be disembarking soon.

"Hey...you doing all right?" Naomi asks, joining me at the railing.

"Yeah, I guess," I answer, turning to face her. "Head's sort of...spinning still. You know what I mean?"

"As well as anyone else here," she replies.

"I wish this was it," I say. "I wish this was our last stop. That everyone could just go back home from here. Try to pretend this never happened."

"Same," she says. "Somehow, I feel like that would be kinda hard to do."

"Because you'd have to adjust to being out there again?" I ask.

"Yeah, that's the biggest part," she says. "It'd be a little weird walking away from everyone, though. Not sure I would be able to forget all of this."

"I didn't really mean it in the literal sense, but...I dunno," I say. "You think we'll survive this next part?"

"I don't see why not," she shrugs. "We survived McGinley's, didn't we? Probably the hardest part. Not that it gets much easier from here. Or at all. I guess the point is that I'm hoping we will."

"What did you mean when you said it'd be weird walking away from everyone?" I ask. She shrugs.

"It'd be weird," she says. "We've been through some rough times. I'd wonder about you and everyone else. That's all. Not like, in a sappy way or anything, I just...I don't know if I can put it into words. It's like the end of an era. Or it would be if we split off."

"I suppose we all will eventually," I say, looking away from her. "One way or another." The two of us watch the ferry pull up to the dock and slow to a halt.

"Beckham! Teymouri!" Rashida says, walking past us. "This way!" She beckons for us to follow her toward the stern. Rochelle, Savannah, Fulmer, and everyone else pass by us, leaving me and Naomi alone by the railing.

"I guess we'll cross that bridge when we come to it. For now we're stuck with each other," Naomi says with a grin, walking past me. She stops a few feet away and beckons for me to follow. "Come on, let's go. The story doesn't end here."

Author's Note and Acknowledgments

Closed Campus could not have been created if not for the assistance of the many people who had a hand in the process. During the time I spent writing this book I had the pleasure of working with a number of wonderful individuals, many of whom were strangers who generously volunteered to speak with me under the condition of confidentiality. I met with people who immigrated to this country from various regions of the world, people who spent time in various prisons here in the United States, some as correctional staff, others as inmates. I spoke with mental health specialists, former police officers, lawyers, and people whose lives have been and still are being effected by racism, xenophobia, and other forms of discrimination in this country. From the bottom of my heart, I sincerely thank every one of you for sharing your stories with me.

Input from various individuals wasn't the only part of this book's development. There were locations with similarities to McGinley's School for Girls that were the basis for the book's setting. One such place, though it was not a reform school, was Alcatraz Island in San Francisco, California. Back in 2011 I took a trip down to California and visited the island for the first time. Much of the architecture and the island itself played a big part in the creation of the island where the story takes place. I frequented places in Washington State such as Fort Worden and Fort Flagler as a kid and these locations also played into the descriptions of various structures in Closed Campus.

One of the most challenging parts of Closed Campus was writing the solitary confinement scenes. Things such as Sarita communicating with another inmate through a vent and her way of pacing back and forth in her cell while counting her steps, are both taken from real-life stories of three people I spoke to who suffered that punishment while incarcerated. Sarita's apparent hallucinations and complete loss of time, as well as Naomi's aggression and difficulty thinking are common problems reported by inmates who suffer through solitary confinement. In the story, Sarita is only in "the bunker" for days at a time, but in real life, people are often left in solitary for weeks, months, and sometimes longer. Currently there are efforts to abolish the use of solitary in prisons, but it still lingers in many.

Closed Campus took me three years to complete, starting in April of 2017 and finishing in April 2020, only a few days from the exact date I began writing it. All the research I compiled in that time will be used for more than just this book as I intend write other books like it. Since many of those I spoke with requested anonymity, I changed some of the names here in the acknowledgments, with the permission of those involved. Others requested that I not use any names at all and so have not been added to the list, but I still want to make sure that I make it clear how much your input was appreciated and that I simply cannot thank you enough for your involvement in this project. The first people I want to thank are my family members, specifically my mother and her fiance', who I just call my step-father at this point. You both encouraged me in my endeavor to become an author and gave me that much needed push to start publishing my books, as well as provided me with some of the necessary tools to create this novel.

Next I want to thank Katrina, whose vital input regarding the story's villain, Ava Halsey, was crucial to making her into what she eventually became; my long-time friend Ken for providing me with a laptop we sarcastically referred to as "the craptop", as it became a vital addition to my ragtag set up. I'll have to thank my step-father Greg for some of that too as he also provided me with an old netbook that I typed a large portion of this book on, as well as used to complete all of the book's edits prior to sending it to my publisher. Next I want to thank Ben, Stephanie, Jason, Roxy, Kerry, Mo, Eva, and Rick, who are just some of the people who sat down to speak with me one-on-one about their personal experiences regarding discrimination, serving time in prison, immigration, and religion. Your input was so very vital and I hope that I've done you all proud with the creation of this book.

I'd also like to thank Roberta, Lexi, and Margaret for their financial contributions that helped get this book off the ground, all of which came at a time where I was flat broke. My thanks also goes out to my good friend Janelle who helped me get out of my own head at times where I had some of my worst instances of writer's block. I also very much appreciate her assistance in helping sort out some of the more complicated details of the characters' escape plan. Since I began writing, I've also had the assistance of Ana, my wonderful friend who has been gracious enough to read through my books before they go to print and provide invaluable feedback. Last I want to thank my publisher for believing in my books and continuing to work with me.